A Song of Sorrow

Robert Faulk

Violetta Archivio Storico Ricordi ICONOO1115

Book Two in the Five Book Series

The Songs of War

A Song *of* Sorrow

Robert Faulk

A Song of Sorrow

Galleon Publishing, Moncton, Canada
www.galleonbooks.ca

ISBN
    Print book: 978-1-7750820-6-4
    ebook: 978-1-7750820-7-1

GALLEON

Dedication

I dedicate this book to the wonderful, brave woman who inspired Juliette. She won the Croix de Guerre for her bravery and sacrifice and I held it in my hand as she recited her story.

The spirit of the story is true, but some details are not factual. When telling a story, even dramatic lives must be condensed and modified to convey the power of events. Using the limited tools at my disposal, I have endeavoured to capture the spirit of the Juliette I knew, not necessarily her history.

Contents

Preface

I was born in a farmhouse to hard-working parents. During the summer, my mother ran a boarding house for my father's lumbering crew; during winter, she cooked for twenty men in his lumber camp. In her spare time, she raised three children.

When I was three, I reached over the edge of the wood stove where my mother cooked dinner and planted both hands flat on the hot cooking surface. They stuck, I screamed, and my mother ripped them off the hot steel, leaving burnt flesh behind. Fortunately, I don't remember the incident or the pain—I must trust my mother's memory— She continuously updated her library of my misdeeds until her death.

I was older, about four, when I decided to help mummy wash the clothes—I began by sticking my fingers between the powered rollers of her wringer washer. They sucked in my hand, then my arm up to the elbow, and then the rollers spun against the joint, ripping and tearing at the soft flesh until Mum got to the plug. The scar is quite grotesque, and that particular episode is burned into my brain...there's no need for Mum to remind me.

During the next few years, I wrecked two or three bicycles, one of them when I drove in front of a fuel truck, putting me out of commission for a few days. And then, at fourteen, my friend shot me in the leg.

Most of my friends didn't last long. Their cautious mothers eventually refused to let them play with me lest they be killed or permanently maimed.

In my last year of school, I missed forty-two days due to various alleged illnesses that I neglected to mention to my parents. My marks deteriorated at an alarming rate, but on the positive side, I made a few dollars playing pool.

I wrote my own excuses, and I forged my father's signature. Dad caught me through a quirk of fate and took advantage of the situation, offering me a deal I couldn't refuse.

Dad had told me that his teacher had expelled him for putting shotgun shells in a stove that was unfortunately located in the centre of the classroom, and looking back, I hoped, reasonably, that my father would sympathize with me. But hope evaporated when Mr. Colburne got Dad on the phone and compared notes. Eighty-four excuses with Dad's forged signature and one with his genuine signature were hard, even for me, to explain.

Goodbye driver's license, goodbye Volkswagen. There would be no fishing trips that spring, and if my marks didn't improve...a lot...Dad promised, "Young fella, Hell will freeze before you see your driver's license again!" My traitorous mother took my father's side, and between them, they got me into university.

Putting it in polite terms, the university was inconsistent with my nature—books bored me. I hated studying, I hated sitting still for more than five minutes at a time, and I hated authority —a deadly mixture for a university student.

My extra-curricular activities during this period set a terrible example for my future progeny. However, the Fredericton police may still be able to find the case files, so I won't go into that now. It's enough to say that if young men committed those acts today, they would probably spend considerable time in an appropriate institution. My wife and I successfully kept that part of my life quiet until our children were ten—when they lost interest in anything we had to say.

I proved I wasn't all bad when I married my childhood sweetheart in my second year of university. She saved me from total disaster and humiliation. I loved her too much to say no, so she leveraged that to train me to respect society's rules. Well, maybe that's an exaggeration, but I haven't stolen any more paddy wagons.

One day...actually, it wasn't just 'one day,' it was a momentous day because it changed my life. It was the day my wife said, "You had better wear a jacket and tie to the audition."

"Audition?" said I.

"Yes. Why do you think I've been teaching you those songs from 'My Fair Lady' and 'Oklahoma?' And why do you think your father gave you Saturday afternoon off?"

"Uhh... I didn't think... Wait... Dad's in on this? Uh...when?"

She looked at the kitchen clock. "You've got an hour. She lives on Cameron Street, opposite Victoria Park. Your clothes are on the bed, and the sheet music is on the kitchen table."

"Who is she? Is she a famous singer?"

My wife, who didn't and still doesn't trust me to dress myself, talked as she followed me to the bedroom.

"She was an opera singer in Europe during the war, and yes, she was famous then." She sniffed my neck. "You've got time to shower."

I'll skip the audition, thereby sparing all of us the embarrassment. It's enough to know that this fine lady took me in—a redneck from the wilds of Albert County, like a wet cat that appeared on her doorstep. She nurtured my soul with beautiful music and miraculously taught me to love music that wasn't sung on or to a horse. And it had more than three chords. I even started listening to the CBC's "Saturday Afternoon at the Opera," singing along with the tenor while working on my race car—I almost lost my pit crew over that.

In the end, I actually learned to sing—I became a real Mario Lanza... well...that could be an exaggeration. In any case, she accomplished a miracle.

A few years later, when she was more or less satisfied with my technique, Juliette sent me to study repertoire in Toronto with a famous accompanist who played for many concert stars. Thinking back, he must have laughed when I first sang for him—it helped that he was a bit eccentric; he chewed tobacco and spit the juice behind the piano. And he smelled like a brewery.

I drove to the big city on bi-weekly weekends in a Chevy station wagon, sleeping on a piece of foam in the back and eating food my wife had supplied. That way, I wouldn't stop at those sleazy truck stops where the wrong kind of women hang out.

I will skip a couple of years of hard work to the audition for the manager of the Canadian Opera Company, Mr. Herman Geiger-Torel. At the audition, the music director of a small opera house in Germany, who happened to be in town, offered me a contract, but Mr. Geiger-Torel put a pin in that balloon. He said my musicality was of the raw, underdeveloped variety, and my technique needed work. Mister Geiger-Torel said, "Go and get your wife; I want to talk to her," and I did.

With that kind of power against me, I refused the offer and followed Mr. Torel's advice. With my wife's permission, I applied to the Nordwestdeutch Musikakadamie Opernschule, a German university in Detmold specializing in remedying such minor musical imperfections as I possessed. They accepted the challenge and gave me a scholarship.

We sold the house, packed our suitcases and the kids in a plane and arrived in Germany without an Auf Wiedersehen or a Guten Tag to our names.

Anyway, the most meaningful consequence was that my family and I (three daughters), had the most fantastic seven years of our lives. My brutish past forgotten, we grew up as a family, immersed in Germany's incredible culture, and I found out what civilization feels like. Friends in the world arts community found our Canadian ways interesting, and, as a result, we accumulated three Godchildren, one of whom is a singer, another a pianist, and the third does something I can't spell.

The person I credit for all this is my first teacher, that wonderful lady my wife tricked me into learning to love. She is the star of this book; she is Juliette, and she is my hero. As I am wont to do (actually, legalized lying attracted me to fiction), I embellished a bit in places, but A Song of Sorrow, the second book in The Songs of War series, is based on her heroic deeds.

The Songs of War series is a journey through the chaos of the Third Reich's rise and fall. The stories are of ordinary people forced to be heroes, facing unimaginable and overwhelming violence in their extraordinary lives.

A Song of Sorrow begins at a 1937 Nazi party rally in Nürnberg, where Fools, Angels and the Devil left off, and it is already too late to save Germany. The power of the vote has been eliminated, along with every political party except the National Socialists. Hitler is free to use intimidation and terror—he has no need to hide his ambitions—and Germany and the world will soon have a desperate need for heroes.

Chapter One

8 September 1937

Sie können alles erreichen, wenn Sie bereit sind, den anderen Ehre zu geben.
(You can accomplish anything if you are willing to give credit to others)

WHEN JULIETTE AND PETER ARRIVED at the National Socialist Party rally, the morning twilight had yielded to a hazy dawn that coloured Zeppelin Field pink. Scheduled to begin at ten, the rally would play to a packed house, and Peter wanted good seats. Thousands of rabid party members had already swarmed into the stadium, and the only places Juliette and Peter could find were high in the stands. As a consolation, they had an excellent view of the vast arena.

It was Wednesday, 8 September 1937, the sun was already warm when it peeked over the trees, and the weather promised to be perfect. Although the long summer days were past and dawn was late, there was no hint of autumn's chill in the quiet morning. Peter and Juliette sat on their folded coats as they placed their bags filled with the day's supply of food and drink on the boards between their feet.

The opening chords of the orchestra were still two hours in the future when, to kill time, Juliette and Peter quietly sang their roles in La Traviata, the next opera on their schedule. They would perform it in the Nürnberg Staatstheatre, the city's cultural heart, where Peter was the company's leading lyric tenor, and Juliette was their coloratura soprano. They sang together in all the romantic opera productions, so it was natural for them to have fallen in love in real life. This season, it was performances of Puccini's La Bohème carried over from last year and a new production of Verdi's La Traviata. Their love scenes came naturally, and the couple's deep bond connected them to their audience in a way that made them the city's darlings.

The stands around them quickly filled with talking and laughing people, but the opera singers' clear, resonant voices pierced the chatter, and they didn't notice when the crowd became silent. As they worked on the Act One duet from La Traviata, their singing became more enthusiastic, and the crowd's silence spread from row to row. Their audience avoided looking at them for fear they would stop—most looked at their feet; others pretended to find something interesting in the cloudless sky.

When they finished the duet, they embraced, and the audience clapped and laughed as Juliette, playing to her fans, passionately kissed Peter.

Juliette and Peter bowed, and when their audience had settled back into chatter mode, Juliette pulled Peter's arm close and rested her head on his shoulder.

"Why are we here, Peter?" She wanted him to reconsider his passion for the dictator she believed had stolen Germany from fair and reasonable people and given it to hoodlums. Although a Belgian citizen, Juliette was keenly interested in German politics and understood their intricacies far better than the average German—certainly better than Peter. She distrusted Hitler and his party; only her love for Peter had brought her here. She had finally relented because she needed him to see the danger that Hitler represented, and although she hadn't said it out loud, this rally would be his last chance.

Peter considered the question while looking down at his hands. He had hoped that Juliette would attend her first National Socialist rally with an open mind.

"I need you to see why I want to be a part of the new labour movement, the reason for this rally. The National Socialists are committed to a classless society, and I believe that is a good thing."

Juliette looked straight ahead, beyond the stadium, surrounded on three sides by groomed forests. She didn't want to argue against Peter's enthusiasm for the rights of the working class, but they both knew her nature would not permit her to remain quiet.

"Your goals are admirable, but you can't ignore the excesses of National Socialism." Frustrated, she turned to look at him. He raised his gaze to meet hers, and she saw the hurt in his eyes, but she was committed to her mission and forged ahead.

"Your mother has effectively lost her citizenship; you are a second-class citizen in your own country, and you still believe that Hitler has good intentions?" She immediately regretted making her argument personal.

Peter closed his eyes, breathed audibly and said, "Juliette, the Nürnberg Laws are temporary. Hitler only instituted the law to appease anti-Jewish factions in his party, and Jews will be citizens again when..."

"No...," Juliette interrupted... "How can you say that? The SA and SS persecute the Jews under Hitler's direction. They arrest them and beat them; they use any excuse to steal from them! Even now, Hitler is looking for an answer to the Jewish question—something he invented—and the answer he seeks is not one your mother and her parents would agree with!"

Juliette looked at Peter, defiance carving trenches in her beautiful face. Already in deeper water than she had intended, Juliette knew she was over a line she had vowed not to cross.

"Why don't we have a snack?" Peter's voice broke; he swallowed, cleared his throat, and began again. "I packed enough for the whole day, and you can take your pick." He opened his pack full of food, beer and juice, wishing he could be anywhere but here. His hopes for a beautiful day with Juliette had evaporated; even Hitler's speech wasn't worth a fight with Juliette. He was terrified as he tried to find something she would like.

Juliette wasn't ready to quit the subject, but she loved Peter, and the look on his face told her not to go further. She pawed through his pack, quickly found his black bread and cheese, and turned up her nose. Turning to her much smaller pack, Juliette pulled out a croissant with an apple jelly filling. Making a show of biting into it in front of him, she sweetly smiled as she pulled the delicate pastry apart. He lifted a piece of black bread coated with butter in a salute to her ravaged croissant, ceremoniously slapped a generous slice of Gouda cheese on it, and took a huge bite, grinning as he bit, knowing his future happiness hung by a thread.

Peter forced a laugh and spoke with his mouth full, spraying crumbs on her. "You're going to get fat, and I'm going to get strong!"

She asked, a playful tone forced into her voice, "Will you still love me when I'm fat, Liebling?"

He said, too quickly, "I will always love you, fat or thin—but what about you? Will you still love me if I join the National Socialist Party?"

The shock on Peter's face instantly told Juliette Peter knew what he had done, and she forced herself not to respond. She fought back the urge to scream at him, bit her lip, turned to the forest scenery bordering the field and viciously took another bite of her croissant. Turning to Peter, she swallowed most of the chunk without chewing and put all the force she had behind her words.

"Yes, I do love you, as I know you love me, but if you join that party, I swear I will never speak to you again!" She fought in vain to control her anger. Her voice burst out of everything she had held back for the past year.

"I came here hoping that if you could see what a propaganda farce this is, you would convert to reason. National Socialism is evil, a terrible plague that threatens to infect the world, and I will have nothing to do with anyone who joins those animals!" She stamped her feet on the boards behind the row of seats in front of her.

"Meanwhile, Liebling, if you still want to save what remains of the day, I suggest you not say another word about joining Hitler's Party of Fools!" Her resonant voice had risen, and the sarcasm was sharper than she had intended. People near them tried awkwardly to avoid her gaze.

Peter hung his head, and the Vollkorn black bread in his hand fell on the planks between his feet. He attempted to pick it up, but it broke into small pieces.

He spoke softly, leaning over as he fiddled with the crumbs. "If you don't leave me, I promise I will never join the National Socialist Party." He straightened but kept the sound level for her ears only, "Please don't ask me to lie by saying I disagree with their philosophy of all work being equally valuable. I came to the rally to hear Hitler's plan for working men like my father, but if you want to leave, I'm ready to go with you." Peter looked at her, and the mixture of fear and longing on his face saved him.

Juliette hugged him with her free arm, pushing her croissant under his face—he had to lift his head or have her shove it into his mouth. She said sweetly, "Here, my love… Try some real food." Her affection returned as suddenly as it had left.

At precisely ten o'clock, a stirring fanfare began, played by dozens of trumpets in the back row of a one-hundred-piece orchestra. A ripple of applause rolled through the seats as rows of men with shovels on their shoulders marched onto the perfectly cut grass on the eastern side of the field. Cheers from seventy-thousand throats greeted the Führer as he approached from the west, standing in an open car, his head and torso above the windscreen. His head high and his back straight, gripping the windscreen's frame with his left hand, he waved to the crowd with his right. The Mercedes crossed in front of the main grandstand to park beside the route the mass of marching workers would take. The bare-chested men approached from Hitler's left as he saluted them, his arm straight out in the Nazi image. They carried their shovels as one would a rifle, over their shoulders, a pair of white shorts their only clothing. As they passed the Führer's car, they raised their right arms to return his salute. Hitler held his arm iron straight until every man had passed him.

Juliette and Peter stood with the crowd, clapping along with the beat as forty-five thousand men marched past, eighteen rows together, a flowing river of bare-chested men. Juliette caught Peter watching her, his broad but tender smile indicating his pleasure at seeing her enjoying the spectacle.

He asked, "Are you impressed yet?" and gently laughed as hope returned to tease him again.

She shouted over the noise, "The sight of forty-five thousand bare-chested men always impresses me! Now, if I pick out two or three, can you get me their names and addresses?" Her musical laugh tortured him as he shook his head in feigned jealousy.

"Liebling, those are the RAD, the Reichsarbeitsdienst; they're only good with shovels!"

The men marched past in four groups. When the fourth group cleared the intersection, the first had circled the field and entered again, now thirty-six men wide. Then, to a deafening roar of approval, Hitler left his car and mounted the steps to the speakers' platform.

Juliette yelled in Peter's ear, "He certainly knows how to make an entrance!"

"Yes, he does, and wait until you hear him speak!" When Peter smiled down at her, his eyes glowed. She didn't have the heart to rupture his balloon again. She silently vowed to take her father's advice and leave Peter's political views with Peter.

The shovel-carrying men smoothly formed organized groups on the green field in front of the grandstand, standing at attention in front of their Führer. A shouted command resounded in the open theatre, and forty-five thousand shovels slammed down between their owners' bare feet, all striking the ground at the same instant, the impact reverberating above the closing chords of the orchestra. The stadium was suddenly silent. There was no sound until a loud voice commanded the men to raise their weapons, and the shovels whipped through an intricate routine designed to resemble a rifle drill.

The shovels' blades glinted in the sun as the men whirled them around their heads, twirled them like batons, then threw them at the ground between their feet with a single tremendous clap and a guttural roar from forty-five thousand working-men's throats.

Hundreds of banners and swastikas ringed the field, and, with the cheering crowd waving thousands of flags, the scene became an exciting spectacle of colour and movement.

"Okay, I am impressed with their choreographer," Juliette shouted, "We could use him in the theatre." Peter clapped and cheered, and she added, "I am more impressed that not one man dropped his shovel or stabbed himself in the foot!"

"Yes, I did notice that," Peter nodded vigorously, "That's equivalent to one man doing that routine forty-five thousand times without making even one tiny mistake!" He clapped with renewed energy as the routine ended.

Juliette pulled on Peter's arm, smiling impishly. "It is coordination, my love—some men have it, and some don't. I know from experience that yours is excellent!"

Peter grinned like a little boy, and his face turned red. Hope had given way to joy.

RAD Leader Hierl then stepped to the microphone at the front of the stage and said to Hitler, his amplified voice echoing back from the wall of trees surrounding the field, "Mein Führer, forty-five thousand men of the Reichsarbeitsdienst have come to this event for you!"

The Führer shook hands with him, took his place at the microphone and shouted, "Heil, working men!"

The men answered with one great voice, "Heil, Mein Führer!"

A rousing fanfare signalled flag carriers to wave them in unison, and forty-five thousand voices sang to the Führer. A speaker then stepped to the microphone and asked:

"Is anyone too good..." and the shovel army responded... "to work for Germany?"

"Is anyone too simple…" the men shouted louder... "to work for Germany?"

"Everyone has the right—everyone has the duty…" the men shouted with one thunderous roar... "to work for Germany!"

The dialogue continued, and the men's enthusiasm for work, the Fatherland, and the Führer spread through the crowd. The final phrase from the leader echoed across the field, "The Führer wants to give the world peace!" and forty thousand men responded with one voice, "We will follow wherever he leads!"

The men's chorus then sang of proud work to create a better future for Germany and the world. When they finished, the speaker shouted, "Your shovels become weapons for the battle against those who have no faith in their country or their Führer. We march into the future, true to Hitler's commands. We are the shock troops of faith, and with our hoes, shovels, and spades, we will again make Germany strong!"

The thrust shifted to comrades who had fallen in combat for the Fatherland, and also to those who were killed or injured on the job while working for their country. The men sang of their eagerness to work on the road to power and freedom for Germany, the greatest country in the world. The movement climaxed with another mighty fanfare.

Juliette and Peter stood with the crowd for the entire program, Juliette's anxiety growing as the people shouted, waved flags, and worked themselves into the fervour planned by Nazi organizers. Tears filled her eyes as the Führer removed his hat and stood, his face turned toward the sun, reflecting the light. Finally, he bowed his head, apparently in submission to the people. Juliette felt something stir in her bowels as Hitler waited a perfect moment, then gestured with both hands for his worshippers to sit down. He paused, as he always did, and it was several long minutes before he spoke, and seventy thousand people sat in silence.

Juliette swallowed the bile climbing into her throat and declined the piece of bread that a grinning Peter offered, but when he opened a bottle of beer, she took it from him. He smiled and opened another for himself.

"He hasn't spoken yet, and the crowd already loves him." Oblivious to Juliette's sorrow, Peter couldn't restrain his excitement. "Wait until you hear him!"

Juliette looked away, then back to Peter; she swallowed the long pull on the beer bottle and paused to think. She wanted him to see what she saw but knew he couldn't. Nonetheless, she had to try.

Juliette spoke quietly so their neighbours wouldn't overhear, acutely aware that the respectful, subdued crowd waited expectantly for Hitler. "I understand how work is important, and it is good to instill that in people, but this is much more than that. I'm not arguing against the principle of honest work here, but I am frightened when I put this façade in the context of the power that Hitler has transferred to himself."

She turned to look at the Führer just as he raised his head from what Hitler intended to appear to be prayer, but what Juliette the *Shauspielerin* recognized as pure theatrical timing.

Peter opened his mouth, but before he could respond, the Führer stepped to the microphone and immediately began his speech. Hitler addressed the men standing before him; his words echoed across the country through the miracle of radio—and beyond, through history.

Juliette saw only satan bewitching his disciples.

The Führer used the occasion to congratulate the National Socialist movement on their progress toward a better-educated country... "fully employed, except for those too lazy to work." Hitler then shouted a perfectly timed rant. "The National Socialist movement has led Germany out of the abyss created by the disgraceful Versailles Treaty and, above all, out of a worldwide depression engineered by Jewish banks. The inner nature of the German people is changing to create a better sense of community, and the birth of a new Volk is the result!"

He waited for the applauding crowd, then continued in his naturally strident voice, "The new Reich Labour Service will obligate every young boy and many girls to six months of manual labour after graduating from school. We will unify the idea of labour, and everyone will value work equally, regardless of occupation. The proudest accomplishment of the National Socialist Party is the founding of the Reich Labour Service, the RAD; it will unite the working man and guarantee him honourable work for the common good of the German people. The theme of this party congress is labour. By working tirelessly to create the Reich Labour Service, you have shown us how working men can change a country, and your number one worker is your leader, Party Comrade Hierl." Hitler waved his hand in the leader's direction, and his men cheered. The crowd took the hint and clapped furiously.

He waited until the commotion began to wane, then went on, "Within the space of a few short years, your movement has become an integral part of the great German people, a part we cannot now do without. You belong to the German people as much as the Wehrmacht does, and you are as essential to us!"

He stopped for a ripple of applause, drank from a glass, and then went on, "It gives us comfort to know that long into the future, generation after generation of working men will shoulder their weapons, the tools of their trade, in the interest of everlasting peace and the service of our German community. You have renewed the eternal strength of Germany, and you are the guarantors of your country's eternal greatness and strength, and your country will never again take you for granted!"

Peter and Juliette clapped with the crowd until it became too much for Juliette, and she clasped her hands tightly together. She began to watch the people around her, and when she turned back to Peter, the fanatical worship she saw in his eyes stunned her. His expression quickly changed when he saw the expression on her face, and he leaned down to speak to her.

"What's wrong? He's an incredible speaker—the people love him!" He returned his eyes to Hitler, who tirelessly waved to his enthusiastic admirers.

Juliette looked up and waited for Peter to look at her again. He finally lowered his eyes and leaned over so she could speak into his ear.

"I agree, but he has seduced the people with lies—he is a master at making people feel good. He never says 'I' or 'me,' and he says 'you' and 'your' more than he says 'we' and 'us.' Nothing is more empowering than the enthusiasm of others... But don't you see what he's doing? He has systematically organized a mob of people who would kill for him, and if he told them to, they would destroy their country because their loyalty lies with Adolph Hitler, not Germany! The French Revolution had the same lofty goals, but ultimately, wasn't it at the expense of the educated and the artistic communities—what they called the bourgeoisie, what we call the elite? Hitler has declared war on truth, reason, and intelligence, and this pandering to the working man and stirring of nationalist fervour is nothing more than manipulation for purposes which I predict you will not like!"

Peter straightened and looked across the field. When the crowd sat down, Juliette retrieved another croissant and a small bottle of milk from her bag. Peter slowly dug out another beer and a piece of bread and cheese. He slapped the small slice of cheese on the black Pumpernickel bread and bit a mouthful off, sliding the cheese ahead, carefully portioning it to last for the entire piece of bread. Juliette waited, but Peter wisely said nothing.

While Hitler and his guests watched, the SA, 'Brownshirts,' represented by thousands of marching troops, filed past the reviewing stand, waved flags, and sang their anthems for the Führer while the orchestra played in the background. Hitler stiffly returned their salutes so often that Juliette was amazed he could keep lifting his arm.

Finally, Peter spoke to Juliette during a short break in the colourful parade.

"I love you too much to fight about this. I understand what you are saying, but I will keep my reasons for disagreeing to myself." He touched her arm affectionately. "Can we just watch for a while?"

Juliette nodded and looked down. When she looked up at him, he still stared at her, and she relented. She bit her tongue and said, "That sounds like a good idea."

The Hitler Youth filed past in eight rows, four of the rows opposing one another on each side so that they zippered together in front of the grandstands, their flags touching as they met, singing their *Fahnenlied*, the 'flag song' of the Hitler Youth.

Thousands of young girls, members of the BDM, *Bund Deutscher Mädel*, the League of German Girls, danced for the Führer, their white dresses flowing behind them. Hitler left the reviewing stand to drive amongst the performing youths in his Mercedes motorcar, often stopping to wave, sometimes singling out a young man or girl, getting out of his car to shake their hand. Juliette had to resist the urge to vomit.

She suffered through the remainder of the daytime part of the rally, then happily followed Peter as he navigated through the crowds out to the streets. They strolled toward home, arm in arm, exhausted but happy to be in each other's company, and Juliette put her head on his shoulder.

Peter asked, "What do you think of Hitler now?" From the tone in his voice, his political position hadn't changed, and Juliette, her mood shattered, paused to prepare her response. She lifted her head from his shoulder and looked straight ahead.

"I am impressed with how he has manipulated his Volk, which is any politician's job, but now that I've experienced his charisma, he terrifies me. Satan is alive and well in Adolph Hitler!" She looked up at Peter's face and waited for him to speak, allowing him to steer her on the brick sidewalk. They slowly, almost aimlessly, walked toward home, recognizing that the conversation was becoming more important than the journey.

Peter took a long breath…he didn't want to go where Juliette was leading him. "Why would you be frightened of him? What about three years ago? Didn't he arrest the leaders of the SA and execute those guilty of treason? And when the Brownshirts rampaged through Munich, beating and murdering Jews, he rounded them up and executed them, including Röhm, head of the SA in Munich. He put the SA under the Army's control so we could have peace and order, and that's why we can walk home knowing no one will bother us!"

Juliette waited for Peter to go on, but he didn't, and she replied carefully.

"Another way to think of *Unternehmen Kolibri,* but more appropriately, the 'Night of the Long Knives,' is to recognize that Hitler and his band of thugs officially murdered eighty-five people, although the truth is probably much higher. He arrested thousands, yes, but not all were members of the SA. He also executed two top generals in the Wehrmacht who likely were not guilty of anything." She held up two emphatic fingers.

"None of these people had the benefit of a trial, and none had the opportunity to defend themselves." She stopped, let go of his arm, and spread her hands hopelessly. "Hitler simply passed a law that he could murder anyone he thought was plotting against the government, without trial or defence, and he specifically clarified it to include any action against the Führer. And since he passed a law forbidding other political parties to exist, he is now an unopposed dictator—he can legally execute anyone who dares to oppose him!" She looked up at Peter, taking his hands and pleading, "Don't you understand what this means?"

Peter looked away, then began cautiously, "Yes, I do understand the power Hitler has taken." He pulled his hands away from her and waved at the sky, lit by the searchlights ringing the field they had left, aimed upward and inward to form 'Speer's Cathedral' at twenty thousand feet above the street. "But I also see how he has organized the people to work toward the common goals of peace and prosperity. He has thrown out Versailles—no one can defend that outrage—and there's work for everyone. He couldn't have done that if he'd had to work around political opposition."

Juliette started to speak, but Peter was on a roll. "I've told you about Germany five years ago; people were starving, businesses were going bankrupt, and there was no money to modernize our industries. At M.A.N., where my father works, everything was outdated, and they were trying to develop a direct-injection diesel engine that would revolutionize the industry..."

He paused. Juliette knew there was more. She wanted to tell him to stop—that he had told her about Hitler's 'miracle.' She wanted to tell him the price was too high, yet Hitler wanted more! But she loved him too much to burst his balloon, so she remained silent.

"...And M.A.N. would have joined the thousands of companies declaring bankruptcy had it not been for Hitler's initiatives." Peter waved his arm in a circle. "Before Hitler, companies had to fire thousands of workers because there were no markets for their products. Now those workers are back, and the companies can't fill the orders coming in!"

He was preaching now, and Juliette could hear Hitler's cadence infecting his voice. She prepared herself, then turned to face him, but Peter had anticipated her rebuttal and was ready. His face was red... he was shouting.

"If Hitler's methods are necessary to achieve a decent wage for hardworking people like my father, then I am prepared to accept that."

Juliette put her finger against Peter's chest, too involved now to let Peter have the last word.

"You know Hitler won't stop here! He has made no secret of the hatred he spreads for anyone non-Aryan. Have you suddenly forgotten that you are one-half Jewish?" She put her hands on her hips, "You are officially a Mischling, and that's not going to change! If I am considered Aryan, we can't be married, and if we continue to have sexual relations, the Gestapo might arrest us!" She was shouting now. "Peter, Hitler will use the people he has inflamed with his passion to destroy you, your mother, and your grandparents. He's mad! He wants a 'pure' race of Germans to control the country, and who knows where he will stop?" She waved her hands in frustration and turned away.

He waited until she turned back to him before beginning again, this time softly. He had gone too far, and he was in deep trouble.

"I don't dispute Hitler's power, but he will not attack the people who run businesses in Germany. Without Jewish money and expertise, the German economy would disintegrate in a year, destroying everything Hitler has accomplished. As for my Mischling status, the law permits me to have sexual relations with an Aryan. I would need to have one more Jewish grandparent before my classification would not permit it."

Juliette replied quickly and reflexively, regretting her words as she said them.

"All right, if you want to have sexual relations with some blonde Aryan girl, you go right ahead—it's for sure you won't be having any more sexual relations with this nice non-Aryan Belgian girl!"

The fire in her tone had an immediate effect: Peter blanched and tripped on a sidewalk paving stone.

Juliette felt tears welling in her eyes, but she couldn't stop. She turned on her heel and picked up a driven pace, her face reddening and the tears multiplying as she walked.

Peter skipped ahead to catch her.

"I don't want any girl but you!" He was suddenly desperate, "I want you to marry me and have children with me!"

She stopped and faced him, the frightening fire in her heart unquenched by the tears in her eyes.

"I won't marry you because you can't see the truth! I love you, but I hate what you believe! Even if you are not a National Socialist, you might as well be if you believe they are right. Right now, you represent everything I hate in this country, and you can go to Hell with your fascist idol!"

Juliette could see her words cutting through Peter's soul. He silently accompanied her to the steps of her apartment and waited while she unlocked and opened the door. She barely heard him sob as he stood with his head down, his eyelids squeezed shut, trying to force the tears to stay behind them.

Juliette fought off the urge to put her arms around him. She had tried to understand his devotion to what he considered a just cause, but she could hear the crowd's fanatical cheers, their adoration for a criminal, and she slammed the heavy oak door behind her as she hurried upstairs.

She ran to the bay window to look through the crack between the drapes. Juliette watched as Peter walked past two buildings to his apartment in the light of Albert Speer's Cathedral, her tears becoming a stream as he stopped in the open doorway to look upward at the cone of light over the city.

Juliette had never felt so sad in her short life and couldn't imagine ever being happy again. An uncontrollable shiver sapped her strength;

she fell into the soft chair she kept beside the window and curled into the fetal position.

Juliette woke an hour later, the noise of stamping feet and a military marching band crashing into her consciousness. She turned in the chair, wiggled to her knees, and cautiously pushed the heavy drapes apart.

Dozens of torches approached, bobbing to the rhythm of a military march played by a band leading twelve lines of men in three tightly grouped rows. The men were in full battle dress, carrying rifles on their shoulders, packs on their backs, and marching in the familiar goose step. Torchlight reflected from their young faces, and Juliette watched in horror as row after row passed under her window and continued down the street. She looked at Peter's doorway to see if she could find him in the crowd. People crowding the sidewalks gave the men a 'Heil Hitler' salute and waved flags. Every window was open, filled with cheering people. Juliette looked for Peter but couldn't find him.

For the second time, an uncontrollable shiver surprised her. She quickly closed the drapes, but the tramp, tramp, tramp of Wehrmacht boots was interminable, and Juliette went to bed fully clothed. She pulled the Federbett over her head, but the sound seeped into her. Even after the marching stopped and the band died away, she couldn't shake the feeling of dread. Finally, as the pre-dawn light filtered into her room, Juliette slept.

She woke three hours later, her cheeks wet, her stomach heaving. She got out of bed but threw up on the floor before reaching the bathroom.

CHAPTER TWO

Christmas 1937

Liebesschmerz
(Love's pain)

THE NÜRNBERG AUTUMN OF 1937 was exceptionally sunny and beautiful but nonetheless miserable for Juliette. She sang love scenes with Peter, working professionally on the stage as though nothing had happened, overwhelmed by sadness every time she performed. When Peter, as her lover Alfredo, confronted her in the dramatic La Traviata gambling scene, it broke her heart when the role forced her to crush Peter's spirit. She had difficulty controlling her voice in the last-act death scene, and Juliette and Peter's naked sorrow captivated the audience. Every time Peter took her in his arms, pleading with her to live, to stay with him, his voice reflected the same heartbreaking sadness, and tears blurred her vision. On the final performance of La Bohème, the day before they left for Christmas break, Juliette impulsively kissed a renegade tear from Peter's cheek as she turned to leave the stage after their first curtain call. The audience shouted, laughed, and cried, but Juliette couldn't return. She cried as she ran to her dressing room, despite the stage manager's pleadings for her to join Peter for yet another crossing of the stage.

The following morning, as Juliette went home to Brussels, she boarded the train with the hope that Christmas with her father and Mother would somehow relieve the pain and loneliness in her heart.

Peter and his parents arrived on his Jewish grandparents' doorstep in Munich two days before Christmas. Moshe and Hannah Metzger greeted their family at the door to their third-floor apartment, and after much hugging and chattering, everyone found a place to sit in the modest living room. The interior was not luxurious, but it was comfortable, with large windows on the front and back walls. Sunshine burst through the pristine glass, splashing across the floor and furniture, warming the room.

At just under six feet, Moshe was almost as tall as Peter but more slender. He wore a neatly trimmed beard, and only his receding hairline spoiled the impression of a much younger man than his sixty-six years.

Peter had dark brown hair and brown eyes identical to Moshe's, and they had the same twinkle when they smiled. But there, the similarity ended. Peter had a clean-shaven Germanic face, and his grandfather was a srereotypical bearded Jew.

Peter's Mother, Elisabeth, was, apart from signs of age, the image of her Mother. Both were slightly overweight, had round cheeks and green eyes, long pulled-back hair, and a shared taste in almost everything. When they met after having been apart for months, they resumed their relationship as though only a few hours or even minutes had passed.

Peter's father, Heinz, had no formal education past high school and spent the last two years of his schooling in a machine shop. A competitive swimmer, Heinz met Elisabeth in the Munich Hallenbad, the city's indoor swimming pool, and they were married a week after receiving his journeyman's papers at M.A.N.

Elisabeth was the intellectual head of the family, and under her direction, Heinz played the role of husband, father, and provider. Peter's father loved his family with a passion he tried not to show, but his clumsy attempts to hide it made it more evident. Heinz was as tall as Peter but built like a truck. He wore his scarred, calloused hands like medals—he was proud of his trade and who he was. His confidence in his abilities, supported by Elizabeth, gave him a natural air of authority among his peers, but he left it at the workplace. Elizabeth ran the family and the household, and it didn't occur to Heinz that it could be otherwise.

Pleasantries out of the way, the family gathered around a low table in the living room for ersatz Kaffee and Kuchen. Genuine coffee had become impossibly expensive, and ground hazelnuts, chicory, and grains replaced authentic beans. The kuchen was the same on every visit: an Apfeltorte for Peter and a Käsetorte for his father.

When the chatter slowed, Moshe deliberately embarrassed Peter, obviously enjoying himself as he did.

"Peter, I hear that you have a heart problem. Why don't you tell us about it?"

Peter had expected his grandparents to ask about Juliette, but not so soon. They had met her at Peter and Juliette's closing concert in the Odeon Theatre at the Munich Musikschule, where they had studied together. After the performance, the family had eaten dinner at a restaurant with Moshe and Hannah, where Juliette had been the centre of attention.

Peter poured himself a cup of the nut-flavoured coffee and began, "Juliette and I had a difference of opinion, and she can't forgive me."

Elisabeth and Heinz put down their cups. Peter guessed this would not end well.

Elisabeth asked quietly, openly disappointed, "You didn't tell me about this, Peter... What did you fight about?"

He waited a few seconds, buying himself more time by cutting a piece of Apfeltorte and sliding it onto his plate. "I took her to the Party's Labour Rally, and we disagreed about Hitler."

Moshe, eyebrows raised, asked Peter, "What do you think Hitler intends to do?"

"I think he's trying to motivate the German people to work together and build a more unified nation. He wants the privileged and the workers to unite, and I believe his plan to have all young men and women work at manual labour for six months after graduation could do that."

Moshe sipped his coffee before he asked, "And what about those of us who are now non-Germans? Will he include us in his plan to unite workers?"

Peter replied, "Hitler will eventually rescind the Nürnberg Race Law, and the Party will concentrate on building a future for all Germans, including non-Aryans such as Jews and Romani. Meanwhile, it would be devastating economic policy if Germany were to cut off the Jewish hand that feeds them." Peter had rehearsed that little speech until it sounded logical when he said it aloud.

Hannah set her coffee cup carefully on her saucer, lifted her eyes, and, openly disturbed, said to him, "Peter, you are wrong, and if this is the reason Juliette won't speak to you, I applaud and understand her reluctance." She paused, and Peter waited, surprised as he watched the kind expression on his grandmother's face harden.

"Hitler is not who you think he is. Remember, the Sturm Abteilung is his creation. The SA killed David Cohen and his wife Nitza just before the 'Night of the Long Knives.'" She paused, then said as she looked into Peter's brown eyes, "They dragged our innocent friends out of their shop and beat them to death!"

Peter couldn't hide his shock. Onkel David had been like a second grandfather to Peter. His voice was weak as he said, "It was Hitler who punished the SA leaders and stopped the violence against Jews."

Hannah nodded, but Peter knew it wasn't because she agreed.

"Yes, Hitler killed the SA leaders, saying that they were too aggressive against us, but, in reality, he was afraid that the animals he had created were becoming too powerful. He proved it when he placed the SS and Gestapo where the SA had been, with Himmler now in charge. That is hardly an improvement for Jews."

She pointed at the floor, determined to open Peter's mind. "On the ground floor under our feet, thugs have robbed Aaron Rinzler's clothing store twice in the past two years, and the police will do nothing. Aaron and Louise have carefully built a clientèle in this city, but by order of the Führer, they are losing their Aryan clients, and their business is struggling."

She folded her hands in front of her, pushing them down hard onto the table. "And in case you've forgotten, Moshe's teaching job is only there until the National Socialists decide to take it away, and the Party has told me mine will disappear in the spring. Hitler's National Socialist Party gave us the option of renouncing our religion and joining them, and we made a choice we will have to live with. I've paid into my pension for twenty years, but I am no longer eligible to collect it because the man you worship has stolen it from me, and he has made it clear that the only reason is that I am a Jew!"

Oma Hannah stopped to breathe, but no one interjected. She tapped her finger on the table in time with her words. "Is this the future Hitler is promising?" Peter knew it would be better to stay silent. His Grossmutti was in a mood Peter had never imagined. "Peter, don't you think that it might be possible he has something even worse in mind? Do you think Hitler will stop when he takes our jobs and our pensions?"

Peter respected his grandmother and didn't want to argue with her. She was upset; he had no answer to her questions, so he waited for her to go on. The silence became very long.

Moshe tried to save his grandson. "Don't you think that's a little harsh, Hannah?" But Peter could hear that his heart wasn't in it. He knew that Moshe and Hannah never disagreed on anything…Moshe knew Hannah was right, and he was trying to protect his naïve grandson from his grandmother.

"The streets are much safer now, and even though we are not citizens, we are legal residents of Germany, with the same rights as citizens except for voting… and, of course, we can't hold government jobs." He pointed half-heartedly at Peter while looking at his wife of over forty years. "Peter has a good point when he asks what the German economy would look like if we withdrew our money and left. Why, the country would be bankrupt in a year!" He sat back, satisfied with his argument and the effort to save Peter.

Hannah's voice was more intense for its softness, "But what if they throw us out of the country and take our money, along with our houses and businesses… that seems like the more logical outcome to me."

Elisabeth leaned forward and spoke with the same soft strength as her Mother, "And what if they take everything from us and don't allow us to leave? How will we live?" She waited in the silence that followed, her face betraying her astonishment at where logic was taking them. And then she blurted out the nightmare that woke her almost every night.

"What if they make us work for them for no pay, like the people in work camps?" Elizabeth looked at her husband and put her ugly dream into words. "Heinz… What if they take all we have and then kill us?"

Heinz, his intellect just a little behind the others, jumped eagerly into the awful silence.

"This is all ridiculous talk," he said, much too loudly, "Elisabeth is Jewish, yes, but officially, she's protestant, and I know what would happen to anyone who tried to take her away from me! We are not leaving Germany, not as long as I breathe, and no one will hurt my family!" He looked around the table, and, misinterpreting the expression on everyone's face, he said, "I'll break the neck of any man who tries!" He made a neck-wringing motion with his big hands.

Peter put his hand on his father's shoulder. "Dad, you and Mom have nothing to worry about; you are both protestant German citizens. We're talking about Oma and Opa's status."

Heinz continued, confused but determined. "I mean… I won't let anyone harm my family, no matter who they are… and Elizabeth's parents are my family!" He looked at his parents-in-law as he slammed his fist on the table and then became embarrassed when everyone smiled. He vaguely gestured toward Peter as he went on, "I'm like you; I don't believe Hitler has any intention to hurt people, and I'm sure he won't hurt Hannah and Moshe. I believe that Hitler has done a lot for the country and will make it right with the Jews as soon as he can."

Heinz stopped and looked around the table. Hannah gave him a warm smile, and he took it for encouragement.

"As far as this six months of labour for kids just out of school goes, why would that be so bad? The young people today don't know what a good day's work is, and when we get them in our shop fresh out of school, they still haven't learned…" He hesitated, looking for words he had heard Hitler say… "That laziness is the key to poverty. If we paid them nothing and had a shop full of them, we would go bankrupt paying for the material they ruin. Yes, sir, Hitler's labour camp idea is just what those kids need!"

Moshe nodded at his son-in-law and raised his cup of coffee in a salute. Peter smiled sympathetically at his father and raised his cup.

Looking pointedly at Heinz, Moshe began, "Heinz, I teach these children, and I agree that young people aren't like they were when I was young. I worked on my father's farm—I was up an hour before dawn to milk the cows, then off to school three kilometres away, rain or shine. Today's kids have a school within a kilometre, they don't have to be there until eight, and they've cut the class time down so that the Hitler Jugend can play soldier all afternoon." He banged his fist on the table so hard the cutlery jumped. "Young people need to learn to work!"

Hannah broke in, looking sympathetically at Heinz and not-so-lovingly at her husband.

"Moshe, you remember things differently than I do!" She wagged her finger in his face. "I knew you when you lived on that farm, and I don't remember you milking any cows. Your sister often helped, but your father had to pull you out of bed to get you to school on time."

Moshe hung his head.

"I work in the school office, my dear husband who can't remember what day it is, and I know the children you speak of. You are wrong about them and a lot of other things! They are smarter than their parents, and they work as hard as their parents ever did. I do not like Mister Hitler's idea of forcing every child to move away from their parents to a work camp when they are still children. Some may learn something about hard physical work, but others will suffer because that's not what the Lord intended them to do. The best of those children are not aggressive physical people; they are sensitive and artistic and work with their intellect. A work camp would destroy those children—you know very well what would happen if they couldn't escape from their less-gifted tormentors!"

Before Moshe or Heinz could reply, Elisabeth cut in on the women's side.

"Mother is right," She looked at her husband, who shrank back like a whipped dog. "You know how children bully the most intelligent students." She then looked at Peter; he knew he and his father had lost the argument and just wanted her to stop, but his Mother punched the table with her finger and kept going.

"Those children are the country's future, as are people who work with their hands. We need engineers and professors to deal with new technologies and teach them, and we need workers to turn engineers' and architects' ideas into reality—but first comes the idea. Everyone is necessary and equally valuable, but the shovel is not more valuable than the pen or an artist's brush, and the artist is as essential as the engineer is. Hitler's idea will destroy the artist as surely as it will eventually destroy the engineer. The man who works with his hands will then be redundant because, without an educated vision, there will be nothing for him to do!" She turned to Moshe, who looked at his folded hands. Peter waited for the coup de grace with his head down.

"Is it unfair that a labourer with no papers receives lower pay than a master machinist like Heinz? Men like him have spent many years learning their trade, and there must be a reward, or no one will do it. Meanwhile, the engineer that designs the engines Heinz builds receives more pay than Heinz does... and is that not his right?" She looked at her husband. "Heinz? Am I right?"

Heinz lifted his head to look at his wife, knowing what he had to do. He spoke to her with undisguised respect and admiration.

"You are right, Liebling; I hadn't thought about it enough. The engineer that I work for is worth every pfennig he gets. I help him with his designs when he asks how I would build a part, but I could never put it down on paper or figure out how strong it has to be; I don't have the head for that." Heinz turned back to Hannah. He had seen the light, and it was confession time.

"Yes, I know what you mean about those kids in school. Some boys couldn't lift a shovelful of dirt if their life depended on it, and if they were all put in the same place, the aggressive boys would tease them and probably hurt them."

All eyes in the silent room turned to Peter. He knew it was time to lay down his arms.

He lifted his hands in resignation and said, "All right, I know when I'm beaten. If they had forced me into a work camp, I would never have survived to become a singer!" He looked at his Mother. "The idea of equalizing the classes appeals to me, but..." He searched for the thought, found it and went on... "People just aren't all alike, and trying to force them together would be a mistake. Everyone needs respect, and for many of the children, work camp will accomplish the opposite." He was suddenly shocked and embarrassed as he recognized his about-face, and turned to his Mother for help.

Elisabeth looked into her son's brown eyes, and he melted. She took his hand.

"Will you say that to Juliette when you get back?"

He replied quickly, "Yes, if she will let me." And then, dreading that Juliette might not, Peter looked down and fiddled with his fork.

His grandfather smiled and broke the silence.

"I think we should discuss Hitler's plan for Jews like us. Peter, I cannot share your optimism that Hitler's Race Law is temporary—he passed that law so the National Socialists could validate what they intend to do. They now have a description of a Jew, and because Hitler makes the laws and appoints the judges, the existing laws against Jews will be applied. That is what dictators do, and Hitler certainly is a dictator."

"But why...?" Peter began, but Moshe went on.

"Hitler's National Socialists want the Jew's property and money, and to get it, they first must remove their rights. The Race Law finally does that. It was construed by men without ethics for or against Jewry or a 'pure' race. Except in a few cases, the law has little to do with ideological racism and everything to do with power and greed. We and our religion mean nothing to those men. We are a thing they can use, like a shovel or a hammer."

The room was silent. Moshe broke it again when he said, "We need a plan. We can't fight them—we need a hole to run to."

Heinz asked Moshe, "What do you mean?" and Moshe explained.

"I mean a place where we can go before the government takes everything we own. Once they prove they can rob us without consequence, the door is open to worse things. It will be like an earth dam breaking. It begins with a trickle, and then... Only God knows!"

"Where could you go," Elizabeth asked, "And what would you do there?"

"I've been thinking about the possibilities, and there aren't many. For example, Poland is not allowing its Jews to return home, even though Germany will not allow them to stay here—the Poles are terrified of incurring Hitler's wrath, and the same goes for all the countries east of here. Italy, France, Belgium, and Holland all have strict laws against taking Jews unless they are married to citizens. Even England will not accept us, nor will America or Canada, unless we have barrels of money. Currently, Shanghai and Palestine are the only countries accepting Jews, and I have heard the Philippines is considering it. But Shanghai's high visa fees and other stipulations block most Jews. We have enough to pay the bribes and fees, but we would have nothing left to live on and no job when we got there. That disqualifies us, even if everything else works."

He stopped to look around the table, but no one spoke. Moshe began again.

"There is a possibility that we could go to Palestine. The British and French allow a few Jews to return, but they must apply well ahead of time, and there is no guarantee. I will also look into the Philippines."

Peter suddenly needed to be with Juliette. He wanted to tell her he loved her, that nothing else mattered. He was confused, and Juliette would know why. He was suddenly afraid that he would never be with her again.

He asked, "What have we done that everyone hates us?" He suddenly realized he had admitted to being a Jew.

Hannah said, "That's a good question. We are supposed to be God's chosen people." With a hint of weariness, she said, "But sometimes I have the impression that God doesn't know that."

Elisabeth interjected, "The Jewish people prosper everywhere because we are all one family; we recognize no borders between us as individuals, so we don't waste time or money fighting one another." She looked at Heinz. "Sometimes, a Jew falls in love with a non-Jew and goes to their church, but they are still a Jew."

Heinz hung his head, but Peter rescued his father. "Dad, you are German by heritage, but that does not make you an enemy of Jews.

If you defend Mother, Hannah, and Moshe because you consider them your family, the National Socialists will target you because you are defending Jews and are not one of them. If you don't hate Jews, family or not, you can't be a National Socialist." His face reddened as he thought of the implications.

Heinz spoke again, his face indicating a new idea was taking form, "Why can't Elisabeth and our children be baptized in the Lutheran church? Then they won't be Jews anymore!"

Peter said, "No, Dad, we would still be Jews under the race laws. We are descendants of Jacob, and therefore, we are Jews. Juliette told me that since the middle of the nineteenth century in Germany, a Jew could convert to another religion and become Aryan, but she said the Race Laws would remove that possibility. If you are the son or daughter of the line of people of Jacob, you are officially a Jew, and you cannot change that. You are who you are, an Aryan and a German, but you can become a National Socialist by accepting their beliefs. I am a Jew only because my Mother is a Jew."

"But you are also my son!"

"That's why I am officially a Mischling, but Juliette said that classification may give me no more protection than if I were a hundred percent Jewish."

Peter stopped talking and stared at the wall. The truth he had spoken was Juliette's, not one he had ever admitted to himself, and he could think of no counter-argument. He searched his soul and found that he didn't believe Hitler would ever repeal the law now that he had admitted to its intention.

Hannah picked up the coffee carafe and headed for the kitchen. "That's enough of this depressing talk. The coffee is cold. I'll make a fresh pot if you talk about something else."

Everyone said, "Agreed," approximately together.

Juliette crept back into Peter's mind. He longed to see her again. He had to see her again, even if she rejected him.

Hannah said, "Peter, why don't you stay with us for the holidays?"

He nodded and said, "Yes, I would like that."

Chapter Three

6 January 1938

Liebesfreude
(Love's joy)

Peter arrived back in Nürnberg on Wednesday, the sixth of January, the day of the final performance of La Traviata, and walked straight to Juliette's Wohnung. Juliette watched from her window as he approached the door to her building, listened to his feet on the stairs, and heard his tentative knock on her door. She sat in the upholstered chair under the window, her feet curled under her, trying to remember the feeling that had caused her to reject Peter and then torture him for four long months. Juliette forced herself to stay there while he tried again, a little louder this time. Finally, she jumped up and said, "Peter, wait, I'm coming!" as she heard him trip running down the stairs.

She waited ten minutes before leaving for the theatre.

Choir members and stage personnel filled the cafeteria, but Juliette found Peter alone at a table in the corner. He faced a window, his blank eyes looking outside at nothing. Juliette was sure Peter hadn't seen her, and she noticed he didn't have his usual beer in front of him, so she bought one. He didn't see Juliette until he stood to go to the bar, and Juliette set her tray opposite his. She smiled sweetly and said, "Never mind, I've got a beer for you." Peter looked at her, confused, then sat down heavily. She sat opposite him, and he asked, "Where did you come from?"

"I just got in on the train from Brussels. How about you?"

"I arrived from Munich a few hours ago and went to your house. You weren't there, so I came here to practice, but..." He took a breath. "I love you, Juliette, and I beg you to forgive my stupidity at the rally.

I've spent the past two weeks with my grandfather and grandmother and..." He paused, then started again.

"I understand now why you warned me about Hitler. I can't believe I was so blind. I can't stand you being angry with me, and I don't know what I'll do if you don't forgive me!"

Juliette removed the paper from her croissant and then put her hand on her glass of milk. Though tempted for a moment to torture him, she was so pleased with his change in attitude that she wanted to kiss him, so she said sweetly, "I forgave you a long time ago." She looked across the table at his puzzled expression. "I love you too, but I've been waiting for you to understand that politics in Germany is not a game; it is, without exaggerating, a matter of life and death for you and your family!"

Juliette's hands left her croissant and milk and gently rested on Peter's hands. "Now that we have that out of the way, I want to talk to you about our options. I have done some research, and Hitler has something to say about that, so let's have dinner somewhere quiet after the performance and get down to specifics."

La Traviata has always been a heart-breaker opera, and grown men cry when Violetta sings her last gasped note. Juliette and Peter portrayed the tempestuous love affair between Violetta and Alfredo with a passion that devastated the audience when Violetta died. No one wanted the night to end, but after eleven curtain calls, the exhausted lovers finally returned to their dressing rooms, and the people in the seats finally gave up and went home.

It was almost ten when Juliette and Peter left the theatre and began walking more or less in a northerly direction toward their apartments.

"I still feel light-headed after that ovation." Peter squeezed Juliette's hand, looked down at the cracks between the paving bricks, then stopped. Their eyes found one another, and four months of misery evaporated.

"Were you serious about dinner with me?"

"Yes, I would like to go out for dinner. It's late, I'm famished, and I want to talk to you about love." Juliette squeezed Peter's arm.

Peter picked the most expensive restaurant in the city, "How about the Steichele? I've heard they have an excellent wine cellar, and they're on our way."

Juliette looked up at him. She had planned on a smaller, more intimate venue but decided not to mention it. "If you like it, I'm OK with the Steichele. It needs to be romantic, so choose our table wisely."

Peter didn't try to hide a catch in his breath, and when he stopped, Juliette pulled Peter's arm. She was cold, and snowflakes were beginning to cover the cobblestones. The Steichele was three blocks away, they would close soon, and she wanted to get there as quickly as possible.

"I promise it will be romantic." Peter's excitement aroused Juliette. "The food is excellent, and it's open until midnight." Happiness sparkled in his brown eyes, and Juliette shared the feeling for the first time since the rally.

They walked fast, breathing out puffs of frozen mist, and less than five minutes passed before they entered through the heavy wooden doors. The maître d' showed them to a corner table, expertly lit a candle with a flourish and asked if they would like to order a bottle of wine. They each took a copy of the wine list, but Juliette knew what she wanted. She ordered a bottle of white Spätauslese, and Peter quickly closed his leather-bound folder. She defended herself.

"I want something sweet tonight." He grinned like a schoolboy.

Peter wisely said, "Tonight belongs to you."

The theatre audience had made their preference for her Violetta over his Alfredo starkly evident during the solo bows, so she decided to throw him a bone.

"I'll let you drink your sour wine when we're married, but tonight, I want everything to be sweet." Juliette watched Peter melt, and her heart jumped.

He hadn't missed the coaching. "When we're married? Shouldn't I ask you first?"

Juliette chuckled and held her hand under his face; he took it gently and asked, "Juliette Durand, will you marry me?"

Juliette widened her smile. "Yes, darling Peter, I will marry you..." She pulled her hand back, and, although puzzled, he kissed it before he let go.

"But there are conditions, and you may want to change your mind when you hear them." She set her purse on her lap, opened the clasp, unfolded a piece of paper and pushed it in front of him.

"This is an official copy of the chart explaining the Nürnberg Race Laws. I got it from the Einwohneramt, and it explains why we can't get married if we're going to live in Germany."

With questions written all over his face, Peter read it in the faint light of the single candle. He took five minutes to figure out where he would fit in the description of who was a Jew and what it meant to their relationship. Juliette waited patiently for his reaction.

"If I am reading this correctly..." Peter looked down at the paper and followed the words with his finger... "I am officially a Jew..." He said it without emotion. "And that means I can't marry an Aryan." He looked up at Juliette. "You are Belgian; doesn't that make it all right?"

She shook her head, Peter's expression darkened, and she explained.

"No, Peter, I am Aryan." She pointed to a line on the document. "The definition of an Aryan under this law is any white European who is not a Jew or a Gypsy. The Romi are Gypsies, as are the Sinti, and, worse than that, they and the Jews are Untermenschen. Hitler has designated a third of the country, and the world for that matter, as Untermenschen, the equivalent of Neanderthals, and he has assigned the ultimate race of Germanic Nordic-Aryan like your father, the title 'Master Race.'" She slid her finger to the bottom of the page.

"No, that can't be true..." Peter, exasperated, tried to rationalize what was in the document, "How can my mother be a subhuman and my father a member of the Master Race? They are the same!" He stared at the paper, and Juliette put her hand over his.

"We can get married in Belgium, but we would never be allowed to return to Germany as husband and wife. Marriages like your parents' can continue because they were married before this law. However, our marriage would be illegal in Germany, even though we would legally be married in Belgium. If we have sex together in Germany, the police could arrest us. And worse, I'm afraid we can't even live under the same roof here." She looked into his frantic face. "Do you understand what the Nazis have done to us with this law?" She took his hand in both hers, lifted it to her mouth, and kissed his fingers.

They silently waited as the smiling waiter poured the wine. Peter tasted it, looked at the waiter, noticed he was a member of the master race and said, "Yes, that will do," without enthusiasm. He waited for the waiter to disappear before he continued.

"My God! Who could be so inhuman? How did this happen?" Peter's face reddened, and Juliette was afraid he would scream. She began speaking quietly, and his face softened.

"Hitler set this up with the precursor of the present Race Law two years after he became chancellor. The law, which forbade Aryans to buy from Jewish businesses, didn't define a Jew, so most people ignored it. Before the Nürnberg Race Law, the lack of a definitive legal description of our situation would have allowed us to marry. But now, this paper is available at every Einwohneramt in every city, town, and village in Germany. The Polizei, or worse, the Gestapo, must now arrest Aryans who go into a Jewish store, and we don't want to think what they will do to the store owner. Of course, marriages like ours are now forbidden."

Peter looked down and said quietly, "This is just more proof that I am a fool." He absently folded and unfolded his hands, then gripped them together so hard his fingers turned white. Finally, he looked into Juliette's eyes. "And I voted for that monster. May God and you forgive me!"

She wrapped her hands around his clenched fingers. "I forgave you in September after the rally. I wanted to hold you then, and I want to hold you now, but at that moment, I couldn't do it because you didn't understand the implications of Hitler's power. Tonight, I don't dare because we are in public, we don't know who's watching..." She tilted her head toward the hovering waiter... "and...it's illegal."

Juliette watched Peter try to resign himself to his fate. Finally, he said, "Ich liebe dich, Juliette!" and she pushed back tears.

Peter's plans had evaporated, and his romantic mood had dissolved with them. He hadn't realized the implications when he first looked at the document, but now...

Peter shook his head and asked, "What are we going to do? Our contracts in the opera house run until the end of this year. There are about ninety opera houses in Europe, and sixty-five are in Germany. Where are we going to get a contract if we leave here?"

Juliette picked up her glass, saluted Peter, and bought some time by downing half the glass. Then, forcing a confident tone, she said, "You are an excellent singer, but your French, Italian and Latin are terrible, not to mention your Bach interpretation!" She pointed at him. "You and I will work on your diction and your Bach, and by the end of the year, Mademoiselle Desjardins will have contracts for us all over Europe! Brussels and Antwerp have good opera houses, and we will audition there. We will spend the summer singing in small festivals to polish up our language skills, and we will be married in my parents' church at the end of the year when our German contracts run out. My mother will arrange all of that, and we will honeymoon somewhere warm, like Greece or Spain or southern Italy."

"How long?" Peter asked, his face expressing a mood that rose like a hot balloon.

"How long what?"

"How long have you had all this planned, and when were you going to tell me if I hadn't asked you to dinner?"

Juliette laughed mischievously. "My mother and father and Monique Desjardins—she's a talent agent now—helped me work it all out while I was home, and I was going to tell you as soon as you figured everything else out. I didn't think it would be possible for you to visit your Jewish grandparents and not return enlightened, but you surprised me by turning completely around." Juliette took Peter's hand, took a long drink of the last of her Spätauslese, and felt its warmth course down her body from her throat to below her belly button, "And if you think about it, I invited you to dinner."

Chapter Four

July 1938

Liebe kann viel, Geld kann alles.
(Love can do much; but it takes money to do everything)

THE SPRING REPERTOIRE INCLUDED productions of The Bartered Bride by Bedrich Smetana and Don Giovanni by Amadeus Mozart. Everyone in the theatre knew that Peter and Juliette were now 'steady,' but no one said it, not wanting to be responsible for what it would mean if the Gestapo got involved. Peter had asked Juliette to sleep with him, but although no one in the city would have believed it, she refused. Consequently, the open secret that was not a secret remained a secret, and the Gestapo stayed away from Juliette.

Peter sang the rejected lover, Don Ottavio, a thankless and forgettable role in Don Giovanni, except for one understandably famous tenor aria about a furtive tear. Juliette sang Zerlina, a dazzling diva role, to roaring applause.

After their curtain calls, Peter led Juliette backstage and stopped outside her dressing room door. When Juliette opened it, Peter put his arm across the opening, blocking her.

He said, "I feel that I'm deceiving my fans by depicting an illegal, intimate relationship that, well, isn't happening. I am living a lie!"

She gently slapped his hand and said, "Stop feeling guilty…your fans understand that deception is our business. In fact, how can I be sure you love me? You've become such a great actor… How can I be sure?"

"But I do love you!" He said it far too loudly and looked down the busy hall before he whispered, "I'm not pretending—in my heart, I'm a criminal—the worst kind! Everyone thinks… everyone knows we are breaking the law, and it's dishonest of us to deceive our friends and fans!"

Juliette put her finger on his lips, playing the role he set for her, "shh."

"So," she whispered in his ear, "what you are saying is that I should make you an honest man by sleeping with you?" Juliette laughed and pointed her finger at his nodding face. "Yes, I see you want to sleep with me. But you're a criminal just for thinking about it!" She poked him in the side; he put his hand on the spot and groaned as though she had broken a rib.

"Shh." She somehow made it sexy to put her finger on his lips again. She pointedly looked down and chuckled at his embarrassment as he turned sideways, thankful that her desire didn't show as his did.

She stepped through the door. "In that case, it's up to me to save us from the Gestapo—so goodnight, sweet prince!" She closed it in his face.

Juliette and Peter began the six-week-long summer break on the third of July by crossing the Belgium border using first-class train tickets donated by Juliette's parents. At the Brussels station, Juliette led an astounded Peter to a new Rolls-Royce 25/30. Peter stopped and stared at it as they approached, then moved aside as the chauffeur—he recognized Marcel dressed in the ridiculous uniform—took their bags. Juliette led Peter to the back seat, where she snuggled beside him on the leather seat.

The open-topped Rolls was perfect for this beautiful day—the breeze in the backseat was magnificent, and Juliette used her hand to deflect the soft, warm air onto her face.

Peter looked for a canvas top, but there wasn't one. "What do you do when it rains? What about winter?"

"Oh, this car has a top that Marcel can install," Juliette said matter-of-factually, "but Papa found it was a nuisance, and there was room in the garage for another Rolls, so he bought a second one with a permanent roof."

She suddenly realized she had answered as though he had asked a silly question.

"Are you aware that one of these cars costs more than my father's house?"

Juliette, miffed, answered quickly, "Yes, I know I'm spoiled, but I can't help who I am any more than you can. I like being rich, but I think I could be just as happy without money..." She quickly revised the exaggeration,

"Well, not with no money, but with very little money… Like normal people. As a matter of fact, and you know it's true, I lived with a roommate at the opera school, I didn't have my own bathroom, and I even made my own bed…sometimes."

Peter laughed. "You had better not marry me if you can't live without a lot of money."

Juliette straightened her hat. The wind tried to blow it away. She adjusted the pins that held it on her head. "You think I'm a spoiled brat, don't you?"

Peter touched her hand. "I wouldn't say you're a brat…but spoiled… I'm worried that I won't be able to earn enough money to keep you happy."

Juliette smiled and tried again. "Would it be an affront to your German pride to let Daddy help?"

Peter laughed, "That doesn't solve anything. Let me meet your parents, and I'll try to fit in somewhere."

Juliette decided to leave it there. Her parents were ethnic French, but both spoke Flemish and German. Her mother struggled with German, mostly because she hated the language, and her father was also fluent in Italian and English because of his occupation as an international art dealer. While Peter struggled with French, his English was good enough that he wouldn't starve in England, but his diet would be limited to fish and chips. Despite her diligent work to prepare Peter and improve his French, Juliette sensed he was apprehensive about meeting her parents, especially her father. Peter had spoken with her father on the telephone, but the conversation had been short and intense.

The Rolls-Royce glided quietly down the circular drive of Avenue de Saturne 6 and stopped in front of a two-storey Tudor-style house with a red roof covered with dormers. Its exterior of black beams and white stucco promised a warm interior.

A woman rushed out to greet them, with a tall man calmly following her. The woman's black hair and green eyes demonstrated the source of Juliette's genealogy, but she didn't appear old enough to be Juliette's mother.

Veronique Durand hugged her daughter, turned to Peter and said, "You didn't tell me he was so handsome!" She reached up and wrapped her arms around his neck, kissed him on the cheek, said, "Thank you for protecting my daughter from those thugs," then scolded her daughter, "Were you afraid I would steal him from you?"

"Welcome to our home, Peter!" Juliette's mother spoke musical French. "My name is Veronique, and my husband is Jacques."

Peter said in passable but harsh French, "Thank you, Madame Durand. I'm looking forward to getting to know you and your husband." Juliette smiled at her mother, and her mother winked. She had forced Peter to memorize that phrase, and, unfortunately, that was exactly how it sounded.

Although a few years older than his wife, Jacques Durand had the same youthful appearance, emphasized by his square shoulders and athletic waist. He had a slightly oversized—some would say large—French nose and a dark complexion. Jacques held out his hand to him; Peter took it, and Jacques said, "Welcome to our family," as he pulled Peter close to hug him. Juliette stifled a laugh at Peter's attempt to avoid it.

Marcel the chauffeur took the bags into the house, and Juliette followed him, walking ahead of Peter. They stepped into a wide foyer opening to a beautiful stairway rising out of a polished hardwood floor to the second floor, wide enough to accommodate four abreast. A chandelier hung over the centre of the opening, and doors led to rooms on either side of a long hallway.

"Where do you want Peter to sleep, Mother?" Juliette asked.

"Of course, I assumed he would sleep with you, my dear. Charles moved a double bed into your room." She smiled at a handsome, middle-aged black man who appeared and picked up the bags. Juliette and Peter followed him up the stairs.

Her mother called after Juliette, "Take your time freshening up. As soon as you're ready, we will have wine on the terrace."

The bedroom was more like a suite of rooms, with a private bathroom and dressing room. The sleeping room furniture was Colombo Louis XVI made with inlaid walnut roots. A Persian rug covered the dark oak floor except for a narrow strip around the outside, and a white embroidered canopy with a matching bedspread covered a black four-poster spool bed.

Charles put the bags in the centre of the room, and Peter offered his hand before the servant could turn to leave.

"Thank you for your help, Charles." He shook the man's hand. "My name is Peter."

Juliette touched the black man's arm and said, "It's good to see you again, Charles, and thank you for helping."

Charles winked at Juliette, nodded at Peter, and left without speaking, softly closing the door behind him.

Juliette looked at the bed and then at Peter.

Peter grinned. "I guess your mother doesn't know about the Nürnberg Laws."

"No, I haven't told her about that," She returned the grin, "She obviously thinks that since we're engaged, we're sleeping together."

"I'll sleep on the floor." Peter looked at the carpet, then the bed; it was clear to Juliette he had something else in mind. She laughed and said, "Nonsense, Belgium has no such law, so you'll sleep in the bed with me." Still laughing, she went into the bathroom, shaking her head at Peter's failed attempt to look serious.

Juliette and Peter walked into the drawing room fifteen minutes later, Juliette wearing a long, summer-flowered dress that stopped just above her ankles, and Peter, constrained by his limited wardrobe, dressed in brown cotton pants and a tan shirt. Veronique's eyes lit up, and she let out a soft but audible sigh when they walked into the room.

"What a beautiful couple you are!"

Veronique stood to meet them before they reached the centre of the room, where a Steinway grand piano and a row of potted plants visually cut the lengthy area in two. Windows on one side spanned the entire length; trees and flower gardens filled the openings that looked out into a spacious yard. Outside, on a wooden terrace running the length of the building, Charles had set four places at a table covered with a white tablecloth.

Veronique took Peter's hand, guiding him to the table, and Juliette and her father followed them. Not confident of the protocol, Peter waited until everyone else had chosen their chair before he nervously sat in the only one remaining, beside Veronique and opposite Jacques.

Charles appeared with a tray of cheese and bread and a bottle of white wine. Jacques poured the wine, filling every glass to precisely the same level.

"I propose a toast to the betrothed." He stood and raised his glass. "May you give us many grandchildren."

Peter and Juliette exchanged glances, and everyone stood to take a symbolic sip before sitting down again.

Juliette turned to her mother, "Our contract goes to the end of the year, leaving me no time to come to Brussels to arrange the wedding. Can I leave all of that in your hands? I will have my wedding dress made in Nürnberg, but I'm afraid everything else will be yours."

In no hurry to answer her daughter, Juliette's mother took a sip of wine and picked up a piece of Gouda cheese. She nodded at Jacques, and he looked at Juliette as he spoke.

"Veronique and I have discussed this constantly since you were here at Christmas, and we think you should get married this summer. We can make the arrangements and get you married before you return to the theatre. You do have six weeks, don't you?"

Juliette said as she nodded, "Yes, but there is still the problem with Peter's citizenship and racial designation." She took a sip of wine, let that settle in, then took the discussion further. "His mother is Jewish, and his father is German, making him a Mischling."

When Juliette stopped to breathe, Veronique interrupted. "I don't understand what that has to do with anything—aren't Mischlings still Germans?"

Juliette shook her head, "No and yes, depending on your interpretation. A Mischling is a person of mixed blood. Because Peter has two Jewish grandparents, Germany officially classifies him as a Jew for some things while allowing him to remain and have most of the rights of a German citizen in other ways."

Jacques interjected, "In Germany, a Jew can't marry an Aryan, and Juliette is officially an Aryan. So, the question is this: Does his Mischling status extend that far?"

Juliette nodded at her father and explained to her mother, "Germany passed a law three years ago forbidding sexual relations or marriage between Aryans and non-Aryans, but it didn't define the difference. According to that law, Mischlings are technically not Jews… but, unfortunately, they are not Aryan either."

Veronique asked, "Have you two been obeying that bizarre law?"

"Mother, you do get to the point!" Juliette wagged her finger and chuckled. "Yes, Mama, we have obeyed the law since Christmas, when they began to enforce it. The penalty is a prison sentence without the benefit of a trial. We have waited this long; we can wait a little longer."

Veronique turned to a red-faced Peter. "How do you feel about waiting, Peter? There is no Gestapo and no race law in Belgium!"

He cleared his throat, "Juliette will decide…It's not my decision. But I will not put her in any danger."

Veronique nodded, then continued. "That's not an answer to my question, Peter, but I'll assume the obvious."

While Peter's face turned crimson, she turned to Juliette.

"Why can't you get married here this summer? You could continue living separately in Nürnberg, and what you do privately in your own homes would surely be your business. Couldn't you occasionally visit one another?"

Juliette shook her head vigorously, leaving no room for interpretation. "No, no, no…we used to, but not now. I know from experience that the Gestapo believes there is no such thing as privacy in Germany, especially for Jews, and that organization has no heart! If we get married here, the church will register our marriage, and if the German authorities find out, they will arrest Peter and send him to prison. We can't take that risk!"

After a short silence, Jacques said, "I think that in light of the injustice and callousness of the German government, you would both be justified in breaking your theatre contracts, and I will take care of any financial repercussions. I will arrange an audition for both of you in the Monnaie Theatre, and I am sure that Monique Desjardins can find enough work outside Germany to keep you both busy. I would be happy if neither of you returned to that country until Hitler is either deposed or dead!"

Juliette hesitated, but Peter responded immediately.

"Sir, there are sixty-five opera houses in Germany—three times as many as in the rest of Europe. The German government supports their theatres, and if we break our Nürnberg contracts, we will never sing in Germany again. Our careers in Germany will effectively be over." Juliette was surprised at how smoothly Peter explained the situation in French—a few wrong tenses and word endings, but understandable.

Veronique leaned to Juliette and said, "You realize that Peter is taking a risk by staying in Germany and that you will share that risk by staying there with him. It won't matter whether you are sleeping together or not if your theatre friends think you are."

"Yes, Mother, we've discussed that, and I have discussed it with the Gestapo." Juliette wanted to make her mother understand there was no immediate danger if they obeyed the rules.

"We know the risk to us of getting caught having sex in Germany is small, but we can't take a chance; we must wait." She smiled at her mother, then turned to smile at Peter. He was looking at his folded hands, and he was not smiling.

He said half-heartedly, with a bit of heroic self-sacrifice thrown in, "I can wait as long as we are in Germany. I love Juliette, and our whole lives are ahead of us."

Peter looked like his dog had just died, and Juliette noisily stifled a laugh.

Jacques spoke to Peter and Juliette in perfect German. "I want you two to listen to what I have to say. I have many German clients, most of them Jews, but some are National Socialists high in the government. They are all moving their art objects to vaults in Switzerland, and some are selling their collections to convert everything to cash, which they change to Swiss Francs and deposit in Swiss accounts. Many Jews leave Germany if they can, moving to Palestine, Shanghai, or the United States if they have enough money, and I am helping these people liquidate their assets. I can tell you that Hitler's intentions terrify my Jewish clients—they fear the bastard might do what he promised. Most believe that the government, as in Himmler, Heydrich and Goebbels, is impatiently waiting to move on the Jews, take all their possessions, and then force them into labour camps. They believe that the motivation driving this persecution is larceny—that cultivating hatred against the Jews is a deliberate tool for financial gain, not a philosophical one. I don't go that far, but I won't eliminate the possibility either."

Peter tried to respond in French but quickly switched to German, "My mother's parents are secular Jews; my grandfather teaches mathematics in a Munich Gymnasium, and my grandmother works in the school office. They have only a few possessions and barely enough money to keep them going from day to day, so if that's true, I don't think the Nazis would have much interest in them." He coughed, choking on a drop of saliva, and Jacques waited until he drank the last bit of wine in his glass and started again.

"My father is a master machinist in the M.A.N. factory. His job is essential to the German industrial and military programs, and he is very protective of his family. I don't think the government will disturb my family for those reasons."

He looked at Juliette. "As for me, I am a tenor in one of the largest opera houses in Germany, and good tenors are rare. I have influential fans who would be very disturbed if anyone were to bother me."

Jacques looked to Veronique for help, but with her limited German, she had none to offer. He turned again to Peter, "Do not expect German politicians or the Gestapo to follow your rational logic. Nothing they have done concerning the Jews makes sense unless one assumes their intention is robbery. Everything they say about the Jews is a lie, and if they continue on this path, the cost will be so immense that they will surely bankrupt their country. Meanwhile, the men pushing this policy are becoming rich, ergo, the anti-Jew policy. German professionals are leaving the country as fast as possible; in universities, entire science departments have emigrated to England and the United States and are welcomed there with open arms."

Jacques emptied the wine bottle into his glass. No one spoke as he drank, and when he finished, he said, "My income has tripled this year, entirely through helping Jews and Hitler's minions move assets out of Germany. Every month, frightened Jews liquidate their estates, transferring the money and valuables to Switzerland and the United States. A year or two of this, and there will be nothing left for the National Socialists to take! For that reason alone, they must move on the Jews now or lose those assets forever."

He leaned close to Peter. "When it comes to your grandparents, remember this...If they move on rich Jews, they must move on all Jews. The attack will be based on the trumped-up lies of the party's ignorant, fanatically anti-Jewish and anti-communist element, led by Goebbels and Himmler. They will enlist Himmler's SA and the SS to carry it out. If anyone dares resist, Hitler now has the laws and power to eliminate them without interference from the Justice system."

Veronique, speaking slowly for Peter's benefit, switched the conversation to French.

"Jacques knows German politics because he must advise his clients. He deals with many non-Jewish Germans who agree with his assessment of Hitler's intentions; some are very high in the German government. Disturbed with the party's direction, many of them have opened accounts in Switzerland."

Jacques took over in German.

"They quietly move money, jewels, and art into Swiss vaults. Corporations are moving reserve cash to Swiss Francs in Swiss accounts, and a few are sending everything to the United States. Of course, Hitler is blaming all this on the Jews, but that's only one more lie to add to the pile. No non-Aryan German is safe if Hitler decides to persecute the Jews in earnest. The National Socialist Party has become a band of thieves!"

Veronique sat up straight, then leaned ahead to plead desperately to Juliette and Peter, "Please stay in Belgium… Don't return to that dreadful country. Sleep in that beautiful bed I set up for you; get married here; please, please, don't go back!" She looked at Jacques. "We will replace whatever you have there, and you can both live here for as long as you want. Jacques and I have already decided to set up an apartment for you. Tell us how much money you need to live comfortably; it will be in your account every month. Please, do this for us!"

Juliette noted her father's surprise at the offer and rescued him. "Mother, we can't accept your charity." Jacques breathed out audibly. "Peter has a family in Germany, and we have careers there. We will try to find singing work outside Germany for next year when our contracts expire, and I promise we will leave Germany. We love one another and will be married here, but we must try to leave the door open to sing and visit Peter's family in Germany. Perhaps, when and if Hitler sees the error of his ways, we can return to our careers there." She added hopefully, "This insanity will stop somewhere."

Veronique wiped her wet cheeks with her napkin. "If you go back to Germany, I'm afraid I'll never see you again!"

In bad French, Peter said, "I promise that when our contracts expire, we will return to Brussels to be married, and we will remain outside Germany until they repeal the Nürnberg Laws."

Jacques spread a thick layer of butter over a piece of bread and slapped a generous slice of brie on it. He drank the last of his wine before he said, "I think we should celebrate and stop worrying. There is nothing we can do to change the children's minds, so we should work our way forward." Then, speaking directly to Veronique, he said, "For now, I suggest you start making wedding plans."

The family spent the remainder of the afternoon chatting about the wedding. They set a tentative date for Wednesday, 28 December, three days after the effective end of Juliette and Peter's contracts in Nürnberg and the final performance of La Bohème on Christmas Eve. They made plans to leave Germany the day after Christmas.

A week later, Juliette and Peter sang for the manager and general music director of La Monnaie Theatre. The Durand family supported the theatre, and its contributions saved it from closing during the beginning years of the Depression. Veronique served on the board, and Juliette had previously sung Mimi in La Bohème. When Jacques Durand called, the manager did not need to consider his reply.

The theatre had already set the program for 1939 but hadn't cast all the roles. They ambitiously planned to perform the four operas of Wagner's Ring Cycle, which accounted for the first three months of the year. However, they still hadn't cast La Nozza di Figaro, scheduled to premiere in early May, and that would give Juliette and Peter time to attend the rehearsals that would begin in early March.

Juliette and Peter started their audition with the first act duet from La Bohème, and when the manager clapped and said, "Brava," Juliette knew they wouldn't need to sing anything else. Shortly afterward, the theatre manager led them to his office, talking as he walked. He said, "We have con-tracts to discuss, and I have decisions to make about next year's program."

The offer was for Susanna and Basilio in The Marriage of Figaro and minor roles in the Wagner Ring Cycle. He also indicated that he would cast them in leading roles in the operetta he planned to do in the autumn of 1939. The money wasn't adequate for the couple to live on; they would need some oratorio and concert work, but Monique Desjardin assured them that would not be a problem.

Juliette arrived home walking on a cloud; her world was coming together.

She and Peter slept in her 'four-poster' bed for the remainder of their vacation, and every evening, they cuddled on the expansive terrace and watched the sun go down through the trees. Charles kept them supplied with tea and pastries, and Veronique and Jacques avoided disturbing them. Juliette could feel herself growing closer to Peter as the summer evenings counted down and Hitler and his world receded farther and farther from their new reality.

Chapter Five

9–10 November 1938

Die Kristallnacht
(The crystal night - the breaking of glass)

Their grandson's choice of bride delighted Moshe and Hannah despite Juliette's religious beliefs. They had never considered their grandson Jewish; Elizabeth had raised her children in the Lutheran church, true to her husband's convictions. Elizabeth's choice of a Christian husband had not sat well with her Jewish parents, but time had healed the wound, and when Juliette and Peter arrived at Moshe and Hannah's door, it was to a warm welcome.

It was Wednesday, the fifth of November, 1938, the day Hitler would find an excuse to allow Goebbels and Himmler to open their Pandora's Box of hatred toward the Jews. Goebbels had carefully and methodically prepared gullible German society for this day, using his Propaganda Ministerium to drive people who would otherwise never have thought of violence to commit terrible atrocities against their neighbours. On that sad Wednesday, Hitler finally opened the curtain that hid his true intentions, allowing Goebbels and Himmler free rein over their sadistic wills. Nothing could have prepared the country for the inconceivable events that would follow. It was the beginning of the end for tens of millions of people.

It took only a few hours for Juliette and Hannah to become friends, and when, in the late afternoon, the small talk became boring, Hannah took her to the kitchen, determined to teach Juliette how to make Kartoffel knödel.

When they sat in their places for dinner, Moshe opened a sweet and expensive Eiswein for the occasion, and Hannah and Juliette drank most of the bottle before the main course was over. There were a few laughs about Juliette's potato dumplings, but Hannah's Sauerbraten received unanimous approval. When the brown-sugar-encrusted apple pudding dessert appeared, with instructions to wait, Peter pulled his chair back, put one knee on the floor beside Juliette and took her hand, silencing the conversation.

Brimming with joy, he looked into her beautiful eyes and said, "Juliette Durand, I love you more than I thought it was possible to love anyone. Would you give me your hand in marriage? Will you marry me?"

Juliette and Peter hadn't spoken of a formal proposal or a ring, so Juliette's surprise was genuine when Peter opened the small box that magically appeared in his hand. The cluster of diamonds had cost Peter at least six months' salary, and, for a moment, Juliette hesitated. She wanted to tell Peter this was too much, that their future was uncertain, but the look on his face stopped her. She held out her right hand to him, and he slipped the ring on her finger. With shining eyes, she put her arms around his neck and said what true lovers always say, "Yes, I will marry you!"

Moshe and Hannah clapped, and Hannah's eyes shone as she said, "Oh, Juliette, I'm so glad you're joining our family!" She glanced at the knödel and quickly added, "Don't worry, I will teach you how to cook." Juliette forced a sweet smile while everyone else laughed.

They spent the evening exchanging tales of childhood pranks and playing Shafkopf. Moshe and Juliette teamed up against Peter and Hannah, giving them a savage beating. At eleven o'clock, tired and happy, Juliette and Hannah went to bed when Peter and Moshe turned their attention to politics.

Too happy to sleep, Juliette's thoughts were of children and family when, fifteen minutes after she pulled up the covers, she heard someone knocking frantically on the door to the apartment. She heard Moshe open it and invite someone inside.

From the frantic tone of the voices, something was very wrong, and for Juliette, sleep was immediately out of the question. She got out of bed, pulled on her housecoat, and stepped into the hall where she could see two people who, assuming from the conversation, were Aaron and Louise Rinzler, Moshe and Hannah's landlord. They lived in the apartment below them, and an alarm went off in Juliette's mind when she saw them standing in the living room dressed only in their nightclothes.

A terrified, confused Aaron spoke too loud for the small room. "My friend David just called. He told us to hide! We must leave the house immediately!" He whispered as loud as he could, his emotions out of control. "David said SA and SS soldiers and gangs of thugs are breaking windows and doors in Jewish houses and stores; they're looting and stealing, breaking everything! Mobs of people are dragging Jews into the streets and beating them!" He began to cry. "The city has gone crazy—we must leave immediately!"

Juliette arrived in the living room as Peter, still dressed in his street clothes, went to the door that Moshe had left open, checked the stairwell, turned off the light, then closed and locked the solid door, sliding a steel bolt into its pocket. He turned out the living room light, and the sudden darkness stopped the conversation.

"I'll get some candles..." Moshe turned to leave, but Peter grabbed his arm.

"No...no lights, no candles, and no loud talking! If the mob comes, they must believe no one is here." The firmness in Peter's voice startled Juliette; she had seen a glimmer of this side of him when the SA had arrested her, but this was Peter taking control, and she felt a surge of pride.

He started down the hall toward the bedrooms, speaking firmly to Juliette as he passed, "Get dressed as quickly as you can." Peter moved fast, and when he reached Hannah's room, Juliette heard him say, "Get dressed, Oma—we're leaving here now!"

Peter's focused resolve jolted Juliette's mind from fear to panic, and without saying a word, she dressed as quickly as she could in the dark. Before she left the room, she checked that the curtains were tight across the window. Through the open door, she heard Peter say to Aaron and Louise, "You must get dressed here; you can't return to your apartment."

Then he spoke to Moshe. "Do you have clothes to fit them?" and Moshe answered, "I do, I do. Maybe not a perfect fit, but well enough."

Juliette headed for the living room, meeting Moshe, Louise, and Aaron, hurrying to the bedroom. She went straight to Peter—he barely acknowledged her, but she grabbed his hand and insisted.

"Peter, what's happening?" She followed him as he took a wooden chair to the door and wedged it between the handle and the floor. "Can I help?"

"Perhaps, in a moment." He turned to the window looking out on the street and began pulling the heavy drapes across it. He hesitated just before they came together, the sound of angry shouts drawing his attention to uniformed soldiers and a mob of civilians running toward Aaron and Louise's shop. Somewhere in the distance, the glow of fire reflected off the sky, and a cold chill ran down his spine as he drew the curtains together, completing the darkness by eliminating the soft light from the street,

Peter turned, put his hands on Juliette's shoulders and looked into her eyes with an urgency that frightened her. "I'm not sure what's going on, but I'm afraid that Hitler is moving against the Jews, just as your father predicted. This could be very bad; we can't risk staying here, but I'm not sure it's safe to use the streets."

Peter clipped every word, adding driving determination. "Moshe and Hannah must disappear, and Louise and Aaron must go with them! We must take everyone to my parents' house in Augsburg, even if we have to walk fifty kilometres through the woods!"

Minutes later, Moshe returned to the living room carrying an unlit candle. Peter nodded to his grandfather, and Moshe lit the candle. Aaron joined them at the table, and they began to outline a plan to hide in an abandoned factory five blocks from the apartment. A Jewish friend of Aaron's had recently purchased it and had given Moshe and Aaron a tour. They described it to Peter as enormous, with dozens of empty rooms.

Juliette listened, trying to keep her mind on the emergency, but the desperation in the conversation increased her apprehension. For the first time in her life, panic started to overrule her keen sense of logic.

She admired Peter's ability to take control—something she had never imagined him doing—but then remembered how cool-headed he was when things went wrong in front of an audience. Peter didn't lose his head; he never stopped singing, leaving his fellow performers out on a limb.

The sound of boots on the stairs ended the escape-plan discussion and Juliette's reflections. Peter blew out the candle, and everyone stopped breathing to listen. The sound of shouting in the stairwell one floor down, then hammer blows and wood splintering, stirred the hot coals of terror beginning to glow in Juliette's heart. Peter touched her arm in the darkness, then quietly fitted another chair in place to brace the door.

Everyone was in the dark living room, listening to loud voices rising from the street and the sounds of furniture and dishes breaking in Aaron and Louise's apartment, when Peter whispered to Juliette, "Take Hannah and Louise to Hannah's bedroom and lock the door. Block it with whatever you can find, and don't make a sound or come out, no matter what you hear!"

Peter's urgent tone encouraged the women to scamper down the hall to Hannah's bedroom, where Juliette quietly closed and locked the door. As silently as she could, she braced a chair against the door as she had seen Peter do, then slid a dresser against it. She sat down on the floor next to Hannah.

A minute later, Juliette heard hard-soled boots stomp up the stairs and stop in the stairwell in front of the apartment door. Hannah grabbed her hand and squeezed it. Louise wrapped her arms around Hannah. Fists beat against five centimetres of oak, voices yelled curses at the Scheissjuden hiding behind it. Minutes later, the beating and cursing stopped, and hope replaced panic, but moments later, something more solid and heavy than a man's fists or boots hammered on the thick oak door. Hannah whimpered, and Louise made a shush sound.

The apartment door, solid black oak fitted against a solid oak frame bolted into a concrete block wall, was too much for fists, boots, and now, even the blunt instrument the thugs were using, and Juliette began to hope they would give up. Her hopes became more optimistic as a loud, harsh baritone voice shouted, "We know there are Juden in there, but if you open the door, we won't hurt you."

Juliette held her breath and prayed that the men would tire and leave—there would be easier targets. But more boots ran up the stairs. And then, more hammering, using a different tool, one that cut into wood. Juliette's heart stopped as she heard splintering. Something crashed against the door, tearing pieces away.

Someone shouted louder and more clearly; there was no longer anything between the voice and the living room. "Schmutzigen Scheissjuden!" It was a shout of triumph—another crash, more splintering—the shouter was coming through the door to get at the men in the living room. Heavy boots crossed the floor.

"No!" Juliette heard Peter shout, "Don't do it!" And then, a thud, followed by what could only be a body hitting the floor.

Juliette's heart stopped but started again when she heard a cry of anguish from Peter; he was still alive! The shouter's terrible, triumphant voice revelled in his work, and Juliette covered her face, overcome by fear and panic. She bit her lip to keep from crying out.

A new voice said, "Grab him, but don't kill him—they will pay us good money if we send him to a work camp!" Juliette's heart jumped again when Peter screamed in rage. Her Peter was alive and fighting!

The sound of blows and grunts carried to the bedroom; the new voice yelled in pain. Peter cursed his tormentors, and the struggle continued. Juliette tried to stand, determined to help Peter, but Hannah pulled her down. Juliette resisted, but a sense of hopelessness paralyzed her when she heard a body fall down the stairs then evil voices laughing. She sat on the floor and leaned hard against the wall, sobbing. Hannah put her arms around Juliette's neck, softly whispering Shush, Liebling in her ear. Juliette cried as quietly as she could.

Aaron's voice shouted out the pain he couldn't bear, and Louise whimpered pitifully. Juliette heard sounds that could only be an object pounding against body parts as Aaron's screams echoed through the building. A final horrible thud ended his cries.

Hannah and Louise rocked in one another's arms, but their whimpers went on. Juliette put her chin down against her chest and cried softly into her hands. Terror filled her as she realized the terrible men in the living room would surely search the apartment.

Juliette heard Peter cry out from the stairwell and stopped crying to listen, but there were no more sounds. She tried to stand, but Hannah pulled her down, whispering, "We must be very quiet. You cannot help Peter now. You must survive!" Juliette slid down the wall to sit on the floor. Louise began to shiver, and Hannah wrapped her arms around her. Juliette thought she could hear Peter's distant voice in the street, shouting for help as she sobbed into her raised knees.

A switch clicked in the hall, light shone under the door, and Juliette heard boots in her bedroom across the hallway. A pair of heavier boots stopped in front of the door where the women hid. Juliette trembled, pulled her legs tighter to her chest to stop the tremors, and asked God for a miracle.

The handle rattled with increasing violence—a boot kicked at the door, but it held. The sound suddenly stopped as a young man's voice in the hall said, "Let's go, Fritz. The others are gone; we should catch up to them."

Louise whimpered softly, and Juliette held her breath.

The man with the boots made a "shh" sound, and then his resonant bass voice, one that Juliette's keen sense of pitch would never forget, said, "There's someone in there; I can hear the Jew bitch whining!" Juliette stifled a cry as he kicked at the solid oak door again, but it didn't yield.

"Get the pick-axe." The deep bass commanded the young voice, then grunted as he uselessly kicked the door.

Juliette locked her arms around her knees and squeezed, begging God to let her die.

Hannah tapped her shoulder urgently, and Juliette looked at her. Hannah pointed down at the floor, and Juliette followed her gaze to a specific floorboard, not different from the rest.

The door splintered on the first blow from the heavy axe, and pieces of wood flew into the room. Juliette jumped to her feet and ran to the dresser, bracing herself against it. Hannah got up and joined her, and then Louise found a corner to push on.

The oak door shattered, the hole widening with each blow. Light burst in from the hall, and Hannah put one arm around Louise. Panic tore open Juliette's soul as she watched the door disintegrate, sapping her strength as a massive man in a brown SA uniform smashed at the edges of the opening with the pick-axe, ripping the pieces aside. Done with the splintered door, he dropped the axe on the floor with a loud clatter and pushed, but the dresser didn't move. Juliette watched in horror as the brute pulled out his pistol. Animal growls rose from deep in his throat as he aimed it at Hannah, bared a crooked set of nicotine-yellowed teeth in a disgusting grin, and pulled the trigger. Hannah fell, and Louise screamed. Juliette cried out as the brute fired, then yelled, "getroffen." He fired again, and Louise's screams stopped.

Juliette was alone, facing a ruthless animal twice her size! Pistol raised, the fat man snorted, proclaiming his victory, and Juliette waited for the death she had prayed for.

But she knew there would be no easy death for her when she heard the fat man say, "No, I'm not going to shoot you yet," and saw him holster the gun so he could push on the dresser.

Juliette gasped as she tried to pull breath into her lungs, but her body needed more. The animal pushed the dresser aside, then grabbed her with his arm around her waist as she tried to get past him.

The fat man yelled triumphantly, "Mädchen, du gehörst mir," and Juliette could see most of two rows of rotten teeth. He distorted his already grotesque face as he threw her on the bed and assessed his prize, holding her arm in a grip that stopped the blood. She tried to twist away, but as quick as a hungry predator, the brute let go of her arm and grabbed her shoulder. Juliette's energy increased with her certainty of his intent—she wrenched herself around to loosen his grip, but his free hand grabbed her other shoulder. His left hand struck like a snake—its fat fingers wrapping themselves around her throat. She tore at his hands, but the harder she fought, the harder he squeezed and pushed her down. Juliette struggled to breathe, twisted her body one way, then the other; he squeezed her throat tighter and let go of her shoulder—he waited as her strength ebbed—she prayed once again for death. He tore at her dress with his free hand, ignoring her waning struggle, laughing, excited by the fight. Her dress ripped—he tore it off, then pulled at her underwear. She kicked at him, clawed at where she thought his face would be, but her strength seeped away, the room began to fade, and her vision became a vague blur.

She heard his voice coming from far away, saying, "This is a lively one, Wilhelm!" He laughed as he squeezed her throat tighter. Her arms fell uselessly to her side; he grabbed one of her now barely moving legs with his free hand, and the voice, farther away, said, "You can have what's left when I'm done."

Juliette's struggle stopped as he expertly choked the life from her. Barely aware of his weight on her, she felt him release her throat so he could spread her legs with both hands. Her brain began to function again, and she tried to renew her struggle, but his weight held her pinned to the bed. She heard him spit on his fingers; she screamed when she felt him pushing into her.

Juliette entered a world of excruciating pain and intense humiliation: Something inside her tore, and she cried out. The animal grunted, drove himself deep into her. She felt wetness on her thighs... He groaned, forced two more violent thrusts, and pushed the pain deep inside her. He increased the power and frequency of his thrusts, then grunted as he slowed, pushed harder, and finally collapsed on her. Panting, he rolled off her.

He laughed deep in his throat as he used the bedsheet to wipe blood and semen off himself. Pulling up his pants, he looked at Juliette with an evil grin. She pulled her feet together, but the beast sprang to the bed, grabbed her left foot and raised her leg. She squirmed, but he held it tighter and raised it higher.

"Well, I'll be fucked," he yelled at the young soldier, "Look at this! The Jew bitch was a virgin! Wilhelm, I fucked a virgin—that's my first!" He pointed his finger; she tried to turn away. He threw her leg back on the bed; she turned on her side, away from him, pulling her legs up until her knees were in her stomach.

"Come on, Fritz!" Wilhelm pleaded, "We've got to go!"

Fritz laughed from his fat belly, and Juliette didn't care when she heard him slide his pistol out of its holster. "OK, I'll shoot her if you don't want to fuck her."

Juliette waited for the blackness; she was no longer afraid; she welcomed death.

But the devil wasn't done with her, and she heard Wilhelm say, "No, Fritz, I want to fuck her. You go ahead—I'll shoot the bitch when I'm finished."

Juliette heard the fat man holster his gun, heard him growl as he went past the young man into the hall. "Be damned sure the Jew bitch is dead when you leave... Better to put one in her head to be sure." He stomped down the hall, through the living room, and Juliette heard him go down the stairs.

While the fat brute was leaving, the young man approached the bed, and Juliette suddenly wanted to live. She felt burning hate rising like a fire in her, and she committed herself to fight with whatever strength she had left. Juliette turned toward her enemy, positioning herself to attack him. She raised herself on her hands, pulled her feet under her and faced him like an animal, teeth bared, a growl resonating from her throat. The young man stayed just out of range. He picked up her torn dress, and, arms outstretched so she couldn't reach him, he threw it over her. She brushed it aside.

He pulled out his pistol and said, "Promise you won't tell on me!"

Juliette closed her eyes. He fired two shots, but she felt nothing. When she opened her eyes, he was disappearing through the broken door.

Juliette lay on the bed for a long time before she moved. She cried until no more tears would come, and then gradually, her strength returned. She swung her legs over to the floor, stood up, pulled the bloody sheet off the bed and stood over Louise. Juliette gently covered her, sobbing, then sat on the floor beside Hannah. Holding Hannah's head in her lap, she rocked back and forth and began singing a Brahms lullaby. As Juliette sang, the humiliation retreated, replaced by a blazing rage she knew would never cool. She whispered through grinding teeth, "I will punish them, Hannah, no matter the cost. I will find the bastards, and I swear to our Gods that you and Louise will see them burn in Hell!"

Juliette sat with Hannah for a few more minutes, grief forging a rising rage and burning hatred that she knew would be part of her until she died. And then a sense of resolve took over, squelching the tears. She stood and went naked into the living room, dreading what she would find.

Aaron and Moshe lay in pools of blood. She cursed in four languages and forced the contents of her stomach to stay where they were while she looked for Peter. A glimmer of hope crept into her mind when she couldn't find him—there was blood on the floor near the door, but not enough to kill a man. There was no body in the living room or the stairwell; Peter was not dead!

A grim determination began to grow out of the havoc within Juliette, its intensity increasing as she went to the bathroom, washed in the tub, and returned to her bedroom. She picked out clothes, combed her hair, put on lipstick, and returned to the room where Hannah and Louise lay dead. She crossed herself, then searched for the floorboard Hannah had shown her. It took three tries, but Juliette found the loose board, lifted it, and found two envelopes—one marked "Last Will," and the other containing two bundles of money, one in Reichsmarks and the other in Swiss francs—a lot of them. She didn't stop to count; it was enough.

Juliette found her purse on the floor in the living room where the fat man had thrown it. Young Wilhelm had called him Fritz... two names and faces she would never forget.

She opened the purse—there was no money, but her passport was still there. She stuffed the thick cash envelopes through the opening, closed the catch and touched her ring with her left hand—they had missed the most valuable item in the apartment.

"I will find you, Peter," she said softly, "I swear I will find you!"

She left the apartment, ran down the stairs and out into the street. Glass littered the vacant sidewalks, and she vowed her revenge over and over as she furiously, methodically, placed one determined foot in front of the other.

Chapter Six

November 1938

Arbeit Macht Frei
(Work makes you free)

Two SA soldiers lifted Peter from the street, stood him on his feet and pushed him to walk. Peter tried, but his feet would not move ahead, and he fell, cutting himself on the rough paving bricks. Blood ran from his head into his eyes. People appeared from nowhere; they kicked him, spit on him, and called him "Saujude!" He couldn't see his tormentors; the world swirled around him; he vomited on the street. He shouted, "Ich bin kein Jude!" at the paving stones. Strong hands slid under his armpits, lifting him. Soldiers grumbled, pushed the people away, accused him of laziness. They half-carried, half-dragged him to a waiting Lastwagen, a truck with the load bed covered with canvas. He cried out again, "Ich bin kein Jude," as strong hands threw him in the rear. He screamed when he landed on a steel floor. He retched on a pair of shoes—a man cursed, and the shoes disappeared.

As the soldier transport moved, Peter rolled onto his side, propped himself up on his elbow and wiped his eyes with his fingers. Three confused and disoriented men sat on a bench facing a young SS soldier holding a machine pistol. The man closest to Peter helped him to a vacant spot on the bench next to the tailgate.

"If you're going to vomit, please do it outside," said the man beside him. He indicated the flap of canvas that didn't entirely close the rear.

Peter nodded, then turned to the soldier, who shifted his machine pistol slightly to indicate it would be a bad idea to try to jump out. The young Sturmabteilung soldier looked through Peter to check on the flap, appearing not to notice his bloodied face, blood-spattered clothes, or the puddle of vomit. Peter looked at his bruised hand, vaguely remembering hitting an SA officer—was that why he was here?

The truck stopped at a security gate manned by four brown-shirted soldiers with red armbands. While one of them checked the driver's papers, Peter read the words over the iron gate and balled his fists.

"Scheisse!" he whispered, "We're in Dachau!"

The prisoners had been quiet, but the man with vomit on his shoes asked, "How do you know?"

"The iron sign on the gate says Arbeit Macht Frei. I've seen pictures of that gate, and it's the entrance to Dachau."

"My God!" The man's voice broke, "Dachau is for criminals…I did nothing wrong…why am I here?"

"Halt's Maul!" The young man with the gun waved it in the prisoners' faces. "If you want to live to see the end of the day, keep your mouth shut." He pointed the gun at the man who had spoken. "If you plan on protesting your arrest, it would be kinder of me to shoot you now. Verstehst du, Jude?" The man nodded that he understood.

The truck stopped in front of a stone building, and two soldiers in brown uniforms with red armbands lowered the tailgate. Peter noted black swastikas on the bands—they were Sicherheitsschutz—the SS.

Peter gritted his teeth against the pain in his ribs and slid out of the Lastwagen, but when his feet hit the ground, a stab of pain in his chest made him cry out. One of the soldiers caught his arm just before he fell and asked, "What's wrong with you?" in an unsympathetic tone.

Peter gasped, "I think they broke my ribs," and struggled to stand.

The guard supported him until he could move without help, then led the group into a building where the first person Peter saw told him to strip. Other men in prison garb led him into a shower room where two prisoners, who appeared to be trustees, sprayed him with disinfectant and told him to wash. Peter did as instructed and then followed one of the trustees out of the room. The man gave him a prison uniform, brown shoes that approximately fit, and two coarse wool blankets. Two guards, one of them armed with a pistol, led him and three other prisoners out of the building and across a gravel yard.

They took them to one of a long row of wooden buildings with

"22" carved into a sign over the door frame. The lead guard opened the door; the one with the pistol stayed outside. They entered a long room lit with three bare bulbs. Their warm orange light shone on four rows of triple-layered narrow cots, one against each outside wall and two down the centre. There were two alleyways and no windows. The guard guided Peter to an empty top bunk and watched him painfully try to throw his blankets onto the bed, helped him pick them off the floor, and, standing on the bottom bed rail, spread them neatly on the thin mattress. The man then pointed to two doors at the end of the room. "Toilets and showers." He looked at Peter without emotion. "Mealtimes are at six a.m. and six p.m. There will be no talking, and you will begin work tomorrow." He turned on his heels before Peter could ask a question.

Peter looked at the men sleeping in the bunks around him…none stirred, but Peter knew some of them had to be awake. He climbed the ladder, curled into a fetal position and pulled the top blanket over him. He tried to control the shivers that suddenly shook him, but the harder he tried, the more violent they became. His tears fell onto the rough woollen blanket between him and the mattress. He lay on his right side with his broken ribs on top, and the pain was bearable, but the anguish in his heart was not. Moshe and Aaron were dead—he was certain of that and wanted to cry out his grief and anger, but fear and uncertainty choked back the sound. He prayed silently to the God he had never been able to imagine, begged Him for a sign that Juliette, Louise, and Hannah were still alive. The rational part of his mind told him they couldn't have survived the brutality he had seen, but his heart silenced it. Juliette had to be alive!

The remainder of the night brought dark thoughts and unbearable grief. Men groaned, snored, shouted, and farted, and sleep didn't find Peter until morning, when a whistle, then the sounds of men whispering and shuffling across the floor stirred him awake. His ribs had stiffened, and it took him long minutes to climb down the ladder.

He was on the floor in time to meet the food cart. Men silently lined up, and a skinny prisoner with a black badge identical to the one worn by the trustees in the prisoner processing building gave Peter a metal bowl and a spoon. The man, who Peter assumed was also a trustee, ladled wheat porridge into the dish, and Peter ate it in four trips to his mouth with the spoon. He followed the other prisoners' example and put the bowl and spoon on a shelf beside his bed. Intimidated by the silence, he didn't try to speak to anyone, and no one said anything to him.

The whistle blew; the men lined the empty alleyway between the beds. Each man appeared to have a set position, and they left a gap for Peter between them. A man with a paper clamped on a board asked each man his name, checked it off, and when he got to Peter, Peter said, "Schweitzer, Peter," in the same order the others had. The man looked at the paper and said, "No work for you today. Your trial is this morning, so you must stay here until someone comes for you." He looked at Peter's bowl, still on the ledge. "You must wash your bowl and spoon before inspection, or we will punish you."

Peter waited until the men filed out of the room before going through one of the doors at the end of the hall where the guard had indicated the toilets would be. He took his utensils with him.

Showers lined the wall with no separation, and there were no sinks. He left the room and tried the other door. He had found the toilets—French-style holes in the floor—a trench against the wall served as a urinal. There was no toilet paper but a small hose with a spray nozzle hung beside each hole. The wall opposite the urinal was lined with a tin trench serving as a sink, with a brass water tap every forty centimetres. The room reeked of excrement, urine and disinfectant.

Peter used the urinal and then went to one of the washbasins to clean his utensils. The basin was clean when he began, and he made sure he left it that way.

Halfway through the morning, a very thin prisoner with two badges, one black and the other yellow, woke Peter from a deep, troubled sleep. He said, "It's time for your trial. You must follow me."

The man patiently waited while Peter climbed carefully down the ladder, gasping in pain on every rung. Peter followed him outside and decided to try to talk to him.

"What does the yellow badge mean?"

The man didn't turn his head. "Jew, and the brown badge on your shirt means criminal. Better your badge than mine!"

He led Peter across the compound to another building, obviously one that housed camp officialdom. They climbed the stairs to the first floor and stopped in front of a door marked Gerichtskommisar. The trustee knocked and opened the door without hesitation. He motioned Peter to enter and closed the door behind him.

A Gestapo officer in black street clothes sat behind a desk, writing energetically. He didn't lift his head as he said, "You are a Jew, charged with resisting arrest, assaulting an SA officer, and opposing National Socialist policies. What do you have to say for yourself?"

Peter said, "I am not a Jew; I am officially a Mischling. My mother and father are registered as Evangelisch; they are officially as German as you are."

The man stopped writing, lifted his head and smiled. Peter waited, but the man said nothing, so he went on.

"The SA officer didn't tell me that I was under arrest. He attacked me, and I defended myself. He and those under his command killed my grandfather and his neighbour in cold blood!"

Peter stopped, but the officer just stared at him and waited, smiling.

Peter suddenly remembered an accusation he had missed, "I have no quarrel with Hitler or National Socialist policies, and I have never opposed them."

The officer finally said, the pleasant smile still on his face, "Before I pass sentence, do you have any assets you would like to donate to the Nazi Party of your own free will?"

Peter hesitated, surprised, then said, "I have about three thousand Reichsmarks that I will gladly give to the Party, and my apartment has some furniture in it that I will also donate. Otherwise, I have nothing."

The officer, still smiling, looked into Peter's eyes. "I suggest that you have miscalculated, or perhaps you have forgotten a hundred thousand Reichsmarks you would like to donate." The smile became a thin, straight line, a threat. "You have one month to find the money; otherwise, your sentence is three years of hard labour."

"What about the murder of my grandfather and his neighbour? My betrothed, my grandmother, and my grandmother's friend were also in the Wohnung... where are they? What's happened to them?"

The officer began writing and speaking without looking up. "I have no report of those people or others who might have been in the apartment, but I will see that the appropriate Polizeipräsidium looks into your accusations."

The Gestapo Gerichtskommisar rang a small bell on his desk. The prisoner trustee immediately opened the door, and Peter silently followed him to the barracks, his mind trying desperately to understand what was happening to him. What had happened to Juliette and his grandmother? Someone had to tell Hitler about this... But was Juliette's father right? Was Hitler under Goebbels, Göring's and Himmler's thumb? Was this the beginning of the end?

Chapter Seven

November 1938

Das Leben ist kein Spielplatz
(Life is no playground)

J ULIETTE CLIMBED THE STONE STEPS into the Reichspolizei building, entered through a massive door, walked up to the front desk and said, "I want to report four murders, a missing person, and a rape!"

She spoke emphatically, concisely, as she imagined the bureaucrat in front of her would appreciate. Then Juliette looked closely; she saw something familiar in the woman—she had stood before her five years ago.

Before she looked up, the officer finished reading a sentence in her Ernst Jünger novel, *In Stahlgewittern.*

"These are serious charges, and I am not authorized to deal with such things—you must come back in the morning at seven." She turned the page and resumed her reading.

Juliette resisted the impulse to scream, took her passport and visa out of her purse, laid them on the counter and waited. She was suddenly aware that she had clamped her jaw so tight it hurt.

When the woman ignored her and continued to read her novel, Juliette said through clenched teeth, "As you could see if you looked at these papers, I am a Belgian citizen, and I am engaged to marry a citizen of Germany. An hour ago, SA criminals murdered my betrothed's grandfather, grandmother and their neighbours. The same SA officers kidnapped my future husband. You must do something!"

The woman sighed, marked the page, and closed the book. She picked up a pen, slid a piece of paper in front of her, and poised her hand to write. "I know who you are... We established five years ago that you are not a Jew and that you have very powerful friends. Who is the rape victim?"

Juliette screamed at her, "I am the rape victim!"

The officer lifted her head and smiled at Juliette. "You are not a child…did you not enjoy it?"

Juliette slapped her hand on the desk so hard it hurt. "If you don't do something, both you and the verdammte Dritte Reich will regret it!"

The woman leaned toward Juliette, almost touching her face. She shouted, her spit hitting Juliette's cheek, "How dare you say that here? You must leave immediately, or I will arrest you for threatening a police officer and the Führer!" The size of her voice fit her Nordic stature.

Juliette held her position while noisily coughing up a large wad of phlegm, and the woman sat down. Then, waiting long enough to make her point, Juliette picked up her passport and visa, swallowed, turned on her heel and walked across the marble floor to the door she had entered. Once through it, she slammed the heavy oak against the frame so hard she expected the glass in it to shatter and fall on the stone steps.

Juliette half-walked, half-ran to the train station, bought a first-class ticket to Brussels, and a half-hour later boarded the first train that took her in the direction of home. She telephoned her parents at the Aachen station, ten kilometres from the Belgian border, changed trains, and crossed into Belgium. An hour later, she arrived at the Brussels station, where the Rolls-Royce awaited. Marcel didn't ask what had happened, and Juliette didn't volunteer any information. She caught him watching in his mirror as she wiped tears away, and they stared at one another for what seemed too long. He finally looked away when she blew her nose, and the look on his face frightened her.

Juliette opened the door before her mother reached the car, jumped out, and stopped trying to control her anguish. Sobbing, she threw herself in her mother's arms, and Veronique held her until Juliette's sobs became whimpers. She turned Juliette toward the house, her voice soothing her daughter as it had since she was a child.

"Don't try to say anything, ma chérie…come into the house, and we'll talk about what happened." Juliette fought to control herself but could only sob when she tried to speak.

Marcel followed them with his head down, keeping a discreet distance but remaining close enough to hear them. Mother and daughter held one another until they reached the door, and Marcel rushed around them to open it.

Juliette broke away and moved quickly across the living room, spotting the morning paper on the table where Veronique had been eating breakfast. She picked it up—the headline screamed: "NAZI MOBS RAMPAGE THROUGH GERMAN STREETS. THOUSANDS DEAD!"

Juliette put it back on the table and turned to her mother, her voice breaking, "They killed Hannah and Moshe and their neighbours! I don't know where Peter is... Papa has to find him!"

Juliette alternately cried and talked for the next half-hour, trying desperately to remember every detail but stopping short of telling her mother about the rape. When she was finished, Jacques walked into the room. Juliette threw her arms around her father's neck and wailed, "Oh, Papa...Peter's gone, and Hannah and Moshe are dead!"

Juliette told an abridged version of the story into her father's shoulder, including the details of the SA brute and his minion breaking into the room and killing Hannah and Louise. When she stopped, he held her at arm's length. "What about you?" he asked, "Did they hurt you?" His voice broke.

Juliette knew he had the answer when she lifted her head to look at him. He asked softly but with hard determination on his face. "Ma chérie, I must know. Did they hurt you?"

She looked deep into her father's eyes but couldn't find the courage to tell him about the brute and what he had done to her. "Papa, I can't tell you what happened. Would you mind if I talked to Mama alone?"

She had answered his question, and his entire demeanour changed as he said, "Before you do that, I need you to answer a couple of questions: How many did you see? Did you hear them use names? Were they SA or SS?

"There were two. Wilhelm, a young man, and Fritz, a fat ugly man with yellow teeth and ten years older than Wilhelm, maybe thirty-five. They were SA."

"Accents?" Jacques spoke through a clenched jaw, his teeth barely parting.

"Fritz had a heavy Bayern accent, almost a Swiss Aussprache. Wilhelm's was the same as Peter's."

A mask of fury drifted across Juliette's father's face, and she hardly recognized him as he leaned over and kissed her cheek. There was brutality in his face that she had not thought possible. She knew a terrible plan was forming behind those hate-filled eyes, and Juliette didn't recognize the man who turned to leave the room. Her father's shoulders shook as he went through the door, and he smashed his fist against the wall as he rounded the corner. He shouted, "Marcel, I need you!" but Marcel was already there.

Juliette took a deep breath, turned to her mother and braced herself for what she had to say.

"That SA man, the fat one with the yellow teeth, raped me. That's why he didn't kill me when he killed Hannah and Louise."

Veronique collapsed into a chair; all colour drained from her face. "Oh, Mon Dieu, no!" She put her face in her hands.

Juliette put her hand on her mother's shoulder. "Fritz wanted to kill me when it was over, but Wilhelm, the younger soldier who was with him, saved me." Her mother raised her tear-streaked face.

"Marcel will kill both of them, and I will help him if I can."

Juliette had more to tell her mother but hesitated when the rage she saw in her mother's eyes equalled what she had seen on her father's face. When her mother turned away, Juliette found enough courage to blurt out, "Mama, there was more blood than there should have been, and there was a lot of pain! I'm afraid that he tore me inside!"

Veronique squeezed the arms of her chair, thought for a few seconds, and then switched to action. "I will call the doctor, and you must go to the hospital immediately." She stood up and shouted, "Marcel, we need the car!"

Ten minutes after her father and mother took their daughter into the hospital, doctors and nurses surrounded Juliette, quickly concluding that they must put her under anesthetic to assess and repair the damage.

Juliette awoke, groggy and nauseated, fighting to regain consciousness with all the will she had. Peter came into and out of dreams, and she cried out his name as he appeared, then disappeared. As her mind slowly cleared, Juliette discovered her mother sitting beside her. She tried to sit up, shouting, "Mother, tell Papa we must find Peter!" Her stomach immediately revolted. Veronique put a pan under her face in the nick of time; Juliette's stomach turned inside out in its attempt to get rid of everything.

The retching lasted only a few minutes before Juliette felt much better and lay back on the pillow while her mother caressed her hair. Her father appeared, surrounded by fog, and Juliette forced herself to stay conscious. Somewhere in the mist, she heard, "I have called the SS client in Munich. As an intelligence officer, he knows everything that goes on within a hundred kilometres of Munich—I will know what happened to Peter before this dreadful day is over."

She smiled, happy, and Peter returned to sing her to sleep.

Juliette woke an hour later and was on wobbly legs in another half-hour. Her father was gone, and her mother took her arm to steady her.

"The doctors said there would be no permanent damage. You need to rest at home for a few weeks." She helped Juliette dress and supported her as she shuffled down the wide hallway.

Juliette stopped as a sense of urgency overwhelmed her. Peter was in trouble; she had to help him! Desperate, she pulled on her mother's arm and shouted, "We must find Peter!" Her mother caught her before she fell.

Juliette was awakening from a nightmare when Marcel lifted her from a wheelchair to the back seat of the Rolls. She was still awake when he cradled her in his arms and carried her into the house.

Juliette had no appetite for food but drank a cup of 'nerve tea' to help her sleep before Veronique took her up the stairs to her bed. She tried to sleep but, despite the drug-laced tea, became ever more restless, her sense of urgency growing. Frustrated, Juliette teetered and tottered to the bathroom and then dressed while sitting down. Carefully negotiating the stairs, she worked her way to the drawing room, where Veronique and Jacques sat in front of a fire. Jacques stood up and said, "Juliette, I'm glad you're here...I expect a call momentarily that will give us Peter's location. But right now, I can tell you with certainty that Peter is alive."

Juliette clapped her hands and looked up, "Thank God, and thank you, Papa. I knew in my heart that he had survived. But I know he is in danger—we must bring him home!"

On cue, the phone beside Jacques rang. Juliette heard her father say, "Dachau?" then, "How much?" And then the conversation went on to the price of a painting. Ten minutes of haggling later, Jacques and the caller settled on a thousand Swiss francs, and he hung up the phone.

"When can he come home, Daddy?" She kissed him on the cheek. Jacques picked up his whiskey and downed the last of it.

"Peter is not injured, but he can't come home." He looked sympathetically at his daughter. "The charges against him are resisting arrest and subversion against the Nazi regime. But his real crime is, of course, that he is half-Jew." He shook his head. "He also broke an SA officer's nose, but, at the moment, that's not important."

Juliette gasped and sat down beside her father. "Peter broke someone's nose? I can't imagine him hitting anyone. But last night, he surprised me in a lot of ways!"

Jacques said, "The Gestapo judge demanded that Peter make a one-hundred-thousand Reichsmarks donation to the Party, the standard amount for this situation."

Veronique looked worried, "Can we pay that much?"

Jacques said, "Yes, I think we can arrange that," holding back a grin, "but I will still have to negotiate, or they won't take me seriously in the future. My Munich SS contact will negotiate for me—I've offered to sell him a painting worth at least a hundred thousand for a thousand Swiss francs. If he gets Peter out of Dachau, I don't care how he does it or how much profit he makes."

He looked at Veronique with a guilty smile. "I bought the painting from a prominent Nazi party leader with a money problem." He chewed on the end of the pencil he had been using and smiled thoughtfully. "...I'm ashamed to say that I bought it for less than a thousand Swiss francs."

"Oh, Papa, thank you!" Juliette kissed him on the cheek. She thought for a moment, then said, "You're making a profit?" Jacques said, "The value of art is subject to the opinion of the buyer and the seller. I make my living by manipulating one or the other, or both, to my benefit."

The mood at dinner was one of hope, and the phone rang again before they finished. Juliette heard from her father's side of the conversation that his contact had more information, and when Jacques returned to the table, he explained, "The SA and the SS have arrested thousands of young Jewish men and sent them to work camps like Dachau. Those with no money will serve sentences ranging from three years to indefinite. Peter's sentence is three years if he cannot come up with the donation to the party, but we can take care of that."

Jacques paused; Juliette looked at him hopefully, and he continued. "As you would expect, some of these young men witnessed atrocities, and the Nazis want them out of the country. The only catch is that I can't get Peter out of Dachau without a visa and a prepaid ticket to another country. Once we have everything and Peter has the papers signed by the proper Gestapo official, they will escort him out of Germany without any contact with anyone. But if he returns, he will return to Dachau—or worse."

"Papa, wherever he goes, I will go with him; I can't lose him."

Jacques nodded. "I understand, but you must appreciate what that means. I don't doubt Peter will be glad to leave Germany, but no European country will accept him. Most of them have openly accepted the Nürnberg Race Laws, and all the Balkan countries have passed similar racist restrictions. Jews are not welcome in England or America unless they have more money than I can afford to give to Peter. A few South American countries might still accept Jews, and there is a possibility in Shanghai and the Philippine Islands. However, Jews who are my clients and have some money still have difficulty finding a country." He looked at his daughter. "Are you sure you want to follow Peter? You aren't married, and you could wait for him here. I promise to get him back as soon as I can."

Juliette didn't try to hide the shock in her voice, "Papa, don't you understand how much I love Peter? I will go with him if we have to live in a cave! You think I haven't the courage or character to survive without all this?" She swept her arm around the room, glaring at her father.

And then she threw everything out in the open. "A Nazi raped me less than forty-eight hours ago, and it was the worst experience I can imagine! But I will not let that pig ruin what will be the most beautiful thing in my life!" She clenched her fists, breathed, and asked softly, "Please, Papa, you must help us!"

Jacques only had one daughter, and his daughter knew what he would say.

"Of course, your mother and I will help you! I am proud of you, and because you want it to be so, Peter is part of our family." Jacques looked from his wife to his daughter. Juliette was manipulating him. She was going with Peter so her father would work harder at getting him back.

He sighed. It would cost a lot more than a thousand marks to get that done!

"You are like your mother…you are both manipulators, survivors and fighters. If you follow Peter, you leave us with no choice. We will support you with everything we have, but I need you to tell me everything." He pointed at her and went on… "We can start with that Nazi SA bastard. I want you to write down as much as you can remember about him while it's fresh in your mind. Write down every detail, even those you think are inconsequential. Marcel and I will find him!"

Juliette stood up, threw her arms around her father, and kissed the stubble on his cheek. "I love you, Papa." And then her expression changed; she was no longer Papa's little girl.

"When you catch Fritz, I want to kill him…just me, no one else! Wilhelm can live."

Jacques looked at Veronique, and she awkwardly broke the short silence. "I hope you reward your father's generosity with a house full of children. I could never give you a sister or brother, and I need babies to cuddle."

Juliette's face changed again, and she winked at her mother.

"I promise I'll be a good Catholic daughter," she said, smiling, then turned to her father, and the smile disappeared. "You know that I will never forgive you if you don't let me kill that bastard with my own hands!"

Jacques said, "Yes, I know," Veronique put her silk handkerchief over her mouth and began to cry.

A few days later, the National Socialist Party received a generous donation on Peter's behalf, and Heinz and Elizabeth received a letter demanding that he leave the country. He must have a valid visa and proof of paid passage to the country named on the document. Peter's mother immediately called Jacques.

Jacques found a way to get two visas for Shanghai. However, before the Shanghai government would issue them, they insisted that he deposit ten thousand British pounds in the British Shanghai Bank in Peter's name. Juliette needed a marriage license to travel with him, so, aided by her father and a sample supplied by Peter's mother, Peter's signature appeared on the document.

Juliette danced around the house, singing to herself, and did her vocal exercises every evening. She looked forward to being in Peter's arms and back in Brussels to sing Susanna in May.

Chapter Eight

11–12 November 1938

Eine Hand wäscht die andere
(One hand washes the other)

ON THE OVERCAST MORNING OF HIS SECOND DAY IN DACHAU, Peter marched through the yard with forty other prisoners from his barracks, herded by four guards. The men entered a building full of machinery to make artillery shells, and each man went to his station. One of the guards steered Peter to a machine that crimped the explosive projectile cartridge into the brass propellant casing; a whistle blew, and the assembly line started. A heavy man who clearly hadn't been a prisoner for long lined up the first shell and pulled the lever that initiated the process of pressing the explosive charge into the brass casing and crimping the edge.

While Peter watched, he studied how the crimping machine worked, his curiosity concerning all things mechanical aroused. An SS officer patrolling the work floor stopped beside him and paid particular attention to the crimper. He examined the newly crimped shell, said to Peter, "Pay attention; you will do this tomorrow," and then moved on.

As Peter watched, he kept the conversation with the worker to questions about the crimping process, and it didn't take long to figure out how little the man knew about what was to Peter a relatively simple machine. When it became apparent the crimps weren't tight, the man tinkered with the adjustments, but Peter could see that the crimps still were not satisfactory—the adjustments weren't the problem. He silently watched the man ruin five shells before he called for help. The SS officer arrived, looked at the shells, and stopped the assembly line. He shouted and waved, and a man with a toolbox appeared.

Heinz Schweitzer, Peter's machinist father, was heartbroken when Peter chose a singing career rather than using his natural mechanical abilities and exceptional intelligence to become an engineer. Peter had worked with his father in the research and development shop at M.A.N. every free day since he was fifteen. Peter's brilliant mechanical talent baffled everyone in the department, and the chief Maschinenbauingenieur took the boy under his wing. Peter's intuitively logical thought process at once grasped concepts far beyond the understanding of normally gifted boys his age, and his father's chest swelled with pride when the engineer shook his head and said to him, "Heinz, you have an engineer on your hands; the best I've ever seen!"

When the mechanic began examining the machine, Peter immediately realized the man knew no more about mechanical systems than the operator. Peter had recognized the problem with the crimper after the first shell but had decided that silence was likely his best bet until he got the lay of the land.

The mechanic adjusted the fingers on the crimper to the limit of their travel, the officer waved the line to start, and Peter wasn't surprised the first shell wasn't acceptable; in fact, it was worse. Peter assumed that someone would reject every one of the shells before they reached the end of the line. But despite that, the operator continued to crimp ammunition that Peter's keen sense of mechanics told him was unacceptable, and he knew the bad crimps couldn't be fixed.

A half-hour later, the SS officer stopped at the station to check on the machine, examined a shell, and, to Peter's annoyance, said nothing. Peter's father had taught him not to accept sloppy work, and so, as the officer turned to leave, Peter faced him and said, "Sir, the machine is not set up correctly, and someone must reject every artillery round this machine is ruining. Perhaps, if you stopped the line for a few minutes and the mechanic let me use some of his tools…"

The SS officer cut him off with a sarcastic laugh. "Saujude, you would be better off to shut up and watch—perhaps you will learn something. You have only today to learn how to operate the machine; if you don't, you will find yourself in a pail of shit!"

Peter told himself that correcting the problem was helping the Nazis—not what he wanted to do right now—but his natural obsession to fix things that didn't work was irresistible. That urge had been pounded into him by his father, beginning when he broke his first wooden toy soldier and continued through repairing his bicycle and sharpening his mother's knives. He had spent three summers working with his father, and if it hadn't been for his addiction to the sound of his own voice, his love for Juliette, and Professor Garcia's stubborn insistence, he would be graduating from Heidelberg University with an engineering degree.

Peter's frustration grew as the day wore on, and defective cannon shells continued to go down the assembly line—hundreds of rounds—faulty ammunition that, when the fuses and primers were installed, could kill the men who handled it. The day seemed endless; the operator didn't permit Peter to touch anything and only reluctantly answered his questions. Peter stood in bored, exasperated silence while the crimp deteriorated with every shell until Peter was surprised they stayed together long enough to be packed in boxes! No one said a word about the crimp, although four SS officers patrolled the assembly line, occasionally examining an artillery shell. Each round had a half-dozen stamps and tags on it by the time it reached the packers, and Peter assumed that was what the officers were examining.

Late in the afternoon, the whistle blew, the line stopped, and the operator left without saying a word.

The prisoners returned to their barracks to an evening meal of bean, potato, and turnip soup, two pieces of unbuttered coarse black bread a little bigger than Peter's palm, and a tin cup of warm water tinged with black tea. Peter thought of the German father's arietta in Engelbert Humperdinck's opera Hänsel und Gretel: "Hunger is the best cook." The dry black bread and the bland soup tasted delicious, and he wanted more!

The following day, when a prisoner trustee led Peter to the crimping machine, there was no operator. Peter looked around, found the scrutinizing SS officer who had chastised him the day before, and the man motioned him to operate the machine. A whistle sounded, the machinery started, and Peter stepped up to the crimper. He guided the first shell casing into the socket designed to hold it, and a projectile dropped on top of the powder. When Peter pulled the lever, the fingers on the crimper jammed the rim of the brass casing against the sides of the cartridge as they should, but the crimp was far from perfect. Peter was certain it would fail well before the shell was in the breech of an 88 mm cannon.

Nevertheless, the finished shell slid away, and another took its place. Peter lined it up, pulled the lever, and, as anticipated, got the same result. He looked at the officer, pointed to the shell and said, "Dass ist Scheisse!"

The SS officer shouted a command, the whistle blew, and the line stopped.

The officer examined the shell, said, "You are not crimping them properly!" and pulled Peter away from his station. "Don't touch anything until I return…I must find out whether this is your fault or something is wrong with the machine."

The officer left and returned with a higher-ranking, older SS officer and the mechanic from the day before. The superior officer pulled Peter aside while the mechanic examined the machine and said, "All of yesterday's production was rejected by the inspectors. I've been watching you… Do you know what's wrong with it?" Peter nodded. "Can you fix it?" Peter nodded again.

The older officer waited patiently while the mechanic and the younger officer fiddled with the crimper. Finally, the mechanic stood back, wiped his hands on a filthy rag, stared blankly at the machine and announced:

"Es geht nicht! Die Maschine ist kaput!"

"Kaput? How can it be kaput?" the young SS officer asked, "The machine is nagelneu!"

The mechanic looked at the officer and stopped wiping his hands. "Yes, it is new, but it was built wrong. It must be replaced!"

The young officer turned to his superior and pointed at the crimper. "This is not built properly. We must shut down the factory until we get a new machine."

"Dass geht überhaupt nicht!" The superior officer pulled his subordinate aside and turned to the mechanic. "Leave your tools and step back." When the mechanic reluctantly stepped away, the officer pointed at the machine and looked at Peter. "Fix the machine, and I will give you Mittagessen, the same meal I will eat, but it has to work perfectly." Peter detected a mixture of anxiety and hope in his blue eyes.

He found a ten-millimetre wrench in the toolbox, loosened the ring holding the fingers on the crimper and lifted it off. He turned the fingers around, adjusted them evenly, replaced the ring and tightened it. The operation took him less than ten minutes, and anyone who knew anything about mechanics would have known that this was the work of a Meister.

He explained to the SS officer. "The fingers weren't properly fitted when the machine was set up. You can start it now, but it might need an adjustment before everything works perfectly."

The SS officer paused as if to say something, then waved his hand in the air. The whistle sounded, the line started, and the first casing slid into place. When Peter had the cartridge lined up perfectly, he pulled the lever; the fingers crimped the shell, and a second projectile slid into place. Peter lined it up, pulled the lever, and—perfect again. The senior SS officer tipped his hat to Peter and walked briskly away, motioning the junior officer to follow him.

Peter crimped shells until one o'clock when the junior SS officer appeared with yesterday's operator in tow. The officer beckoned to Peter, and the operator took over. The junior SS officer then led Peter to a room at the end of the building and told him to sit at a wooden table. The senior officer entered from the other end of the room and set a cloth bag on the table. The contents spilled out when Peter opened it.

Buttered rye bread, wurst, and cheese slid onto the table, and the officer opened a beer bottle on the table's edge. He poured the contents into two glasses, addressing the younger officer as he did so.

"Scharführer Becker, you are dismissed," and the younger officer stretched out his arm in a straight-armed Nazi salute, shouted, "Jawohl, Herr Untersturmbannführer Küster! Heil Hitler!" and held the Nazi pose until Küster acknowledged the Heil Hitler with a gesture that could have been a salute. Becker turned on his heel and marched stiffly across the room, opened the door, and slammed it as he exited. Küster looked at the door, smiled, and sat on the table beside Peter, his right boot on a chair, a glass of beer in his hand. He paused for a moment before he spoke.

"I checked your file, and you have a right to be angry. If you give me a few details, there might be something I can do for you." He thumped another bottle of dark brown beer on the table. "Anything but get you out of here…that will take a while, but I promise I will work on it. Jacques Durand knows you are here."

Peter choked on the piece of bread in his mouth—the officer slapped his back and laughed.

"I heard you and Juliette Durand sing a concert of opera duets here in Munich last year, and I have never heard anything so beautiful. I am amazed that you can also fix machines, but with a master machinist for a father, I suppose I shouldn't be."

Peter put his bread and beer down. Trying to keep his voice calm, he asked, "My fiancé, Juliette—do you know what happened to her? We were at my Jewish grandparents when the SA broke down the door. They murdered my grandfather and his friend Aaron Rinzler in front of me, but Juliette hid in the bedroom with my grandmother and Aaron's wife…"

Küster interrupted, "I can't get justice for you; unfortunately, that is no longer available in our country. But I will find out what happened to your grandmother and her friend. I will also personally contact your father and mother. I have information that Juliette is safe at home."

The officer didn't say anything more; he waited for Peter.

Tears of relief flooding Peter's eyes, he finally asked, "What do you want from me?"

Küster smiled. "Thank you for your offer, but I will understand if you withdraw it when I tell you what I need." He slid off the table, put down his empty glass and stood facing Peter. "If we can't make satisfactory artillery shells, the camp commander will close the operation, and only God knows what will happen to the prisoners who work here. I am also staking my career on making this work." He paused to think and then said, "If you can get the rest of this factory running like you did that machine, I will bring you Mittagessen like this every day...of course, you can eat it here, away from the other prisoners; there will be no repercussions for you."

Still euphoric knowing Juliette had survived, Peter was so shocked he couldn't speak, and the SS officer misunderstood Peter's hesitation and added a sweetener.

"I will also find a mechanic among the prisoners who will do whatever you ask."

Peter thought for a long minute, then pushed the food across the table.

"First, I will not take your food while the others starve. I can't fix your assembly line unless every prisoner working in this building eats the same meal as I do!"

Küster stared at Peter for a long moment, then stood up and paced across the room, one hand holding his other wrist behind his back. When he returned to Peter, he sat on the table again and said, "Yes, I can't give you a guarantee, but I may be able to do that. Of course, the food will not be as good or as plentiful as you would enjoy alone, but..." He hesitated and smiled warmly... "I will guarantee the soup will have meat in it, and the bread will be plentiful and without mould."

Peter looked steadily into the SS officer's blue eyes, took a pull on the beer, enjoying its exquisite taste, and waited. He knew this would be his last beer for a while, and he had another Bitte. Peter waited with his eyes locked on the Untersturmbannführer's until the officer took the brown bottle out of Peter's hand, drank a long pull, and said, "I understand where you are going with this, and I have another offer for you. I could make the quality and quantity of the food dependent upon production. I will allow you to arrange the workers as you wish, without interference, and we will shut the assembly line down for a half-hour for Mittagessen every day at one o'clock."

Peter waited. Küster said, "I will permit the prisoners to talk during the midday meal." He seemed to be searching for something more to give but gave up.

He said apprehensively, "There is a condition. I can't make this work unless you can produce perfect ammunition for our guns, and each month, you must produce more than you did in the previous one." He stood up, put the empty bottle on the table, and extended his hand. "I can't make this work unless you can do that for me. One hand washes the other—do you agree?"

"Einverstanden," said Peter, "However, if we double the output, and every shell is perfect, I want warm clothes and proper shoes for all the men. I will also need three men who know how to make shells, whom I will approve, to inspect them at stages along the line. You will also place an officer you trust at the end of the line to guarantee there is no sabotage. Do you agree?"

Untersturmbannführer Küster looked intently at Peter, smiled, and shook his hand. "I may soon have more information regarding your possible release." His tone implied that he knew the news would be good. And then, before he left the room, he asked, "Why are you concerned with the quality of the shells?"

"Because I love Germany, and I don't want German men to die because I made defective shells."

Peter drained the last drops from the beer bottle, checked on the crimping machine, and gave the remainder of his meal to the thinnest prisoner he could find. Peter took the grateful man's position and marked down several adjustments and deficiencies while he worked. The man wolfed down the food so fast that Peter feared he would throw it up, then returned to his job, heaping a flurry of thanks on Peter that embarrassed him.

Peter spent the rest of the day circulating through the factory, looking for problems and ways to increase production. He had two pages of notes when he finished the inspection.

The following day, Peter asked Scharführer Becker, the young SS officer, if he could have an hour to prepare the assembly line for increased production, but Becker refused; the whistle sounded, and the line started on time. Peter could have asked to see Küster, but the changes could wait, so he decided not to push it.

Peter circulated through the machines with the mechanic, a Bolshevic communist who made his dislike for Jews apparent by refusing to acknowledge Peter's questions and input. Finally, when Peter had had enough, he took the tool cart and pushed it to the last station, where workers packed the ammunition in wooden boxes. The table where the shells were collected for packing wasn't level; the brass casings rolled away from the packers, and they had to lean over the table to retrieve them. The three men working at the table continually stumbled over one another.

Peter picked up the hand level and a micrometre from the tool cart and checked how much he would need to shim the table. He asked the mechanic where he could find shims, got an answer and went to get them.

When Peter returned, the mechanic was talking to Scharführer Becker.

Becker asked Peter in an irritable tone, "What do you think you are doing, Jew?"

"I'm going to slope this table so the shells roll toward the packers."

The SS officer said firmly, "The mechanic says the table is better as it is. You must leave it alone."

From behind the officer's back, the mechanic gave Peter a look of arrogant satisfaction.

Peter said resolutely, "Untersturmbannführer Küster asked me to double the production of this assembly line, and to do that, I need to fix the slope on this table." He ignored Becker, laid the correct shim beside a table leg, found a pinch bar and hammer in the cart, and drove the sharp point of the bar under the corner of the steel leg.

He was sliding the thin spacer under the raised corner when a heavy wrench struck him on the temple. The blow knocked him sideways, the room spun out of his vision, and he saw a black SS boot hit him in the ribs. As blackness threatened, Peter vaguely heard someone laughing and drew himself into the fetal position, protecting his ribs and head with his arms and hands, but the blow didn't come.

He heard a grunt and was barely conscious of Officer Becker falling on the floor beside him. Hands lifted Peter to his feet, and he shouted in pain. He heard Küster say, "Take this man to my room and wait there with him!" Two pairs of arms half-dragged Peter to the room where he had eaten the previous day and sat him on a chair.

A few minutes later, when Peter could breathe normally again, a glass with two fingers of clear liquid appeared on the table in front of him—he assumed it wasn't poisonous and downed it in two gulps. It was Schnapps, and it started a delicious fire in his belly. Küster filled the glass to the mark, and again, Peter swallowed it in two gulps.

"Are you feeling better, Herr Schweitzer?" Küster's voice had a sympathetic ring to it.

"Yes, much better…thank you for asking." Peter felt the Schnapps' warmth working its way from his stomach through his body.

Küster sat on the table beside him, his foot on the chair next to him. "What happened out there?"

The communist mechanic interrupted, "You cannot take the word of a Saujude. It is known that they will not tell the truth!"

The SS officer gave the mechanic a dangerous look, and he shut his mouth.

"Now, Herr Schweitzer, you will please tell me what happened."

Peter grimaced as he twisted his body, trying to loosen the stiffening ribs. Becker had aimed his kick well. Küster noticed. "Do you want to go to the Klinik before we continue?"

"No, Untersturmbannführer." Peter smiled, "But perhaps another schnapps? I will catch my breath, then return to the table Ludger and I were levelling."

Küster filled the small glass level, then slid it across the table to a grateful Peter.

"Do you have a problem working with Ludger?" Peter carefully raised the glass to his lips, sipped the edge, swallowed twice, stopped for a few seconds, and then finished it.

"No, sir; I have no problem with him if he has no problem with me." He decided he liked this SS officer…perhaps the mechanic isn't such a bad guy either, and the Schnapps is excellent!

Peter slurred, "We will work things out," and grinned.

Küster put his hand on Peter's shoulder, and Peter looked into his eyes. "I am going to give you one more chance, Herr Schweitzer. Do you want me to replace Ludger with someone more sympathetic to you? Perhaps one of the Jewish prisoners?"

Peter didn't hesitate; he looked at Ludger as he said, "No, sir— Ludger and I will get along fine…." He looked at Küster, unaware he was smiling stupidly. "We'll be just…" He searched for a word… "ausge… ausgezei… We'll be Okay!"

The SS officer smiled at Peter and shook his hand. "You are a good man, Schweitzer, and you will not see Scharführer Becker again if I can help it. If he regains consciousness, he will be supervising construction elsewhere in the camp. For now, I will count on your help looking after the factory, and I would be happy if you could fix that table. Perhaps it would be best if Ludger did it, following your instructions, of course." Peter nodded enthusiastically, and Küster turned to Ludger. "Stand outside the room and wait until we come. No one is to enter."

Ludger left, carefully closing the door behind him.

Küster's face became serious.

"I have bad news for you, Peter." He said it quietly, and a part of Peter died. "As you feared, your grandmother and Aaron's wife were murdered. The perpetrators are unknown, and I must advise you not to pursue the matter."

Peter asked desperately, "Juliette—how did she escape?"

Küster avoided the question when he said, "That's the good news. I can confirm that Juliette is home, alive, and uninjured." Peter opened his mouth to ask for more information, but fear of the answer made him close it.

"She went to the police station to complain about the incident, and her father has been inquiring about you. You can count on help from the Durand family."

Despite the circumstances, or because of the Schnapps, Peter hugged the embarrassed SS officer. Küster briefly held Peter and then helped him to the door, saying he must check on Becker. Ludger would not meet Peter's eye, and Peter had to make a supreme effort to put his tongue in the right places as he said, "I want to make this factory run like the German railway. You can help me if you want to, and I would appreciate it if you would." He tried unsuccessfully to speak without a slur. "Will a communist shake a Jew's hand?"

Ludger reached out tentatively, and Peter grabbed his hand. He held on for a few seconds, and his mind wandered to something else until Ludger pulled his hand back, wiped it on his pants, and said, "If you are ready, I'll help you with the table. You tell me what to do, and I will do it for you."

After teaching a confused Ludger how to install the shims, Peter, feeling particularly happy, waved to Küster, who discreetly watched them.

Peter focused first on the SS officer's cap, then on the men packing shells at the table. In a sudden burst of clarity, he said loudly and emphatically, "Sir, we don't need three men on the table! May I send one of them for a rest break?" He grinned foolishly, and the packers looked at him.

Küster smiled and said, "You have my permission to reorganize the men in any way you see fit, as long as you get the work done."

One of the men looked in his sixties or older, but was probably much younger. Peter pointed to a bench against the wall and told him to stay there until Mittagessen. The frail man laughed pathetically. "That is not a good joke."

At one o'clock, the whistle sounded, the line stopped, and Unter-sturmbannführer Küster's voice announced over the loudspeaker, "The prisoners will assemble along the west wall."

The terrified men shuffled toward a wall, some checking with others to make sure it was the west wall—a command from the SS never prophesied something good. When they saw tables covered with food, they approached them skeptically, and again, the voice came through the speakers.

"It would be better if you hurried. The Fliessband will start again in thirty minutes."

The men began examining the tables' contents, nervously at first and then with gathering enthusiasm. They grabbed at buttered bread, wurst, and boiled eggs, stuffing it into their mouths. Stronger prisoners took food from weaker ones until they realized there was enough for everyone. The men sat on the floor to eat, backs against the wall, and five prisoner trustees distributed tin cups filled with watered-down apple cider. The men drank and ate silently until the whistle sounded, then returned to their stations, their puzzled and suspicious eyes shifting from one man to another. As they walked past the tables, some checked to see if someone was looking, then picked up whatever they could stuff in their pockets.

The speakers came to life once again. "From today, if you work diligently, there will be food for you at one o'clock. The voice paused, the microphone clicked again, and Küster's voice said, "You may talk during Mittagessen and when you are in the barracks, but not while you are working."

CHAPTER NINE

12 May 1939

Treulich geführt
(The wedding march from 'Lohengrin')
Richard Wagner

EARLY IN JANUARY, JACQUES HAD TO ADMIT FAILURE in his effort to find refuge for Peter in Belgium. To appease its dangerous neighbour, Belgium refused to accept German Jews under any circumstances. Britain and France would not consider Jews, even those with money. North America excluded them from any visa application without a lot of upfront cash or proof of an extraordinary talent that America needed.

But Jacques found another possibility. The Cuban embassy in Berlin offered visas to Jewish families at the meagre cost of five hundred US dollars. To accommodate the anticipated response, the Hamburg America Line booked the MS St. Louis to leave Hamburg on May 13, 1939, sailing to Havana, Cuba.

Unable to consult Peter, Juliette chose Cuba over Singapore, and the Singapore government returned Jacques' deposit minus a fee. Cuba was close to the United States, and her father thought there was a good chance she and Peter could find their way back to Belgium from there once they were legally married and European paranoia had cooled. Juliette wrote to Peter's family to inform them of the change in destination, while Jacques took care of the visas and booked cabin passage on the MS St. Louis.

On Monday, February 20th, Jacques visited Joseph, his SS friend in Munich, and they went to the official office for emigration. The bureaucrats examined Peter's visa and his paid passage, then thumped four rubber stamps on each of six pages of the triplicate document that allowed Peter to leave Dachau on the twelfth of May. He would travel under escort to Hamburg by train and board the MS St. Louis that night. Jacques received one copy, was satisfied with the document and gave Joseph a small piece of paper with a number and a password written in pencil. He gave him the name of the Luxembourg bank, where the painting waited for him.

"Thank you for everything, Joseph; I am in your debt." Jacques shook the SS officer's hand.

"Nonsense, Jacques…one hand washes the other." Joseph smiled and folded the piece of paper.

It was raining and cold in Munich on May 12th, 1939, and there had been no heat in the barracks since May 1st. Peter woke midway through the long night, shivering despite being fully clothed, lying in the fetal position, and sandwiched between two woollen blankets. The cold and the chaotic state of his mind kept him awake until breakfast arrived at six. He wolfed down the porridge, went to the showers, and thought of Juliette, her father, and Küster as the cold water beat on his back. The SS untersturmbandführer had told him of Jacques' efforts in such detail that Peter wondered where he could have gotten his information; as far as he knew, only Jacques, Veronique, and Juliette had access to it. Peter could eliminate the family, but what about Marcel, the chauffeur? He had been omnipresent and quiet, usually the description of one who listens with a purpose.

Küster, the SS officer, was a puzzle; Peter's gut told him that the man was not a committed Nazi, so Peter asked himself, what is Küster committed to? He is a member of the SS and must, therefore, be a member of the Party. Logic didn't support the equation in Peter's gut—Küster was an enigma.

Before the guards led the prisoners to work, they allowed them to gather around Peter to bid him goodbye. Every man in the barracks filed past and shook his hand. When the last man left for work, Peter thought about how he and Küster had made these men's existence in Dachau bearable, and, despite making thousands of rounds of artillery ammunition for Hitler's guns, he felt proud. Küster had lifted the restrictions on talking in the barracks until ten o'clock, and decks of cards appeared. Games of Skat sprang up, spontaneously at first, then organized, with teams playing toward a championship. Life had become tolerable for the prisoners in barracks 22.

As they filed out of the building, Peter wondered how many deserved to be there. What was Hitler doing or planning that he needed to hide these innocent men from the public? Why must he, an opera singer, go to Cuba? He had done nothing to hurt Germany…he was not a shit-disturber…and then he said aloud, "What in the name of God is happening to my country?"

When the last man left, a trustee prisoner took Peter to the Schubraum building, where six months ago, his world had collapsed. He collected his clothes and papers with shaking hands, gave the humiliating uniform to the attendant, and an SS guard led him to a small room near the gate. From the window, he could see the wrought iron arch with the words, "Arbeit macht Frei," over the entrance to the camp.

He thought, unintentionally aloud, "'Work will make you free' has nothing to do with Dachau!"

He was still staring at the sign when Untersturmbannführer Küster, dressed in the dark grey SS uniform worn outside the camp, entered the room. Peter stood, and Küster offered his hand.

"Peter, I am going to accompany you to Hamburg. It is near my home, and I have a few days to visit my parents." Peter didn't hide his pleasure when Küster said, "The trip will take all day, and I would consider it a favour if you called me Alex."

Following Alex's example, Peter switched to the familiar 'du' form when he said, "Sir, I would be honoured—without your help, I might have died here."

Küster waved Peter off, "Since we're being honest, you have done more for me and the prisoners than you probably should have. You increased production threefold, and your shells are perfect. The Wehrmacht tells me that every time they fire one of our shells, they know it will fly precisely the same as the previous round, and, of course, I get all the credit." He examined his hand. "I thought about keeping you here, but there is a limit to what an SS officer will do." He was grinning when he looked at Peter, but his face darkened as he said, "Your shells have kept this little operation going, but I don't know how long it will last. The camp commander believes these men are his mortal enemies, and he wants them to suffer."

The driver threw two suitcases in the SS Mercedes' trunk, then opened the rear door for the Untersturmbandführer. The car stopped at the security gate, and Alex rolled down the window. He passed an envelope and a document to the apathetic guard who, after a short examination and a long look at Peter, returned them. As the car accelerated away from Dachau, Alex handed the envelope to Peter. He pulled out two pieces of paper and read, then slowly reread them. The official black-on-white words released him from Dachau without a word about guilt or innocence, then kicked him out of the country with a list of dire consequences if he returned.

Peter looked back at the gate and thought of the friends he had made who were condemned to remain in the camp for nothing but a lack of money. He carefully folded the papers, slid them into the envelope, and remembered that he had once argued in favour of the Nazis. Sadness washed over him, and he asked himself, "How could I have been so stupid?" After six months in Dachau, it was finally clear to Peter that Hitler had duped him and the entire country by using temporary, superficially logical solutions to complicated problems, to buy his way to absolute power over Germany.

The SS had booked a private cabin in a first-class car on the train to Hamburg for Untersturmbannführer Alex Küster and his prisoner. When Alex lifted two suitcases to the rack over the seat, he left his hand on one of them; it was new.

"You'll find clothes in there and a few things you may need on your voyage. However, I don't want you to open it until you are on the ship."

Peter spotted a short-lived, mischievous grin.

"I don't know what to say; I..."

Küster interrupted, "As is always the case with the SS, there is a condition." He waited for Peter to ask the obvious.

"Okay, what is the condition?"

Alex's voice fell to barely more than a whisper, "I don't want you or Juliette ever to return to Germany. And get your father, mother, and siblings out of the country as soon as possible. Jacques Durand has the money and influence to get that done, and that is his intention, but you must convince your family."

Peter looked out the window at the fields flashing by, then turned to Alex.

"What more can they do to me? They have beaten me, imprisoned me, and taken my career. They murdered my grandparents and did God knows what to Juliette. What's left to take?"

Alex looked at Peter, waiting for something but saying nothing.

Peter reluctantly went on. "Okay, they could arrest every Jew, including my mother, my sister and brothers—and then what? What could they do to hundreds of thousands, perhaps millions of us?"

Alex nodded. "They could shoot you—perhaps millions of you— you know they have the bullets and the artillery ammunition to kill millions of people."

Peter's face registered the shock of the SS officer's words, and Alex immediately tried to temper the impact.

"I didn't mean to imply that… Peter, your family must get out of here. They will conscript your father to work in a factory building Panzers, or ships' engines, or aircraft, and when he's out of the way, they will take your mother to a work camp where she will likely die of typhoid or starvation."

"Has our country gone crazy?" Peter looked out the window; a hunting club had a rabbit cornered, and a dozen laughing men watched the dogs tear it apart.

Küster's voice brought Peter back. "All the rules you believe in do not apply. I am in danger talking to you about this—I've risked my life helping you and am a prisoner of the system that is exiling you. My saviour is the wonderful artillery shell assembly line you created. They need those shells, and I run the factory that produces them, but even that may not be enough. Even now, I am searching for a way to get out."

Peter looked aimlessly ahead at the opposite wall, then at Küster.

"Nothing about this is real to me. I am confused about everything, beginning with you. I don't know who you are, but your heart is not SS, and you are not one of them."

Alex stared out the window without reacting.

Peter said, "I will tell no one," but got no response.

Alex hired a taxi when they arrived in Hamburg and took Peter to the Hamburg America Line pier, where the MS St. Louis towered above the dock. Peter stepped out of the Mercedes, the driver opened the trunk, and Juliette was suddenly there—her father and mother standing a metre behind her.

Juliette restrained herself when she saw the SS officer get out of the car. Alex saw her hesitation, moved out of the way, and Juliette flew into Peter's arms, laughing, crying, kissing Peter's cheeks, mouth, and forehead until finally, she found Peter's mouth. She kissed him passionately—he tried to reciprocate but couldn't and, sensing his embarrassment, she let him go.

Alex put Peter's suitcase beside Jacques; they shook hands, Küster clicked his heels and bowed.

"I am Untersturmbannführer Alex Küster." He spoke using formal pronouns. "I have brought this man to the ship and must see that he boards it."

He released Jacques' hand, let his eyes wander around the dock, and spoke less formally but quieter. "I have heard a lot about you, Monsieur Durand, and I am proud to finally make your acquaintance. Your influence made Peter's stay in Dachau much easier than it otherwise would have been."

Jacques looked at him curiously. "I have heard he had help on the inside, and I believe I should thank you for that."

Alex nodded and said, "Peter and I worked together, mostly to my benefit. I have given him some important advice, which he will need to discuss with you before he boards the ship." He touched his hat and clicked his heels again. "Please follow my suggestions precisely; I know what is happening to my country." He looked around the dock again. "I will trust you to see that Peter boards the ship."

Alex Küster climbed into the taxi, and Jacques watched it drive away, knowing what Peter would tell him. He also knew who Alex Küster really was.

When Peter and Juliette finally stopped touching one another, Jacques took Peter aside while Veronique took Juliette's arm and guided her toward the long gangway. They stopped at the bottom to wait for Peter.

Jacques said, "Peter, Küster has given you instructions, and he said they were urgent."

Peter hesitated, puzzled. "He told me not to tell anyone where the instructions came from."

Jacques smiled, "I deal with secrets every day, and some of them would get people killed. He knows I can be trusted."

Anxious to tell someone what he knew, Peter said, "During the train ride, Alex said there would soon be another attack on the Jews, worse than Kristallnacht. There is a plan to imprison them in camps, and he believes there is a long-term plan to permanently remove them. He insists my entire family must leave Germany as soon as possible."

Jacques spoke quietly, "Yes, I've heard this from all my reliable sources. Germany is moving into a place I would not have thought possible six months ago." He put his hand on Peter's shoulder. "I warned your father and mother, and I have offered to help them, but your father believes there is only a small element within the party that wants to destroy the Jews, and I cannot convince him otherwise."

Peter looked up at the massive ship. "I won't be able to contact anyone for a while, and by then it may be too late. Will you visit my father and contact my siblings? Perhaps you can convince them to leave if you see them face to face. I know and trust Untersturmbannführer Küster, and if he thinks…"

Jacques put his arm around Peter. "You and I are now family because Juliette chose to go with you to an uncertain future rather than remain with us. There is no question where her love and loyalty lie, and Juliette takes ours with her. Whatever we have is available to you and your family. I have business in Munich, and Veronique and I plan to take the night train to Nürnberg to visit your parents. I promise we will get your family out if they will go, and Veronique and I will do everything in our power to convince them. Now, say goodbye to Veronique and enjoy your cruise."

Peter stretched out his hand, but Jacques wrapped his arms around him. Peter stepped back as soon as he could without creating an awkward situation, and Jacques said, "Juliette has had a very rough time. Please be careful with her. She appears strong, but I'm afraid no one can sustain such strength."

To call the accommodations a cabin was to call Versailles a shack. Peter and Juliette's 'cabin' was a suite of three rooms spanning half the stern's width. Juliette giggled as her eyes roamed over the ornate brass and oak trim decorating the sitting room. Peter let his new suitcase fall to the floor as he said incredulously, "My God, is this all ours?"

Juliette flung her arms around Peter's thin chest and found his brown eyes. Despite the extra food Peter and his fellow workers had gotten, twelve hours of work every day had burned every gram of fat from his body. She said, "Yes, my dear, it is all ours, along with twenty thousand United States dollars and fifty thousand Swiss francs in the ship's safe. We are now rich, and you have no more worries." She put her arms around Peter's neck, pulled his head down so that she could reach his mouth with hers, and kissed him passionately.

He gently broke free and walked to a wide pocket door. He rolled both sections to the side and stared at a beautiful bed with a snow-white bedspread and canopy. The "MS St Louis" logo covered the centre of the bed. A round brass-framed window on the outer wall looked over the ship's port side.

Juliette followed Peter into the room, took his arm, and looked up at him, her eyes shining.

She spoke gently, "We will sleep together in that bed—there is no Hitler to say we can't, and no one will arrest us." She chuckled. "You have no more excuses."

Peter looked down. "I want to talk to you about that a little later. I need to find out who I am, and we need to get reacquainted." He raised his head to look at Juliette. "Would it be all right to take it a step at a time? I like the idea of getting married first. We can find a priest in Cuba and..."

Juliette caught herself before she laughed. "As you wish, my love. Now, what can we do until the ship sails tomorrow morning?" She put her finger in a thoughtful position against her lower lip, reached for a long gold cord and pulled it.

Peter said, "Oh, good... We're going to eat now. I'm starved!"

Juliette smiled like a cat with a mouse between its paws. "Soon," she said happily, without attempting to disguise her excitement. A knock on the door interrupted her.

She let Peter go to the door, and when he opened it, a uniformed steward stood facing him. Juliette called from behind Peter's back, "You can tell the captain we are ready whenever he has the time."

"We're ready for what?" Peter looked suspiciously at Juliette.

The steward clicked his heels and left, and a confused Peter looked questioningly at Juliette as he closed the door.

"What has the captain got to do with dinner?"

Juliette pulled a folded paper from her purse, opened it, and passed it to Peter. He read it quickly and then, puzzled, looked at her and held it up.

"This is a marriage license."

"Brava!" Juliette clapped her hands.

"But this isn't my signature; it's not legal."

Juliette said sweetly, "I wouldn't tell the captain that."

Finally, the light came on.

"The captain is going to marry us?"

Juliette clapped her hands again. "Yes, in a few minutes. Mother and Father are waiting, and we are getting married right now." She jumped like a little girl, then controlled herself but couldn't hold back a giggle.

Peter began, "But...."

"You promised, and I have the ring to prove it!" Juliette held her right hand in front of his face. "And it's long past the day you said you would."

There was another knock, and Juliette opened the door to find the Captain standing before her, dressed in an impeccable uniform.

She stepped aside. "May I present my future husband... Peter Schweitzer."

"Peter, this is Captain Gustav Schröder."

"I appreciate your help, sir," Peter said softly, "I love Juliette."

The Captain shook Peter's hand and tried not to laugh. "That's very fortunate for all of us, but especially for your fiancé."

Everyone but Peter laughed while he looked to Juliette for help. "I don't have any clothes to get married in."

"Yes, I think you do; it's time to look in your suitcase, Liebling—we will wait for you."

Five minutes later, Peter entered the room dressed in an elegant, loose-fitting tuxedo. Peter, confused, asked himself, How in the hell did Küster know?

Juliette smiled, touched his nose and said, "Now it's my turn, but I may take a bit longer."

"And how did you know...?" Peter started to ask how she knew about the clothes in the suitcase, but she slid the doors shut.

Fifteen minutes later, Juliette rolled the doors back, and Peter forgot the question. She stood before him in a snow-white wedding gown, a diamond tiara resting atop her veil. She lifted the cloth covering her face and said, "Okay, I think we're ready. Let's get married."

When he stopped opening and closing his mouth, Peter said, "Your father must have paid a fortune for that tiara—maybe we should do this when your parents can be with us."

The Captain pulled the gold cord, the door opened, and the steward led Jacques and Veronique into the room.

Peter waved his hands…everything was out of control.

Veronique ran to Juliette and threw her arms around her daughter while her father stood in the doorway with his mouth open.

Peter laughed, Jacques laughed with him, and Peter said, "Sir, you have a beautiful daughter." Then Peter looked at Jacques and asked, "How did Küster know I was getting married?"

Jacques coughed and looked at his feet, clearly buying time, and before Peter could open his mouth to ask another question, Juliette pulled him to her side. With a sigh of relief, Jacques stepped up to his position on the other side of the bride. Veronique stood on the other side of Peter. Captain Schröder faced the group and got right to the point.

"We are gathered here to join this couple in holy matrimony. Are there any objections?"

No one said anything.

Nodding at Juliette, then Peter, he said, "I now ask each of you to pledge your vows to one another." He looked at Juliette. "The bride first."

Juliette began, "I love you, darling Peter...I have loved only you since the first day we sang together. Do you remember the duet from Der Vogelhändler?"

She magically produced a long-stemmed red rose that her mother had smuggled into the cabin and began singing, I give you a rose to show my love, so you will know my heart is yours. And as I now give you this flower, you have all I am."

Peter took the rose, tears forming, and his silence touched Juliette. She just wanted to kiss him, say, "I do," and get on with whatever came next.

The Captain turned to Peter and waited—everyone waited—but Peter would only look at Juliette.

Captain Shröder tried a more direct approach. "The groom shall now say his vows."

Shröder waved a hand toward Peter, nudged him, and said in a deep voice, "Would the groom please say his vows so the captain can get back to his ship?"

Without turning away from Juliette, Peter sang the second verse of the duet. "Hear the words of the rose; place your trust in me. And if a thorn should sting, you must know I will suffer your pain."

Peter stopped singing, saying, "I will never allow anything to hurt you. I will love you, and we will remember this song every day we are together."

They sang the duet refrain. Peter's voice blended perfectly with hers, and when the vibrations of the final note faded, they kissed.

Peter lifted her chin and said, "I love you, Juliette, more than I love my life. While I was in Dachau, I thought of nothing else. I made a promise to God—I told Him that if he gave you back to me, I would do anything he asked, no matter the consequences. He has returned you to me, and now I owe Him my life. I will stay with you until I die, and then I will follow you wherever you go. I promise to love and protect you beyond death, to eternity and…."

Juliette stopped Peter's soliloquy by lifting her veil and flipping it back over her tiara. She pulled his head down and kissed him tenderly, then pulled him down again and kissed him hard on the lips, opening her mouth so their breath mingled. Something stirred in Peter that he hadn't felt for a long time!

The Captain waited until the mood changed before he said, "I don't know whether sung vows are legal, but I'll take a chance. By the power vested in me by the laws of the sea, I pronounce you man and wife." He turned to the steward and said, "Change the ship's manifest to show that Mr. and Mrs. Schweitzer occupy this cabin."

Following a round of toasts, the Captain spoke to Jacques and Veronique. "Monsieur and Madame Durand, you are welcome to dine with us at the Captain's table. There are two places set for you."

Jacques half-bowed. "Thank you, Captain. We will join you when the bride and groom are less formally dressed."

Fifteen minutes later, Juliette and Peter entered the Captain's dining room to applause from the guests seated at a long rectangular table.

The ship would sail on the tide before daylight the next day, so the Captain left the dinner early. Jacques and Veronique bid the newlyweds adieu in the corridor outside Juliette and Peter's stateroom. When she and Peter were inside, Juliette turned the key, took it out of the lock and laid it on the small table beside the door. It was almost ten, but not yet completely dark. She turned off the light and pulled Peter into the bedroom, rolling the doors together behind them. She was nervous, as many brides are, but not for the same reason.

Chapter Ten

11–12 May 1939

Alle Anfang ist Schwer
(All beginnings are difficult)

Peter whined, "Please, Juliette, I don't know if I'm ready for this. I just got out of a work camp—I don't think I can do what you want."

"My darling, you don't know what I want. We have the rest of our lives to perfect this, but we must start sometime. I have no expectations, and you shouldn't have any either." She sat on the bed and patted the place beside her. "Talk to me about how you got to Dachau, and I'll tell you what happened to me."

Peter reluctantly sat beside her. Juliette had prepared herself for a brutal story, but his words hit her like blunt instruments.

"They tore the door down with a pick-axe and laughed at us like we were animals they had been hunting in the woods. I was so terrified I couldn't move when a big SA soldier killed Moshe with the pick-axe they had used on the door. I screamed and tried to attack him, but he knocked me down and kicked me while a second soldier broke Aaron's arms with a club...and then..."

Peter looked down, breathing hard through his mouth... "he laughed, a terrible laugh. I would gladly have given my life to kill him, but I couldn't! I felt helpless and weak!"

Juliette asked quietly, "Was he fat and ugly, with yellow teeth? And did he have a deep voice?'

"Yes, he was an officer of some kind; he ordered the others around. He was taller and weighed twice what the biggest one did." Peter looked at Juliette, and his eyes were wet.

Juliette sensed he knew how she had known about the fat soldier.

He began again. "I guess I thought I would die anyway, so I tried to get to the man hitting Aaron, but two others knocked me down and started kicking me. They broke some ribs and threw me down the stairs. Maybe the stairs broke the ribs; I'm not sure."

Despite everything, Juliette smiled and asked, "Perhaps someone broke your ribs because you broke his nose?"

"What? How did you know that?"

Juliette smiled, and Peter spread his hands, frustrated, and said, "Oh, never mind," and went on.

"They dragged me down the street. People kicked me and called me Saujude and Dreckige Jude."

Peter looked at the floor. "I'm ashamed…I denied I was a Jew. I wished that I had been born something else—anything but a Jew—I think I actually hated myself for being half-Jewish."

"How did they take you to Dachau?" Juliette swallowed a lump, and it took a herculean effort to keep from screaming.

"They threw me into the back of a Lastwagen—It had a steel floor and a canvas top. I threw up on a prisoner's shoes." Peter lifted his head. Juliette met his eyes but had to look away to keep from sobbing.

His pitiful whine stopped as he asked, "Did you know that there is an iron sign over the entrance to Dachau… And it says, Arbeit Macht Frei?"

Juliette shook her head, "I didn't know that. Do you remember that Hitler said that work is the most important part of our lives…that everyone should work for the Fatherland?"

Peter nodded and hung his head. "Now, I know what he meant."

Juliette slid off the bed, pulling Peter with her.

"That's enough for now." She forced cheerfulness. "Let's have a bath—you probably don't smell anywhere near as good as you think you do!"

She gently steered Peter backward until he sat down in a gilded chair. She pulled his socks off and flipped his braces down over his shoulders. Juliette stepped back, neatly slipped her stockings down and pulled them off, then smoothly pulled her dress over her head, leaving only a support garment covering her breasts. Turning around, she backed up to Peter; she could hear his fast and heavy breathing. Hope invaded her mood.

She said, "It's much easier to get this off if you unfasten the loops for me."

Peter fumbled with the simple contraption, finally succeeded, then loosened the loops all the way down. Juliette let the garment drop to the floor…she wore panties but nothing else. Flipping the girdle up with her toe, she caught it with her hand and walked to the bed with her back to him. Without turning around, Juliette slipped out of her last vestige of modesty and, as neatly as she had with the girdle, picked the tiny piece of cotton up with her toe and flipped it into her hand. She turned around, praying for a reaction.

Peter gasped as she had hoped he would, and she watched his excitement grow in his pants. His face flushed to a deep red. Excited, her heart beating like a trip-hammer, Juliette surmised that he had never seen a naked woman. She also knew he had never had a woman stare at his obvious arousal. Juliette went to him, unfastened the top button on his pants, and pulled him to his feet, holding his waistband in her hands. When she let it go, his pants dropped past his narrow hips to the floor. She quickly unbuttoned his shirt and pulled it off his chest and down his arms. He turned around and looked at himself in the full-length mirror on the wall beside him. She could feel his heart sink as he stared at his thin frame.

She wanted to cry but continued to smile.

"Oh my God, Juliette, I look awful!" He was close to crying as he turned to her. "How can you make love to someone who looks like this? You are so beautiful, and I look like a skeleton under a bedsheet!"

Juliette threw Peter's shirt in the corner and pressed herself against him. He was still standing in his pants, piled on the floor around his feet. She put her fingers under his underwear, leaned over, and pulled them over his erection and down to the pants. Then, taking his hand, Juliette led him to the bed. His penis began its retreat, and Juliette decided to change course.

"All right, you win, we'll have a bath. But first, I want you to tell me about Dachau…." Juliette knelt on the floor and rested her arms on his legs. He pushed them together; she said, "Relax, Peter, I won't bite you," and pried them apart while smiling up at him.

Peter gave up and started talking. He told her everything, from the early despair of his sentence, the meagre food and terrible conditions, to his beating and eventual friendship with Alex Küster. When he told her how the men had increased shell production threefold, Juliette stopped playing with his limp penis and turned sideways. She leaned against the inside of his leg.

"Tell me why you would help those people? They murdered your grandparents, humiliated you, and they raped me!" Tears suddenly filled her eyes; shame replaced her anger.

Peter leaned over, kissed her gently and said, "I know what happened, Liebling…it's my fault…you were right; I couldn't protect you." He slid off the bed and sat beside her on the floor. She took him in her arms, and they rocked back and forth.

The memory of the brute who had raped her lit Juliette's fuse; she wriggled free and climbed onto the bed, her anger in full bloom. Hot blood rushed to her face, and she spoke louder than she intended.

"Don't you dare pity me! I will not let that bastard ruin my life with you! I am no longer a virgin, but I am as far as you are concerned! I have never had another man of my own free will, and I will have a wonderful sex life with you!"

Peter pulled himself to his feet and sat on the bed beside her. Juliette slowed her breathing.

"Yes, I did work for them." Peter chose his words carefully, "I did it to get food and rest for the prisoners in the factory. I didn't really care whether the shells worked perfectly, but I was also not going to put the men who fire those guns at risk because they had faulty ammunition."

Juliette nodded, sighed at the wall. "Enough of that; let's change the mood." She stood and wiggled her buttocks as she walked to the bathroom. Sneaking a conspicuous glance over her shoulder, she happily caught Peter staring at her bottom.

Juliette, a plan in her head, turned both taps on full, and Peter entered the room. She beckoned him, and he sat on a wicker chair beside the bathtub.

When the tub was full, Juliette told Peter to get in. Naked, kneeling beside him, she picked up a bar of soap and washed his legs, slowly working her way up, taking her time, washing, rinsing, and building his excitement as she skirted his danger zone. When he was clean, she drained the water and refilled the tub as she washed him again, finally cleaning the place she had avoided. Peter gasped when she climbed into the bath and straddled his legs.

She lay on top of him until the water grew cold, listening to the sound of their breathing, knowing they were, for now, safe

Chapter Eleven

17 June 1939

Unglücklich das Land, das Helden nötig hat.
(Unfortunate is a land in need of heroes)

Officials from the Cuban government boarded the MS St. Louis the day it anchored in Havana Harbour, cancelled all visas except those of US citizens, and ordered the ship out of Cuban waters. Only twenty-two of the over 900 passengers qualified to land, and after six days of pleading with the Cuban authorities, Captain Gustav Schröder admitted defeat and weighed anchor.

Schröder sailed to nearby Florida, but the Americans refused permission for the ship to land. Captain Schröder threatened to ground his ship and let the passengers disembark on the beach, but two Coast Guard cutters cut the MS St Louis off. He tried an end-run around them, but one of the cutters fired a shot across the ship's bow, forcing Schröder to turn north.

Still desperately trying to find a refuge for his Jewish passengers, the MS St Louis sailed up the east coast of the United States, shadowed by American Coast Guard cutters prepared to intercept any attempt to land the ship on American soil.

Schröder contacted the Canadian government through a group of concerned Canadian citizens. They had taken the case to the Canadian Prime Minister, and two days later, on the ninth of June, the MS St. Louis sailed into the Halifax Harbour entrance. Captain Schröder requested permission to dock, but the Canadian Prime Minister, William Lyon Mackenzie King, refused, leaving the MS St. Louis's owners no choice but to order its return to Germany. Captain Schröder would not take his ship home until the owners could guarantee that a country other than Germany would accept his passengers and continued to sail back and forth in front of the entrance to Halifax harbour. Finally, when the Hamburg America Line promised to find a solution, he headed toward Europe but slowed the ship to give his masters time.

The Saint Louis powered slowly eastward, the passengers becoming more anxious with every mile closer to Germany.

Finally, as the MS Saint Louis approached Britain, Schröder threatened to wreck it on the rocks and take the passengers to shore in lifeboats as refugees. Newspapers worldwide had picked up the story, and the attention embarrassed the US and Canadian governments, forcing them to find a solution. Together with England and the European nations, they reached an agreement just hours before Schröder would execute his plan to drive the ship on the rocks. Britain, France, Belgium and the Netherlands agreed to divide the passengers among them, and Captain Schröder set a course for Antwerp.

On the morning of the seventeenth of June 1939, as the ship sailed up the Scheldt River, the passengers gathered in the main salon for the last time. Every Jew now had a place to go when leaving the ship, thanks to the efforts of Captain Schröder. The Captain humbly minimized his contribution, and when the applause died, asked Peter and Juliette to come to the front.

Juliette looked at Peter, and he shrugged. She followed him to stand beside the Captain.

A steward walked to the small stage with a framed picture in his hands and passed it to Captain Schröder.

"We didn't schedule entertainment on this voyage, but in gratitude for the nightly concerts provided by you, I present this photograph of the MS St. Louis. Two hundred of your fans signed this picture, including me. We have been standing on the lower deck every night, listening to your evening concerts, and I thank you both for the wonderful singing we have enjoyed."

Late every evening, after walking around the top deck to exercise their legs, Juliette and Peter had sung a concert to the sea, choosing solos and duets from their repertoire. They thought they had been alone while they went to the stern rail and vocalized together.

"Apparently," said Juliette to Peter, "we had a secret audience."

The St. Louis docked in Antwerp later in the day, and, finished with immigration, Juliette and Peter met Jacques and Veronique outside the building. They hugged, kissed, and eventually climbed into the familiar Rolls-Royce. Juliette and her mother sat in the rear with Peter between them, and Jacques sat in the front.

Peter leaned ahead to talk to his father-in-law, "I should probably wait until we get to the house, but I would like to know how you fared with my father and mother."

"Nothing was certain until a few days ago, so I didn't write and get your hopes up. But everything came together, and they are waiting for you at the house. Your father has a job here in Brussels, and they are now Belgian citizens. Your brothers and sister have refused to leave Germany, but I haven't given up."

Listening to the conversation, Juliette leaned ahead and asked her father, "What is the danger to them now?"

"There have been no attacks on the Jewish community since Kristallnacht. The attack outraged the world, as well as most Germans. The Nazis don't dare take any physical action against the Jews, but their anti-Jew policies remain, and Hitler and his minions can't be trusted."

Jacques, his frustration apparent, half-turned around and said, "I found a way to sell Peter's father's house for a fair price, but if he had been a Jew, the government would have taken it. Every day, it's becoming more difficult for Jews to live in Germany. They are paying an exorbitant fine for the death of that Nazi bureaucrat in Paris—Mon Dieu; the government even fined them for destroying German property during the Kristallnacht riots! The destroyed German property is the Jewish stores, homes, and synagogues ransacked and burned by the SA and SS!"

The Rolls-Royce stopped in the drive of Avenue de Saturne 6. Peter's parents met him at the door; his mother flung her arms around him, almost knocking him over. She hugged him, tears running down her face.

"I thought we had lost you. I'm so glad you're safe!" She wept into his shoulder.

"Mother, I'm happier than I've ever been." He turned to his father, who put out his hand. Peter shook it, and his father, eyes glistening, slapped Peter's shoulder.

"Dad, I want you to meet my wife." Peter took Juliette's hand, and she stepped forward, threw her arms around Heinz's neck, and stood on tiptoes to kiss his cheek. She was pleased when he blushed, and she said, "Heinz, you and Elizabeth are my parents now—no shaking hands, only hugs from now on!"

Juliette hugged Elisabeth, and when they separated, Elisabeth cried and held onto her new daughter's hands.

"Juliette, I am so proud you've chosen Peter, and I am delighted to call you my daughter."

They worked their way to the luxurious front room, where the evening breeze through the large open windows offset the warmth of the late afternoon sun. Coffee and French pastries waited on a table.

When they all had found their seats, Peter asked for details of his parents' status in Brussels.

Heinz began before Jacques could answer.

"We sold the house in Nürnberg for more than we expected, and Jacques found us a much better house here. I have a good job in the vehicle maintenance department for the city, and somehow," Heinz smiled, "Elisabeth and I are Belgian citizens. We were both born in Liège, and her maiden name is Steingut."

Jacques stood, holding a glass of brandy in his hand and began pacing as he talked. He stood beside Peter's chair as he said, "That makes you, Peter, officially Belgian and Aryan, but I can't do anything about the German records—unfortunately, they still exist. If I could get your siblings to Belgium, their Mischling status would also disappear. The churches will modify baptism records to accommodate Jewish-German refugees for a small donation, and Germany is losing its brightest and best as fast as they can get out of the country!"

Jacques looked at Heinz and Elisabeth. "The Belgian government now recognizes you as Catholics and native-born Belgian. Peter's hospital records confirm he was born in Brussels, and the church records show that you christened him in St. Michael's Church, which we attend. Your new passports and papers are clear and correct, and if

Nazi eyes should search your past, they will find nothing in Belgium that contradicts that."

Peter asked, "My God, Jacques, how do you do these things?"

Jacques began pacing without addressing Peter's question. "At the moment, there is a tremendous amount of anxiety in Europe. Politicians and wealthy bureaucrats are paranoid about the value of money, believing that valuable art objects offer them security. I have a warehouse in Switzerland full of precisely what they want, and the Nazis want to buy them as badly as the Jews want to turn them into cash. They simply change hands in my records." Jacques winked, but Peter didn't understand why. He still had a glass of brandy in his hand and refilled it from the bottle on the small table beside his leather chair.

"I also store much of the art and jewelry the Nazis buy or steal." He sloshed the brandy, sniffed the glass, and went on.

"For example, five years ago, I purchased a painting from the Nazi who stole it, paying him ten thousand Swiss francs, a reasonable price at the time, considering it was stolen. I sold it to another Nazi last week for two hundred and fifty thousand, twice what it's worth on the market today, and it's still in my warehouse. The sad truth for the Nazi who now thinks he owns it is the painting may someday be returned to its rightful owner… But I will keep the profit on the transaction."

The room was quiet while everyone tried to digest the incredible numbers—more than five years' salary for Heinz in one transaction!

Juliette asked, "What about our contracts at the Monnaie Theatre?"

He smiled, "I paid guests to play your roles in the Marriage of Figaro, and now that you are here, the manager has changed the fall schedule so that you can sing another Mozart opera. You start rehearsals for Don Giovanni next week. You will sing Zerlina, and Peter sings Don Ottavio, if that is agreeable."

Juliette screamed for joy so loudly it hurt everyone's ears. Peter laughed, took her hand, and asked, "Are you trying to break your parents' china?"

Jacques said, "Peter, now that I have a son, my good fortune is yours. I am not yet fifty, but I must do some succession planning, and until you have children, you and Juliette are the only succession I have."

"Until you have children," Elizabeth repeated Jacques' words, smiling, nodding at Juliette.

Jacques said, "I want you to work with Veronique and me in planning the future you want. You and Juliette will have the final say, certainly, but we would like to be part of your plans for the future, just as we hope you will be part of ours."

Veronique stood and put her arm around Jacques' waist. "Now, I will embarrass you two a little more; we haven't discussed your wedding present with you yet. Your parents know about it and will show it to you after dinner tonight."

Dinner stretched until nine, and although Juliette tried to find out, no one would tell her anything about the wedding present. Finally, Heinz and Elisabeth accompanied her and Peter to the Rolls, and Marcel, the chauffeur, drove them four blocks, stopping in the driveway of a beautiful, modern two-storey building set in a grove of old oaks. Elizabeth stood beside the car, looking at the house with Juliette beside her. "It has four bedrooms and a private bathroom next to your bedroom, a necessity for a house full of children."

Juliette looked at Elisabeth, and the joy of the moment faded.

"You must think I'm a spoiled brat."

Heinz answered.

"We think you are a fortunate woman, and we're glad you married our son."

Chapter Twelve

September 1939

Blitzkrieg!
(Lightning war)

JACQUES SIPPED HIS COFFEE ON THE TERRACE, sitting with his family under a huge sun umbrella. "I'm afraid war is inevitable—Hitler has taken a step that will surely lead Germany to war with England."

Everyone picked at a pile of croissants on the round wooden table they had gathered around. Jacques put down his coffee and picked out a croissant. "German army units are on the Polish border, and Hitler wouldn't have put them there if he weren't intending to invade."

Juliette swallowed a bite of croissant and a sip of coffee. She raised her finger, and everyone waited for her to speak. "Chamberlain backed off when he negotiated the Munich Pact; he let Hitler invade Czecho-slovakia and did nothing—why would anyone think the English would defend Poland? In addition, Poland is on the wrong side of Germany for England to help them."

Juliette said, "I made a note when, on the tenth of July, Chamber-lain warned Hitler that, according to the treaty with Poland signed on the thirty-first of March, England would automatically be at war with Germany if their army crossed the Polish border. I know that both British houses of parliament have passed a law that would trigger an automatic declaration of war if Germany invades, so surely Hitler's generals will reason with him and…" Jacques shook his head but didn't answer the insinuation, and Juliette said, "Well, wouldn't they?"

Jacques said, "Hitler's generals and minions are bootlickers who will do his bidding without question. They would pee their pants before going to the bathroom without his permission!"

Peter was on his second cup of coffee. His singing voice had returned, and he was on a high that even talk of war couldn't ruin. He asked, "If he attacks Poland, when would he do it?"

Jacques waved his left hand and wrinkled his brow. "Who knows? But probably in the next few months. Perhaps this is not so bad for us—Poland is on the other side of Germany, and Hitler's generals would never start a war on two fronts—the Great War taught them at least that much!"

Juliette said, "But if he invades Poland and the British declare war on him, won't that automatically be the case?" Her father nodded his gratitude for the astute question and explained.

"That threat only works if Hitler believes the British will do what they say, and their record isn't stellar in that department!"

Peter poured another coffee, speaking as he did.

"So, you think the English guarantee to Poland is worthless? Or will England, France, and Poland together defeat Germany?"

"No, they won't defeat Germany unless the war goes on for years. As Juliette pointed out, the British and French can't defend Poland without attacking Germany from the west. They would need to cross Belgium and Holland to do it, and those two countries are determined to stay neutral. Hitler knew that when he signed a neutrality treaty with them. As long as they remain neutral, he will leave them in peace, but only until he wants to attack France at a date of his choosing. For that reason, I'm afraid Poland is doomed."

The speculation became reality when, on the first day of September 1939, at 04:45, German guns began firing across the Polish border, and the world got another taste of Hitler's audacity. At 08:00, without warning, the Wehrmacht Heer, the regular German army, crossed the Polish border without declaring war. The official excuse was a staged attack on a German facility close to the Polish border using dispensible German concentration camp prisoners dressed in Polish army uniforms.

Britain and France issued an ultimatum to Germany, which Hitler ignored. He also laughed at their declaration of war three days later. Warsaw fell at the end of September, and the German and Russian armies met at an agreed-upon Polish partition line, roughly following the Bug River. Neither Britain nor France had fired a shot in Poland's defence, leaving the country no alternative but capitulation.

On the first day of October, Juliette and Peter ate Sunday dinner with her parents. They arrived late in the afternoon and joined Jacques and Veronique in the drawing room, where they all enjoyed a glass of wine. The lights were off, and the fireplace glowed as Jacques poured wine for everyone but him, then sat down, spinning his brandy glass with his fingers. Jacques said what everyone in Belgium knew but tried to ignore.

"The news from the war front is not good. The Allies have spent the past month wringing their hands instead of engaging Germany in Poland. The country now belongs to Hitler, freeing the German army to attack France. They will have to cross Belgium, but Hitler won't lose any sleep over that, and we will not stop them. The French and British appear disorganized, and I predict the Germans will take over our country in a matter of months. We must discuss our options."

When Juliette leaned over to her mother, Veronique whispered, "Do you think you might be pregnant?"

Juliette whispered, "No, Mother, and we're taking precautions."

Peter sat in a comfortable chair opposite Jacques. He had heard the whispered exchange between Juliette and her mother and pointedly asked, "So... are we here to talk war tonight?"

Jacques wagged his head. "No, war is no longer talk. The Germans crushed Poland in less than a month, and we are much weaker. We need to talk about the likely German occupation."

"Surely, the British and French will help us."

Jacques said, "Yes, they've committed themselves to fight the Germans, but they've got nothing to fight with. The German forces have prepared for war—Poland and Czechoslovakia were just practice—while Britain and France have put their faith in rhetoric. Talk is cheap, wastes time, and is ineffective against war machines. The time to attack Germany was when they crossed into Poland with their backs to the British and French.

"The Luftwaffe will neutralize the French and British armour, and German fighting vehicles will push the British and French armies back.

They will fight the war on Belgian, Dutch, and, I believe, finally on French and British soil."

Juliette vainly tried to disguise the distress she felt. "What do you want us to do, Papa?"

"I want to move the family to Switzerland—I will stay here to look after the house and the business, but everyone else must go."

Veronique spoke to Peter in French. His French was more than passable since Juliette had made his French her raison d'être. "Jacques has friends in the Nazi Party, and they will see that he stays safe, but we cannot risk you or your parents falling into German hands." She spoke to Juliette, "Of course, you will want to be with Peter."

Juliette shook her head, "No, we can't...we have another four performances of Don Giovanni, and the last one is on Christmas Eve. We can't leave. Who would replace us?"

As Juliette expected, her father had prepared an answer.

"I have spoken with the theatre management, and they can find someone to do the roles as guests, just as we did when you were on the St. Louis. The danger is too great for Peter, and, in any case, when the Germans attack Belgium, the theatre will probably close."

"Daddy, we won't leave you here alone. Peter and I will stay, but Peter's parents must go."

Jacques looked at his wife and shrugged, "I've never been able to say no to her; you'll have to do this."

Veronique leaned ahead in her chair and spoke to her daughter more urgently, "You do realize the real danger is Peter's. There is no doubt now that the Nazis will move against the Jews, and if they come here looking for him, they will find him. If they look in their German records, they will find out he is a Jew and return him to Dachau."

Jacques added, "And you must know there will be many helpful Nazi sympathizers in Belgium. A few officials know that Peter and his parents have falsified papers, and if even one of them is a sympathizer or is tortured..."

Juliette began pacing, much as her father did when he wanted to make a point. She wanted her father to listen to what she had to say, so she had come prepared. "Didn't Belgium declare neutrality in this war, and didn't the German government agree to respect Belgian sovereignty for that neutral position?"

Jacques nodded, "Yes, Belgium and Holland did that, leaving the British and French without a route to Germany. Hitler won't respect that treaty any more than he respected Austria's, Czechoslovakia's, or Poland's. Now, it's too late to upset Hitler's plan.

Juliette was confused., "Why would Germany break the agreement and attack us... Wouldn't that give the British and French the right to cross Belgium?"

Jacques laughed without joy. "Hitler's agreements to respect Belgium and Holland's neutrality have outlived their usefulness, and he will now take the shortest route to the French—his real target—through Belgium and Holland. The French and British will try to meet the Germans halfway across our country, as they did in 1914, and again, it is Belgium's choice whether to fight the Germans or the French and British. Either way, Belgium and Holland will become bloody battlegrounds." He waved his arms in frustration.

"Our politicians were naive to think we could remain neutral... all they did was give Hitler the time he needed to defeat Poland and turn his army westward. When, not if, the Germans cross the border, we must defend ourselves. Hitler will never respect our neutrality; the road to the French and British is through us, not around us, and Hitler will take that road. That will effectively declare war on Belgium, and we must fight back so the British and French have time to organize."

Juliette sat down, defeated. She looked at her father. "Will you take sides?"

Jacques glanced at Veronique, and she nodded.

"We took sides years ago; this war started for us in 1933, when Hitler came to power, and since then, we have been working against him. I have built a formidable business on the foundation my father left me, a potent tool for good or evil.

"The Nazis persecute communists, Jews and Romani in Germany, and Goebbels' speeches make it clear they intend to abuse them everywhere they find them. The definition of who is a Jew or a Romani is in the Nürnberg Race Law. The authority to detain and fleece the Jews in

Germany, and now in Poland, Austria, and Czechoslovakia, is already in Hitler's hands.

"Our money and connections put us in a unique position to help some of those people escape their fate. We are helping finance resistance groups, and I am gathering intelligence by working with Nazis to fence their loot. King Leopold has plans to stay here and work within the system the Nazis will set up, whatever that means, but it may work well for us. Your mother and I are in a position to appear to collaborate with the Germans while secretly working to defeat them, and perhaps that is the route the King will take."

Juliette's epiphany in any other context would have been comical, "My God, you are spies!" She added the obvious… "But, if they catch you…"

Veronique sympathetically took the inference to its conclusion. "Yes, my dear, we will be shot if the Nazis catch us. However, we must use our advantages to save lives, and we have already earned a huge profit in that department. More than a hundred Jews are out of Germany because of your father, and more are in the pipeline—we can't stop now."

Juliette, defiant, announced, "Peter and I will help you… We can't watch you take this risk while we sit safely in Switzerland."

Juliette noted her father's hesitation but was in no mood to negotiate.

Jacques spoke carefully, convincingly, "I'm sorry, Juliette, but you can't speak for Peter in this, and your mother and I could not live with your death. No! The risk for you and Peter is too great!"

"You have no more right to speak for Peter than I have!" Juliette spoke louder than she had intended, "And you have no right to tell me what to do. Those bastards raped me, and don't you dare tell me I can't have justice!" She pointed at her husband while still looking at her father. "Why don't you ask Peter what he wants to do?"

Peter spoke before anyone else could, "Juliette and I have discussed these possibilities, and I told her I would fight the Nazis any way I could. I won't run away, and I must be a part of what you are doing!"

Juliette deliberately toned down her aggression, "Papa, you misunderstand. I didn't ask a question—I made a statement. If the Germans occupy Belgium, as you say they will, Peter and I will join the

Résistance with or without you." She softened her tone, becoming her father's daughter again.

"We will have a better chance of success and survival if we work with you. You know our talents intimately and will know how best to use them while keeping us out of danger. I want you and Mother to work out what our role will be. In any case, our singing careers are probably over until the war ends. Peter cannot be in the spotlight anywhere the Nazis have power, and I doubt they will hire me in Germany, even if they keep their theatres open."

Jacques looked at Veronique, who dropped her eyes. "I told your mother that this would be your response. I am scared to death for both of you."

Typically, dinner at the Durand house on Sunday evening was full of cheerful chatter and laughter, but tonight, the table was quiet. When the meal was over, the family gathered in the drawing room.

Jacques left the room for a few minutes and returned with the 'chauffeur,' Marcel, and Charles, the servant. They sat with the family, and Veronique poured the tea. Charles put French pastries on a large china plate and set it on a small table where everyone could reach it.

Jacques swept his hand toward Marcel and Charles. "These men are not who you think they are—Marcel is British military intelligence, MI6, and Charles was in the Deuxième Bureau, French military intelligence, until the British hired him. They are dangerous men if you are the enemy."

Juliette laughed, "I knew you two were something special. You act like servants, but I sensed that you aren't."

Marcel didn't laugh. "Then we're not very good actors. If we didn't convince you, then perhaps someone else will figure it out."

Juliette shook her head, "Oh, no, I didn't know anything; I just sensed that you were not servant material."

Jacques went back to business. "Every mission we discuss must meet Marcel and Charles's approval. Their interest is intelligence-gathering, and my connections within the Nazi government are a gold mine for them. The Jews we've helped escape are often excellent sources of information, as was Peter's report on the munitions produced in Dachau." He looked at Peter.

"Report...?" Peter was surprised; Juliette wasn't. "I didn't write a report."

Jacques smiled and explained, "No, but you told me about your experiences in Dachau in great detail, including the relationship you had with... What was the name of the SS officer...?" The tone told Juliette that her father knew the answer.

"Untersturmbannführer Alexander Küster," interjected Charles, "He runs the munitions assembly line."

"Yes, that's right." Jacques nodded innocently at Charles, then returned to Peter.

"Perhaps you remember Charles was present when we discussed your time at Dachau? Well...he has a phenomenal memory."

Chapter Thirteen

23 October 1939

Mimi è una Sirena…
(Mimi is a flirt...)
Giacomo Puccini, *La Bohème*

Juliette's telephone rang on October twenty-second, and Herr Geer, the manager of the Bielefeld Opera House, was desperate. His soprano was sick, and they needed a Mimi tomorrow night. The opera was Puccini's La Bohème. The manager offered her five thousand Reichsmarks for a single performance as Mimi and a rehearsal and two thousand for each additional Bohème, should his soprano remain sick. Juliette accepted, with the condition that she must return to Belgium on the thirtieth. Herr Geer agreed, and Juliette ran down the stairs to tell Peter, almost tripping in her excitement.

"I just accepted a Gastvertrag in Bielefeld, and it's for more money than I made in Nürnberg in two months!" She wrapped her arms around Peter, who, in the process of preparing a schnitzel for their dinner, had a carving knife in one hand and a long fork in the other. He stood with his arms spread, afraid he would cut or stab her. She said, "I've always wanted to find out if I could sing a role on such short notice!"

Peter asked, "What's the role?" She let him go; he trimmed the fat from one side of the schnitzel, and she pilfered a piece of lettuce from his salad.

"It's Mimi; I know that role so well I could sing it in my sleep." She contemplatively crunched the lettuce. "I hope the tenor isn't an ass."

"How about this tenor—am I an ass?" Peter laughed.

Juliette pinched his bum and pulled herself tight to him. "Yes, that's your best quality, my handsome husband." She released him, a thought suddenly grabbing her attention. "I wonder if Daddy had anything to do with this."

"Your first guest contract in the city where my sister, who wants to leave Germany, lives? Now, why would you think that?"

After dinner, Juliette and Peter walked down the Avenue de Saturne to her parents' house. Juliette went straight to her father's closed office door and opened it without knocking. She caught him sitting behind his desk with her mother on his lap. Veronique immediately stood and smoothed her dress.

Juliette grinned at her, then turned to her father, "Papa, I just received an offer to sing Mimi in Bielefeld tomorrow night for an obscene amount of money...uh... You didn't have anything to do with that, did you?" Juliette tried for a touch of annoyance in her tone.

"Why would you think such a thing?" Jacques was only partially successful in mixing a generous bit of hurt and innocence into his dodgy reply.

Juliette gave Peter an "I told you so" look.

"Will there be anything else, ma chérie?" Jacques asked as she turned to leave.

Juliette looked at Peter as she answered her father, "No, that's all."

"Then, since you will be in Bielefeld anyway, there is one small thing you could do for me." Jacques stood up, and Veronique headed for the door.

"You do remember that Peter's sister Louisa and her husband live there?... Well..." He fished around his desk... "I have some papers for them, and it would help me a lot if you could deliver them. They are travelling to England via Belgium, and on the way, I thought they could stop off here to visit Peter." Jacques smiled sweetly. "And you wouldn't mind if they travelled back with you, would you?"

Juliette tried not to laugh. "No, I wouldn't mind at all. Will there be anything else, Papa?"

"There is just one more tiny detail. I'm sending Marcel with you as your valet. You will treat him well, won't you, ma chérie?"

Juliette ran over to his desk. "Papa, I love you," she leaned across it to kiss him.

Peter reached for Jacques' hand, said, "Thank you, sir," and pulled back before Jacques could get up and hug him.

"I'm working on your brothers." Jacques grinned at his son-in-law. "And I think we're close."

Jacques turned to Juliette. "Marcel has the tickets, and he will drive you to your house—your train leaves Brussels in two hours, and you change in Frankfurt. You have reservations in a very nice Bielefeld hotel close to the opera house, commensurate with your opera diva status. Dress like a star, and don't forget to act like one…don't be too gentle with the paid help."

Waiting outside the open door, Marcel grunted, and Jacques added, "Sing well, ma chérie."

Veronique intercepted them at the door, and the nervousness in her hug brought Juliette back to the reality of the mission. Her mother said, "I packed some extra clothes for Louisa and Wolfgang, just in case they don't have anything appropriate for first class."

Juliette smiled sympathetically, recognizing her mother's worry. "Thank you, Mother. I will give the clothes to them, and I will be careful. And don't worry, you know that Marcel will protect me."

The first-class compartment on the train from Frankfurt to Bielefeld was luxurious and private. Marcel stowed the luggage in the overhead racks while Juliette waited, then graciously held the door as a loyal servant should. He sat opposite her, maintaining a respectful distance. When the conductor slid the door aside to check the tickets, Marcel spoke to him in perfect German. Once situated in their compartment, he opened a French book, and Juliette stole a glance at the cover. It looked a little more risqué than the previous one, and Juliette smiled as she reviewed her La bohème score, humming her role.

A tall, handsome, clean-shaven and well-built young man met the train in Bielefeld at ten o'clock in the evening, and when Johann Finke told her that he was the second violinist in the opera orchestra, she barely hid her amazement. He was not what Juliette expected any violinist to be—he was built like an athlete and had the face of a Greek God. When he reached for her suitcase, she shooed him away. "My father pays Marcel to do that; if you do it, Papa will be angry, and he won't pay him."

Johann pointed to an old gray Benz parked at the curb. He said, "I have a car to drive you to the hotel." And then, apologetically, "It's not far."

"Oh, dear," said Juliette, "I'm used to Papa's Rolls… But, I suppose Marcel can get everything in." Marcel was already arranging the luggage in the rear when Juliette said, "Marcel, please be careful with the hats!"

He ignored her, carefully fitting all but one of the suitcases and a hatbox into the Mercedes' luggage space.

"I suppose that means I must sit with a suitcase beside me." Juliette deliberately sounded distressed. "I guess that will be acceptable since it isn't far."

Marcel opened the door for Juliette while Johann put the surplus case and the hatbox on the other side of the rear seat. He opened the front door, slid into the passenger seat, and winked at Johann as they drove off.

Johann met Juliette and Marcel at their hotel at nine the following day. Juliette complained about the uncivilized hour from the moment she climbed into the Mercedes until Johann slowed down as the car approached the rear of the theatre. Juliette tried a few arpeggios, announced that her voice would not work at such a dreadful hour, and that the rehearsal would be a complete waste of time.

Ignoring Juliette, Johann stopped at the stage entrance. Marcel opened Juliette's door, and she stepped elegantly out of the back seat. They waited outside while Johann parked the car, and when he returned, Juliette let him open the stage door, then swept into the hallway and gave him her arm.

"Are you married, Johann?"

"Yes, happily married, Mademoiselle Durand. Barbara and I have two children, a boy and a girl."

She said, "What a pity!" as Johann opened her dressing room door.

"The wardrobe lady will be here in a few minutes to fit your costume, and we will meet on the stage when you are ready. I will be your pianist for the Stellprobe." Juliette started to speak, but Johann continued, "Don't worry about my playing; this rehearsal will only work on the staging, not the music. If you want or need to, you may 'mark' your way through if you like, but the rest of the cast will use their performance voice most of the time."

Juliette decided that no real diva would sing full out in a staging rehearsal. She looked at Johann and pouted, "Could you ask them to please 'mark' too so I won't be the only one? My vocal cords won't work until at least noon."

Juliette knew Johann wanted to laugh, but instead, he said, "I'll ask them to be nice to you." She chuckled as he closed the door.

A few minutes later, the wardrobe lady arrived with Mimi's plain poor-girl dress and a coat and nightdress for the last act. Everything fit perfectly. The dress's neckline barely concealed her breasts' essentials; she leaned forward and looked down; she could see her nipples. She leaned back, and her nipples' outlines barely showed through the thin material—she decided not to wear a bra.

"How did you know my size?"

The wardrobe madam said, "The theatre in Nürnberg had all your measurements, and you can stop your diva acting around me. I know the people you worked with; I worked there before I came here, and when I heard you were coming, I called to find out your size. According to them, you are the sweetest thing this side of honey."

"I'm nice enough if I get what I want, but isn't everyone? I've learned that if people I work with think I'm nice, they treat me differently than if they're afraid of me. If I'm mean, no one dares to criticize me—they're glad if I sing!"

"I won't tell a soul, dear." Her clicking tongue and wagging head said what she was thinking.

Juliette sat in front of the mirror and dabbed makeup on her shiny nose. She wanted so much to hug Johann and tell him what a lovely man he was to put up with her, but the diva act was a necessary distraction for future operations, and Johann must believe it. Her father had said that she must establish a reputation as a difficult woman if she were to be effective at the border. What self-centred, empty-headed diva would be interested in anyone or anything but herself? A woman like that wouldn't risk breaking a fingernail for a just cause. Self-absorption came with the territory.

She finished applying her makeup in a few minutes, and Johann had pointed out the stage door, but she decided to wait in the dressing room until he came to get her.

The knock on the door came ten minutes later, and she asked, coquettishly, "Who is it?"

Johann answered, "We are ready whenever you are, mademoiselle. Everyone is waiting."

She said to the door, "I don't see how you expect a beautiful woman to go on the stage in this shabby costume. It's horrible!" She brushed a stray hair back from her forehead, smiling as she did.

There was a pause, then Johann said through the door, "Will you be out in a few minutes, madame? We have a lot of music to go through; you're in almost every scene, and we cannot begin without you."

Juliette opened the door with a flourish, and Johann almost fell backward as she swept past him. She said, "Well, come on then..." and walked as fast as she could.

She stopped at the door marked "stage right" and waited for Johann to open it. He held it open; she straightened her shoulders and flounced grandly onto the stage. She immediately picked out her Rudolpho. He was short, slightly taller than she was, and almost as broad as he was tall—it would be a challenge to imagine being in love with him—but Professor Garcia had taught her well.

Juliette stretched out a limp right hand, and he bent down to kiss it.

She thought, At least you're not dumb, and said, "Darling, such a handsome Rudolpho, and with manners too." She turned to the rest of the cast, standing in a group watching her.

"I'm here, darlings; we can begin now." She said it loudly, in thick French-accented German.

The stage director and conductor introduced themselves, and they too kissed her hand.

Juliette looked around the stage. The first act set represented a Paris Atelier, a cold attic where Rudolpho wrote his novels and poems. Centre stage, a round cast-iron stove was connected to a tin chimney that disappeared through the sloped ceiling, and a table and three chairs stood slightly stage right. Further to the right was an easel, paints and brushes, and an unmade bed. A door exited the room stage left, and two fake dormers in the painted paper roof gave imaginary light. An unlit candle sat on the table, along with the yellowed pages of Rudolpho's manuscript, a feather quill, and a bottle of ink.

Strips of white tape, stuck helter-skelter on the floor, marked where the singers should position themselves during specific points in the score. Juliette noticed hers were wider than the others, with "Mimi" and a number written in black ink.

Herr Kretchmar pointed out the tape locations, singing the passages that signalled Juliette to move from one place to another in numerical order. When she gave him a hostile look, he stopped singing and said, "Our excellent Souffleuse will help you with this. She is a former singer of this role and knows the score perfectly." Kretchmar stepped around the half-shell built into the floor in the centre of the stage and waved at a woman's head inside it. Juliette bent over, waved and smiled sweetly—no singer wanted a Souffleuse as an enemy—then followed Kretchmar from position to position.

Juliette waited until he had pointed out all the movement for the first act before she said, "This is much too complicated. I must place myself appropriately for my interpretation of Maestro Puccini's music. It is impossible to become the Mimi he intended while following those ridiculous spots. Just think how stupid I will look, staring at the floor, searching for the proper place when the Souffleuse says, 'Mimi, go to number three.'" She took a loud breath, looked pointedly at the director, and said, "Only a Prussian would think of something so stupidly arcane!" His mouth flew open, but only a croak came out.

Juliette added, "Herr Kretchmar, I am just not that kind of actress. To act, I simply must have my freedom; otherwise, I won't be able to sing!"

Herr Kretchmar blanched. His hands started shaking, and Juliette knew that she had struck gold. Before a week was out, every theatre in Germany would know the name 'Juliette Durand.'

But now, she had to sing like a goddess.

"B-b-but Mademoiselle Durand," his voice squeaked, "you cannot expect the cast to follow you around the stage—such freedom is impossible!" He waved his hands in every direction.

Juliette tilted her head. "Herr Kretchmar, I am sorry, and I understand your position perfectly." He let out an audible but indecipherable squeak as she started for the stage door. She didn't turn her head when she said, "Would you kindly fetch my five thousand marks while I change my clothes?" She made a point of looking at the round white clock on the wall above the stage door. "I want to catch the train to Frankfurt in an hour." Juliette left the stage, searching for a plan of how she would come back if no one came after her.

As she opened the stage door, Juliette discarded the need for a plan when she heard Johann running after her. She slowed to let him catch her in the hallway, then stopped in front of her dressing room door.

"Please, Mademoiselle, he will have a heart attack! Can't you compromise?"

Juliette's heart broke for Johann, and she made her first mistake—her face betrayed that she was not what she seemed. He caught it and touched her arm. "I don't know why you need to do this, but you've pushed as far as you can. Let's go into your dressing room."

She turned to face him, deciding to use the moment. "There is no need to go into the dressing room; I've made my point. But there is something you can do for me in the strictest confidence."

"If it will get you back on the stage, there isn't much I won't do,"

"You must be discreet; lives may depend on it. And we will need your car. We can talk about it after the rehearsal."

Johann said, "Agreed—we will talk later. Now, can we return to Herr Kretchmar before he kills himself?"

When they returned, the cast had gathered around the embarrassed stage director. They spoke sympathetically, in quiet tones, and Juliette could hear Kretchmar crying. Afraid she had gone too far, she regretted what she had done.

Halfway across the stage, she said, "Herr Kretchmar, please allow me to apologize." The gathering opened a gap to the stage director—there wasn't a friendly face in the group. Kretchmar wiped his face with a handkerchief and stuffed it in his pocket.

"Herr Finke has explained your staging techniques, and although such precision is not in my artistic nature, I will do my best to fit into your vision. My brain is not so... how do you say... élégant? I cannot learn such complicated staging in so few hours. Would it satisfy your requirements if I moved into the vicinity of the marks and left the exact placement to my interaction with the other singers? I don't mind if they take my hand and lead me—if you think that is necessary."

The look of relief on the Regisseur's face was comical, but no one laughed. He stumbled over his words as he took Juliette's arm and led her to the tape marked, 'Mimi 1.'

"Yes, yes, that was my intent, Mademoiselle." Excited now, he waved his free hand as he said, "I'm afraid I did not make myself clear; I don't need precise placement, and I apologize for giving you that impression. On such short notice, you can interpret Mimi as you wish—but with some limitations, of course. I don't need you to stand in a specific spot, but you must be in a specific area so you can interact with the other singers. We will have pandemonium if they have to follow you around the stage!"

Juliette graciously touched Herr Kretchmar's arm. "I've never before jumped into a performance on such short notice, and I hadn't thought about your problems. Herr Finke has explained these to me, and I now understand your intentions."

She touched his face and said gently, "Shall we begin again, ma chérie? I'm prepared to go directly to the music."

Everyone ran to their places, and Johann struck the notes, signalling Juliette to knock on Rudolpho's door. She rapped on it three times; Rudolpho asked, "Wer da?" and the scene began.

The tenor had a beautiful sound, a ringing 'high C,' and his facial expressions were natural. When he ended his aria, he asked Mimi to tell him about herself, and the cast spontaneously applauded. Juliette waited, and when she began her aria, the silence on the stage was palpable. Kretchmar didn't interrupt her; he let her sing using the staging she had developed in Nürnberg. Rudolpho listened intently, with genuine interest, as she explained who she was. His simple "Ja" response to her question in the middle of the aria was so sincere it almost threw Juliette off.

When the Mittagspause arrived at one o'clock, the cast had run through everything except the final scene, and Kretchmar paused the rehearsal until three. Johann met Juliette at the stage door, and Marcel, who had been sitting in the wings watching Juliette, joined them.

Johann said, "If you like, I can take you to the restaurant down the street, or we could eat in the Menza to save time. The theatre is paying either way."

"In that case, why don't we eat where it's more private? The restaurant will be fine." Juliette turned to Marcel. "Of course, you should eat with us, Marcel."

He nodded, and Juliette caught a look of dismay on Johann's face as she went to her dressing room to change, guessing that he had a budget problem. The meal would be expensive, and Marcel was an unplanned expense.

The restaurant was decorated in the old German aristocracy's elegant, formal, and exclusive style and probably hadn't changed for two hundred years. Juliette hadn't eaten breakfast, and when she looked at the menu, she saw prices that would have made her father hesitate. She heard Johann suck in his breath, and the expression on his face told her he hadn't planned on these prices. It was time to end his misery and seal his allegiance.

"You do know that I come from a wealthy family?" She smiled at him as sweetly as she could; he nodded hopefully. "I will make a small donation to the Bielefeld Theatre by paying for meals, including Marcel's and yours."

Johann relaxed. "Our Intendant, Herr Geer, will appreciate the gesture, and he would fire me if I refused your kind offer."

Juliette ordered a 'hunter's schnitzel' with sliced roasted potatoes and red cabbage. Johann and Marcel tripled the order. And then, without asking anyone's opinion, Juliette ordered an expensive bottle of sweet chardonnay.

Johann, his hands folded on the table, said to Juliette, "I believe we made a deal so you would go back to the rehearsal, and you kept your side of it. So, tell me what dastardly deed I must do!"

Marcel looked at Juliette; she nodded, and he said, "Despite your deal with Juliette, we will understand if you decide not to honour it, but we would be grateful if you could help us."

Juliette put on her pleading face, touched Johann's hand, and watched him melt as she said, "I really need you to do this, Johann."

Marcel said, "Juliette has a sister-in-law in Bielefeld, and she and her husband are returning with us. We need you to quietly bring them to the hotel before picking us up tomorrow morning. After they get to our room, we need an hour to prepare them for the journey, and you must time everything so that we all get to the train just before it leaves, with very little time to spare."

Johann hesitated before he asked, "What's so complicated about that? I understood this was an exceptional favour...perhaps even a bit risky."

Juliette examined his face, found nothing that disturbed her, and decided to tell at least part of the truth. "My sister-in-law is half-Jewish, a Mischling, and when she leaves the hotel, she and her husband will have new identities. The star of David she must wear will disappear before she leaves the hotel room."

She was pleased when Johann didn't hesitate nor ask why. He said frankly, "In that case, I will be careful, and you can count on my discretion."

Juliette and Marcel decided, after meeting Johann and seeing his car, a model and colour seen on every street in Germany, that they would ask him to pick up Peter's sister and her husband. No one would pay attention to something that happened many times a day, but a taxi stopped on a residential street could draw attention, and the driver would be a random risk—things could get complicated if they had to explain something to what could be a loyal Nazi.

Although she had only known Johann for a few days, Juliette trusted him. The chances were good that she was right—there weren't many Nazis in the arts community, and everyone knew who they were.

La Bohème was a huge success, and the death scene was Juliette's diva moment. As she died, the tenor's heart-rending cries of "Mimi" on a 'G' mingled with the sobs from the audience. When the rest of the cast had bowed and waved to the weeping throng, Juliette and her Rudolpho took their bows; the audience clapped and shouted, accompanied by shouts of "Brava." It took three solo curtain calls to quiet them down.

Opera singers take every opportunity to party, and the cast of La Bohème was no exception. Juliette joined them at the hotel restaurant, where she met Johann's wife, Barbara, and their children. When Johann introduced them, Juliette felt she had known Barbara for years, and they stepped aside to talk about women's things and children. When the evening was over, Juliette's maternal instincts had kicked in, awakening an urgency to have babies. She left the party when Barbara and Johann took their children home, retiring to her room.

She thought of Peter as she went to sleep, but Marcel's face, a mask of pity, invaded her dreams. When she woke the following morning, she couldn't shake a feeling of intense sadness.

Joliette was dressed and ready to go when Johann pulled his car to the front of the hotel. She watched as Louisa and Wolfgang exited the Mercedes and entered the hotel, dressed for travel, an unmistakable yellow 'Jew badge' on Louisa's coat. Johann parked the car on the street, then disappeared through the wide door behind them.

Marcel rapped his unique code on Juliette's door; she let him in and had barely closed it when Johann knocked. She opened the door, and the new arrivals stepped into the room. Johann said, "I'll be waiting in the lobby," then discreetly left without coming in.

Wolfgang said loudly, "Why did we come to the hotel? If we're going to visit Louisa's parents, why didn't we go directly to the Bahnhof?" He pulled out his pocket watch and looked at it. "We don't have any time to waste!"

Marcel's expression told Juliette that she was on her own. She spoke to Louisa, "You have a star on your coat so the Nazis can find you. The Belgian customs won't let you cross the border if you wear it."

She turned to Wolfgang. "I thought you understood… This isn't about a visit to see Louisa's parents… Louisa won't return, and I thought you would be going with her."

Wolfgang turned to Louisa and asked angrily, "Do you intend to stay in Belgium without me?"

She hung her head but didn't answer, and he asked, "How long will you be there?"

Juliette anxiously interrupted, acutely aware that German trains ran on time. "She cannot remain in Belgium—the Nazis will invade any day, and you and Louisa have papers and passage to immigrate to England. If you want it, you have a job as a draftsman in an aircraft factory. My father has also arranged a flat for you in Sheffield, near the factory." Juliette looked at Louisa. "I thought Louisa had told you that!"

Wolfgang sat down, and Louisa took over.

"Liebling, I couldn't tell you. If the Gestapo suspected I was leaving, they would have arrested me and sent me to a camp!"

Confused and hurt, Wolfgang asked, "You didn't trust me?"

"It wasn't a matter of trust," Louisa said quietly, "You are a lousy actor, and when you drink with your friends..."

"But I am your husband! Don't I count?" He spoke too loudly.

Louisa looked at Juliette, then returned to Wolfgang, hurrying the conversation.

"I will be travelling on a Belgian passport as your wife. You will be using your German passport, and you can return here whenever you want to, but I must go to England." She pleaded with him, "We both have good jobs waiting for us, and if you stay with me, I'll help you learn English." Unsure of what her husband would do, Louisa wrung her hands and said, "You can do it, Wolfgang… But we don't have time to discuss this. You must decide now!"

"But what about our house? I built it with my own hands!"

"The house doesn't matter as much as we do. If you go to England with me, someone will sell the house for us and forward the money. Juliette's father has guaranteed that, and I believe him. We can use the money to buy another house in England, or we can rent, and you can buy a new car!" Louisa was desperate—there was no more time.

Juliette was ready to stop the conversation and go to an alternate plan when Wolfgang put his arms around Louisa.

"I can't bear the thought of losing you, and lately…well… I've been scared to answer the door, afraid it was the Gestapo coming to take you away. I didn't think there was a solution, and so I...I hoped the law would change—but it didn't, and it won't. And now, I suppose this has gone too far to turn back."

Wolfgang stroked Louisa's hair. "I love you, Louisa, and I will go anywhere to keep you safe. I hate the Nazis, and I don't want to stay here and work for them. Someday, when those people are gone, perhaps we will return."

Suddenly, he stepped back, laughed nervously, and ran his fingers through his bushy brown hair. "Wow, I can't believe we're doing this!" He said, "Good morning," in English, with a thick German accent, then, "How are you this morning?" And everyone laughed.

Wolfgang, suddenly serious, asked Marcel, "What would you have done if I had said no?"

Marcel answered, smiling, "You didn't say no, did you?" He put his arm around Wolfgang's shoulders.

When the foursome arrived in the lobby, Johann rose from his chair. Marcel had a suitcase under his right arm and one in each hand—Wolfgang carried two more. The car's trunk was already half-full with Wolfgang and Louisa's luggage, so Johann tied four suitcases on the roof.

At the station, Juliette hugged Johann and kissed him on the cheek, and he blushed.

"Thank Barbara for me, Johann—and I hope we meet again."

Johann said, "I've never heard a better Mimi, and I've never met anyone as strong as you are, except perhaps Barbara. In a different world, we would be great friends."

Inside, Juliette unlocked the window in the compartment and slid it down to put her head out and look back at the platform. Johann was standing where she had left him, and she waved at him. He waved weakly back to her, but even as the distance grew, Juliette thought she could see fear in his face. She wondered whether it was for her, his family, or his country.

Sitting on the leather seat beside her, Marcel took Juliette's hand as she pushed herself against him. She put her head on his shoulder and wrapped her other hand around his. She closed her eyes to hide the tears, but they squeezed past the lids and down her cheek.

"Marcel, will we live to see the end of this?"

He squeezed her hand and turned his face away.

SS soldiers boarded the train at the Belgian border, blocking the exits. Officers went from compartment to compartment, checking the passengers' papers. A young SS soldier examined their documents and then said to Louisa in Germanized French, "I see that you were born in Liège. On what street lived you?"

Louisa answered without hesitation, "Avenue de Brion." The young man nodded, and as he handed her papers back, he said, "Au revoir, madame. Bonne Voyage."

The SS left the train, and Belgian customs officials entered, working their way through the first-class car as they examined passports. A middle-aged woman looked at Louisa's without a word, stamped it, and left the compartment. Ten minutes later, the train was on its way to Brussels.

Marcel furrowed his brow. "Is there an Avenue de Brion in Liège? I know the city well and..."

"I have no idea," Louisa answered, "I've never been in Liège.

Wolfgang looked confused.

Juliette explained, "Her papers don't give a street address for her birthplace, just Liège—the SS officer was testing her French."

Louisa said, "I wasn't sure what he asked; his French was bad, but I knew it had something to do with a street address."

Juliette laughed, but not because she thought it was funny.

Chapter Fourteen

January 1940

Geduld, Geduld…
(Patience! Patience…)

A YEAR AFTER DACHAU and a few days before Christmas, Peter and Juliette met Jacques and Veronique in the drawing room. Before they sat down, Jacques said, "I'm afraid I have bad news. Dieter and Rolf have been arrested and taken to Dachau."

Juliette asked bitterly, "On what charge?"

"Being Jewish, of course."

Jacques looked at Peter sympathetically. "At the moment, I can't free your brothers, but the SS will transfer them to a Zwangsarbiter slave labour camp near one of the German factories, perhaps in Wolfsburg, building the new Volkswagen. Your brothers have skills the factories need, so they will be well-treated. The Wehrmacht has taken most of the skilled mechanics to fix their Panzers and Lastwagen, and German companies need workers. They are happy to take all the three-marks-per-hour labour they can get."

"They get paid?" Peter was skeptical. "I thought they were slaves."

"They are indeed slaves, and they don't get paid—the Nazi Party does.

Juliette asked, "What about their wives, and Dieter's children?"

Veronique explained, "Their wives are Aryan, and therefore free to leave the country or stay. They can choose where they want to go, but both have already said they want to stay in Germany, near their husbands."

Juliette's feeling of hopelessness had been growing since Bielefeld. "But how will they live? Neither of them has a job or any education."

Veronique said, "We will transfer whatever money they need from a

Swiss account. They will have enough, and they can find jobs. Jacques has a client who knows someone in the Arbeitsamt who will see that they find work near the factories where their husbands will be."

Juliette, frustrated, gestured with her hands as she said, "Why are the Nazis doing this?" She saw tears in Peter's eyes and took his hand.

Peter said, "When I think they can't hurt us anymore, they still find a way to do it."

The final performance of Don Giovanni took place on Christmas Eve, and because Peter and Juliette hadn't renewed their contracts, the theatre had nothing more for them. But despite that, Peter and Juliette had a full calendar until spring. Peter had scheduled oratorio concerts in Belgium and Holland, and Juliette had three more guest contracts in German theatres.

Juliette's first contract was in Heilbronn, arranged by her father. The theatre had scheduled rehearsals for La Traviata beginning the second week in January, and Juliette's obligation was for three performances of Violette before the end of the month.

Before Juliette's scheduled departure, she and Peter feverishly worked on music, mostly his. Hitler had not yet invaded Western Europe, and there was hope in Belgium that he might be satisfied with half of Poland. The English and French couldn't attack Germany as long as neutral Belgium and Holland blocked their way, so perhaps the stalemate would hold until sanity returned. Having invaded Finland, a peaceful land with nothing for its conquerors but ice, snow, and reindeer, the Russians seemed a greater danger to European stability. The people of France, Belgium and Holland relaxed, dubbing the war against Germany a 'fake.'

Determined to pay his way, Peter took every gig he could, from Bach to Stravinsky. His studies and career had concentrated on opera, not oratorio or concert repertoire, and all of the singing he now accepted was new to him. Peter contracted to sing two of Bach's cantatas and his massive St. Matthew Passion without looking at the music. He was horrified when it became painfully obvious how challenging and lengthy the Passion was. Juliette was an excellent interpreter of Bach, and when he threw the piano score across the room, she offered to help him transition from opera singer to Baroque musician.

Flopping down in a big armchair, Peter said, "How could anyone who knows anything about the human voice write music that can't be sung?" He was furious because he could not sing the "Geduld, Geduld" aria in Bach's St. Matthew Passion. "I need help, Bitte! Bitte!"

She laughed at him, increasing his frustration. "Bach wrote his music for the instruments of the time, usually tuned about a half-tone below the four-forty 'A' we use now. You could use that excuse for your problem, but it won't help you sing the music."

He looked at her with evil intent, picked up the score, took it in both hands and feigned tearing it in two. She laughed again.

Juliette said, not without a bit of mocking in her voice, "Bach isn't difficult to sing; it's a balm for the voice—if you know how to sing it. You're trying to make every note full and round, like nineteenth-century Italian opera, but that's impossible, even with baroque instruments tuned to a lower pitch. Not to mention that it sounds terrible and won't carry over the edge of the stage.

"You must learn to relax; let your voice find the notes, not your mind. Each note is individual, and you must learn to sing them clearly, exactly on the pitch from the beginning of the note to the end. Then, you must delineate the vowels cleanly, separating the pitches but smoothly connecting the notes without sliding. Do you understand?"

"No—" he waved his arms around, with no apparent purpose— "I don't understand. How can I separate the pitches but connect the notes?"

She winked at him. "We are separate, but sometimes we're connected."

Peter smiled at her coquettish solicitation, but she could see he was frustrated. She sat on the arm of his chair and ran her fingers through his hair.

"No," he waved her away, "I want to get this right...I sound like a dying animal in a thunderstorm!"

Juliette took his arm and pulled him to his feet, "Come; I'll give you a lesson in Baroque singing technique."

Peter tried to resist, but she pulled him with her, leaning back and tugging his arm until he gave in and followed. She led him into the bedroom, closed the door and turned the key in the lock. The expression on his face asked whether that was to keep others out or him in.

"You can stand there and sulk, or you can participate. But I'm your only hope if you want to sing Geduld." She began unbuttoning her blouse.

Peter waved his arms helplessly; Juliette laughed at him, turned away, removed her blouse, and neatly slid her skirt to the floor. She turned to face him, removing her bra, panties and stockings in ten seconds. Juliette said, "Sit on the bed," and he sat down, grumbling nonsense. She pulled his knees apart and pushed her breasts in his face.

Peter turned his head, "I can't do this right now—my mind is on Bach."

"J. S. Bach had umpteen children. If you want to understand him, you must act like him—he didn't buy those kiddies at the market!"

Juliette pulled his braces over his shoulders and pushed Peter back until he lay on the bed. He whined, "No, Juliette, I really can't do this!"

Juliette went to work on his fly buttons.

She peeked up at him; he opened his mouth to protest again, but she was quicker. "Don't talk! I'm going to teach you how to sing Geduld. Just lie back; this won't take long." She tugged on his pants, pulled them out from under his buttocks, stepped back, picked up one foot at a time and yanked the pantlegs off. She repeated the process with his underwear. He whined, "No, I can't," and she ignored him.

She got on her knees.

Peter stopped whining. He caught his breath enough that Juliette knew she was winning. Then, his tone changed. "Juliette, what are you doing?"

"Don't be so curious. Stand up and take off your shirt. I'm going to fix your Bach problem."

She stepped back; Peter got up, his penis hard. He removed his shirt and asked, "What do you want me to do?" not quite eagerly, but the whine was gone.

She pushed him back on the bed; he lay with his legs hanging over the edge. "I want you to relax, close your eyes, and think about those Bach passages you think you can't sing. When I tell you to sing them to me, sing softly."

Juliette kissed his stomach and abdomen and said, "Sing," as she moved lower. Peter started singing and was halfway through the first phrase when he gasped and moaned. The first high 'A' that he hated was at the end of the second phrase.

"No moaning… keep singing!"

He chickened out and began the phrase again, singing softly, "Geduld, Geduld… Ge…" Another moan.

"Peter, you must keep singing. Remember, Geduld means patience." She swung her leg over his and sat on his knees, stroking him with both hands.

Peter began the second musical run as he had sung the first—softly. Juliette quickened her pace, and Peter arched in anticipation. The 'A' came next, and again he chickened out.

"Keep singing!" She let go of him. "Start over; sing the whole passage to me. I want those notes clear—you are sliding around like a provincial Italian tenor who learned to sing by imitating a donkey. Sing the notes clearly and distinctly. Concentrate, or that 'A' will splatter, and you won't have any fun."

Juliette didn't move until Peter started singing. She stroked him slowly, tantalizingly, and Peter almost lost control, but she stopped in time. To save himself, he concentrated on Bach, and when he had finished the first two phrases, his voice was relaxed and clear; the 'A' suddenly seemed a possibility.

Juliette stroked him again; Peter concentrated as he sang, his voice bright and beautiful, and the 'A' went by like just another note. She could feel his joy as he sang the next phrase perfectly, another beautiful 'A' sliding out like oil.

Juliette pushed hard against him until he was deep inside her. Finally, after the third top 'A,' and a phrase that seemed to live on top of his voice, sprinkled liberally with the once-dreaded notes, she said, "Stop singing!"

Peter stopped, and Juliette cried in delight as he filled her, driving her to climax.

He pulled her hips down and thrust until she collapsed on his chest.

"So, how was the voice lesson?" she asked Peter when she found her voice a few minutes later.

"I think I can sing the hell out of that aria now, but I will need to reinforce what I've learned—we will need to practice every day for a while."

Juliette waited a few seconds, then giggled when she said, "Don't worry about that. From now on, I'm going to give you a lot of singing lessons!"

Chapter Fifteen

11–31 January 1940

Heidi…Komm nach Haus, find dein Glück!
(Heidi, come home, find your happiness!)

Juliette and Marcel checked into the Heilbronn Hotel, opposite the theatre on Berliner Platz; it was Thursday, the eleventh of January. The bellhop carried a load of Juliette's suitcases to her room, and then he and Marcel went to the lobby to get the four that remained. Juliette had left the door open, and a few minutes later, a soft knock on the jamb distracted her from unpacking. A tall, thin, blue-eyed and lightly-bearded man stood in the doorway.

He said pleasantly, "I'm sorry to bother you, but my name is Matthias Bergman."

Juliette hesitated, wondering if she had forgotten something she shouldn't have.

"That is a wonderful name…" She smiled, could think of nothing she had missed, then asked, "Should I recognize it?"

The embarrassed man fiddled with the cloth cap he held between his hands. "I'm sorry…I must have the wrong party. I'm looking for Mademoiselle Juliette Durand." He twisted his cap.

"No, you've got the right party, although my married name is Madame Juliette Schweitzer."

Marcel arrived with the bellhop and peeked around the stranger in the doorway. He put a finger in the air and explained, "Mm… Juliette, I haven't told you about him yet." He nodded in the direction of his room. "Let him in, and I'll be right back." He left with his suitcase.

Juliette stood aside, and the bellhop followed the bearded man into the room, unloaded the bags and promptly disappeared. She waited until they were alone, closed the door, and said, "We might as well wait for Marcel, but I would appreciate it if you would tell me what's going on. Who are you, aside from your name?"

Matthias shifted his cap to his left hand, leaving his right hand free to gesture toward the corridor. "Perhaps we should wait for your valet; he seems to know what's happening."

Juliette looked warily at Matthias. "Yes, but he doesn't necessarily tell me."

Marcel knocked on the door, entered, and closed it behind him as he said, "Now, where were we?" He looked at Juliette as though he had stolen her cookies.

She said sweetly in French, "You were going to tell me who he is and what he's doing here… I assume this is another of Daddy's little jobs?"

"Yes, I'm afraid so. Pastor Bergman is going to help us, if I can talk him into it."

Matthias raised his free hand, coughed, and said with a Belgian French accent, "I'm afraid I must confess I have a Wallonian mother and German father."

Marcel made a face at Juliette and continued in French.

"This is Pastor Matthias Bergman of St. Killian's Church, just around the corner. We drove by it on the way here."

"The church with the beautiful Renaissance steeple?"

Matthias said, "The same; I am the pastor of the most beautiful church in Germany!"

"If this has something to do with Daddy's usual business, shouldn't we have proof that he is Pastor Bergman?"

Marcel smiled, "Do you think he's an impostor?" Juliette deliberately turned away.

He turned to Pastor Bergman. "I have information that you are responsible for the emigration of a great many Jews from Germany…is that correct?"

Bergman smiled and nodded. "Of course, I must now trust you and incriminate myself to prove who I am. But I suppose I must admit to being at least partly responsible for some Jews leaving Germany."

Marcel said, "I had no doubt about who you are, only whether your reputation is based in fact." He took time to arrange his words, then went on.

"We have an important client who must get out of the country. He is officially only a quarter Jew but is in grave danger because he publicly disagrees with the government. He has a sensitive job and is one of ours, and we expect problems for him in the very near future..."

Matthias's nodding stopped Marcel's explanation. "Yes, I have the details from Monsieur Durand." He shifted his feet, impatient. "When can I expect this man to arrive?"

"He could come any day; the timing will depend on the opportunity. Juliette sings her last performance here on the thirtieth of January, and we will take him to Zürich the next day—she is singing there in February."

"How is he travelling here?" Matthias was all business as he ran through his list.

"By automobile," Marcel answered.

"His automobile?"

"No, he will be driven. We can trust the driver; he is also one of ours."

Juliette raised her eyebrows.

Matthias didn't hesitate. "We can hold him as long as we need to. He won't be comfortable, but he will be safe."

"Very good—I will contact you when I have an arrival time. We can make the final arrangements then."

Matthias shook Marcel's hand. "Come to church this Sunday and every Sunday until you leave..."

Juliette interrupted him, smiling. "I'm afraid we are Catholic, and that would make us sinners."

Marcel looked at the floor, but Matthias returned Juliette's smile. "I will meet you at our kaffeeklatsch after the service. If it is safe, I will connect with you there; if I ignore you, I am being watched." He turned to go, put on his cap and stopped in the doorway to look at Juliette. "We let Catholics in if they promise to be good and refrain from speaking Latin." Matthias laughed and bid them a good day with a wave.

Juliette's fury had grown to a storm. Embarrassed and angry, she faced Marcel, who waited for the onslaught.

"Did Daddy get this job for me? Can't I earn anything on my own merit?"

Marcel smiled convincingly. "The truth is, we organized the mission around your contract."

Despite Juliette's assumption that Marcel had just lied to her, she relaxed slightly.

"Alright, how does this work?" She sighed, resigned to her father's interference.

"Two Mercedes automobiles will take us to Zürich. I'll be in the lead one, and you will travel behind me in the second with Herr Gronau."

"Uncle Hébert?"

"The same; he is coming from Switzerland to hear you sing and is taking you home with him." He smiled; the storm was over. "Uncle Hébert sends greetings to his little Heidi."

Juliette smiled, remembering her summers in Switzerland, climbing over rocks, marching on mountain trails behind Uncle Hébert….

She shook it off and said, "You said this man is important... How important?"

"As important as they get! He's the chief engineer on a radar beam project—I don't know how it works, but it allows an operator in a plane to see other aircraft on a green glass display. The inventors, Siemens AG, call it Lichtenstein. The system is called radar."

"Why would he leave Germany?"

"His wife is half-Jewish, officially a Mischling, and she is terrified the Gestapo will send her to a camp. Many of their friends have disappeared. We must get her out first, and when she's safe, he will join her."

"Why wouldn't you take them out together?"

"If they go anywhere together, the SS follows them. As we speak, she is visiting her sister in Cologne, and they will be in England by the end of next week. Her husband must be there before the middle of February, and by the end of March, the British will know how to find the beam coming from those radar sets. They will then be able to follow the beam to any plane that is operating one." Marcel shrugged. "Again, I don't know how that works, but apparently this man does."

"Doesn't England know how to build this radar thing?"

"I think so... " Marcel looked thoughtfully out the window, then turned back to Juliette... "But what is most important is to know the frequency of the signal the Lichtenstein set uses. The Luftwaffe will install them in their night fighters so they can find British bombers in the dark. If the British know the frequency, they can find the night fighter by turning his radar against him. The British bomber will see the aircraft's location on some sort of instrument, and they can then choose whether to avoid it or try to shoot it down."

Juliette said, "I suppose it is important to prevent the Germans from knowing that the British have this frequency thing." She thought for a few seconds, and a thought sprang into her head.

"But when this engineer disappears, wouldn't the Siemens company change the frequency? Is that easy to do?"

Marcel smiled and shook his head. "You're not as dumb as you try to make people think you are!"

Juliette tried to kick him, grazing his leg as he stepped out of the way. Marcel laughed, then neatly dodged her second attempt, so she gave up.

"The Siemens machine has the frequency fixed in the design, and it would take a major redesign to change it. If they think the engineer is in England, they will do it, but if we prevent the Germans from finding out that he absconded...."

"And...?"

"And that is why he will die in a car crash, burned beyond recognition."

Juliette appeared satisfied but had one more question.

"Who will die?"

Marcel smiled. "People die every day. One that is just the right fit will turn up in a specific burned-out car. The driver will escape and tell the SS what happened."

"But why would the driver?...

Marcel smiled. "The Nazis have made some very dangerous enemies! Indeed, you are not the only one."

Juliette decided not to examine that explanation too carefully.

Juliette had sung Violette in Nürnberg and refreshed it in Brussels, so she knew her role perfectly. The tenor and baritone were both excellent singers and easy to work with, leaving Juliette with nothing to complain about, so she toned down her diva attitude. But no one in the theatre ensemble would have believed it. She stepped on the tenor's toes to make a point and shrieked at her poor operatic maid Annina when she missed an entry.

However, Juliette sang like an angel and convinced the audience that Violette was in love with the tenor. She kissed him twice during their many curtain calls, and he took heart that perhaps she did love him, until she brutally crushed his ego when he propositioned her at the première party.

Juliette didn't meet the Siemens engineer when he arrived; Marcel told her that Matthias hid him in a crypt in the largest cemetery in Heilbronn. Someone took food, water, buckets of warm bricks, and a clean bedpan to him every day.

Juliette sang three performances in twelve days, completing the first run. She would return in June for three more Violettes, but right now, she looked forward to seeing her Godfather, Uncle Hébert Gronau, one of the wealthiest men in Zürich. But even his wealth would not save him if Juliette flopped in the most critical performance in her career—the one at the Swiss border.

Marcel brought Uncle Hébert to Juliette's room on the thirty-first of January, and she squeezed him in a hug reserved only for her Godfather. A short man, barely taller than Juliette, they fit like a hand in a glove. He was thin, sported a neat moustache, and wore well-cut clothes, which immediately categorized him as wealthy.

"Hébert will fill you in while I pick up the engineer." Marcel backed out of the room and closed the door.

Juliette hugged her Godfather again. "It's been such a long time, Uncle Hébert. I'm all grown up, but your Heidi still looks forward to hiking in your mountains with you."

"It's January, Juliette; that will have to wait, but I'm looking forward to your visit with me in Zürich." He smiled. "But first, I'm told we must play a little game at the border."

It was three in the afternoon when Marcel, loaded with suitcases, followed Hébert and Juliette to the two shiny Mercedes cars. Juliette and Hébert sat in the rear seat of the second Mercedes, and Marcel climbed into the back seat of the lead vehicle, where Hébert's bodyguard was already sitting. Juliette peeked at him through the side window as she walked past, half-heartedly waving when he raised his hand in greeting. He was a stranger to her and looked very much like an engineer.

Juliette's automobile followed Marcel's out of the city, and for the next three hours, they twisted and turned through the countryside on a narrow road that connected the villages strung around the edge of the Schwartzwald. Although her luxurious Mercedes was quiet and comfortable, the combination of anxiety and corkscrew road churned Juliette's stomach. When they reached the border, where she must give the performance of her life, there would be no applause, no curtain call, only survival for the engineer and the hundreds, maybe thousands of British flyers that German night fighters would not shoot down.

She swallowed the bile that tried to erupt, made a face, and quietly said to herself, toi, toi, toi, the German equivalent of English performers' 'break a leg.' Uncle Hébert squeezed her hand.

There were two crash bars at the border, one on the German side, guarded by two SS soldiers holding machine pistols, and one on the Swiss side, where two bored officials sat in a small open-sided hut at one end of the barricade bar. Juliette's Mercedes pulled up behind Marcel's on the German side, and the young SS officers motioned with their weapons for the occupants to get out.

Hébert exited and went to the front fender to stand with the chauffeur. The soldier approached Juliette's window and motioned with his hand for her to leave the car. Despite a desperate need for fresh air, Juliette deliberately turned away and looked straight ahead. The young man straightened and eyed the chauffeur, who was standing at the front fender as instructed. The second soldier, still at the front of the car, kept his machine pistol trained on the chauffeur and Uncle Hébert.

The chauffeur shrugged. The young man tried again, putting his face a centimetre from the window while he rapped it with his knuckles.

Juliette turned to him and mouthed emphatically in French, *"Imbécile! Ouvrez la Porte de la Voiture!"*

The young soldier said to the chauffeur in German, "I think she said she wouldn't get out, but the lady must understand that she has no choice!"

"She wants you to open her door and help her get out," the chauffeur explained, "She's a famous opera singer."

The young man nodded as though that explained everything, opened the door, and Juliette swung her bare legs out, put her feet gracefully on the ground, and stretched out her hands so the young man could help her stand up. Embarrassed, he looked at the machine pistol in his hand, searched for somewhere to put it, and decided to balance it on the round rear fender. He clumsily turned to her and took both her hands. She stood up gracefully, wobbled, stumbled, and fell forward against him, letting her perfumed hair brush his face. He lifted her hands to save her from falling, and, as his partner looked enviously at the scene, Juliette guided one of his hands so that it cupped her breast. She took her time recovering, her stomach still churning from the drive.

"Thank you so much for saving me, monsieur," Juliette said in heavily French-accented German. She put her mouth close to his ear and breathed deeply while holding onto him. The young man steadied her, then cautiously stepped back.

His partner waved his gun at the young man and shouted, "Your gun, Hans, your gun!"

Hans stuttered an "Excuse me, Mademoiselle," stepped around Juliette, and almost dropped his machine gun when he lifted it from the slippery fender.

An SS officer, at least fifteen years older than the young border guards, appeared in the building's doorway and motioned the nervous soldier standing next to Juliette to come over. He pushed the young man through the door, then reprimanded him loud enough that everyone at the border crossing could hear every word. When he finished, he pushed the soldier out, pointed him at Marcel's Mercedes, and went to face Juliette. He quickly extended his hand and barked, "Papier bitte!"

Juliette started to speak, blanched, gagged noisily, then threw up on his shiny black boots. The officer was too slow to react—Juliette threw up again, this time on his shirt, and immediately, she felt much better. She wiped her mouth with a glove and said, in horrible German, "Papier? Do you want Papier? J'ai peur... Je... I don't know what you mean."

The SS officer tried to maintain his composure, but Juliette started to shake and cried inconsolably. He delicately brushed the front of his uniform as he cautiously leaned toward her, manoeuvring his position so that she would miss him if she were to have another misfortune. Softly, slowly, he said, "Ich brauche nur ihre Ausweis bitte." Juliette repeated it in a thick mixture of French and German, "Mon Dieu... Ausweis? Qu'est-ce-qu'un Ausweis?" She wobbled on her feet, swaying dangerously close to falling. He reached for her, but she straightened up on her own.

His eyebrows rose as he self-consciously said again, softly enough that no one but Juliette would hear him, "Passport, s'il Vous plaît?"

Suddenly, Juliette stopped crying and kissed him on the cheek. "Passeport! Mais oui, passeport!" She opened her oversized purse, but on the wrong side, and the contents—a grand assortment of handkerchiefs, makeup in various forms, combs, papers, and money—a lot of money—fell in the snow. The cold breeze blew snow, documents, and cash across the yard. Juliette started to cry, wailing like a child whose mother had just died. The officer bent over and chased the documents and Swiss banknotes. The two young guards ran to help—the wind scattered the money—they laid down their guns to go after it.

It took five minutes to gather everything, and when they gave it to the officer, he held the items away from his soiled shirt. Brushing away the snow, he passed the documents and banknotes to Juliette, one at a time, until finally, he found her passport, a work visa for Germany, and a second visa for Switzerland. The young men had collected over a thousand Swiss francs in fifty and twenty-franc notes and over two thousand Reichsmarks. Juliette had six months' wages for a high-ranking SS officer in her purse.

Juliette kissed him and put on her sexiest voice, "Merci beaucoup, monsieur. Merci! Merci!" She kissed him again, this time on the lips, and brushed his face with her hand. "You are so sweet. Is the Papier correct?" She leaned over to see the papers he was examining and accidentally touched his bare hand with her barely covered breast.

He quickly returned the visas and passport to Juliette and removed his hat as he assured her, "Oui, mademoiselle, all is correct." He gave her his hat. "Please, Mademoiselle Durand, would you sign the inside? Please sign it, 'Mit Liebe, Juliette Durand.'" He pointed at the place where she should write.

Juliette became excited and coy, "Oh, Monsieur, I must use your name, n'est-ce pas?"

He gave her a black pencil. "It's Frederick, mademoiselle," he grinned like a little boy peeking at his older sister in the bathtub.

Juliette signed the SS hat and gave it back to him. He carefully put it on his head, turning it just a little to the side.

She said, "You are so handsome, Monsieur," and touched his cheek.

When the drama with Juliette was over, the soldier at the front of the car examining the chauffeur's papers noted, "Your Swiss work visa runs out in two weeks. You had better get it renewed; the Swiss have no patience with Germans these days."

The chauffeur whispered his response. Juliette noted that Hébert had moved toward the rear and behind the car, but she plainly heard, "Herr Gronau hasn't signed my employment papers yet—he won't do it unless I agree to take a salary cut."

The young soldier said quietly, looking at Herr Gronau, "Those rich bastards are all alike!" He glanced at the sequential license plate numbers he had meticulously written in a notepad. "He owns both of these fancy automobiles, and still won't pay you a decent wage...." He shook his head, said "Bastard!" under his breath, and the chauffeur nodded in agreement.

The older officer went around the car to Uncle Hébert, who handed over his papers, staying as far from the stench as his short arms would allow. He waited patiently, leaning against the rear fender to increase the distance from the officer to his nose.

"You live in Zürich?" The officer didn't look at Hèbert as he searched the papers for something.

"Jawohl, Herr Oberscharführer, since I was born." Hébert had been holding his breath, and the first word came out louder than he intended.

The officer said, "I know Zürich very well," returned his papers and said, "I see you live on Müllerstrasse. That's a couple of blocks east of the lake, isn't it?" as he offered Hébert his documents.

Hébert couldn't avoid taking a breath to answer.

"Nein, Herr Oberscharführer, Müllerstrasse is north of the lake, close to the railway station." He forced himself to breathe in again. "The street by the river is Mühlebachstrasse. Even people who know Zürich very well get those streets mixed up."

The officer touched his hat, said, "I wish a good day to you, sir," and returned to his building, smiling sweetly at Juliette as he passed. She coyly dropped a fifty-franc note, and the wind blew it to him. He bent over to brush snow off his boot and put the money in his pocket. She waved, blew him a kiss, and wiggled her fingers.

The young soldier, who had quickly finished with Marcel and the bodyguard, looked at Juliette longingly as he passed her car.

The road to Zürich was smooth and empty, and Juliette was in the hotel half an hour earlier than expected. Hébert and his chauffeur drove away, leaving Juliette's suitcases in the lobby. She went to her room without them, and Marcel knocked on her door fifteen minutes later, a bag in each hand.

Wound up like a clock spring, Juliette greeted him with, "Thank God that young man didn't figure out who the bodyguard was! I tried to stage my diversion away from him!"

Marcel chuckled. "There was nothing for the young man to figure out. He is Hébert's bodyguard."

"But he actually works in Berlin at the Siemens AG plant. If they had figured that out, we would all be at Gestapo headquarters or already dead!" Juliette was puzzled. "Wouldn't we?"

"Lorenz Martillo is a close friend of your parents," Marcel said, his smile widening, "He runs a security business here in Switzerland, and, on the side, he's your Godfather's bodyguard."

Juliette had trouble putting her words together.

"But...we were supposed to bring the engineer from Siemens with us and...."

"We did. The engineer was your chauffeur, the one with the almost-expired visa." Marcel laughed at her confusion. "By the way, your performance was superb. We could have been transporting the Mona Lisa, and they would never have found it!"

Juliette laughed tentatively at first, then heartily and full-throated.

"You and Father knew I would try to draw attention away from you and your partner, which would deflect attention entirely away from the driver. Brilliant!"

"I told your father this would be your reaction."

"And what did he say my reaction would be?"

"That is top-secret information and shall never cross my lips." He left quickly, and Juliette ran to catch him, but he was already going in the door to his room when she reached the hallway. Returning to her room, she softly closed her door and asked, "Then, who was the other driver?"

Chapter Sixteen

9 May 1940

Der Zweck heiligt die Mittel
(The purpose justifies the means)

WHEN JULIETTE SANG SUSANNA in Mozart's The Marriage of Figaro in Zürich, a role she had performed in the Monnaie Theatre in Brussels, her performance was a huge success, and guest contract offers poured in from opera houses in Germany. Juliette had acquired a reputation for being difficult and arrogant, but she was a singer who knew her music when she arrived. And Juliette Durand could not only sing, but she was beautiful, shorter than most tenors, and she could act. Theatre managers let the conductors and stage directors handle the rest. Most importantly for Juliette, she didn't look like a people-smuggler... not a chance this beautiful singer would take that risk!

Juliette received another guest contract to sing Mimi, this time in Aachen, and her correlated mission was to bring a married couple back with her. The man was one-quarter Jewish and the chief engineer with a chemical company in Dortmund. Hoesch-Benzin GmBH manufactured synthetic gasoline and lubrication products from coal, absolute necessities for the German war machine that required a high level of expertise.

At Juliette's briefing, Jacques told her that, until now, the engineer would not leave Germany without his Aryan wife, and she refused to leave her friends and family. But his wife changed her mind when their Jewish friends began to disappear.

Juliette's mission was to get them into neutral Belgium, and from there, they would follow the human pipeline used by British Intelligence to get strategically important Germans to England.

Aachen is less than one-hundred-and-fifty kilometres from Brussels, travelling by automobile through Liège, and is only seven kilometres by road from the Belgian border. The Aachen Opera Theatre engaged Juliette to replace another ailing soprano as Mimi in La Bohème, and Juliette suspected her illness had something to do with Jacques.

Marcel and Juliette left Brussels at seven in the morning on the day of the performance, arriving in Aachen two-and-a-half hours later.

Despite Juliette adopting her usual diva personality, the rehearsals went well. The Turkish tenor was a post on the stage; his voice had all the endearing qualities of a squeaking wheel, and his "C" was barely a "B-and-a-half," but he was handsome. Marcello, sung by an Italian baritone from Milano, was exciting and romantic, and he could sing. Juliette found him charming and sexy and worked that into their stage relationship. The audience ate it up, forgetting the painful tenor.

A half-hour before the first curtain call, a middle-aged woman with a perpetually wrinkled brow entered Juliette's dressing room carrying a makeup kit.

"Are you ready for me, Fraülein Durand?"

"Yes, that would be fine." The woman closed the door and put the kit on the table beside the mirror. Evidently nervous, she fidgeted with her hands, rubbed them together, locked and unlocked her fingers.

Juliette sat in front of the mirror, humming to focus her voice and encourage blood to flow to her cords. When the woman remained fixed to the spot, Juliette said, "You may begin now."

The woman continued to wring her hands. "I'm Frau Sonnenberg. Marcel told me to bring this kit in here and do your makeup, but I don't know the first thing about it."

Juliette turned around, "What's your first name?"

"Mechteld."

"All right, Mechteld, I will do my own makeup, but when we leave this room, you are my exclusive makeup person. Is Mechteld the name on your new Ausweiss?"

"Yes," she said, "the official name is Mechteld Kraus. My husband is not my husband; he is Jürgen Krüger, and presently he is sitting in the audience with Marcel."

Juliette quickly applied the foundation layer. "Yes, Jürgen is officially my pianist, and you are my makeup and wardrobe expert."

She turned to face the nervous woman. "Mechteld, this is not the first time we have done this—you will be safe if you follow our instructions precisely."

The woman sat on the only other chair in the room, still wringing her hands and looking at the floor.

"I trust you; that isn't the problem."

Mechteld was upset, and Juliette sensed a crisis. She watched the nervous woman in the mirror while finishing her makeup and didn't like what she saw; Mechteld was close to a breakdown.

She continued, still looking down, "I don't want to leave Germany. My parents live in Düsseldorf, and I'm afraid I will never see them again." She looked at Juliette in the mirror and said softly, "I'm afraid of what the Nazis will do to them if we leave."

Juliette turned around in her chair. "You don't have to worry about your German Aryan parents, but if you don't go, you must realize that the Nazis will send your husband to a labour camp, and you will never see him again. The Nazis plan to intern every German who is one-quarter Jewish or greater by the end of this year. They'll send them to slave labour camps, and there is no plan for them to return home. We have reliable information that the Nazis are building a "final solution" camp in Poland, and you can figure out what that means."

Mechteld's face hardened. "That is Communist propaganda! My husband's job is essential to the war effort now that the treacherous English and French have decided to attack us! The Nazi Party will not send him to a Zwangsarbiter camp where the SS will waste his talents!"

Juliette turned her attention to finishing her hair. She brushed it out, then asked Mechteld, "Would you help me pull my hair back and tie it in a bun?"

Mechteld stood behind Juliette, twisting her hair into a neat bun. Juliette talked while watching Mechteld's expression in the mirror, trying to assess the danger this nervous woman represented.

"You know that you must go through with this, Mechteld. Why are you here if you haven't already committed yourself? If you don't leave with us now, all of us will be in danger!"

Mechteld manipulated the ends of Juliette's hair into place.

"I did agree, but I've changed my mind." She stabbed the bun with a round wooden spike. "If I say no, you can't drag me over the border!"

Juliette turned around.

"This is not a children's game, where you can change your mind if you don't like the rules. You have been playing with your husband's life, and now, you're endangering my life and the lives of others. You must go through with this, at least to Brussels. When your husband is safe, you may return if you want to."

"What can you do about it if I leave right now?"

Mechteld's childish defiance was dangerous; it was time to tell her where she stood.

"If you do anything other than the plan you have agreed to, I'm sure you are intelligent enough to understand the inevitable consequences."

Mechteld put the comb on the table and sat down. "Is this all so serious?"

"Mechteld, the Nazis have already executed thousands without trial or inquiry. If your husband leaves without you, they will torture you to find out where he went, and they will not hesitate to kill Marcel and me when you tell them who we are. Of course, before they kill us, they will torture us to find out what we know. There are no rules except survival, and we must protect ourselves!"

Mechteld began to cry. Her distress forced her to stand and begin to pace. "I love my husband, but I also love my family and my country. You are asking me to betray both, and I don't know whether I can do that."

Juliette had to be on the stage in less than ten minutes, and the stage manager would be at her door in five.

"I am married to a Jew, as are you. He is also officially a Mischling but classified as a Jew, as is your husband. His mother is Jewish, and his parents now live in Switzerland to escape the Nazis. You don't believe the Nazis will kill Jews, but my husband Peter was in Dachau for five months, and he could explain to you how they are already killing

Jews and others by starving and working them to death. If not for my father's help and influence, my husband would be among those who have already died."

Juliette could see that she was winning and decided to go all the way.

"Peter is one of the best operatic tenors in Europe and has never been a threat to the Nazis. He even took me to Hitler's labour rally, and we broke up because he supported the Nazis' labour program." Mechteld remained silent while Juliette gathered her courage, then went on.

"But that all ended on Kristallnacht when I visited his Jewish grandparents with him. A disgusting SA officer and two other soldiers broke into the apartment, killed his grandfather and the neighbour, then beat Peter. The SA officer broke into the bedroom where we were hiding and shot Peter's grandmother and her friend in front of me." Juliette paused, then decided to tell everything. "He then raped me and left me to die."

Mechteld's face lost all colour. Juliette knew she had won.

"Mechteld, that's why I do what I do, and it is why you must go with your husband. I will sing now and leave you to think about what you must do. If you are gone when I return after the second act, I will know that you have decided not to go and that I am in grave danger, but you will not make it to the authorities. If your husband chooses to remain in Germany, the Nazis will arrest him, and the best you can hope for is that they take him to a slave worker camp."

Mechteld collapsed in the chair, and Juliette knelt in front of her. "You must decide what to do, but remember this: the Nazis are not your country, and Germany is not the Nazis. They are liars, bullies and crooks, a brutal gang of thieves and criminals who have taken your country from you. We need you and your husband to help us get it back!"

Juliette opened the door. She took one last look at Mechteld, and the shock on the woman's face told Juliette she would be there when she returned. She decided to trust her instincts and headed for stage left.

Juliette's tenor partner was painful to listen to but turned out to be a passable actor with the face and body of a Greek god. Despite his regrettable voice, the audience brought the house down at the end of the first act, and the festive second act's street scene was the best Mimi had experienced. The act ended with a parade across the stage; the cast bowed to thunderous applause, and Juliette apprehensively returned to her dressing room.

She opened the door, and relief swept over her with a rush; Mechteld's frown that had seemed permanent had disappeared, and she smiled at Juliette from the dressing table where she had everything perfectly organized. Mimi's third-act costume lay draped over the back of the chair.

"I see you've made a decision." Juliette closed the door. She had twenty minutes to change her costume and adjust her makeup; there was no time for drama.

"Yes, I have," Mechteld turned on the stool to face Juliette. "I have spent my life in my kitchen, sheltered from the world, and it is time I stood up for what I know in my heart to be true." She melodramatically placed her hand over her heart, then lowered it and went on. "Six months ago, the Nazis took my husband's best friend, also a Mischling, and we haven't seen him since. I have tried to tell myself that he is off doing something important for the government, but I have no doubt what happened to him." Mechteld stood, and Juliette took her hand.

"I will do whatever you need me to, and I will stay with my husband wherever he goes. Perhaps the English can find a way for me to help defeat the Nazis."

Juliette hugged Mechteld.

The opera played out to everyone's satisfaction, and the General Music Director who had conducted the performance met Juliette in the wings, hugged her and kissed her cheek.

"I wanted to catch you before you leave." He spoke French. His German accent was thick, barely understandable. "You are the finest musician I have ever had the pleasure to work with! Would you consider singing for us in the fall season? I want to stage Norma, and you would be my perfect leading lady!"

Juliette touched his hand. "I will have to think about that; Norma may be too dramatic for me right now. My father manages my career, and I will tell him I want to sing for you, but there is no guarantee. He will contact you, but, unfortunately, we may soon be enemies."

The conductor looked hopeful but anxious. "I don't understand political things and don't want to get involved. My Führer would never attack your country because Belgium is neutral, and he only wants peace."

"I think you can count on a call..." She touched his arm... "If you are correct about Herr Hitler's intentions."

He smiled broadly, clearly full of optimism. He kissed Juliette's hand and said, "Have an uneventful trip back to Brussels."

It was the ninth of May, a month of short nights, and darkness hadn't yet wholly vanquished the twilight when Marcel and Jürgen met Juliette and Mechteld at the stage door. Mechteld, dressed in everyday clothes, carried only Juliette's makeup case. Juliette, dressed like a nineteenth-century "Lady of the night," wore a gaudy pink hat with a long red feather, a long pink dress that covered the top of her high-heeled black boots, and white gloves that stretched to her elbows. She carried an enormous sequined purse covered with baubles.

Marcel laughed when he saw her and, still snickering, opened the rear door of the Rolls-Royce.

The border, only seven kilometres from the centre of Aachen, took less than fifteen minutes to reach. The last two kilometres passed through a forest, and Marcel pointed out several Panzers parked on the service roads. As they drove, it soon became evident that every opening was plugged with tanks, and soldier transports filled with men.

Marcel said, "Those tanks have their engines running; I can see smoke from the exhausts."

Juliette saw dark shadows sitting between the trees everywhere and more behind them, all with rising smoke. Jürgen said uneasily, "Something is going on, and we should report it at the border."

Marcel looked at another group of tracked vehicles, counting them. "I wouldn't mention anything to the SS, but I am sure the Belgians will be interested."

Juliette took Mechteld's cold hand, willing the next hour to be over.

The SS guards looked at their papers and then ordered everyone out of the car. One of the young border guards opened Juliette's door, and she brushed against him as she exited. He smiled and decided to question her.

"Is this your car, Madame?"

"It's mademoiselle, young man. I am technically married, but spiritually I am still free." She touched his shoulder. "You do understand, don't you?"

He blushed and said self-consciously, "Yes, mademoiselle, I understand." His smile widened. "Who are these people to you?" He waved in the direction of Jürgen and Mechteld.

"I am an opera singer…" she said grandly, lifting her chin… "Mechteld is my wardrobe and makeup coordinator." She motioned to her, Mechteld curtsied, and Juliette swung to Jürgen. "Herr Jürgen Krüger is my extremely talented accompanist. No, I must correct that; he is much more. Jürgen is my confidant when I am depressed and my companion when I need company…" She winked… "I could never perform without Jürgen…" She winked again… "He attends every rehearsal with me, and I can count on him to…"

"Yes, yes, I can see that he is important to you." Juliette almost laughed when the young man interrupted at precisely the right spot. "Is this your car, mademoiselle?"

"Oh, Liebling, heavens no," she laughed, "That is one of Daddy's cars. He lets me use the little one whenever I want to." She motioned to the Rolls. "Of course, I have no time to learn to drive—my fans demand all of my time—so my chauffeur Marcel drives it for me." She put her finger under the young man's chin. "He is an excellent driver!" She laughed like a barmaid.

A senior officer stepped out of the small building adjacent to the barrier and approached. He asked, "Who is your father, and where does he live?" Evidently, he had been listening.

Juliette pouted, pretending the question had offended her. "Why does everyone want to know who my father is? He is Jacques Durand, and he lives in Brussels, as I do."

"What is your father's occupation?"

Juliette lowered her voice, "He buys and sells valuable paintings and jewellery. He is very wealthy!"

The officer turned to the soldier. "Don't bother this young lady any longer—I will vouch for her and her father."

He took Juliette's hand, guided her to the car, and closed the door. When everyone had returned to their seat, Marcel started the engine. The SS officer spoke to Marcel through his open window. "Drive immediately to Brussels—I recommend that you bypass Liège.

The bar lifted, and soldiers, instead of the usual customs officials, greeted the Rolls on the Belgian side of the border. Two of them approached the car quickly and asked for the occupants' papers, which one of the soldiers passed to an officer who joined them.

Marcel told the officer, "You might want to know that we saw Panzers and transports filled with soldiers parked in every hole in the woods on the other side of the border."

The officer looked up from reading the papers. "How many did you see?"

"At least twenty, and as many Lastwagen or more."

The officer passed the papers to Marcel.

"Are you sure?"

"Yes, I am certain there were at least twenty, but likely several times that number..." Marcel was becoming impatient. "All of them had their engines running." He added, "The German border guards told us to avoid Liège."

The officer thanked Marcel and waved them on.

The drive home was peaceful, even though Marcel did drive through Liège. Jürgen and Mechteld were in a safe apartment, and Juliette was in Peter's arms at one-thirty.

Marcel picked up Juliette and Peter at nine the following day and broke the news as soon as they were in their seats.

"The German Wehrmacht invaded Belgium and Holland this morning. They've crossed the border everywhere from Luxembourg to the Dutch beaches."

Juliette squeezed Peter's hand. "It has begun, hasn't it? Everything will change now."

Five minutes later, they pulled up at the Durand residence.

Jacques was in his favourite chair, nursing a coffee while reading documents. When Juliette and Peter entered, he put the papers in a folder and stood to greet them.

Veronique entered the room. "Marcel told you that the Germans have attacked us?"

"Yes," Peter replied, "as expected. So much for the 'fake' war. Now we get to see the real thing."

Jacques pointed at the folder. "There isn't much detail yet, but I have some information from my contacts. German armoured divisions crossed the border near Aachen and are heading toward Liège. German Panzers crossed the Dutch border near Maastricht and will quickly cross Holland into western Belgium. Paratroopers landed behind our lines in Belgium and Luxembourg and are attacking our fortifications from the rear. The French have moved to intercept them, but I wouldn't get my hopes up."

Jacques stood up, talking as he led the way to the breakfast table.

"It looks like the Belgian plan is to withdraw to the centre of the country, giving up the eastern half. The Belgian army will set up a defence line twenty kilometres from Brussels, and if the Germans cross it, and they will, their Panzers will be in the city centre a couple of hours later. The British and Belgian Generals cannot agree, and the French act as though they are the only ones fighting the Germans! King Leopold, a man who couldn't organize a dogfight, makes all the military decisions for the Belgian army.

"The German intention appears to be a frontal assault across Belgium into France to attack the British and French armies."

Marcel joined them, emphatically contradicting Jacques. "I don't believe that for a minute! The British, French and Belgian Generals are stuck in the Great War, and that is going to cost them dearly!"

Marcel snatched a croissant from a pile in the centre of the table. "They captured a Messerschmitt pilot who crash-landed in Mechelen early this morning. He carried papers indicating the Germans would thrust directly through Belgium and Holland as they did in 1914, not through the Ardennes, which would make a lot more sense. With modern Panzers and transports, the Ardennes is the more logical route.

If the French and British commit everything to defend the centre, the Germans will trap them between two forks." He looked around the table. "Why would a fighter pilot carry top-secret battle plans? The Germans have telephones, telegraphs, and radios! Besides, the battle plan was fixed months ago!"

Jacques looked thoughtfully at his hands. "Of course, the French and British want to believe this document confirms their assumptions and are committing their forces to the centre of Belgium. If you're right, German Panzers will surround the British and French forces within weeks, and, within a month, German soldiers will be goose-stepping in Brussels' Grand Square!"

Veronique looked at Peter and Juliette, and Marcel voiced her concerns.

"When the regular German army takes over, the SS and Gestapo will move in. Most local civil servants will remain, becoming collaborators rather than lose their jobs, and the Nazis will use them to find Jews and Romani. Some will cooperate, some will not; those who don't will disappear. In Poland, local authorities are helping to herd Jews into ghettos!" He looked at Peter. "Juliette and Peter should immediately leave for England or Switzerland."

Marcel leaned toward Peter, emphasizing his words with his finger. "It will be impossible to hide your records from the Gestapo. Within a few days, they will break down your door!"

Peter pushed his breakfast aside.

"I am the one in danger, and I am the one who must hide. Juliette can remain with her family and continue her work. Am I right?"

Jacques answered, "Yes, you are right. And you will not be safe in Belgium."

"What if I change my name and have a new identity that's not on the records? I understand I entered the country as Juliette's husband, which is now a problem. But I could hide in plain sight with a new identity; I could join your Résistance and continue to fight the Nazis as Juliette is doing."

Juliette suddenly became desperate—her eyes glistened as she bitterly said, "Peter, you would be a spy, and the Germans would kill you if they caught you! And if you leave, we won't be able to see one another..." She started to cry, angry at her helplessness.

Veronique covered Juliette's hand with her own. "I don't see any solution except for you to flee to England or Switzerland together."

Peter answered, "No, I will not run away and let others fight my fight...I will fight the Nazis, even if it costs my life!" He faced Juliette. "I love you more than my own life, but if we run away now, we will have no right to a country. The Nazis are forcing us to fight them. They expect us to be passive, but we will shorten the time it takes to defeat them if we fight. Your father and mother are in grave danger, but they will continue to work for the Rèsistance, and I won't do less."

Juliette stamped her foot. "No, I won't let you!"

Peter turned to Jacques. "I am not going to run!"

Jacques sighed, thought a moment and said, "I will have papers for you within a few days, and before the Germans march into Brussels, we will figure out what to do with your talents. I want you to learn the ropes; we have people who can teach you. We will decide how all this will work once we know how successful the Germans are."

Juliette wiped her red eyes, furious with her father and Peter. In a tone that left no doubt of her intentions, she said, "I will fight the Germans too; I must fight them, and I must win!"

Chapter Seventeen

25 May 1940

Zwischen Plänen der Männer und Vollendungen haftet Schicksal seine Gabel
(Between man's plans and their fulfillment is where fate puts his fork)

THE OUTCOME WAS INEVITABLE when Juliette and Peter met Jacques, Marcel, and Veronique in the drawing room on the afternoon of the twenty-fifth of May. The day was cloudy and dark, underlining the mood.

Juliette took her mother aside.

"Mother, I think I'm pregnant... So much for the rhythm method," she laughed sarcastically.

Veronique asked, "Have you been to the doctor?"

"No, I haven't, but I'm a month overdue, and I've never been a month overdue in my life."

Veronique took Juliette's hands. "Under the circumstances, I shouldn't be happy at this news, but I am so glad you and Peter are giving us a grandchild." She got Jacques' attention with a wave. "Your father has to know this. He may want to change things."

Jacques joined them in the comfortable chairs. Peter and Marcel remained at the table, out of earshot, sipping coffee and talking about the impending invasion of England.

Veronique said, "Juliette thinks she's pregnant," as Jacques sat down.

"That's wonderful, Juliette!" He leaned over and hugged her. "In almost any other context, that would be the best news I could hear. However, in this case, we must work around it."

Jacques said, "I also have good news. I didn't want to raise any hopes, but I have managed to get Peter's German records expunged. If they are going to connect him with his Jewish past, they will have to look for precisely that, and I can't think of a reason they would want to. The Belgian records of his immigration on the MS St. Louis are gone; he was never on the ship. Peter's parents are Belgian citizens living in Switzerland, and Peter's birthplace is, according to Belgian records, Liège." He shifted his attention to Juliette. "Taking this and the announcement that Juliette just made into consideration, I must change our strategy."

He said to Juliette, "I hope your news wasn't too much of a shock to Peter."

"I haven't told him yet..." Juliette walked across the room to stand beside Peter's chair.

"You haven't told me what?" Lost in war talk with Marcel, Peter switched his concentration to Juliette. She put her hand on his shoulder; he put his hand on hers and looked into her eyes.

"I'm not positive yet, but I think we should make our plans considering an additional family member." She smiled; Peter's face drew a blank.

"I'm pregnant!" She laughed at him. "We're going to have a baby!"

Peter's mouth opened, but no sound came out. He tried again.

"A baby? My God, how did that happen?"

Marcel jumped in. "Remember all that fun you two have been having?" Everyone laughed, "I'm pretty sure it's connected with that."

Marcel stood and walked around the table to hug her. "Congratulations, Juliette; I'm so happy for you." Tears wet his eyes; he quickly wiped them and turned to Peter, shook his hand, and growled, "You are one lucky bastard!"

Veronique appeared with glasses and two bottles of champagne. Juliette sat beside Peter; Veronique sat at one end of the table, Jacques at the other. One toast followed another until the bottles were empty. They saluted the baby, Juliette, Peter, the grandparents, and their Catholic religion that had made it inevitable.

Veronique removed the glasses and returned with a large platter of pastries. She put them on the table and turned to Jacques. "You were the one who sent Charles to Switzerland; you can get up and help me."

Jacques jumped up and helped Veronique distribute the plates and napkins. He poured the coffee, they sat down, and he began his prepared speech.

"As you know, on the tenth of May, while the French and British forces defended the centre of Belgium, German armour and infantry attacked through the Ardennes Forest. The Wehrmacht is fighting a well-planned campaign while the French and Belgian armies are descending into chaos. The British Expeditionary Forces, under-equipped and under-manned, are paying the predictable price.

"The Luftwaffe has complete control of the skies, making the Allied armour irrelevant. The German army has encircled 340,000 Belgian, French, and British troops like herring in a purse seine and is tightening the loop, forcing the Allied armies toward the sea." Jacques paused.

The shocked, silent room waited for him to continue.

"King Leopold will surrender our armed forces within a few days, and our seat of government will be Paris. I don't know what the King will do, but he must decide whether to follow the parliament or stay here as a German prisoner. Either way, there will be German soldiers in the streets, martial law, and a curfew."

Jacques' gaze moved around the room. When the truth had sunk in, he said, "Although the Germans have completely encircled the British and French armies, the British Navy may yet evacuate part of the cornered armies across the channel, but the casualties of such an endeavour will be high."

Jacques waited for comments, but none came, so he shifted his attention to Juliette and Peter.

"In light of the news we have just received, I would prefer you go to Switzerland. Peter can work for me there, or he can sing—the choice is his." He stared at Juliette, waiting for her to digest the implications.

Juliette looked at Peter, and he nodded. She turned to her father.

"Papa, I will not tell our child that we ran away from you and our country. We will fight here, with you and Mother. We will make the Nazis suffer every day they occupy Belgium!"

Jacques nodded slowly. "All right, Juliette, but I will want you and Peter to use your intellect and your voices, not guns. I want you to sing in Germany. Fulfill the contracts you have, and we will see about new singing engagements that fit our purposes. There will be Jews to rescue, information to carry, Allied pilots to rescue, and Germans important to our cause to get out of the country."

He shifted to Peter. "You will not go to Germany until the Nazis are defeated; you will remain in Belgium and France and sing short-term oratorio and concerts. I want you to help set up communications networks in the Nazi-occupied countries. Marcel will teach you how to operate the shortwave sets and set up a system of stations that the Germans can't locate. Some are already in place, but we have only begun."

Peter smiled from ear to ear. "This means that Juliette and I can live together."

"Yes, it does, but your careers will blossom in different directions. Even in Germany, the arts communities hate the Nazis with a passion that will become stronger as Hitler abuses them. The majority are willing to help, and they know where to find others."

Marcel took over. "I will coordinate Juliette's performances and travel so everything goes smoothly, and it will be my job to connect all this to British Intelligence. Neither of you"—he looked at Juliette and Peter—"will ever speak on a radio or write anything down!"

Jacques addressed Peter. "Do not meet anyone face-to-face unless I clear it first. You must never use your real name, and you should assume that everyone else is doing the same!"

Juliette asked, "How will Peter pick up and deliver messages or papers if he can't meet anyone?"

Marcel smiled and looked at Peter. "The oldest game in the espionage world. We use drops and exchange points. If you know nothing, meet no one face to face, you can't reveal anything..."

Juliette interrupted, "...in case the Gestapo is questioning us in their cellar."

"Yes, Juliette," said Marcel, "but it's just as important if customs agents, border guards, or the police on the street are questioning you. Most of them are trained to pick out a liar; if you aren't lying, you will look and sound innocent."

Chapter Eighteen

15 June 1940

Helden ohne Tragödie sind wie Bücher ohne Worte.
(Heroes without tragedy are like books without words)

Hitler's modern panzers brushed the Belgian army aside and squeezed the British and French into a shrinking pocket with the sea at their backs. The German Heer and Luftwaffe had decimated England's army and the British Royal Air Force, and the shocked world resigned itself that Hitler would now turn his Blitzkrieg on Britain. The world's newspaper headlines screamed the imminent fall of all of Europe.

However, Hitler focused his forces on humiliating the hated French, not wiping out the British army and following them across the channel. He ordered his forces to halt, giving Churchill time to reconsider an agreement with Germany, but also allowing the British Navy an opportunity to pluck the British Expeditionary Force off the beaches.

Hitler found it "Regrettable but unavoidable" that a hundred thousand French soldiers escaped with what remained of the British army.

The German army occupied Paris on the fourteenth of June 1940, parading Wehrmacht soldiers through the city in a brazen demonstration of military supremacy. People in Germany danced in their streets as goose-stepping Wehrmacht and SS soldiers marched through the Arc de Triomphe de l'Étoile and down the Champs-Élysées before a silent, fearful crowd.

Hitler completed his revenge on the twenty-first of June 1940 by dictating the terms of unconditional surrender to the disgraced French in the same railway car where, twenty-two years earlier, the Allies had forced Germany to sign the armistice that ended the "War to End all Wars." Germany had laid down her arms, believing American President Woodrow Wilson and the European Allies' promise of a fair "Peace without Victory." Instead, with Germany disarmed and helpless, France and Britain broke their commitment to be 'fair' by drafting the humiliating Treaty of Versailles, creating the lever Hitler would later use to unite the German people behind his Fascist Dritte Reich.

Juliette and Marcel arrived in Heilbronn on the evening of the fourteenth. People flooded the streets, celebrating the crushing defeat of the country that had been the focus of their revenge for over twenty years. Exchanging Nazi salutes, they chanted Adolph Hitler's name—and red flags impregnated with black swastikas hung from almost every building.

The following morning, Juliette attended a short staging and ensemble rehearsal to refresh the opera, and sang the first of her three remaining performances of La Traviata at seven that evening. The mood in the theatre was euphoric; not even Violette's death could sadden the audience.

Juliette's pregnancy changed her voice from its pretty childlike quality to a woman's rich, vibrant, sexy tones. Her range was still wide, but her low notes were honey-coated, and her top notes rang with a new-found vitality. The audience responded appropriately; the reception from the joy-filled crowd overwhelmed Juliette, but she made only a single solo bow.

As Juliette walked to the hotel with Marcel, a wave of sadness swept over her, and Marcel, sensing her mood, entwined his fingers in hers. He said affectionately, "I have never heard anything as exquisite as that."

"Yes," she said. "I love that opera; it has everything: beautiful melodies, exquisite lines, and a touching story. We can all relate to Violette and Alfredo's pain."

"No," he said, "I specifically meant your singing."

Juliette looked up at the handsome man who guarded her so diligently, sensing pain in him. He looked back with something more than fondness, and she blushed and lowered her eyes. She looked at the sidewalk as she spoke. "I find it hard to be cheerful while the German people celebrate humiliating a country." She looked down the street at rows of red and black flags, people walking arm in arm, laughing and kissing, and her sadness deepened.

"The Nazis will ravage France, Belgium, and Holland—I don't think we can imagine the damage they will do, especially to the Jewish communities!" Marcel squeezed her hand, and they walked the final hundred metres in silence.

The following day, Juliette and Marcel went to St. Killian's Church for the Sunday morning service. Pastor Bergman began his sermon with words taken from Jesus' 'Sermon on the Mount.' Stretching his arms over the congregation, he said, "Blessed are the meek, for they shall inherit the earth."

His restless flock made it clear that love and forgiveness were not on their agenda, but Pastor Bergman stuck to his guns, chastising his community for celebrating the denigration of others. When he said, "Love thine Enemies…" a voice answered, "Sure, right after we crack their skulls!" The congregation chuckled, and Pastor Bergman smiled at the culprit, a young soldier, and said, "Perhaps we should remember that the road to victory is a two-way street," and the tittering stopped.

After the service, Juliette and Marcel poured themselves coffee and circulated in the room, warmly welcomed by members of the congregation.

A Luftwaffe officer and a beautiful woman Juliette assumed was his wife approached them; she smiled and offered her hand to Juliette. "I am Marita Stephanie, and this is my husband, Erik." The officer clicked his heels, half-bowed, and graciously kissed Juliette's hand while his blue eyes looked deep into hers. He gently lowered her hand as he said. "Oberleutnant Stephanie at your service." He released her and said, "Marita and I heard you sing last night, and we were spellbound by your interpretation of Violette." He continued to look at Juliette, but she didn't have time to think of a reply before Marcel moved beside her, and the officer's gaze turned to him.

Marcel said, "I am not a judge of these things, Oberleutnant Stephanie, but despite hearing Juliette sing almost every day, I was also mesmerized." He took the hand the Luftwaffe officer offered. "I am

Marcel, Juliette's manager when she travels. I heard your wife introduce you as Erik. May I call you by your first name, Herr Stephanie?"

Erik quickly adjusted. "Of course, and with your permission, I shall call you Marcel." He seemed accustomed to making small talk. "Do you accompany Mademoiselle Durand to all of her performances?" Erik switched to the informal "du" pronoun, and Marcel replied carefully—familiarity so quickly with a curious Luftwaffe officer rang an alarm. "I work for her father, and it's my job to see that everything goes smoothly."

"Then, you are her bodyguard…" Erik clarified and added… "as well as her manager."

Marcel smiled and took a sip of coffee to buy time. "Yes, to both. It is dangerous for a woman, let alone a famous one, to walk the streets and travel on the trains without an escort. Many details must be taken care of, and Mademoiselle Durand must concentrate on her art."

Erik's wife rescued Marcel. "Is my husband being a pest?"

"Not at all; I was telling him what I do for Juliette." He took another sip of his coffee.

Marita touched Juliette's hand and steered her away from the men. They each picked a piece of sweet Kuchen from the table and began a conversation as though they had known one another for years.

Juliette bit the corner off her Krüller. "This was my first performance since I became pregnant, and I can't believe how much my voice has improved." She bit off another corner. "Do you have children, Frau Stephanie?"

"We have one active little boy. He goes to school this fall, and I will be glad to have some free time."

"When you were pregnant, were you sick every morning?"

Marita took Juliette's arm, guiding her to an empty area of the room.

"Yes, I was sick in the mornings, but it only lasted a few weeks. Everything was wonderful until the last month when I became tired of pregnancy and just wanted to get it over with!"

Juliette whispered, "How badly does it hurt? I don't take pain well."

Marita finished her Kuchen and put her hands on Juliette's shoulders; Juliette was a head shorter than Marita, so she had to tilt her head back to look into the woman's eyes.

"It is the worst and best hurt in the world. The pain is excruciating, but bringing a child into the world makes it so exciting you don't remember..." She hesitated and smiled. "In fact, you will look forward to doing it again. I can't have any more children, and I would give anything to feel that pain again!"

She raised herself on her toes and waved to her beckoning husband. "Ah, I see my Erik wants attention. It was such a pleasure to meet you, Juliette."

Juliette said goodbye, waved to Erik and returned to the sweets, where Pastor Bergman approached Marcel.

Marcel extended his hand to Matthias. "Pastor Bergman, despite the reception you got from your congregation, Juliette and I enjoyed your sermon very much. However, under the present circumstances, it's difficult to understand how the meek will inherit anything but grief."

Juliette picked out an Apfelstrudel; Matthias put his arms around her, and she almost dropped her Kuchen. He said, "The meek must work very hard, and they must enlist the help of the strong, but eventually they will win." He said it confidently, as though he knew events always played out in favour of the underdog.

He looked at Juliette, then Marcel. "Is there anything I can help you with?"

She brightened. "No, we're fine; I am happy, and Peter and I will have our first child in early February. And, since my voice is working very well, I guess it's a perfect world."

Matthias's eyes shared her joy, "That's wonderful news in these times; I wish you well."

He lowered his voice so that no one could hear him but Marcel in the echo of chatter bouncing off stone walls. "I would be pleased if you and Juliette could join us for coffee and Kuchen at my house this afternoon."

Marcel checked with Juliette, then said, "We would love to. Juliette has no performances until Tuesday, and the hotel becomes a prison for her."

"Fine, then we'll expect you right after Mittagspause."

It was precisely three when Matthias met Juliette and Marcel at the door and led them into the dining room. Marita and Erik rose to greet them, and a young woman about Juliette's age stood up and pushed her chair back. Two babies played on a blanket spread out on the floor.

"You've already met Marita and Erik," said Matthias, "This is Monica Kuhlmann, and the babies are Brigitte and Elke."

Juliette and Marcel shook hands with Monica, and everyone sat down. A carafe of coffee, two Apfeltorte, and two large bowls of whipped cream stood by unmistakable design where everyone could reach them. Matthias put a square of torte on each of two plates, added a fork, and passed them to Juliette and Marcel. All joined hands while Matthias said grace.

When every cup was full of coffee appropriately laced with sugar and cream, Matthias opened the conversation.

"I have taken the liberty of telling Erik, Marita, and Monica that you two may have a way to get Monica and her children out of Germany." He looked at Erik. "I would like to hear Erik's thoughts on this before we go any further. Our position is sensitive, as you know, and his political leanings are unknown to our Belgian friends."

Erik began, "I am an Oberleutnant in the Luftwaffe, and I am committed to defending my country. I will be true to that promise, although I believe the people running our country are gangsters, and I do not support their brutal acts or plans." Erik returned Marcel's steady gaze. "I will not stand by while the Nazis take Monica and her children to a labour camp. What are their crimes? Monica's parents are Jewish."

As Juliette watched Erik, she tried to figure out why she trusted him. The table remained quiet until she spoke.

"My husband is a Mischling, and he only escaped from Dachau because my father has enough money to facilitate such things. But I doubt money will help Monica. She and her children must leave Germany as soon as possible, and of course, we will help."

Marcel nodded, "I believe we can arrange for Monica to leave with us, but I will have to think about how we can get the children out." He looked at Erik and then spoke to Marita. "If I can't find a way, could the children remain with you and Erik until we figure it out?"

Marita checked with Erik, and Erik confirmed, "They can stay as long as needed, and we would consider it a privilege to help."

Erik had passed Marcel's little test, and Juliette turned to Monica. "Monica, where is your husband?"

She bowed her head briefly, sighed, then said, "He died in Hannut, Belgium, in a Panzer."

Juliette wanted to touch Monica, but she couldn't reach her. She leaned toward her and said, "Oh, Monica, I'm so sorry."

"I don't care what happens to me now, but I must live for my children."

"We will get them out of Germany when you are safe." Marcel's voice took on an urgency. "But you must go as soon as possible. Where are you staying?"

"At home. I am a Wehrmacht soldier's widow, and they leave me alone."

Pastor Bergman shook his head. He hadn't touched his Kuchen. "That will not continue. Your husband here and alive may have delayed the inevitable, but now that he is dead, they will come for you and your children. It happens every day in this small city."

Marcel said, leaving no room for argument, "The children must go to Marita and Erik's house this afternoon." He looked at Matthias. "And Monica cannot remain here—you cannot jeopardize what you do. What about the hiding place?"

Monica interrupted, "I will not leave my children! There must be a way to get them out!"

She went to the children and picked up Elke. "If you hide her, she won't cry. I can tell her what's happening, and she will listen." Elke made a motor sound with her lips, and Brigitte laughed at her. No one spoke.

Marita picked up Brigitte and put her on her knee. Monica wrapped her arms around Elke and focused her pitiful gaze from one person to another.

"Damn the Nazis!" said Juliette.

"Amen," said Pastor Bergman.

Chapter Nineteen

28 June 1940

Das Ziel des Rechts ist der Friede; das Mittel dazu der Kampf.
(The goal of the righteous is peace; the method is battle)
Rudolph von Jhering

J ULIETTE CONTINUED TO SING LIKE A GODDESS, her voice filling out and relaxing more with every note she sang. Violette suited her voice and personality, and Juliette never failed to draw a full house. The following Saturday night, she sang her third sold-out performance of La Traviata.

On Sunday morning, Juliette and Marcel again attended church at St. Killian's and stayed for kaffeeklatsch. Marita found her way to them.

"Hello, Marita, isn't Erik with you?" Marcel glanced around the room.

"Erik has gone back to his squadron." Marita sipped her coffee. "Walther and I walked him to the train this morning before church."

Juliette asked, "When will he be home again?"

"He gets two weeks of leave every six months."

"I couldn't live like that; I'm miserable when Peter and I are apart for a week!"

Marita looked at her as a mother would a child. "Erik and I have no choice in the matter. He is obligated to serve or go to jail, and there are no married quarters for an Oberleutnants' wife and children."

Juliette realized she had been foolish, but before she could apologize, Marcel jumped in. "We must all bear the cross we are given—war removes all choices."

He checked to see if anyone was close enough to hear before he said, "How is it going with Monica? We have the arrangements made—we leave on Tuesday."

"Monica is fine," she said, "Erik had a telephone installed for her, and she is staying inside."

Marcel shook his head. "That is not what I said—she should not be staying in her home. Compromise is not a good policy in this game where survival depends on a willingness to sacrifice anything to minimize risk."

The walk to the hotel was short—less than ten minutes. Without thinking, Juliette reached for Marcel's hand as they walked from the rectory to the street, and he gently pulled it back. She grabbed it again and held it tightly, but he didn't object.

Juliette asked, "How will we get Monica's children across the border?"

"What children? She doesn't have any children."

"Elke and Brigitte are not her children?"

He shook his head. "Monica is the nurse you hired when you became pregnant. You needed help, so you hired Monica Freiwald to accompany you and care for the children." He looked at her as though he had taken a bite out of a green apple. "Good God, Juliette, you don't expect me to look after your children, do you?"

Juliette laughed, "Was this your idea or my father's?"

"For once, I can take the credit. However, there is one small problem. The children don't know you, and they will call Monica Mommy anytime, anyplace." He asked, hopefully, "Do you have a solution to that problem?"

They walked for five minutes before Juliette spoke.

"I think you should pretend to be Monica for a moment."

"Okay," he released her hand.

Juliette's face changed so much that Marcel laughed. She wagged her finger at him. "Monica, if you don't teach those children that I am their mother, I'll have to fire you! I know I am away from my children more than I should be, but they must know that I am their mommy, and you are their nanny. Someday, you will have children, and you can teach them to call you mommy, but these are my children, and if you don't teach them who I am, then I will find someone who will!"

On Tuesday morning, Marita went to stay with Monica until it was time to go to the hotel early in the afternoon. Just after noon, with the children asleep and Monica lying quietly on the sofa, Marita decided to prepare a light lunch. She was searching the cupboards for food when the knocker on the heavy door slammed against its plate.

"No," she said, as loudly as she dared, and ran from the kitchen to intercept Monica just as she unlocked the door. She pulled Monica back, and her heart sank as a brown-shirted SA officer pushed the door fully open. Two soldiers stood behind him, and the officer asked, "Monica Lindenbaum?" as he looked down at a sheet of paper.

Monica nodded, then corrected herself, "No, that is incorrect; Lindenbaum was my maiden name. My name is Monica Kuhlmann—my husband died in Belgium fighting for the Vaterland!"

The large man, unimpressed, smiled in a very unfriendly way. "You have fifteen minutes to pack one suitcase, and then you will come with me!"

Suddenly panic-stricken, she asked, "Where am I going?" and the large man said, "I will not wait; pack the suitcase, or you will go without it!"

Marita pulled her to the bedroom, took a suitcase out of the closet and began filling it with clothes. Monica ran around the room, picking up things, throwing them on the floor, then picking up something else. When the SA officer entered the room a few minutes later, Monica had only managed to gather her toothbrush and a hairbrush to add to the clothes Marita had packed. The officer grabbed her arm roughly and pulled her out the door. Marita tried to fasten the suitcase while carrying it, running behind Monica to a grey car parked in front of the house. She put it on Monica's lap, still not fully closed, and said the only thing she could think of: "Don't give up hope; do whatever they tell you to; and Monica, listen to me…we will find you!"

Monica wept; her entire body shook as one of the soldiers slammed the door. Monica pressed her face against the window as the car drove off, and when it was gone, Marita sat on the curb, her head in her hands, sobbing.

A moment later, she suddenly stood up and screamed, "The children," as she ran into the house. She gathered clothes, packed a suitcase and a large bag, woke the children, and, five minutes later, had them dressed. Brigitte, two years older than her sister, sensed the urgency and decided to cooperate, and Elke, although only a baby, followed her big sister's example.

It wasn't until Marita pushed Brigitte past the kitchen door that the little girl decided she needed more information before going further.

"Where's Mommy?" She twisted away from Marita.

Marita tried to steer Brigitte toward the door while carrying Elke, the bag and the suitcase, but the confused little girl headed for her mother's bedroom, crying, "Mommy! Mommy!"

Marita put Elke, the suitcase and the bag on the floor, told Elke to stay there, and ran after Brigitte. She intercepted the little girl as she came into the living room. Brigitte looked on the sofa, saw her mother's coat and shouted, "Mommy!" one more time and then looked up at Marita. "I want my mommy!"

Marita squatted down so her eyes would be on the same level as Brigitte's and stroked her hair. The little girl put her thumb in her mouth and became quiet.

"Bad men took your mommy away. I couldn't stop them, and I am afraid they will come back here for you and Elke if we don't hurry." Marita's eyes filled with tears, and the desperation in her voice appeared to satisfy Brigitte that she must obey.

Marita picked up Elke, the suitcase, and the bag. "Brigitte, follow me as fast as you can," Marita ran down the stairs and onto the sidewalk with Brigitte on her heels. Fifteen minutes later, they were at Wacksstrasse 21.

Marita carried Elke and the suitcase into the house, leaving the bag on the steps, and Brigitte followed. Marita's mother, Annalisa, appeared and took Elke from Marita, who went back for the bag, checked that the street was empty and closed the door behind her.

Marita's mother sensed the adrenalin surging through her daughter as she took the bag from her.

"What happened, Marita—where's Monica?" Annalisa carried Elke and guided Brigitte into the living room.

Marita gasped, finding it difficult to breathe. "The SA took Monica... I'm afraid they will come and take the children!"

Brigitte stood in the middle of the rug with three fingers in her mouth, watching Annalisa guide Marita to the sofa. Elke was on the floor beside her, sucking the same three fingers.

"Marita, Liebling, you must sit down; I will care for the children." She took Elke in her arms, and Brigitte sat beside Marita. Annalisa sat on the other side of Marita with Elke on her lap. "If they had an interest in the children, they would have taken them when they took Monica. We must take a moment to think—I'm sure the children are safe for now."

She thought for a moment, then asked her daughter, "Did the SA ask for your name?"

"No, they didn't."

"That's important. The SA or the Gestapo would have no idea where to look for these children, even if they wanted to. I doubt that they will bother them now."

Marita's breathing slowed, and she brushed her hair back with her hand. "I hope you're right, but I must talk to Juliette and Marcel right away—they were planning to take Monica and the children today. Perhaps they can do something."

Marita stood up and looked at Brigitte, who was listening carefully. "We are going to try to find your mother," She stroked the little girl's hair, "I promise we will take care of you until we find her." She turned and walked out the door toward the hotel.

Juliette went to Marcel's door, knocked so hard it hurt, and he opened it at once.

"Marita's here without Monica, and something is wrong. She wants you to come to my room."

Marita was pacing when they entered the room. When Marcel closed the door, she grabbed his arm, panic-stricken. "The SA took Monica, and we've got to get her back!"

Marcel shook his head, frustrated. He guided Marita to the bed, sat her down, then found a notepad and pencil on the bedside table and pulled a chair beside her.

"Tell me what happened. Speak slowly, and try to concentrate on every detail."

Marita shuddered, took a deep breath, then told her story while Juliette sat on the bed beside her. Juliette's father had told her of concentration camps for women, and she feared what would happen to Monica if the Nazis sent her to one.

She held Marita's hand until she finished, then said, "I'm so sorry, Marita, but my father and Marcel will do everything they can to get her back." She tried to sound hopeful, but there was no hope in her heart.

Marcel asked, "What about the children? Who is looking after them?"

"I took them to my house. They've spent a lot of time there, and we love them like our own. My mother is looking after them."

"Without their mother, where will they go?"

Marita had been looking at her hands while she spoke. She raised her eyes and looked hopefully at Marcel. "Do you think we can keep them until we rescue Monica?"

Marcel stood up. "That's possible. The Nazis have no interest in those children, and they certainly must value your husband. If we can't find Monica quickly and you formally ask for custody, you will likely get it."

He tore the pages of notes he had made from the pad and put them in his pocket.

"I'm going to the lobby to make some calls. You should stay here with Juliette, and we will eat when I return. Juliette has to be at the theatre by six, so we must eat early."

Marita shook her head. "No, my mother is looking after our son Walther and the girls, and she will want to know what I found out. I hate to have to tell her."

Marcel escorted Marita to the lobby, waited while she walked out the door and then went to the telephone.

Chapter Twenty

18 February 1941
Kummer, sei lahm! Sorge, sei blind! Es lebe das Geburtstagskind!
(Sorrow be quiet, Angels beguile! Long live the newborn child!)
Theodore Fontane

AS HER BELLY GREW, SO DID JULIETTE'S DISCOMFORT, and as the birth of her child approached, she acquired the personality of a witch. And since Peter was the only whipping boy close enough to hit, he had to accept the appropriate punishment for whatever crime she decided he had committed. Retaliation or defence was out of the question, and pleading for mercy made it worse.

Fortunately, Peter's December schedule had no slack on weekends, and Juliette sensed he wasn't sad to leave for his two-day singing excursions. She even accused him of purposely going a day early and staying longer so he wouldn't have to come home—an accusation Peter vehemently denied in one of her frequent screaming matches. When Peter was away, Juliette slept in her room at her parents' home, where Veronique took advantage of the proximity to fuss over her. She had the special love and patience given to prospective grandmothers by a sympathetic God, and Juliette didn't miss an opportunity to test it.

Juliette sang the first half of Bach's Weihnachtsoratorium in Brussels on December 21 and the second half the day after Christmas. She felt her voice had never worked better, but it was her last obligation before she and Peter moved into her parents' home to await the inevitable. Peter knew from experience that Juliette needed a lot of space—which he gladly gave her—if she couldn't sing for the usual reasons like colds or flu. But her voice was the best it had ever been, and he dreaded the coming weeks.

The days came and went with monotonous precision, and Peter

was surprised and happy when Juliette seemed to resign herself to the wait. She sang at the piano every afternoon, concentrating on Brahms Volkslieder and French lullabies. Several times during the day and just before she went to sleep, Juliette stroked her growing belly and sang the "Song to the Moon" to her baby.

One night, as Peter stroked Juliette's huge stomach while she sang to the baby, he said, "Our child had better be a girl—otherwise, a boy will sound ridiculous singing Rusalka's 'Song to the Moon' as he exits your womb."

"You are right," said Juliette. "We don't want to confuse the baby, so perhaps you should sing to her, just in case."

From that day until 'the day' arrived, Juliette's belly heard tenor arias, soprano arias, and love duets every night, and Juliette said the baby was for sure a girl because she reacted more to tenors than she did to sopranos.

The doctor had predicted a birth date in the first week of February, but it came and went uneventfully. By February 15th, Juliette was running out of patience as she waddled from room to room, spending most of her time in her father's favourite chair in front of the fireplace. Jacques didn't complain out loud and substituted Veronique's leather chair. Veronique knitted in Juliette's cloth-covered equivalent.

Marcel hovered close to the house twenty-four hours a day, and as the days came and went without a twinge, everyone became restless. Peter sang every weekend he could get a gig, and Juliette worried he would miss the event, but Peter wasn't as concerned with missing it as he was with avoiding it. He had heard stories from reliable sources like her Papa of the abuse prospective fathers took when their wives were having a baby, and he didn't want to imagine how venomous Juliette could become when she was in pain he was responsible for.

Finally, the doctor gave her a bottle of drops to take with herbal tea, increasing the dose each day until… But the next day, February 18, in the middle of the afternoon, Juliette rose from her chair in front of the fire and announced, "Peter, it's time to get Marcel...."

Peter got up, tripped over the edge of the Persian rug, and fell to his knees. He struggled to his feet, asked, "Are you sure?" and Juliette gave him a look that started him moving toward the door. Then, loud enough for the entire occupying German army to hear, he shouted, "Marcel, hurry! Juliette's finally going to have the baby!"

Juliette rolled her eyes and headed for the door, and Marcel was there when she reached it. Veronique ran down the stairs with two small, soft bags, and Jacques exited his office. He hugged Juliette and said in her ear, "I'll be at the hospital in an hour. You will wait for me, won't you?"

"Yes, Papa, but I doubt anything will happen for a while. Why don't you come in a couple of hours?" She winced as another pain announced the inexorable course of events.

He kissed her cheek. "Don't be too hard on Peter…you'll need him when this is over."

She laughed; "Oh, Papa, I won't blame Peter—I'm grateful to him for giving us something so wonderful!"

Peter arrived with the third bag Veronique had packed three weeks ago. He asked suspiciously, "I heard my name, and you laughed. What did I do now?"

"Nothing bad, darling." Juliette took his free arm. "Help me get to the car."

Ten minutes later, the Rolls pulled up in front of the massive Brussels hospital, and Peter and Marcel helped Juliette up the steps and through the double doors. Two nurses were expecting them and whisked her away in a wheelchair, leaving her entourage in the waiting room.

They each picked a seat, and Veronique told a reluctant Marcel he could return to the house to wait for Jacques.

She sat down beside Peter and patted his knee. "This will be over in a few hours, and you will be a proud father." She looked at him with something like pity. "The past few months have been difficult for you, haven't they?"

He refused to incriminate himself, and she looked at the wall across from her, smiling as she remembered.

"I made Jacques' life hell for the last two months of my pregnancy, and I hated him until the moment Juliette was born. But everything changed when I saw my baby. I forgave him, but I'm sure he will tell you I was…uh…difficult for another month." She looked out the window, remembering, then said, "But it could have been longer."

A few minutes later, a nurse announced that Juliette was indeed in labour but that it would be a few hours before the birth—there would be time for them to eat. They agreed to walk to a nearby restaurant, ate quickly and talked very little. It was dangerous to speak in public in occupied Brussels; the war was all most people talked about, but one never knew how other topics would be interpreted. Neighbours disappeared, protesters were violently dealt with, and even the once-friendly local police obeyed their goose-stepping masters. Belgium had settled into the Nazi reign of terror, and once-noisy bustling restaurants and cafés had become nothing more than a place to fill one's stomach.

The Juliette support team returned to screams from somewhere down the hall. Jacques arrived and smiled at Peter as he said, "That sounds familiar."

Peter waved his hand toward the screams' source. "Yes, that's Juliette…I would recognize that 'C' anywhere!" He looked at the floor as he said, "I wish I could do this for her."

Veronique's laugh was a ringer for Juliette's bar-maid guffaw. "Do this for her? No, you don't wish any such thing! If it were up to men to have the children, humans would have become extinct when Adam and Eve died!"

Jacques said, "And that begs the question I keep asking the bishop… who was the mother of Adam and Eve's grandchildren?"

He laughed and said as he pointed to Peter, "You know she's right." Jacques shook his head. "Believe me, you don't want to take Juliette's place right now."

Peter said nothing but looked at Jacques with an expression that said, "You don't know me!"

The screams suddenly stopped, and Peter got up to look around the corner. A nurse exited a room down the hall, shaking her head. He worried about what that might mean and met her when she reached the waiting room.

The nurse continued shaking her head as she said, "I've never heard such a racket—that voice could cut granite!"

"Is everything all right?" Standing behind Peter, Veronique asked the question before he could find the correct French words.

The exasperated nurse said, "Yes, she's fine. She's begun to dilate; we've called the doctor, and he'll be here in a few minutes."

Peter asked, "Is the pain terrible?" The nurse gave him a nasty look, shook her head and left.

Juliette noted bits of cloth sticking out of the nurse's ears but felt no sympathy. Screaming was the only outlet for her suffering, and she was going to use it! The memory of Professor Garcia's using a baby's cry to illustrate resonance came back to her, and Juliette thought it was obvious he had never heard a woman in labour… But she had to admit that Garcia had taught her to make a helluva lot of noise without damaging those tender little vocal cords!

The birthing team had tied Juliette to the hard bed, and the only help anyone offered was an instruction to pant like a dog. She tried it, but screaming worked much better. She tried re-pe-te-ke and sh-sh-sh-sh, but both were useless. The situps on the piano bench worked, and that's when she figured out why her hands were tied where they were. It helped when she added the last letter in the alphabet, but the combination of situps and screaming was still way out in front!

As the pains came closer together and lasted longer, Juliette concentrated on protecting her vocal cords by carefully placing the resonance as Professor Garcia had taught her, and focusing on the sound deadened the pain. However, on the negative side, it effectively amplified the sound, driving everyone out of the room. Returning when the pain eased, they abandoned ship again when Juliette accompanied the next wave of pain with sounds they agreed they had never heard in a collective thirty years of delivering babies!

At the apex of her pain, the doctor entered the room and quickly asked for ether, "so the dead may rest in peace." Two whiffs deadened the pain, and Juliette lost the urge to scream. All was suddenly well with the world.

The actual birth was not what Juliette expected. There were moments of sharp pain but a feeling of joy so intense that the pain was bearable. When the doctor announced, "It's a girl!" Juliette struggled onto her elbows so she could see it. The slimy red bundle the nurse took away began to kick, then drew a breath and emitted a familiar scream... not perfectly pitched and as musical as Juliette would have liked, but she could work on that later. Juliette leaned over to see the nurse washing her daughter in a basin, still kicking and yelling her tiny lungs out. She smiled as she thought she heard the sound improve. Perhaps that was the resonance Professor Garcia had been talking about!

The doctor helped a second nurse get Juliette off the birthing table and into a wheeled bed. As nurse number one handed Juliette a bundle, she pushed the edge of the cloth back to reveal the most beautiful baby Juliette had ever seen.

The doctor asked, "Are you ready to see your husband?" and Juliette nodded without taking her eyes off the baby.

When Peter saw Juliette, he hesitated, giving his mother-in-law an opening.

"Oh, you poor dear," Veronique said, stepping quickly in front of Peter to the side of the bed. "You look terrible! You must be tired—we will go soon."

Juliette smiled at her mother and turned the bundle so she could see it. Veronique pulled the cloth back, revealing a wrinkled face squeezing its eyes shut. It made a sour expression as it moved its lips.

Peter watched the mother, daughter, and granddaughter from a respectful distance. Jacques leaned over and said in his ear, "All women think their babies are beautiful. I advise you to agree with them."

Peter whispered, "Did Juliette look that bad?"

"Worse, if that's possible. She was yellow. Juliette had to stay in the hospital for a month, and we had lost hope when she gradually improved. She was a year old before she closely resembled a human being."

He put his hand on Peter's shoulder as they stared at the wrinkled face.

"Veronique always thought she was beautiful, so I kept my mouth shut. Secretly, I thought we would be stuck with her for the rest of our lives!" Peter turned so he was face-to-face with his father-in-law, who said, "Fortunately, you came along in the nick of time."

Peter laughed, edged over to Juliette, and Veronique reluctantly backed away.

"She's beautiful," he said as Juliette held the blanket back so he could see the grimacing red face preparing to scream. He looked at Juliette, tears in his eyes, and said, "I love you." She took his hand and pulled him down to her. They kissed tenderly, carefully avoiding squeezing the little bundle.

Chapter Twenty-One

Easter, 1941

Nach rechts hinsprechen, aber nach links hinausschauen!
(Speak to the right, but watch out to the left!)

Monique Desjardins, Peter's talent agent, found oratorios and concerts for Peter somewhere in France or Belgium every weekend, and with each gig came an opportunity to connect the growing network of Résistance cells through radio sets dropped into the German-occupied countries. Marcel taught Peter the protocol setup to keep the radios safe from detection, and Peter showed the cells that received a radio how to operate it.

Under ideal conditions, the Germans could triangulate a transmitting set in less than five minutes, but could not locate a receiving radio. The transmission of messages, the lifeblood of British Intelligence, had to be as short as possible. Every second the transmit key was down, the Germans narrowed the search area. If the transmitter switch was on 'send' too long, or the radio wasn't relocated often enough, the next time the operator keyed the transmitter, the searchers could begin where they had left off after the previous transmission, taking them ever closer to the source until they struck.

The limit to transmission time was arbitrarily set at two minutes, once a day at random times, and even then, the transmitter's location had a finite shelf life. Radio locations had to change frequently, and decoy stations had to be set up, moved, and then set up again. The Résistance learned how to use portable radio units to confuse the radio hunters and keep them busy chasing ghosts.

Despite the precautions, operators lost track of time, transmitted too often or at regular times, and became complacent if nothing happened when they broke the rules. Cunning hunters lulled operators into false confidence, then pounced on an entire over-confident network of chatterboxes. The penalty for those the hunters captured was always death, but not until they were tortured. Experts at inflicting pain, their captors kept the Résistance member alive until they were convinced they had extracted everything they knew.

Peter set up a new cell every two weeks, but twice in three months, he had returned to find a group or several connected groups destroyed, their members captured, tortured and killed because they had broken the protocol. He protected himself by becoming a nameless ghost and strictly adhering to Marcel's instructions. Whenever Peter left his hotel to contact a cell, he used a false name and varied his clothing and beard as much as possible. The only names Peter used when in contact with the Résistance were René or Camille.

He sang under his Belgian name, Peter Schweitzer, and Mademoiselle Desjardins' singing engagements appeared magically coincidental with a communications setup or information retrieval.

Peter began to hate leaving Juliette; he was forming a deep relationship with the now beautiful bundle of joy, his daughter, Nina, and the danger was becoming palpable. They were becoming a family, with all its love and commitment.

But Peter and Juliette could not forget Kristallnacht in Munich when the Nazis murdered Peter's grandparents and raped Juliette. Their hatred for the swastika and the need for revenge overwhelmed the obligation they felt to their family. Peter convinced himself he must carry on to protect his family from what he knew would devour them, even if it meant death.

Every night, without waking Juliette, Peter changed Nina's diaper and fed her in the living room. He softly talked and sang as he tended to her, and his daughter soon caught on that Peter would pick her up, feed her, and sing to her if she whimpered softly. Most nights, when Peter was home, Juliette slept until morning. When Peter was away, Nina howled, and Juliette got no sleep.

A week before Easter weekend, Monique Desjardins called Peter to offer a contract to sing the Evangelist in Bach's St. John Passion at the Amiens

Cathedral on Good Friday. The scheduled tenor had suddenly fallen ill, and Peter had sung the Evangelist in both of Bach's Passions and, thanks to Juliette, had learned to love the baroque style, particularly Bach. Mademoiselle Desjardins booked a room for Peter at the Hotel de Berny for Wednesday night. It was close to the cathedral and had a good restaurant.

He arrived at the rehearsal Thursday morning to find the choir and a twenty-piece orchestra already practising. A young girl led him to a quartet of chairs set up beside the conductor.

Peter marvelled at the church's perfect acoustics as he listened to the conductor work on Ach Herr, lass dein Lieb Engelein with the choir and orchestra. The tiniest sound carried to the farthest niche—singing the Evangelist here would be salve for his voice, if he got the balance and resonance right. A lot depended on the conductor, and what Peter heard from the orchestra and chorus told him this one was excellent. He looked forward to the rehearsal.

One by one, the soloists arrived, and when the soprano finally made her entrance, the conductor introduced Peter to the choir, orchestra, and the other soloists, who all seemed to know one another. The polite clapping told Peter they did not expect him to reach the standard set by the original. The role was demanding for any tenor, and as the piece developed, most tenors faded, some barely surviving to murder the last recitative.

The first tenor aria, Ach, mein Sinn, ended his role in part one, followed by a chorale that finished the section. Before the choir sat down, the conductor turned to Peter and began clapping. The choir and orchestra joined him, and applause rebounded from the stone walls and Gothic arches. Peter had to bow before the conductor would end his clapping and lower his hands. Maestro Renaud stretched his hand to Peter, and when Peter took it, he pulled him into a hug.

Peter sang the entire oratorio rehearsal without sparing his voice, and when the Passion ended, his final recitative was as fresh and vigorous as his first had been. The conductor took him aside as the orchestra put away their instruments.

"Monsieur Schweitzer, I would like to know who has taught you how to sing Bach. I have never heard such singing!"

"Monsieur Renaud, I must give credit where it belongs. My wife,

Juliette, taught me how to sing Bach. I was truly a terrible singer of this wonderful composer before she worked with me."

The conductor put his finger on his generous nose. "I teach singing here in Amiens, and I am always searching for a better method. Could you tell me how your wife approaches the teaching of singing? I am, of course, specifically interested in the baroque works. You sing so very relaxed, sans travail. Perhaps you could demonstrate your wife's teaching technique for me, monsieur?"

Peter looked at the floor, swallowed hard to avoid a coughing fit, and bought a little time to make up something. A few seconds later, he looked at Monsieur Renaud, patiently waiting to hear Juliette's secret with his head tilted back.

Peter spoke slowly, choosing words carefully. "She taught me to sing Geduld, Geduld while I immersed myself in...uh...physical activity, which took my attention away from my voice. I concentrated on muscle motions unrelated to singing, leaving me no choice but to relax my voice muscles. Previously, I had been over-thinking and consequently over-singing Bach."

Monsieur Renaud put his fingers over his chin and mouth, walked around in a tight little circle and returned to stand in front of Peter.

"Monsieur Schweitzer, I would be so very grateful if you would be so kind as to demonstrate the physical activity you performed while simultaneously singing."

Peter pulled out his pocket watch, looked at it, then feigned a look of shock on his face. "I'm afraid we must continue this discussion tomorrow, monsieur. I have an appointment that I cannot miss. Would you please excuse me?"

The conductor stepped back to give Peter room to exit by the west door. He paused before opening the door to say, "I will make time tomorrow morning, monsieur." and Monsieur Renaud said, "Perhaps you could demonstrate in front of the choir at the party tomorrow evening!"

"Au revoir, monsieur." Peter disappeared out the door, pretending he hadn't heard the last remark.

Later, in his room at the Hotel de Berny, Peter chuckled as he changed his clothes. He checked his new identity papers before he put them in his pocket. His Belgian passport was under the name of René Bouchard, who lived in Florennes, Belgium. The expiration date on the wrinkled and cracked passport was two months from now.

Marcel had drilled him on his identity until Peter knew everything about René Bouchard. He had a Wallonian father and a German mother whose maiden name was Gertrud Greitschutz. René was a fruit and vegetable buyer for his family's firm, and Marcel assured him that if someone were to call the firm's number in Brussels, they would receive confirmation of Renè's location and the purpose of his trip.

Peter exited the hotel's side door, avoiding the lobby, and headed for the Hortillonnages, an extensive agricultural marsh cut into blocks by narrow canals. He crossed the Somme River to a pier where a small square-nosed boat picked him up, following a short exchange with the pilot about the weather. The man, at least seventy years old, stood in the stern, pushing the boat with a four-metre pole. His heritage had blessed him with a large, hooked nose.

When they were underway, Hooknose kicked a paper bag over to Peter and told him to open it. Inside were a piece of rotten-smelling cheese and half a loaf of dry white bread. He pointed to a black, four-litre bottle and said, "Take some wine with the bread. My son made it with grapes from my garden."

Peter pulled the cork and sniffed the wine; it smelled unpleasantly of fermented blue grapes. He tipped the bottle up to slosh just a little on his tongue without swallowing—the taste was strange—a little mouldy, but probably safe to drink. Peter broke off a handful of bread, scraped fungus off a small piece of cheese, squeezed it into the folded bread and took a bite. He hadn't eaten since his early breakfast, but despite acute hunger, the combination was foul.

Rather than spit it out and offend the old man, Peter took a long pull on the wine in an attempt to overwhelm the terrible taste. When it passed his palate, the wine tasted like vinegar laced with rotten grapes, and he had to force himself to swallow. It took all of his strong will to hold the noxious mixture down.

Old Hooknose laughed, slapped his thigh and crowed, "Monsieur, you are the first man to take a second drink—my son makes the worst wine in all of France!" He doubled over, and Peter put the cork back in the bottle. Hooknose reached under his seat, pulled out a 'seven-tenths' litre bottle and passed it to Peter with a wink. A cautious taste confirmed the wine was much better—he took a second pull and sloshed it in his mouth until his taste memory righted itself.

Hooknose laughed again, less uproariously, with more respect, while waving his free hand around in circles for emphasis. "I made this wine. Can you tell me how a son who has watched his father make such wine could make something as poisonous as that?" He kicked the big bottle. Peter returned it to the paper bag, ready for its next victim.

Using his hands to express his respect, Peter chuckled and said, "You did fool me with that wine, monsieur. Now, tell me the truth—who made the bad wine?"

Hooknose smiled sadly. "My wife made it; I have no son. The Germans killed him in 1918 when the Canadians pushed them out of Amiens. The Boche shot him, even though he was too young to be a soldier and was not in a uniform."

He looked at Peter, aimed a finger at him. "You are German, not Belgian—your French is very bad."

Peter made his first mistake when he said, "I was born in Germany. My mother is Jewish, and my father is German—he's a machinist with M.A.N. They left Germany before the Nazis could send my mother to a concentration camp. I married a Belgian woman and joined the Résistance."

He immediately regretted giving accurate information—the first rule of elementary espionage.

Hooknose nodded, and Peter nervously ended the conversation. "I can't tell you more than that." He had a sick feeling that had nothing to do with wine or cheese.

The old man silently poled the boat up the river, then swung it into a side canal. A hundred metres past the turn, he pushed it into a narrow opening in the right-hand shoreline, almost entirely hidden by overhanging bushes. As the canot slid into the canal, Hooknose whistled a few bars of a French folk song. Two men sitting in the long-dead grass, one on each side of the narrow ditch, waved to him as the boat glided past. They carried German Gewehr 98 rifles from the previous war.

Grinning at Peter, Old Hooknose noted, "If you had lied, I would have whistled a different song, and you would now be dead."

Half an hour later, the old man leaned on the pole and pushed the flat-bottomed boat up a grassy bank until half its length was high and dry. Tall trees grew on the strip of land next to the narrow canal, and, as they walked up the bank, hidden by the trees, two shacks with single panes of irregular glass in their small windows came into view. Hooknose took him to the door of the first building and knocked once, then twice. The door opened, and a tiny woman stood in front of Peter. Behind her, a man twice her size cradled a German rifle in his muscular arms.

The woman waved Peter and the old man into the room, then invited Peter to "Search the room and find the radio." The big man with the rifle went outside.

Peter had been challenged to 'find the radio' before and knew it would almost certainly be in the cupboard, the worst possible hiding place and the first place the Gestapo would look. He opened the doors, removed a sack of beans and then a bag of flour. He put one hand under the bottom shelf, the bottom of the cupboard, and another over it, and the thickness was correct. The valance at the top extended to the ceiling with no openings. He stood on a chair, banged on the top, the front, and the bottom—everything was solid. Methodically searching the walls for a hidden door and the ceiling for an opening into the attic, he found none. The only visible wires fed a single electric light bulb hanging from a spike in the centre of the room.

Peter stamped his feet, looked for loose boards, and opened the curtain under the short counter, but there was nothing to find.

Finally, he gave up, saying, "I can't find it," as he waved his arms around the room. "If there's a radio in this room, no one will find it without tearing the building down!"

Hooknose smiled, reached under the cupboard, curled his finger around something, and pulled back with his hand. A latch released with a clunk, and the old man caught a section of the cabinet that dropped to the counter. He slid the valance sideways, revealing a standard British Paraset short-wave radio. When he flipped a switch, the frequency dial lit up, and while he waited for the tubes to warm, he twisted the coarse frequency knob, then the fine adjustment, and plugged in the headphones. A few seconds later, with the radio warm, Ici Londres! Les Français parlent aux Français came on over the short wave frequency, and he passed the headphones to Simone.

Old Hooknose proudly smiled as he said, "I built that for my granddaughter."

Peter ran his fingers over the perfect joinery on the sliding valance and said, "Beautiful work."

Simone's grandfather winked and left to join the big man on the verandah.

Over the next two hours, Peter taught Simone how to broadcast messages using keywords on the station. Once an hour, on the hour, an OSS operator read nonsensical sentences over the air, one hundred percent meaningless except to a listener who had the code words. Each cell had a different designator that changed periodically, and if they heard that word, the following message contained coded instructions or requests. Peter explained how agents passed keywords from cell to cell and left coded messages at drop stations. A prearranged innocuous sign, such as a child's drawing, could indicate whether a drop was safe. If there were two trees in the picture, it was safe; one tree meant danger; walk past it. If the cat's tail pointed up, run away. The simpler, the better.

Peter gave her the first sequence of code words, and Simone memorized them. He taught her how to choose a transmission frequency crystal from the several that the SOE had sent and how to tune it. She learned how to confirm that her morse code was going to her intended target.

Simone switched the radio to 'transmit,' broadcast a short morse code message verifying that she was now a station in the Résistance. She flipped the selector switch to 'receive,' and a British Radio operator confirmed receipt. Simone replaced and tuned a new transmission crystal, changing the transmission frequency for the next time she used the set.

She finished in under a minute, and Peter continued to look at his watch until two minutes had passed, then said to her, "If you take this much time, the SS will find you, and you will be tortured and killed. Stop in mid-sentence if you have to, but you must stop! The second most important thing to remember is to broadcast on your schedule. Never send at another time; an operator is listening to your specific frequency at that specific time. And never set a schedule that is not random." Peter looked at the big man with the rifle.

"You must post a watch whenever Simone broadcasts, preferably placing several people to guard every possible route to the house. They must signal at any irregularity, and when they do…" He looked at Simone…" You must immediately stop broadcasting and hide the radio."

At Simone's signal, everyone disappeared, leaving Peter alone with her.

Simone demonstrated her morse code keying ability, and when Peter finally expressed his approval, she breathed deeply. She returned the radio and the cupboards to 'hidden radio' status and sat at the table with Peter.

"We don't know what we want to do with this cell," she confessed, "My husband will be in charge, but he doesn't want to waste time spreading propaganda leaflets. I am afraid for him; he only wants to kill Germans."

"Where is your husband now?"

"He's outside with my grandfather… the man with the rifle." She suddenly lost her disciplined composure and said desperately, "I don't want him to die! We have three small children, and they need him!" She stood up, went to the stove, took a steaming kettle off the steel top, then added wood to the firebox. "We have hunting rifles against machine guns; my husband is an auto mechanic. His friend outside is a carpenter, and you saw my grandfather. They are half of the only Résistance cell in Amiens. We have only eight members, and none are soldiers, but every week or so, another joins us. The Pétain traitors are trying to find us, even though they aren't sure we exist. We can't even trust our French brothers and sisters!" She waved her arms in frustration.

"These men think they can fight the Wehrmacht, the Gestapo, and the SS with guns! How can my unsophisticated husband and my grandfather fight the German Army?"

Peter turned in his chair to speak to her as she forced coffee through a filter. "Eight is sufficient for one cell. You should help someone outside this cell begin a new one with no connection to this one, except through the radio or safe drops. When you tell me they are ready, I will find another radio, but be very careful—this is how the SS locates and destroys cells. They use Pétain's Milice, his version of the Gestapo, to infiltrate a cell, and then, when they have enough information, the Gestapo destroys any affiliated cells. Never forget that most of France supports the Germans, and they do not brag about it—you might think you know who they are, but you must assume that every Frenchman is working for the Germans in some way."

Simone shouted a French word Peter had never heard before, and the door opened. Three men came in and sat down. Simone began the discussion.

"Monsieur René will now tell us what the British want us to do."

Peter said to the big man sitting beside Simone, "You are Simone's husband?"

"Yes, I am. My name is..."

Peter quickly raised his hand. "Do not use your real name! All women are Simone, Jacqueline, or Rachelle, and men are René, Camille, or Jacques unless those are their real names. You must use the most common names and change them as often as you change your socks."

Simone gave an "I told you so" look to her husband.

Peter looked at the big man's grease-stained hands and his partner's rough, calloused hands and said, "Those are the hands of working men, not soldiers. Your weapons"—he looked at the old Gewehr 98's leaning against the wall beside the door—"are no better than throwing stones at the Germans. The British are building bombers by the thousands, and they have fighters that can cross the channel to attack the Germans in minutes. The Allies are making thousands of bombs and shells every day, and they are training dozens of pilots every week." He waited for what he said to sink in. "And if you had a thousand men with a thousand rifles, you couldn't damage the Germans as much as one bomber can with one load of bombs!"

Simone's husband interrupted, "I haven't seen any bombers."

Peter smiled, "Because they don't know what to bomb. The British want to kill Germans as much as you do, but to do that, they need to know where their barracks are, the locations of their big guns and tanks, and which trains they should bomb or attack with fighters. They need to know the location of Luftwaffe aerodromes; how many planes are there, what type, one engine or two? Does it have guns on the front… are there guns on the rear? Where do the Germans store fuel and ammunition? If you can find out where those things are, the bombers can do a lot of damage." Peter watched the lights go on in their faces. "If you have information, you can draw a map, take a picture, or write a description using code for locations and other vital information. Simone will send a specific radio message, and someone will pick up what you leave at a drop station."

Simone said, "I could get a job at the airfield," pointed at her husband, "and you could start fixing Nazi cars in your shop." She looked at him—it was plain that he was disgusted at the thought. She told Peter, "My husband refuses to fix their cars, and if they make him do it, he sabotages them."

Peter nodded. "And that is the natural reaction, but it is the wrong one." He leaned on the table and stared into the man's eyes.

"You should fix their cars and give them good deals. Find some fine French cigarettes for your German customers, and perhaps you can find some French chocolate and American stockings for their girlfriends. Bring them to your shop for every little problem. Become friends… give them German beer. Drink with them and listen to everything they say, but don't act curious. Above all, do not ask questions! Everyone likes to brag to their friends, and that is how you will get information and live to pass it on."

Hooknose spoke for the first time, "I could take pictures of the barracks and hotels where the Gestapo is staying. They've taken over a building near the river—the grounds are beautiful, and maybe I could get a gardening job there." He chuckled at Peter. "I could grow grapes, and my wife could make wine for them."

Peter laughed, delighted with the change in attitude. "That's the spirit, but perhaps you shouldn't give them any of your wife's wine! For that, they will hang you." A roar of laughter cut him off, and he waited before beginning again.

As he swept his eyes around the group, he said, "A sketch from memory is much safer than a camera and can be as effective."

He looked from Hooknose to Simone's husband and his carpenter friend. "If anything changes, such as troop or equipment movements, you should report it, no matter how insignificant you think it is. Do not filter anything; let the experts in England decide what is important to them."

"What about the Communists?" asked Simone, "Should we let Communists into our group?"

"Yes, the Communists hate the Germans at least as much as you do, and most are French patriots. The Pétain hate the communists almost as much as the communists hate the Pétain."

Peter thought at least half the group in the room were communists, or at least socialists at heart. The French communists and socialists were the main reason most of France sided with the Nazis. They feared the communists and socialism more than they feared Hitler.

Peter said, "You are right to fear the Pétain, and, as you know, you will have to watch out for their supporters; they're everywhere. They've infiltrated many cells, and in every case, the Gestapo dragged everyone away."

Peter pointed to the rifles against the wall.

"If you carry those things around, you'll look like members of the Résistance. You should only carry a gun in the dark, and then only if you plan to kill someone. Otherwise, they are a flag that says you are an enemy of the Third Reich and the Pétain."

He pointed from one to another as he said, "Do not discount the danger of the Pétain! Even though they are Frenchmen and your legal government, their enthusiasm for the Nazi cause is often more vicious than the Gestapo's. The Gestapo depends on the Pétain to root out members of the Résistance. Members of Pétain's Milice are your most mortal enemies, not the German army, the SS or the Gestapo."

Simone gave her husband another "I told you so" look.

Chapter Twenty-Two

Good Friday 1941

Du weißt nicht, wer wahrhaft dein Freund ist ehe das Eis bricht.
(You won't know who is truly your friend until the ice breaks.)

PETER ARRIVED AT THE AMIENS CATHEDRAL an hour before he was to sing. He had eaten a light meal and drunk a glass of white wine, something Juliette never did before a performance. She believed wine dried out her vocal cords, but Peter was confident it didn't affect him. He felt physically and emotionally prepared.

When Peter entered the choirmaster's office, Monsieur Renaud sat behind an ornate Louis XVI desk.

"Peter, I'm so glad you came early." He stood up, walked around the desk, vigorously shook Peter's hand and put an arm on his shoulder. "I've been thinking about your idea for relaxing the voice, and I tried it myself, but I can't seem to get the hang of it."

"What type of exercise did you do?"

"I tried running on the spot and doing situps, but nothing seemed to make any difference. Perhaps I'm doing the wrong exercise—what is it that you do?"

Peter momentarily blushed, then resigned himself to telling the truth... sort of.

"Monsieur, do you mind talking about sex?"

Monsieur Renaud laughed without embarrassment. "Of course not...I am French, non?"

"To tell the truth, Juliette made me sing while we were having sex." He blushed, confirming his German heritage.

The conductor thought for a few seconds while looking straight ahead without focusing. "I'm trying to visualize that. Was she on top, or were you?"

Peter felt the blush increasing, so he directed his eyes to his feet and spoke to the floor, "She was on top."

"Ah! Oui, I can see how that would work," Monsieur Renaud was clearly having an erotic epiphany.

Renaud stood and walked around the desk, pinching his chin as he looked down. He then turned to face Peter, a huge grin on his face.

"Monsieur, I thank you very much for being so forthright—I shall try this for myself. My wife hates my voice, but I have at least one other option."

Peter had never sung better, and the performance in the cathedral went perfectly. The audience was initially undecided about whether to applaud in the church, but once a few brave souls began, it grew to a crescendo and lasted long enough for the participants to take a bow.

When the performers had shaken hands, kissed cheeks, and wished everyone who was going to the train station Bon Voyage, they gathered in groups to go to the party. Peter was staying in Amiens overnight, so he met Monsieur Renaud in his office to get his fee before going to his hotel room.

As Renaud handed him a white envelope, he said, "I will be calling you for more work if you want it, and when you return, I will let you know how it goes with my singing lessons. They laughed and talked about singing and playing Baroque music for a few minutes until Peter left for his hotel room to change out of the tuxedo.

When Peter exited the west wing door, an SS officer walked up the sidewalk to intercept him. Peter considered running but was relieved when he recognized Untersturmbannführer Alex Küster. Alex put out his hand when he reached Peter.

"Peter, I've never heard anything so beautiful; your Evangelist was divine!" He let Peter's hand go. "It's not late; would you have something to eat with me?" He spoke using the familiar "du" form.

Peter stumbled over his words, "Yes, of course, Alex, but there is a party for the local cast, and I must attend for at least a few minutes. You are welcome to come along."

"No," Alex laughed, "I'm afraid I would destroy the mood." He hesitated, then said, "If your train doesn't leave too early, could we have breakfast together?"

"Of course, Alex. My train leaves at noon, and I will be ready for breakfast at eight."

Alex reached for Peter's hand. "I will meet you in the hotel lobby at eight."

"It's the Hotel de Berny, a hundred metres up that street." Peter pointed at the entrance to the hotel.

"Yes, I know where you are staying."

Peter awoke tired and nervous. Alex Küster was SS—he wore a black SS uniform—but Peter still considered him a friend. What was Alex doing in Amiens? What did he want from Peter?

He washed, shaved, dressed in his travelling clothes, and arrived in the lobby a few minutes before eight. Alex waited for him in an oversized upholstered chair.

The restaurant was a ten-minute walk; the morning was cool but sunny, and they talked about Dachau and Peter's voyage on the MS St. Louis.

"How did you get into Belgium?" Alex asked as they walked.

"I married Juliette on the ship—I think you know we tied the knot before the ship left Hamburg. Her parents stood with us..." He turned to face Alex. "It was a fantastic day, and I'm quite sure you had something to do with that. I met others on the boat who had to leave Germany, but my story doesn't fit theirs."

"I am glad to have been able to help."

Neither spoke for several minutes, then Peter asked, "Should I ask how you knew? About Belgium? The tuxedo?"

"No, you must not ask questions. If you knew the answers, you could endanger those you love."

They walked the rest of the way to the restaurant in silence.

The restaurant was upscale, and the cheapest breakfast was more expensive than dinner in the Hotel de Berny. Alex saw Peter's concern as they stood outside the door, reading the menu. "Herr Hitler is buying your breakfast, Peter. I suggest that you eat well."

Without hesitation, Peter decided on a ham, egg and cheese crêpe with mixed fruit, coffee, and juice—the most expensive breakfast on the menu.

The crêpes arrived quickly, and Peter and Alex ate heartily.

Peter said, "Juliette and I have a daughter. We called her Nina Veronique."

Alex said, "Veronique is Juliette's mother's name. What did you use for the last name?" He grinned, knowing he had surprised Peter.

Peter gave the point to Alex but was not surprised that he knew Veronique's name. "We decided to keep Durand and add Schweitzer."

Alex asked, "And where was her father born?" with a wide smile.

Peter answered carefully, "He was born in Liège, as were her grandmother and grandfather Schweitzer."

Alex said thoughtfully, "Are the father's papers recognized by the Belgian government?"

Peter reached into his pocket, withdrew his official passport and handed it to his friend.

Alex examined it closely. "Yes, I can see that Peter Schweitzer is of Belgian birth. This document is genuine." He handed it back to Peter.

They finished their crêpes and sat back to enjoy the excellent coffee, a rare find in war-torn France.

Alex sipped his coffee, put the cup back on the saucer, and said, "Have you heard that the English are forming an underground army in France?"

"Yes, Alex, I have heard, but isn't that inevitable when another country's army occupies the country?"

"I suppose it is." Alex carefully put the cup down and looked straight at Peter. "I have a new job now; I am the director of the Amiens Prison, in partnership with the local French authorities. The Gestapo uses the prison to interrogate Résistance prisoners, but I have no part in that."

"I understand. Is this a promotion for you?"

"Yes, I am now Obersturmbannführer Küster."

"Then, congratulations, Alex." Peter drank the last swallow of his coffee.

"Peter, I have a question." Peter sat up straight. "How can a Jew sing an anti-Semitic work like the St. John Passion?"

Peter smiled and said, "I don't know any Jews who sing the St. John Passion... do you? But if you know one, why don't you ask him?"

Alex smiled and waved the waiter to the table. He wrote a series of numbers on a piece of paper and folded it.

"Thank you for having breakfast with me, Peter." He handed Peter the piece of folded paper. "This is my telephone number. If you return to Amiens, call, and we will do this again. Meanwhile, say hello to Juliette and Nina for me. And a special greeting to Jacques, your father-in-law."

Chapter Twenty-Three

February 1942

"...Wenn es dem internationalen Finanzjudentum in und außerhalb Europas gelingen sollte, die Völker noch einmal in einen Weltkrieg zu stürzen, dann wird das Ergebnis nicht die Bolschewisierung der Erde und damit der Sieg des Judentums sein, sondern die Vernichtung der jüdischen Rasse in Europa..."
Adolph Hitler, 30 January 1939 at the Reichstag.
(...If the international Jewish financiers in and outside Europe should succeed in plunging the nations once more into a world war, then the result will not be the Bolshevization of the earth, and thus the victory of Jewry, but the annihilation of the Jewish race in Europe...)

JULIETTE AND PETER HAD A STANDING INVITATION to Sunday dinner with Juliette's parents, and, following the meal, her father, a glass of brandy between his hands, leaned forward in his chair. "I have something I want to discuss with the family." He let his eyes wander from one to another, gauging their reaction.

"British Intelligence has asked us to accept a dangerous mission, and Juliette is the only possibility to get it done."

Veronique, watching Nina try to feed imaginary food to a porcelain doll, reluctantly turned her attention to Jacques.

"I will listen, but I can't agree to Juliette taking great risks now that Nina is in our lives."

Peter and Juliette said nothing, and Jacques went on.

"MI6 suspects, and the Résistance is certain, that the Nazis have set up a murder machine in Auschwitz to kill Jews, Gypsies, and others that Hitler designates as 'undesirable.' The Free Polish government in England has been warning the British about this, but the British and American governments demand proof. A sane person cannot believe that even Hitler could organize the systematic murder of thousands without the civilized world knowing. The physical task of killing that many people is beyond imagination, and to keep it secret seems impossible."

Jacques had Juliette's unwavering attention. She had decided in the Munich police station that whatever he asked her to do, she would do it as long as it hurt the Nazis.

He continued, "On the twentieth of January, Heydrich chaired a secret conference at Wannsee on the outskirts of Berlin. Hitler ordered Heydrich to find a 'final solution to the Jewish question,' which is a less than subtle way of asking his staff to find a way to exterminate an entire race of people. In the end, with the natural efficiency that Germans possess, the conference decided to build gas chambers to kill masses of them, away from prying German civilian eyes. And they would build crematoriums to dispose of the bodies."

"Why can't your sources simply reveal this plan and discredit Hitler?" Veronique was desperate to keep her daughter out of this mission.

"Because no one would believe it, and we would expose an entire network of people working against Hitler without gaining anything. His core supporters will sow enough doubt to negate what we reveal. Even in Britain and America, there are powerful Nazi supporters who twist the facts, repeating their lies until they bury the truth."

Jacques took his time preparing what he would say, but everyone waited until he went on. "We have a witness, a French Jewess who was in Auschwitz. We also have photographs and signed documents, but our witness and the documents are in Germany."

Peter began to speak and spilled his wine on the small table beside his chair—fortunately, it was white wine, and the glass was nearly empty. He spoke while sopping it up with his napkin before it fell on the expensive rug. "And is this the only witness we can find to put against the entire Nazi propaganda machine? Whether the witness speaks or doesn't, people won't believe this is happening without those photographs and documents, and that evidence should be enough without the witness!"

Jacques opened his mouth, but closed it when Peter held his hand up in a 'stop' sign gesture.

"Hitler has said that he will annihilate the Jewish Race in Europe—he said it in the Reichstag in '39 and again this year in his yearly diatribe at the Sportspalast. So why wouldn't people believe him if your sources supply the evidence, even without the witness?"

Peter had the same motive as Veronique, but Juliette had decided that her father was right, and she wanted the conversation over. She gave Peter a look that said, "Stop talking!"

Jacques shook his head, sympathetic to Peter and Veronique but knowing that Juliette had to do this, no matter the risk. Juliette's silence was her endorsement, but he still had to convince Peter and Veronique.

"The most persuasive argument against the possibility that this is true is an economic one. The cost of doing the physical deed would be tremendous, and the loss of skilled Jewish people would cost considerably more. They have done nothing to hurt the German economy—au contraire, they are an essential economic asset to the country. If Hitler successfully eliminated all the Jews and other undesirables from Europe, there would be no benefit, and the damage would be immense. The entire concept is unreasonable." Jacques put his brandy down on the small table next to his chair. "For that reason, it's difficult to convince anyone that it's already happening!"

Peter spoke again, calmer now. "From experience, I can say that nothing about Dachau is reasonable. "Arbeit Macht Frei" is not the objective... I saw the deliberate abuse of good and talented people without benefit to anyone. The workers received inadequate food and clothing; the guards beat them—sometimes to death, and production was a fraction of what it should have been. If you want good workers, you feed them; you don't starve and beat them. If the objective of Dachau is anything but punishment for no other reason than hate for people who are not members of the master race, I saw no evidence of it."

Peter paused for breath, and Jacques interrupted, "And then there's greed. Jews control or possess a large percentage of the wealth in Europe. Hitler is telling the German people that with the Jews gone, this wealth would transfer to them—he doesn't tell his Volk that Nazis are putting that wealth into their own pockets by shipping most of it out of the country. The profit to a very few Nazi individuals and businesses from the extermination of Jews in Europe will be enormous—I see this firsthand in the art and jewellery I handle for the Nazis who are taking a direct approach by eliminating the owners."

Jacques paused, and the room remained silent. He waited, but no one said a word.

"This is what we know. First, it is unlikely that the Nazis will use the concentration camps in Germany, such as Dachau, to systematically murder people. We know that they abuse, beat, and starve the inmates, as Peter has confirmed, and many of them die, thousands of them, but if you split the hair, the Nazis don't intentionally murder them. Second, we do know that the Nazis are building so-called labour camps in Poland. The publicized purpose of these camps is cheap labour for respected companies like IG Farben, Siemens AG, and Friedrich Krupp AG. This will ultimately only benefit German people who are not Jews. But, in the end, hidden from view, their purpose is the organized murder of Jews and other undesirables.

"Auschwitz, a camp near Krakow, was initially built as a labour camp for the Polish Jews and many other Jews from neighbouring countries. But secretly, in the past year, they have built gassing rooms where guards push the victims down an assembly line to a room filled with deadly gas. And we now know they are using Zyklon gas as the most efficient method of killing thousands…and it's a miserable way to die!"

Veronique gasped, and Peter shook his head as though he couldn't believe the gruesome news. Juliette thought of Monica and fought back her tears.

Jacques went mercilessly on. "There have been several escapes from Auschwitz. The escapees have reported such atrocities, but their reports are third-hand when we get them, and the Free Polish Army's motives in bringing these witnesses forward are suspect. The world needs an actual firsthand witness and, above all, irrefutable documentation. Hearsay from third parties doesn't help; documents alone won't convince the newspapers and politicians; Nazi supporters simply smother the quiet truth with loud lies."

Juliette took advantage of the pause. "And you have both your witness and documentation, and you want me to go to Germany and bring them here."

Jacques nodded. "Yes, precisely! The witness is a French Jewess. She escaped with another prisoner, and the Free Polish Army took her to the German border. The German underground will get her to a city we choose in Germany—it's our job to get her from there to England." Jacques sipped his brandy, then set the glass on the table beside his chair.

"A Free Polish Army officer has been in Auschwitz since 1940. He volunteered to go there as a prisoner and has sent several detailed reports of inhumane activities in the camp, but British Intelligence classifies the reports as exaggerations and illogical. In essence, British Intelligence is saying this: The Free Polish Army reports of atrocities must be exaggerated because no human being would do that to other human beings.

"The report that will travel with the escaped prisoner we will escort out of Germany contains pictures and depositions written by inmates shortly before their execution. This combination of the report and the eyewitness account will be undeniable proof and, if it reaches the world press, which the Nazis can't control, will turn German public opinion against Hitler's minions. Many German officers want to oust Hitler and negotiate peace, but they need the support of the people to stage a coup."

Juliette could see no alternative. "I have the best chance to succeed because I am in a unique position to do it, and I will." She turned to her mother. "Mama, I must do this. You know I am very good at acting and deceit, and I can use my singer status to get into and out of Germany. If Papa has papers for this woman, Marcel and I will find a way to get her back here."

Veronique looked at her daughter with a sense of resignation, and Juliette pressed her argument further. "Mama, the SA took a woman I met in Heilbronn to a work camp, even though she had young children, and we don't know where she is or whether she's still alive. They killed Peter's grandparents, raped me, beat my husband and threw him in Dachau prison. We all have a choice whether to hide our heads and pretend there is nothing we can do, or to fight with every tool we have… You and Papa have chosen to fight using money and influence, and you must allow Peter and me to do what we can using our talents!"

Veronique looked down at Nina, who was singing quietly to her doll. "Yes, I understand, and you know that I will always be here for Nina." She lifted her gaze back to Juliette. "I don't know whether I could live if I lost you and Nina."

Juliette touched her mother's hand. "Mama, I know the danger, and I will be as careful as I can, but we must succeed! Marcel will be with me, and Papa will always keep watch using his quiet power. Many people fight the Nazis with much less!"

Peter looked at Juliette, resignation and anguish in his eyes.

"Why hasn't someone killed Hitler?" he asked no one in particular.

Jacques said softly, "There have been many planned attempts— at least ten, probably many more. A group of German officers, the Schwarze Kapelle, is committed to killing or deposing Hitler, but he is a suspicious man with very effective security. He intentionally avoids routine, cancels appearances without notice, and turns up unexpectedly."

He sipped his brandy. "Those who want to kill him believe that if he dies, the army will revolt against the war, but that would mean German soldiers fighting against German soldiers, and there is no appetite for that.

"The Schwarze Kapelle is our source of information on the Wannsee conference—someone who was at the conference is a member. If, through this prisoner and those documents, we can prove that Hitler is committing mass murder against his people, and if the international press recognizes and publishes this truth, the Schwarze Kapelle could get the support of the army and the people it needs. At that point, Hitler's assassination will become either unnecessary or easier to accomplish."

He focused on Peter. "You are bitter because you must risk losing your wife and the mother of your daughter, but you take the same risk on your own life on every mission that Marcel gives you. If we fail, Veronique and I will lose our only daughter; if you fail, we will lose our son-in-law and Nina's father. All over Europe, parents lose their children, wives lose husbands, and husbands lose their families to battles and bombs. Men willingly fight in hopeless situations, knowing they will die. Women and children on both sides die in their homes, killed by bombs dropped from German and British planes. There is no justification for any war, but this war goes beyond conflict between nations; this is a battle for civilization itself! There is no alternative, no diplomatic solution—Hitler and his Nazi monsters must be stopped! Our tactic cannot be to let the body count rise on both sides until governments and people who support them can't stomach it anymore!"

Jacques was on his feet, his expression one of desperation. "We must succeed in this mission because it is our only hope to stop the war now, and the difference we can make is enormous compared to the sacrifice we might make. If we succeed, we will have done more to change the course of this war than battalions of soldiers, thousands of aircraft, or a fleet of ships!"

Juliette took Peter's hand and turned to Jacques.

"We will do whatever we can. If a God is hiding somewhere out there, perhaps he will help us end this insanity."

Jacques shook his head and smiled. "If there were a God who could interfere in our lives, the name Adolph Hitler would be unknown, and we would be talking about the weather or the possibility of another grandchild. I don't believe God has anything to do with this or any war!"

Veronique looked at her husband reproachfully. "I wouldn't assume that God has given up on us. Perhaps he is letting us fix the mess we have made. Humanity may be learning its ultimate lesson."

Jacques said, "While humanity is learning its lesson, I plan to shorten the time it takes, with or without God's help."

Jacques looked around the room. "Detmold is staging I Pagliacci, and, as usual, Cavalleria Rusticana is on the same program. The house soprano sings Santuzza in Cavalleria, so they need a Nedda for Pagliacci... and I volunteered Juliette's services."

"Interesting," said Juliette. "When do I go?"

"Orchestra rehearsals begin on Monday, and the première is a week from Saturday, February twenty-eighth, I think. I told the conductor..." Jacques stopped to search for the name, found it and said... "Herr Finke, yes, that's right... that you may have sung the role here in Belgium... but I wasn't sure whether that part was true."

Juliette laughed uneasily. "I've never heard the opera in my life—I don't even own the score. And I certainly have never considered singing

Nedda!" She stood, taking the last pastry from the plate. "Do you, by chance, have the score, or must I learn it without the music?" She enjoyed the pastry's sweetness.

"Marcel found a copy somewhere, and your accompanist is ready to start whenever you are."

Juliette tried hard not to smile. She pointed her finger at her father and said, "You assumed I would do this; you know damned well I've never sung that role, and I will bet anything that you've already signed the contract!"

"Guilty on all counts, except I thought that perhaps you had sung something from the opera—an aria, maybe a duet… You've sung so many arias and scenes that I thought you might at least know the major bits."

Juliette kissed her father on the forehead. "I will learn the role, and Peter can help me with the inevitable tenor-soprano moments."

She picked her daughter up from the floor, sat her on her hip and said, "Even a provincial theatre like Detmold wouldn't wait until ten days before the Première to hire a soprano." Nina stretched her arms to Veronique, but Juliette held her tight.

Jacques pulled his hand out of the cookie jar. "Uh…her mother in Bayern suddenly became ill, and she had to go home to care for her." He smiled, satisfied with his lie.

Juliette shook her head and, as she turned away, said, "Come, Peter, we've got work to do."

Marcel met her in the foyer and handed Juliette a piano score of Pagliacci before opening the door for her. She passed Nina to Peter, opened the score and checked for the German translation; it was there.

"Thank you, Marcel. You think of everything."

He returned her smile and opened the door, but his eyes were sad.

Chapter Twenty-Four

February 1942

Ein Freund in der Not ist ein Freund in der Tat.
(A friend in need is a friend in deed)

DETMOLD, IN 1942 a small northern German city of thirty thousand, is located twenty kilometres from Bielefeld where, two years earlier, Juliette had sung Mimi. During the Third Reich, Detmold was the beating heart of Nazi support, and, as Juliette stepped onto the platform, she tried to suppress her apprehension about performing there. Marcel, carrying her small suitcase, walked behind her as she left the first-class railcar behind.

Juliette's dark mood changed instantly, and she squealed with surprise when she saw Barbara Finke approaching her.

She cried out, "Barbara! I'm so glad to see you!" and threw her arms around her friend; Barbara returned the hug and held Juliette at arm's length.

Juliette asked, "Are you my chauffeur?"

Barbara nodded, "Johann's father asked me to pick you up. He's rehearsing the orchestra, and it's my job to get you to the hotel. He will see you tomorrow at nine. I'll pick you up at the hotel at eight-thirty."

"I'm singing for Johann's father?" Juliette was delighted, her unease now completely gone. She hadn't associated the names and couldn't think why she hadn't put it all together. But why hadn't Barbara written to her? And then, she knew the answer…the censors, and, of course, her father.

"Yes, I'm sorry I had to keep you in the dark, but your father has been planning this for a while, and he said.…"

"Yes, I know all about my father."

Barbara said, "I didn't dare tell you anything in a letter… the Nazis read everything, and I assumed your father would tell you when…"

"He doesn't tell me anything unless he can't think of a way to avoid it."

Barbara smiled. "Well, Theo is the theatre's music director. I told you he found a house for us when the Wehrmacht conscripted Johann, and we moved here to be close to him…" A cloud swept across Barbara's face.

Juliette took both of Barbara's hands. "I just can't imagine Johann in the Wehrmacht, and I was so sad when you told me about it in your letter. I sensed there was much more you wanted to say."

"Yes, but there is no point in crying about it now. Sometimes, I can't believe it, but Johann seems to have adjusted, and so have we. In fact, they promoted him; he is a company commander, and we believe he's in Ukraine… somewhere near Kharkiv. Everyone says the Russians will surrender soon."

"I'm so sorry, Barbara. I can't imagine Johann as a soldier. What a waste!"

"The war may be over everywhere soon, and I pray for that every day." Barbara smiled, and the cloud disappeared.

Marcel arrived with a cart loaded with suitcases, and Barbara led them to the exit where the car waited. They pulled up in front of the Detmolder Hof after a five-minute drive.

Barbara checked Juliette and Marcel into separate rooms, and Marcel took both keys.

Barbara told Juliette, "In the morning, I will wait for you in the lobby and, whenever you're ready, I'll walk you to the theatre. Theo wants to run through your role as soon as you get there. He's a wonderful musician and teacher, and I'm sure you two will get along well."

The following morning, Marcel and Juliette met Barbara in the lobby, and she walked them to the theatre. She took Juliette and Marcel to Theo's studio on the first floor and introduced her father-in-law, who sat at the piano, playing a Beethoven sonata.

A bearded man with sparkling eyes stood up, and Juliette instantly liked him. He sealed her impression when he bypassed Juliette's outstretched hand to hug her and kiss her cheek. She felt as though she had known him all her life.

He said, "Johann told me all about you when you sang in Bielefeld, and I want you to know that we will do everything we can to make this work for you."

Marcel didn't hesitate to interrupt. "Yes, and we do need help sooner than we anticipated. The young woman Jacques told you about will arrive this evening at six. She can't stay in the Bahnhof where curious people will ask questions."

Theo nodded slightly. "I was referring to the opera and Mademoiselle Durand's special requirements, but yes, Monsieur Durand did make arrangements with me and my wife Maria. My wife and I discussed it and concluded that when she arrives, the safest solution is to take her directly to our house, where she can stay until you are ready to return to Brussels."

Marcel spoke before Juliette could. "We thank you very much for your cooperation." He nodded and left the studio, heading for a telephone.

Theo asked to see Juliette's vocal score, flipped it open and compared it to the one he was using. He walked over to a shelf, pulled down a dog-eared pale green Peters edition and held it up.

"This is the one we'll use. The differences are slight, and you are free to sing the translation you've learned, but I would prefer you have a copy with bars numbered identically to mine and the stage director's; we will then have common reference points."

Juliette had the role memorized and only intended to use the score to mark the blocking, but she decided to leave things as the conductor wished.

She shrugged. "Okay, let's see how it goes."

Theo allowed Juliette to interpret her aria as she had learned it, and when she had finished singing it through, he shook his head and asked, "This provincial theatre is too small for you, mademoiselle! Never have I heard such a voice or such musicianship!"

Aware that the aria was not yet polished—Juliette thought it was barely acceptable for the first run-through— she waited for the "but...."

Theo turned on the piano bench so that he faced Juliette. "You are far too good for this theatre." He closed the cover over the keys and rested his elbow on it. "Your father told me something about your mission, but if I am going to be a part of this, I want to know more about this Jewish French woman."

"Did you talk to your son about our little adventure in Bielefeld?"

"Yes, I did, and he told me that you are a courageous young woman, among other things. I understand your saving the Jewish woman and her husband, but what is a French woman doing here?"

Juliette decided that since her father and Marcel trusted Theo to care for Yvonne, she could tell him a little more.

"That Jewish woman is my sister-in-law, so yes, that is understandable." Juliette sat on a chair at the end of the piano bench.

"Theo, you must realize that more information increases the danger to you and your family, and you don't need to know more than you do...."

Theo spread his hands in an expression that said, Oh, what the hell, then said, "We are aware that we are already in so deep that the Nazis will probably kill us if they catch us...or you."

Juliette hesitated, decided he was right, and that she would have to tell him everything she knew.

"Yvonne is a French Jewess who escaped from Auschwitz, and I'm taking her to Belgium with me. From there, she will go to England and appear as a witness of Nazi crimes in Auschwitz."

"Auschwitz? Your father didn't mention that name."

"Auschwitz is a work camp in Poland, about fifty kilometres west of Krakow, but It's different from the work camps in Germany. In German slave labour camps like Dachau, murdering inmates is more random than in an assembly-line system like Auschwitz. The purpose of Auschwitz is to eliminate Jews, Romani and other 'undesirables' from Europe—running a work camp is secondary and could be a smokescreen. This woman has evidence that the camp murders thousands of people each and every day—forced labour is secondary—necessary for income and providing cover for the Nazi extermination policy."

Juliette waited for Theo to digest what she had said, and when he said nothing, she continued.

"Yvonne and another inmate escaped by hiding in a woodpile, then climbing over an electric fence. The Free Polish Army set up the escape; someone inside turned off the electricity, and Polish partisans waited for them in the woods.

"The Free Polish Army hid Yvonne for a few weeks, then smuggled her to the German border, and anti-Nazi Germans have been hiding her in Magdeburg since then. She now has papers showing her to be a Wallonian Belgian from Brussels, and she will be accompanied by a German woman who lost her husband in Dachau. Yvonne will carry documents proving the purpose of Auschwitz, and our mission objective is to get both the woman and the documents to England via Brussels."

Theo's head dropped as he listened, and when he raised it, the part not covered by his beard was the colour of chalk. His voice cracked, he swallowed and whispered, "My country... murdering thousands..."

Juliette said quietly, "Yes, but no one knows about it. Many suspect something is going on, but no one has seen conclusive proof until now. The British, including Churchill, don't believe Hitler is exterminating Jews or anyone else. They demand proof, and that is what Yvonne will produce."

Theo said, his colour returning, "Thank you for trusting me. We will protect Yvonne until you get her out of Detmold—it doesn't matter how long it takes. Nothing else but your mission matters now."

Maestro Finke gathered himself, elbows on his legs and his head hanging down. Juliette waited, and what seemed like a long time later, he turned to the piano. As he played the lines before the aria, he said, "Why don't we see what you can do with this scene? Perhaps you can show me how you would like to interpret it."

Juliette smiled. "I've been singing in Germany for five years, and no conductor has ever asked what I wanted to do with the music."

"I want you to make the music—I will use my humble skill to assist you." He looked at her while he played a few improvised chords, and Juliette immediately began to get a different feel for the aria.

Theo added, "If you don't mind, perhaps I will make a suggestion or two."

Juliette began singing, stopping to repeat phrases, incorporating Theo's subtle suggestions. When they finished working on the musical phrasing, she sang the aria uninterrupted, recognizing that this provincial Kuhdorf conductor, while giving her almost total freedom, had guided her to the best performance of anything she had ever sung.

He stood up and said, "No need to waste more time on that now… we'll touch it up later." Juliette laughed giddily, genuinely excited, and Theo said, "I'll go find our Silvio; we'll work on the duet."

He returned with a short, fat baritone and introduced him as Gil Léger. Gil smiled broadly, took Juliette's hand and kissed it. He stayed down a little too long, and Juliette said in French, "Enough, Romeo. Let's sing."

"Of course, we will sing… but afterward?" He wiggled his eyebrows up and down.

She laughed and touched his chin with the end of her finger. "My husband would not approve; he is big, strong, and as mean as a rat."

Gil pointed in the direction of the door. "Is he the big guy out there?"

"Yes," she lied, "and don't let the kind face fool you… That man is a professional killer!"

The baritone spread his hands and, with an expression of disappointment, said, "Alas, my wife would kill me if he didn't!"

Waiting for them at the piano, Theo said, "I don't know what that was all about, but it sounded like you two will get along fine."

From the first note, Juliette liked singing with Gil. He teased her as Silvio would and then became seriously romantic in his role, adjusting perfectly to her. Their first time through the love duet felt flawless, but Theo worked them through it twice more, improving small things that, in the end, united them musically in a way Juliette had not thought possible. When they finished, Theo suggested lunch in the Menza, where the Bratwurst und Sauerkraut was delicious and cheap.

The tenor—shaped like a can of tuna, with almost no neck and a shy smile—waited for them in the studio when they returned.

Horst did not, in fact, sing in the art of Bel Canto; in its stead, bellowing like a water buffalo in pain. But Theo nursed Canio out of him. Canio, Horst's character, was crude, a hot-blooded Italian minstrel clown. Nedda, Juliette's character, was Canio's unfaithful wife and Silvio, a lustful villager, was her lover. At the end of the love scene between Nedda and Silvio, a bellowing Canio interrupted their lovemaking, swearing to kill Sylvio. Canio chased the terrified lover over a fake stone wall, and both men disappeared off the stage, their laughter echoing in the high space around the set. Juliette and Theo laughed and, when Canio and Silvio didn't return, decided to take an Ersatzkaffee break.

Juliette insisted on paying for the 'coffee' and Kuchen, and they chatted like children, laughing and taunting one another. The break should have been fifteen minutes, but Theo allowed comradeship to extend it to a half-hour before convincing them to return to the rehearsal room, ready for the intricate and dramatic final scene.

Horst was no chamber singer, but he was a perfect Canio. He screamed a painful 'A' and an extremely painful not-quite 'B-flat,' threatened to kill his unfaithful wife and her lover, and the angry bellow became appropriate. In this case, drama was more critical than musicality, and drama suited Horst perfectly. His Canio was sympathetically pathetic despite the character's ignorant and violent nature. Horst left Juliette no choice; she had to play Nedda as a cheating, lying, and generally rotten wife. Silvio had to be a lecherous, disgusting, slimy character, forcing Gil to turn his interpretation around during the rehearsal. The love scene became a lustful parody, and Theo smiled his approval at the change he and Horst had wrought.

Horst invited them to his apartment later in the evening for "schnapps and fun!"

Juliette and Marcel met the train at 18:00h, and Yvonne and her escort arrived according to plan. Barbara, whose official job was to monitor passengers' movements, recorded their arrival, adjusting her record to suit Marcel's purposes.

Juliette welcomed them to Detmold, and Marcel drove everyone to Gartenstrasse 18 in Theo's old car. Theo's wife, Maria, led them into the living room, and everyone sat around an oak coffee table. Yvonne's chaperone, a large, muscular woman, hair pulled back tight into a tight bun, spoke first.

"My name is Gudrun, and I'm from Düsseldorf." She began as though she were reading from a book. "My husband died in Dachau—the Arschlöcher beat him to death, but the government says he died of fever. His mother is Jewish, and the SA took his mother and father away on Kristallnacht. I haven't seen or heard from them since that night, and the Nazis came for my Josef the next morning." She pointed to Yvonne. "This woman will force those Scheissköpfe to admit to their crimes, and the German people will rise and kill the Verdammte Verbrecher who run our country. She slammed her meaty fist on the coffee table, rattling the teacups resting on it. "I have made a list!" She banged the table emphatically. "They will pay with blood!"

Theo stood up and cleared his throat. "Can I get everyone some tea? I have a performance and can't stay, but I could fetch the tea before I go."

He headed toward the kitchen before anyone could answer, but Gudrun intercepted him.

"I don't need tea—I must go back to the station now. My sister lives in Bielefeld, and the train leaves in an hour. I will drive with you immediately so I don't need to walk later."

Gudrun pushed past Theo and yanked the big oak door open. Luckily, it wasn't locked; otherwise, Gudrun might have pulled it off its hinges.

Theo shrugged, kissed Maria goodbye, and followed Gudrun, running to catch her before she tried to open the car's locked door.

Juliette and Marcel stayed until the tea was gone, and Yvonne had fallen asleep in her chair. Juliette offered to help Maria put Yvonne in bed, but Maria herded them to the door and said goodnight.

The sidewalk on Langestrasse was narrow, and Juliette slid her arm inside Marcel's, snuggling close so they could walk comfortably side-by-side.

Juliette asked, "Do you trust Gudrun not to reveal anything? She seems so bitter and rash."

"Yes, I trust her; she is ignorant, aggressive, and impetuous, but the woman has been smuggling people for us since her husband died. That woman is clever, or she wouldn't still be alive."

"Where are the documents?"

"I'm not going to tell you anything about the documents. They will arrive in Brussels when we do, but you will not have anything to do with them."

"You don't trust me?"

"If you don't know where the documents are, you won't reveal the hiding place. For your information, Yvonne doesn't know where the papers are either. You must trust me."

Juliette stopped and pulled Marcel's arm around so that she faced him.

"Marcel, you know I trust you with more than my life." She looked deep into his eyes; he nodded, and she took his hand. They walked silently into the Detmolder Hof.

Chapter Twenty-Five

14–28 February

Es gehen viele Freunde in ein kleines Haus.
(Many friends will fit into a small house)

Juliette and Marcel met Theo at the main door to Horst's apartment building across the street from Gartenstrasse 18 at precisely nine o'clock, and together, they began to climb three flights of narrow stairs.

Juliette said to Theo as they climbed, "You seem to know Horst quite well—more than the connection between singer and conductor."

"We've been friends since the beginning of the war when the Wehrmacht imprisoned Horst during the invasion of Poland. He was a soldier for less than a month when his entire company surrendered without firing a shot. He was at a prisoners' compound when a German officer heard him singing—Horst knew all the traditional German drinking songs—and the officer requisitioned him to sing for his men. It only took a few weeks for Horst to become a hit throughout the German front. Word of his talent spread, and the Bundeswehr sent him to Germany."

They stopped at the second landing to catch their breath, and Theo continued. "I found him singing in the Kaserne at the Flughaven Detmold base here. I auditioned Horst—a short affair since no other tenors were available—and the Wehrmacht released him to the theatre. I took personal responsibility for him because, although his heritage is German, he is technically still a prisoner of war."

Theo pointed up the stairs. "We found an attic apartment, and I gave him an old piano we had in our cellar. It took Horst and four stagehands half a day to drag it up there."

"So…" said Theo as he slowly began climbing the last row of stairs… "This is a housewarming party. Neighbours and friends at the theatre donated furniture, helped with painting and decorating, and now they are contributing fuel—Dienst ist Dienst und Schnapps ist Schnapps." He stopped outside the door and held up the bottle. "Kangaroo schnapps, the creation of a white-haired Russian chorus singer."

Theo opened the door, and a large white dog with a few black spots greeted him. He rubbed the dog's ears while Juliette slid past, working her way through a gauntlet of well-wishers to a soft chair.

Everyone asked where Theo had left Maria, and he told them she wasn't feeling well.

The food appeared, and when everyone had filled a small plate, Theo sat at the piano and surprised Juliette by asking her what she wanted to sing.

She had her mouth full, and her answer came with breadcrumbs. "I haven't prepared anything," she swallowed a bite of asparagus rolled in bread. "What music do you have?"

"I have whatever you want to sing... How about Nedda?"

Juliette stood up, wishing she could avoid this impromptu singing she assumed was expected when this gang had a party. She had no idea what would happen when she opened her mouth, so she hedged her bet. "All right, but I don't have it to performance standard yet." She realized she had just made an amateur booboo by laying out an excuse before she sang.

Theo smiled without sympathy, modulated through a few related chords, circling the fifths until he reached the proper key, and then nodded to Juliette. The room became silent; the dog sat in front of her and stared into her eyes. As she sang, he didn't move his eyes off Juliette's, occasionally whining as though attempting to sing. When she finished, the room exploded with applause, some of it for the dog.

Everyone sang something or played an instrument, and eventually, it was Horst's turn. He chose Siegmund's first sword aria from Wagner's Die Walküre, a noisy affair, and Theo again played from memory, as he had all night. Horst had been enjoying kangaroo schnapps and was feeling no pain.

When Siegmund's loud plea for the sword his father had promised in his hour of need filled the room, the dog looked for cover. At first, he crouched as low on the floor as he could, then struggled to push his head under the sofa, gave up, and tried to wiggle himself under an oversized stuffed chair occupied by the opera house's dramatic soprano. She had no place in her life for pets and shooed him away by digging her stiletto heels into his back. Finally, in desperation, Bruno, the dog, sat in the centre of the room beside Horst, put his head back and joined him.

When Horst finished singing, he made Bruno lie between Juliette and Marcel as he began the second sword aria, the Nothung aria that ended the first act. Marcel successfully held the dog down for the first minute, but the dog escaped when Horst cried out for the promised sword to release itself from the tree his father had thrust it into. He scrambled over to Horst, looked around the room, stuck his nose in the air, and howled on Horst's note. The dog wailed, Horst held his arms as though he were pulling the sword out of the tree, and everyone laughed. Horst succeeded in extricating Nothung from the oak tree and ended the aria with the imaginary sword in his hands. Between gales of laughter, everyone agreed that the dog should learn all of Horst's roles and sing on the Detmold stage.

Now, with his voice warmed up and the schnapps in full effect, Horst began the Winterstürme aria, also from Die Walküre, his next role in Detmold. Wagner's atypical lyrical outburst of song announcing the arrival of spring triggered the dog to begin waving his head back and forth as he howled, mimicking Horst's habit when he sang anything approaching romantic. Horst, laughing so hard he had to sit down, stopped singing. The heartbroken dog sat in the centre of the room, looking woefully at his master, waiting for him to resume.

Juliette listened to the laughter, looked at the unhappy dog, then, unable to control her mind, looked at the floor to hide her tears as the image painted by Yvonne of the world in Auschwitz and the certainty that her story was one of many, suddenly seized her. Where was Monica? Would her children ever see their mother again, or was she already dead, deliberately murdered in a gas-filled room? She controlled a sob; Marcel's hand touched hers and held it for a brief moment.

The audience knew and expected the heartrending ending of I Pagliacci. They gasped in shock when Horst, on his way to kill his treacherous wife, Nedda, clumsily kicked a rubber chicken left on the stage by another character, clobbering the first flute and eliciting a squeak out of the instrument. A few impolite individuals tittered, but the majority gasped on cue when Juliette met her violent end at the hands of her brutal husband. The curtain closed while beautiful Nedda lay bleeding on the stage, her abusive husband crying pitifully over her body. No one made a sound as Horst sobbed, his shoulders shaking, tears streaking his makeup. The curtain swept together, but Horst stayed on his knees until Gil helped him to the wings, where he breathed deeply, trying to recover.

The silent audience waited; a tiny ripple of applause began, grew slowly at first, then exponentially, until they stood, one by one, shouting and clapping. Juliette and Gil pushed Horst out onto the stage. He bowed, then returned to the wings and headed for his dressing room. Juliette caught his arm and tried to turn him back to the front of the curtain, but he yanked his arm away and ran from her.

Gil caught Juliette and turned her back to the stage when she attempted to follow him.

"Leave him alone. He got some bad news about his wife just before the performance."

Juliette had a dozen questions, but there was no time to ask them—she and Gil had to take their bows.

The crowd would not stop, and when Theo came out for the conductor's traditional bow, the applause and shouts intensified to a crescendo Juliette had never before experienced. Finally, the cast stopped taking bows, and the audience slowly filed out.

Juliette said as she walked with Gil to their dressing rooms, "I didn't know Horst had a wife. Where is she? What happened to her?" They stopped in front of Gil's dressing room.

"She and her mother were in the Krakow Jewish ghetto. Horst has been getting a letter from her every week since the ghetto was set up, but he hasn't heard anything for a month. Today, he got a letter from his father. A month ago, the SS put his wife and her mother on a train, and he is afraid they are in a concentration camp."

"She's Jewish?" Juliette was afraid of the answer.

"His wife's mother is Jewish, but her father is Christian. Her father disappeared when the Germans invaded."

"How far is it from Krakow to Auschwitz?"

Gil shrugged his shoulders. "Not far...about forty or fifty kilometres, I think... Why do you ask?"

Juliette's heart sank. She said, "There's a camp in Auschwitz, a terrible place... God help her if they sent her there!"

She went to her dressing room to find a distressed Marcel waiting outside the door.

Chapter Twenty-Six

28 February 1942

Dem Teufel wehrt man mit dem Kreuz, den Leuten mit Fäusten.
(One defeats the devil with the cross, people with fists)

MARCEL SAID, "YVONNE IS TERRIFIED the Gestapo will find her and send her back to Auschwitz—She's threatening to kill herself—I need you to talk to her!" He opened the door to Juliette's dressing room and stepped back. She passed him; he closed the door behind her. Juliette opened it, beckoned him to come in and said, "I won't bite… we can talk while I get ready." She sat at her dressing table and began wiping off her thick makeup. "I don't sing again until Thursday, and the train ride is only six hours, including the stop at the border. Why don't we leave in the morning?"

Marcel nodded in her mirror. "That might be a good idea. We would be home tomorrow evening, and she could be on her way to England on Monday."

Juliette pulled her white stockings down over her ankles.

Marcel started for the door, but Juliette grabbed his arm. He said, "I should leave. We can talk later."

"I'll only be a few minutes, and I want you to tell me your plans for the trip. If you're embarrassed, you can turn around."

He turned away from her, looked at the door, and said, "I think we should go to the house before we go to the première party at the Lippische Hof. We must talk to Yvonne as soon as possible and tell her we will leave tomorrow; that will calm her down. Your father has suggested that Yvonne travel as your assistant, and I agree. We have documents showing her to be a former member of the Paris Opera staff—she is a very talented souffleuse. You hired her to teach you your roles—she would then be your private coach."

Juliette's costume rustled when she put it on the back of a chair, and she was picking up her bra when Marcel turned around to speak. His jaw dropped halfway to the floor; his mouth opened and closed like a guppy…Juliette was dressed in nothing but her panties, her bra dangling from her hand.

Juliette thought it best not to laugh but couldn't hold back a giggle. It didn't occur to her to cover herself with the costume. Fascinated with Marcel's reaction, she held her pose until Marcel finally connected sound with mouth movements.

"Oh God, Juliette, I'm sorry…I thought I heard you put on your dress." Although he stopped talking, Marcel's jaw remained open.

Juliette said, "Close your mouth and help me fasten my bra." She slipped it over her shoulders and turned around, chuckling. "Am I the first naked woman you've seen?"

Marcel reached out to hook Juliette's bra together. His hands shook so hard he couldn't line the hook with the eye.

"What's the matter, Marcel?" Juliette laughed, knowing she was increasing his suffering. She wanted to wordplay with 'mate' and 'hole' so much that she had the words on her tongue, but wisely bit it off and remained silent.

Marcel said frantically, "I have to leave!" and was gone, leaving the door partly open. A second later, he slammed it shut.

When Juliette came out of her dressing room, smiling, she said, "I'm sorry, Marcel, I shouldn't have teased you. Please forgive me." They locked eyes on one another, knowing most of that wasn't true, and Marcel didn't return her smile… Juliette walked behind him as they walked down the hall.

Theo intercepted them on their way to the stage door.

Juliette told Theo, "We will talk to Yvonne before going to the party. We've decided to leave early in the morning."

Theo opened the door, let Juliette and Marcel walk ahead, and caught them at the sidewalk.

"That might be a good idea. Maria called me; she's been trying to calm Yvonne down, but each day the poor girl becomes more frightened. I fear what happened to her in Auschwitz is more than we've been told." His tone softened. "Yvonne made Maria promise to kill her if the Gestapo comes to the house." He looked at the ground. "To calm her down, Maria told Yvonne she would."

As the trio hurried along Langestrasse past city hall, Theo worried that if they went to Brussels the following day, Juliette would not return for the last three performances. Marcel was still assuring him they would return when they climbed the stone steps to Gartenstrasse 18, and a hysterical Maria opened the door.

"Yvonne is in the cellar. She has a knife, and I'm afraid she will try to kill herself!"

They found Yvonne in the coal room, cowering in a corner, covered with soot and holding a long knife Maria used to slice bread. Marcel pulled Juliette back. "I'll talk to her; she can't hurt me."

Yvonne thrust the knife at him, narrowly missing his outstretched hand. Her mouth open, Yvonne's alert eyes flicked around the room as she tried to speak, but the sounds she made were meaningless. Marcel's anxious expression didn't change when he added a tiny smile.

"No one here will hurt you, Yvonne. We're here to help you." She stared back through lifeless eyes, half-heartedly thrusting the knife while Marcel easily dodged it.

Juliette put her hand on his shoulder. "You are a man and perhaps therefore dangerous to her. Perhaps you and Theo should leave the room and let Maria and me talk to her."

Marcel reluctantly backed away, keeping his eyes on Yvonne. "I can't let you do that, Juliette—your father would kill me if anything happened to you!" His eyes told Juliette her father probably wouldn't have to—Marcel might kill himself."

Juliette spoke quietly. "Believe me, Marcel, nothing will happen to me. Yvonne doesn't want to hurt Maria or me; she just needs to talk to us privately… isn't that right, Yvonne?" Juliette looked at her, and Yvonne nodded.

Juliette pushed Marcel toward the door, and Theo followed him through it.

Juliette asked Yvonne, "Is it all right if they wait outside the door? I will shut it if you like."

Yvonne nodded, then changed her mind and shook her head. "It's okay if they stay outside the door, and you can leave it open."

Yvonne slid down the wall and sat on the floor in the coal dust, dangling the knife from her fingers. Juliette stepped slowly ahead to stand beside her, then crouched and reached for the hand holding the knife; Yvonne put it on the floor and gave Juliette her hand.

"They did terrible things to you, didn't they?"

Yvonne began to cry. "Yes, and now I can't have children!" She put her head on Juliette's shoulder.

Maria bent down until her head was parallel to Yvonne's. "I will make some nerve tea if you like."

Yvonne stopped sobbing and inhaled loudly.

"Okay, perhaps that will help." She looked at Juliette, then Maria. "You are both getting so dirty here." Yvonne picked up the knife, handed it to Maria, and struggled to her feet with Juliette's help. She was unsteady as they moved toward the door. Maria shooed Theo and Marcel away, suggesting they go to the première party, then led Juliette and Yvonne up the stone stairs into the kitchen.

Maria took Yvonne to what had been her son Johann's bedroom and removed her coal-dust-covered dress. Juliette exclaimed without thinking, "Yvonne! Didn't they give you anything to eat?" as she sucked in her breath. Yvonne answered the question in front of the sink built into a corner of the bedroom.

"Most of the time, all we had was a bowl of potato soup and some-times a small piece of bread." She looked down at her navel. "I look awful, don't I?"

Juliette found it hard to look at the young woman's emaciated body. Yvonne looked like a seventy-year-old skeleton, and it took all Juliette's will to keep her gaze steady and a smile on her face.

Maria said, "No, you don't look awful, but you need to eat good food for a while, and I will take care of that!"

Juliette touched the number tattooed on Yvonne's arm.

As Maria tried to dress her, Yvonne said, "They burned that on me when I arrived at the camp. It hurt a lot!" She sat on the wooden chair, "They tried to glue me shut."

Juliette began stroking Yvonne's brown hair, cooing softly. She couldn't restrain her tears, and she couldn't talk.

"They tested the glue by letting the guards rape me to see if it would break. When it broke, they tried again with a different one… they tested dozens of glues, but they kept breaking!" She fiddled nervously with her fingers.

"I bled a lot, and then one day, they said I was no good to them anymore and sent me to the gas room with some other women. They called it the shower room, but we could hear people screaming half an hour after they entered the building, and we never saw them again. Lots of prisoners saw Sonderkommandos wearing gas masks go in and come out with the dead people."

"Sonderkommandos?" asked Maria.

"Yes, they're the prisoners who work for the SS guards."

Juliette couldn't believe prisoners would help the SS, but Yvonne explained, "The guards pick them out and torture them if they don't do it. The Sonderkommandos get extra rations and a better place to sleep, but every month, they shoot some of them, or, if there's room, they kill them with the gas, and new ones take their place." She paused, took a deep breath, and went on.

"As soon as we went into the rooms before the gas room, SS women guards made us remove our clothes; they still pretended we were going to have a shower, and some women believed it. Many of them began to cry when they saw there wasn't any soap or even soap dishes.

"But someone had counted wrong; there were too many women, so they told a few of us to put our clothes on, and the guards took us back to the grass area at the entrance and told us we would have to wait for the morning group."

She looked at Juliette and Maria, and Juliette thought she was done, but Yvonne wrung her hands and continued.

"I still wasn't positive that the showers were really gas rooms, but when, about an hour later, the Sonderkommandos carried the bodies out, put them on carts, and wheeled them away, I recognized a few as having undressed with me. We all knew they would dump the bodies in a ditch and pour Benzin on them so they would burn—that happened every night." Yvonne looked out the window. "The smoke was very thick and black, and when the wind blew it through the camp, the air smelled horrible. We all knew what the smell was!"

Maria and Juliette waited, and when Yvonne began again, her gaze fixed on a point somewhere outside, her voice quivered like an old woman's.

"The guards left two Sonderkommandos with us, and after dark, one of them hid me in a woodpile until late in the night. I think the other one turned off the electricity for a few minutes so the Sonderkommando and I could climb over the fence. Two men from the Free Polish Army found us, and we ran through the woods until morning, then rested where the trees were so close together that almost no sunlight came through the branches. The man who escaped with me joined the Free Polish Army, and a farmer hid me in his barn.

The next night, a woman led me through the woods, and a week later, we reached the German border. We slept in cellars and barns during the day and walked all night. When we got to the river at what used to be the German border, a Polish woman gave me an envelope full of papers, and a man took me across in a little boat. Gudrun met me, and we walked through the woods for three nights to another farm. I stayed in a cold cellar for a few weeks, and then Gudrun brought me here on the train."

Juliette continued stroking Yvonne's hair while Maria poured cups of herbal tea.

"Thank you, Maria." Yvonne took the cup in both hands and told Juliette, "You must promise you will kill me if they find me—I can't return to the camp."

Yvonne said it so naturally that Juliette lowered her head before she said, "I'll ask Marcel if he will talk to you about that."

It was almost midnight when Marcel and Theo returned from the party, and Juliette and Maria came from Yvonne's room to greet them. The quiet talk quickly turned to Yvonne's physical and mental health.

Marcel listened to the story, took a sip of the bean coffee Maria had found somewhere, and said, "We must postpone everything until she is physically and mentally ready. If she were to break down at the border, we would all be killed, or more likely, something much worse."

Juliette said, "She isn't just thin; no combination of clothes or makeup can hide the fact she's been starved, and it will take time to fix that!"

Maria said, "I will prepare Yvonne for the journey as quickly as possible, but you can't go until Yvonne is ready. And, for the next few nights, either Juliette or I must sleep on the floor next to her bed; Yvonne can't be alone for even a few minutes."

The following morning, when Yvonne got out of bed and said she was going to the bathroom, Juliette yawned, stretched, and washed in the sink. When Yvonne returned, Juliette found the hairbrush, asked her to sit down, and began stroking the woman's brittle hair. She said as she brushed, "We want you to eat as much as possible—we must get some flesh on your bones before we leave Germany."

"We aren't going today?" Yvonne's face warped as though she would cry.

Juliette spoke as gently as she could, unsure what Yvonne would do.

"When Marcel returned last night, we discussed going but decided to wait a few weeks because you are too weak, and, more dangerous, you look like you've been in a prison camp. You must eat and gain weight before you can leave Detmold. Don't worry; you will be safe here for as long as you need to stay."

Juliette was surprised when Yvonne smiled and asked, "Are you going to stay here with me?"

A relieved Maria hugged Yvonne, and Juliette said, "Yes, one of us will always be with you; until you are ready, you will never be alone."

Juliette went into the kitchen and found Theo setting the table for breakfast. The knocker thumped, and he opened the door for Marcel. When they entered the kitchen, Marcel put a bag of warm Brötchen on the table, and Juliette dumped them into a basket. Marcel tore one in half, spread strawberry jam on the piece he kept, and leaned on the doorjamb as he said to Juliette, "I assume you had a rough night—no sleep?" Juliette shook her head.

Juliette used a large spoon to remove half a dozen boiled eggs from the hot water and put them in a bowl. Maria came into the kitchen and said to them, "In a few minutes, I'm going to bring Yvonne out for breakfast, and I want all of you to wait for us." Marcel's mouth was full of Brötchen and jam, and he grinned stupidly as Maria gave him a stern look before she went to get Yvonne.

Juliette said, "Yvonne is in a better place this morning." She nodded toward the table, "Why don't you pour the juice and coffee?" She set the bowl of eggs in the middle of the table beside the basket of buns.

Marcel stuffed the rest of the Brötchen in his mouth, took a pitcher of apple juice from the counter and filled the glasses. Juliette brushed his arm, and he spilled some apple juice but wisely kept his mouth shut as he wiped it up with his sleeve.

Maria entered the kitchen through the living room door behind a colourful Yvonne. Maria's clothes hung loosely on Yvonne's almost bare bones, but she looked cheerful. Yvonne's red dress had white cuffs on the sleeves, hiding her tiny wrists. A silver clasp held her hair in a bun, and if one could get past Yvonne's sunken cheeks, she was charming.

Yvonne looked at the table, and Theo motioned her to the place at the end. "Mademoiselle, breakfast is served!" His French was terrible, and Yvonne smiled as he pulled her chair back from the table.

"Merci beaucoup, monsieur." She sat down as he slid the chair under her.

The communal breakfast broke the ice where Yvonne was concerned, and everyone laughed with her as she corrected Theo's terrible French. Maria had evidently paid better attention in school than Theo had; her French was decent enough to keep up her end of a conversation. Maria apologized for her terrible grammar, but Yvonne assured her that no one she knew used proper French grammar.

Yvonne ate a second bun, covered with as much apple jelly as would stay on it, and an egg chopped into tiny pieces and coated with butter. She drank a glass of juice and a cup of Theo's strong ersatz coffee laced with five teaspoons of sugar and enough cream to leave only a tinge of the original brown. Juliette liked her coffee with about the same ratios, and Yvonne laughed as they matched teaspoons of sugar, spoon for spoon, while Maria cringed. The beet sugar in the bowl was the last she would have before the government issued her new ration cards.

Chapter Twenty-Seven

22 March 1942

"Women defend themselves by attacking, just as they attack by sudden and strange surrenders."
Oscar Wilde, The Picture of Dorian Gray

JULIETTE SANG THE FINAL PERFORMANCE of I Pagliacci on March 21, and the Lippische Hof hosted another party. She sang too much, drank too much, and laughed too much, and when the party ended, Juliette reluctantly put on her beautiful ermine coat and met Marcel in the lobby. She took his hand as they left the hotel.

"I'm still worried about the trip." She let Marcel steer her across Hornschestrasse. "Yvonne frightens me... There is something incredibly sad and unsettling about her."

Juliette squeezed his hand. "Have you spoken to her about the possibility of being captured?"

Marcel waited before he replied. "Yes, and she made me swear I would kill her."

Juliette pushed against Marcel, then pulled on his arm. "Can you do that?"

"I have a pistol in my pocket, and I will kill everyone before I will let the SS capture us."

"Could you shoot me?" Juliette said the words softly.

"Yes"—he didn't hesitate— "and then I would shoot myself!"

The following day, Theo, Maria, and Barbara came to the station to see them off, and Theo presented Juliette with the score of I Pagliacci he had confiscated the first day they had met. It was bound in expensive leather; Juliette Durand was embossed in gold-leaf lettering on the top left corner, and "Detmold Theatre, 1942" was embossed on the bottom right.

"I will always treasure this, Theo." She hugged him and kissed his cheek.

Yvonne hugged Maria tightly, and when she let her go, Maria stepped back to admire her work. Yvonne was thin but not starved, and she carried herself well, with a face so beautiful there was not a hint of Auschwitz left on it. Yvonne said, "Auf wiedersehen," with a pleasant French accent, and then, "Danke schön," with so much energy she very nearly shouted it.

There were no first-class cars on the train, but they found a second-class compartment they could have to themselves. Marcel put the luggage in the overhead racks and sat opposite Yvonne and Juliette wearing his suit coat—his little Beretta 418 tucked into the inside pocket.

They changed trains at Herford, then to Essen, where they would change again for Brussels. As they travelled through the heart of the Ruhr, Juliette saw clear signs of Allied bombing, but roads, bridges, and the railway all appeared intact. She was still wondering why when she fell asleep.

It was midnight when they arrived in Essen, and it would be thirty minutes before the train left for Brussels. Juliette led Yvonne to a bench while Marcel went to a vendor to buy coffee.

The air raid siren began to wail before Marcel returned, and Juliette became anxious until she saw him running toward her without the coffee. Everyone else ran away from the platform on their way to shelters.

Marcel gasped, trying to breathe, "You should both go to the shelter..." Marcel gasped again... "I will stay here to watch the luggage."

Juliette took his arm. "No, we all go, or no one goes. The luggage doesn't matter."

He pulled his arm free and straightened up.

She pointed to the guard on the platform. "The suitcases will be fine...I want you to come with us!"

Marcel intercepted the Wehrmacht guard, who was pacing the platform. "If I leave the luggage here, will it be safe?"

The guard grinned and showed him his rifle. "It will be here when you return, and so will I. You must take your lady friends to the shelter."

"What about you?" Juliette asked the young man.

"I'm paid to stand here, bombs or not." Juliette looked concerned, but the young man waved her away, saying, "It's a lot better than the Russian front!"

Marcel led the way to the shelter, and the 'all clear' sounded forty-five minutes later. A few bombs landed in the city, but none near the station. Most exploded so far away that their 'crump' was barely noticeable.

Five minutes after the siren's wail announced that it was safe to resume ordinary life, the train to Brussels pulled into the station an hour behind schedule. Juliette and Yvonne boarded the train, and Marcel followed with the luggage.

As the train began to roll, the door to the compartment opened, and a young man in a Gestapo uniform glanced at the women and asked Marcel, "Would you mind if I sat next to you, sir?"

Marcel smiled and slid to the window, leaving the empty seat next to the door. The young man sat down opposite Juliette, missing the look of terror on Yvonne's face.

Juliette leaned ahead and stretched her hand to the young officer, smoothly drawing his attention to her. She adopted her sexiest French-accented German as he kissed her gloved hand.

"Oh, monsieur, that is a splendid uniform. I love men in uniform, especially when they are so handsome!" She pulled her hand back with a bright smile.

The young man's neck reddened a little, and he showed a set of perfect teeth as he said, "I am Kriminalkommissar Kristof Gärtner. Please call me Kristof."

Juliette used the affectionate "du" form when she answered, "I am very impressed to meet you, Kristof. I am Juliette Durand, and I live in Brussels."

Kristof leaned ahead with his forearms on his knees. "If you don't mind my asking, madame..."

Juliette immediately cut him off, "Oh no, monsieur, it's mademoiselle!"

He began again, a broad smile lighting his face. "I was wondering, mademoiselle, what has brought you to Germany?"

Juliette laughed, and the sound rippled musically in the compartment, just loud enough to be exciting. She watched Marcel turn to look out the window, but there was nothing to see with a blackout curtain covering it. Nevertheless, he pulled the corner aside and appeared to find something interesting in the blackness.

"Oh, monsieur, I am an opera singer. I am returning to Brussels from Detmold, where I sang Nedda in I Pagliacci."

Juliette noted the young man's embarrassment when he said, "I don't know very many operas. Is that an important one?"

She spent the next half-hour telling him all about the roles she had sung, and he listened with rapture as she sang the most melodic and alluring lines. Then she leaned over so she could whisper in his ear. He leaned over to meet her, and she said, "Do you know the song about the girlfriend waiting for her lover under the streetlight?"

He whispered, "Is that the one Goebbels forbids us to listen to?"

She said, "Yes, I feel like doing something bad with you. Will you allow me to sing it to you?"

Kristof swallowed hard and said hoarsely, "Yes, please, mademoiselle."

Juliette sang a version of Lale Andersen's hit song that would melt a stone statue's heart. When she sang the last verse and the soldier died, then rose from his grave to meet Lili Marlen under the streetlight, just as he had in life, the young man's eyes became wet. Juliette wiped them gently with her perfumed, embroidered silk handkerchief—then leaned over and kissed him lightly on the lips.

Juliette stole a glance at Yvonne, who was watching the drama with ever-increasing wonder. Her expression had gone from fear of the Gestapo uniform to fascination at the young man's foolishness.

Juliette slowly drew back from Kristof and steered his eyes toward Yvonne with her hand. "I have been a naughty girl...I didn't introduce you to my friend and teacher." She put her arms around Yvonne and kissed her cheek. "This is Yvonne. She teaches me all my roles, but she cannot speak German except for a very, very little bit." Juliette put her finger and thumb together, squinted one eye and fluttered the other. Kristof kissed the hand Yvonne graciously offered.

She said sweetly in her musical French, "I'm very pleased to meet you, monsieur." Coyly, she looked down, then lifted her brown eyes to look deep into his steel-grey pools. His jaw was strong and square, and his forehead was flat. He had blond hair and was taller than Marcel—Kriminalkommissar Kristof Gärtner was the master race personified.

The women spent the next fifteen minutes playing with him. Yvonne was shy and reserved, while Juliette carried on as the gregarious lover. Kristof swore when the train slowed at the border.

Juliette touched Marcel; he still gazed out the window. "Do you mind changing places? I want to sit beside the window."

She explained to Kristof, "He is the man my father hired to protect me when I travel."

The door suddenly opened, and an SS guard, a corporal, said sternly, "All passengers must leave the train for inspection!"

Kriminalkommissar Kristof Gärtner pulled rank on the younger SS officer. "They are with me, Unterscharführer. There is no need to bother them." He passed his identification disc to the corporal, who looked at it, then handed it back with a click of his heels.

Marcel gave a bundle of papers to the SS guard; he examined them and then stepped into the compartment. He pulled down one suitcase after another until he had opened them all, then picked up the score of Pagliacci that Yvonne had on her lap and flipped a few pages. He said in French, "This is a beautiful book, mademoiselle."

Yvonne sweetly smiled as she said in terrible German, "Thank you, monsieur. It was a gift to my mistress. She sang the opera in Detmold."

"Ah, Lippe Detmold—yes, I have been there. It is a beautiful town."

"Oui, monsieur, I agree."

The inspector left. When he had closed the door, Juliette brushed Kristof's leg with her foot, then lifted it to the level of his lap. "Kristof, would you remove my shoe, please? My foot is itchy, and it would be so nice if you could scratch it for me." She remembered a scene in Act Two of La Bohème…Kristof was the rich fool, Alcindor, and Juliette played Musetta.

Ten minutes later, the train began to move, and Juliette snuggled against Kristof's shoulder. She placed her hand on his lap and appeared to drift off to sleep. He put his hand on hers and wiggled around until he was sure Juliette was as comfortable as he could make her. She sleepily left his shoulder and put her head in his lap, whimpering a little in her sleep. She hid a smile when she felt Kristof stop breathing.

Marcel woke Juliette and Yvonne just before Brussels, and when the train stopped, Kristof helped him carry the luggage to the platform. The Gestapo officer reached for Juliette's hand, but she wriggled inside his outstretched arm and wrapped her arms around him. She said, "Thank you so much, Kristof," put her head back and looked into his eyes. "I hope I will see you again. If you are in a city where I am singing, I insist you come backstage—promise me you will come?"

Kristof looked down at her. "Yes, Juliette, I will come, and Paris will be lonely without you."

He stepped on the train as it started to move, waving to Juliette and Yvonne until they could no longer see him.

Marcel shook his head. "Why do men think they are in charge? You two turned a murdering bastard into a foolish little boy—I damned near felt sorry for him."

"You feel sorry for a Gestapo officer?" Juliette wrapped her arms around Marcel's arm and laughed.

"I said, 'almost.' What I really meant was I wouldn't enjoy killing him as much as I would have a couple of hours ago."

Chapter Twenty-Eight

23 March 1942

Mit der Wahrheit kommt man ins Geschrei.
(With the truth comes frustration.)

MARCEL DROPPED JULIETTE AT HER HOME at four in the morning. She turned the key in the door and quietly went in, trying not to wake Peter or Nina. She was hanging up her coat when she heard footsteps behind her.

Peter said, "I love you," as Juliette turned to him. She wrapped her arms around her husband and stood on her tiptoes to kiss him. When they parted, Peter said, "Do you want to eat something? I have everything ready."

"No, I can't stay awake." She suddenly felt she would collapse if she didn't get into a bed. "I'm so tired I'll faint if I don't sleep!"

Juliette felt her systems shutting down as she headed toward the bedroom with Peter behind her. He helped her get undressed and into bed, and she fell asleep worrying that her teeth would fall out because she hadn't brushed them.

She slept until a tiny voice said, "Mama" from far away, but it turned out to be from the edge of the bed.

"Mama!" The voice became bigger, closer and terribly intrusive.

Juliette deliberately didn't move. Nina put her hand on her mother's face and repeated, "Mama!" a little louder.

Juliette still didn't move.

Nina climbed up on the bed, put her face close to Juliette's ear, and yelled, "Mama, wake up!" loud enough to wake the dead in the next city.

Juliette didn't move, and Nina started to cry.

Laughing, Juliette rolled over and pulled Nina tight to her breasts.

"I'm sorry, darling—Mama shouldn't tease you. I've been waiting for you to come and wake me."

Nina wiggled free, slid down on the floor, happy again. She pulled her mother's hand and said, "Come, Mama... Viens! Mangez!"

Juliette put on her housecoat and allowed her daughter to pull her to the kitchen, where Peter had prepared fried eggs on pan-fried bread with apple juice and genuine bean coffee. A plate of croissants filled with blackberry jam was in the centre of the table, but Peter pulled them away when she reached for one of them.

"No sweets until you've eaten some real food!" He kissed her; she tried to get to the plate; he swung it around behind his back. Nina giggled and wrapped her arms around Peter's legs while Juliette circled him. She neatly picked a croissant from the plate and bit a corner before he could move it away.

While Juliette ate, Nina climbed on a chair and sat with her legs curled under her, elbows on the table, watching her mother's every move. Occasionally, Juliette gave her a piece of her croissant, and Nina devoured it. Peter put a glass of milk in front of the little girl, and she drank it in one go.

"Don't you ever feed this child?" Juliette gave her yet another bite of the croissant.

"She had breakfast early this morning, and she ate lunch just before she went in to wake you up. It's all your fault; you've given me a monster to feed." He tickled Nina, and she laughed.

"Lunch... already?" Juliette looked at a clock on the wall and was surprised to see it was after one o'clock.

Fifteen minutes later, Juliette kissed the top of Nina's head and said, "I'm finished eating...why don't you take Nina to the living room while I have my bath?" and headed for the bathroom while Peter steered a protesting Nina to the living room.

Juliette returned half an hour later, feeling soft and relaxed, and found Peter working on the St. Matthew Passion and Nina listening intently. He stopped singing before Juliette got comfortable in her favourite chair.

"Jacques wants you to report on the trip as soon as possible—Yvonne has to move on, and he needs your input."

Juliette, suddenly depressed, sat on the sofa and pulled Nina up on her knee. Nina rested her head against her mother's shoulder, and Juliette slipped her hand under Nina's thumb as it headed for her mouth. She got a nasty look from her daughter, but Nina sighed and put her hand in her lap.

Juliette stroked her little girl's black hair as she said, "I am worried about Yvonne; she is so fragile—we were lucky to get her here. A Gestapo officer sat in our compartment, but he was young, and we manipulated him a little."

"You are saying that he is now in love with you."

"Not like you are but, yes, infatuated...something like that."

The meeting with Jacques took place in the middle of the afternoon, and Marcel was already there when Juliette and Nina arrived, sitting in a comfortable chair next to Jacques. Both men asked how she had slept, and Juliette said, "Like the dead," and sat in her chair beside Marcel. Nina climbed up on her mother's lap, and Juliette felt like an intruder as Marcel and Jacques silently looked out the row of windows facing the wooden deck and the front garden.

Finally, Marcel said, "I briefed your father on the trip and what I know of Yvonne's story. We will go into more detail when everyone is here."

The sun streaming through the west-facing windows warmed the room. Veronique opened the door to the patio to let in a slight breeze, and Nina shook her head when her grandmother sat beside Jacques and gestured for her to come. Despite the sunshine, the mood in the room was sombre.

Veronique said, "Yvonne is in her room sleeping, but she will be down later."

Jacques said, "We need to plan the next step, but first, we should all hear what Yvonne will say to the British Royal Commission, and I want to see the documents she brought. I'm afraid Marcel has painted a much more desperate picture than I anticipated. Without the documents, I would find the story difficult to believe."

Juliette stroked Nina's hair, thought about taking her out of the room, then decided to try and control the dialogue.

Juliette put her arms around Nina and kissed the top of her head. "Yvonne knows everything about the camp; they experimented on her, repeatedly trying to sterilize her by gluing her tubes shut. She can't have children now."

"Oh my God, that's terrible!" Veronique stood, raised her voice and headed for Nina. "How could anyone do such a thing?" She reached for the little girl, but she squirmed away, and Juliette said, "Yes, Mother, maybe you should take Nina upstairs for her nap. This gets much worse."

Veronique picked up Nina, who whimpered and stretched her arms to Juliette. When she saw that her grandmother wasn't going to give in, she put her thumb in her mouth and leaned against Veronique's breast.

Veronique glanced at everyone. "I want to hear this, so wait until I return before you go on."

Everyone agreed, and Marcel turned to Juliette.

"You've never told me what Yvonne said or what effect you think it will have on the British politicians."

Juliette looked at her hands, fiddling with her wedding ring. When she lifted her head, she was fighting tears.

"No one can imagine such depravity, and the problem I see is that her testimony will be so graphic and horrible that those privileged old men in the British government will think that because they can't imagine it, what she says cannot possibly be true. Perhaps the documents will be enough proof, but I haven't seen them."

"Ah, yes, the documents." Jacques perked up and pointed at his daughter. " You smuggled them across the border, didn't you? And I believe you have included three photograph negatives."

While Juliette adjusted to that news, Marcel picked up the I Pagliacci score lying on the little table beside him, examined it for a minute, and then opened a pocketknife that appeared out of nowhere. He neatly slit the front and back edges, reached in, and withdrew two bundles of documents and negatives. He passed one bundle to Jacques and thumbed through the other before giving some of them to Peter and Juliette.

As he looked at the documents, Jacques said, "Captain Witold Pilecki of the Free Polish Army signed everything I have here, along with other prisoners who are prominent members of Polish society. We will copy and photograph them before we send anything to England, and they must travel separately from Yvonne."

Veronique returned, and Jacques passed her a two-page document and two photographs. Her eyes froze on the first page.

"This is a record of the number of people executed in Auschwitz gas rooms... Mon Dieu! Seven hundred people every day?"

Jacques said, "Look closer, my dear—I'm afraid it's seven hundred in each group. They gas three groups every day!"

Veronique gasped, "Every day... No, it can't be true! Does this document prove the SS guards kill over two thousand people each day? Every day? And almost all are women... Wait! Some are children... No...this can't be! There must be a mistake!"

Jacques looked at Marcel. "That's precisely the reaction I'm afraid of, but there is an even more incredible number that the British politicians must accept. Using these daily figures, the Nazis annually commit three-quarters of a million murders in Auschwitz alone, and we know of two more extermination camps! There are twelve million Jews in Europe... My God, at that rate, the Nazis will kill them all in six years!

Veronique held up a second document. "This one talks about the lives of the inmates who are building a new IG Farben factory. The plant is seven kilometres from the camp, and they walk there and back. If they can't walk that far, they are gassed!"

Marcel said, "Jacques has reliable information that this chemical company and other German companies pay the Nazi Party three Reichmarks an hour for slave labour, and in this letter, they complain about the quality of the workers!" He held up a sheet that he had been reading. "They are demanding that the camp only send healthy workers! They indirectly say that the camp should execute those who can't work fast enough to make money for the company!"

Veronique worked through the papers, sometimes crying so hard she had to pause.

"The prisoners say nothing about the gassing—they call it delousing, but everyone knows what it is. Most of the camp can hear screams coming from the vents. The guards make the camp orchestra play loudly enough to drown them out. At first, they ran motorcycle engines but found that the orchestra was better—the report says the music calms the prisoners." He held up a report written for the camp commander.

Veronique put the papers on her knee and said, "I can't read anymore." She swallowed hard, trying to control her crying.

Jacques, who had been looking at the floor, raised his head.

"What we are doing has to be done, no matter the cost."

Juliette asked, "Shall I go on with Yvonne's story? Or have we heard enough for now?"

"I can tell my own story." Yvonne stood in the open doorway. Jacques beckoned her to come in, and Marcel carried a heavy chair into the sunlight and set it down. Everyone dragged their chair to form a semi-circle around Yvonne. She leaned ahead with her elbows on her knees and began her story while looking past the trees in the yard.

When Yvonne was finished, Veronique covered her face with her hands, quietly weeping. Everyone silently waited as Yvonne slowly relaxed, leaned back in her chair, and said, "I know it's over, and I know my life is important, but I want to die. I will try to live to tell my story, but only if it will save others."

Jacques asked, his tone full of respect and sympathy, "Can you tell us what a day is like in Auschwitz? If you can, please take us through what you would call a typical day." Juliette gave him a look that could have killed him, but he raised his hand and said, "The British won't give her any mercy..."

Yvonne said, "Don't worry, I can do whatever I need to do to help the others still in the camp—anything is better than being there! I will answer your question."

She paused to organize her thoughts before she began.

"The day begins at three in the morning. If we have any bread left from the night before, we eat it then.

We line up outside so they can count us, and the count must be correct, or they will leave us standing there until they find the problem. If someone dies at night, and almost every night someone does, we must hold the body up so the Sonderkommandos can count them. When the roll call is correct, we leave the body on the ground, and they take it away."

Yvonne stopped and waited for questions, but none came, so she continued.

Marcel wrote as he listened, lifted his head and asked a question when she paused. It took almost an hour, and Yvonne finished with a description of punishment for people with nothing to lose but hope.

The room was quiet, save for the sound of sobs from Veronique and bird songs floating in from the garden through the open windows. Juliette looked out, staring at nothing.

Marcel stood and began pacing. He stopped in front of Yvonne.

"I know you are telling the truth; no one in this room doubts you, but the English politicians will try not to believe you because all humanity is implicated."

Yvonne answered, "It's the truth, and I can't say it any other way."

Marcel shook his head. "I don't doubt it for an instant, but they might try to shut you up somehow rather than deal with the possibility that you are telling the truth. Who would take responsibility for Hitler's rise if you forced them to admit this horrible reality? Everyone is guilty because he unambiguously said that he would do this. He said it in many ways, at many times, and with clarity. Many people from many countries would not stop Hitler when it was still possible for them to do it, and now many more have died fighting his regime. Heads would roll, people would march in the streets, and governments would fall."

Yvonne was clearly stunned at what he was saying, and incredulous, she said, "They won't believe me, even with the reports and pictures?"

"I don't know," said Marcel, "but they won't want to believe you, so we must find a way to present this so they have no choice. If those men want a doctor to examine your uterus, will you let him do it?"

"Yes, of course," said Yvonne, "I will let them do anything if they will believe me. I lost my shame long ago."

Marcel said to the room, "So, how do we make the case believable? Perhaps we should eliminate or adjust the worst of it to make it more credible."

Peter said, "Why don't we give them a little at a time? Perhaps we should send the documents as soon as possible, without the pictures, and then send the photographs a few days or weeks later. When Yvonne begins her testimony, we should have her read from notes. Have the testimony begin with very little shock information, then give a little more as they ask questions, but not too much at a time. We should set the stage for the final act—make it work like an opera or a play. It's all in the timing. We need an introduction, a development, small climaxes leading to the final act where everything comes together."

Everyone looked at Jacques. He nodded in agreement.

"Yes, that's what we will do. We will find a stage director to teach Yvonne and us how to tell her story and, if they attack her, how to respond to their questions. Marcel, you get the photographs developed. Meanwhile, we will send the introductory documents via the Résistance and the Free Polish Army in Britain. I will clear the path for Yvonne to get to England, probably through Spain, if she is strong enough to go over the mountains. The people in MI6 who control Marcel will manage the receipt and distribution of the documents on the other end."

Yvonne was visibly relieved.

"Will I have to stay in England?"

"Would you be willing to go to North America to speak to the Americans?"

"Yes, I can do that, and afterward, I have relatives in Montreal. I could go there when this is all over."

Marcel said, "I will get a guarantee that you can go wherever you want."

CHAPTER TWENTY-NINE

3 April 1942

Keiner wird betrogen als der, welcher traut.
(No one is more wounded by betrayal than one who trusts.)
Niccoló Machiavelli

IT TOOK JULIETTE A WEEK TO ADJUST to home and Peter, and the turmoil in her mind caused by Yvonne's story sent her back to Kristallnacht and the monster who raped her. Sex gave her little pleasure, but Peter made her feel his patience was infinite, and she loved him for it more than she had thought possible. When Yvonne left for England, Juliette returned to music, and its magical power led her back to Peter.

A few days after Peter sang Bach's St. John Passion in Amiens for Maestro Renaud, his agent, Monique Desjardins, negotiated a contract for him to sing the St. Matthew Passion in Amiens Cathedral on Good Friday the following year. Monique also arranged for Juliette to sing two Bach cantatas in Antwerp on Easter Sunday, meaning she and Peter would be apart for almost a week. Juliette told herself that six days would fly past, but unreasonable desperation seeped into her mood as the day approached when Peter would board the train to Amiens.

On Wednesday afternoon, while Nina slept, Peter and Juliette made love so intensely that they slept until the little girl shouted from her bedroom. Juliette pretended to be asleep as Peter slid his arm from under her head, and she smiled to herself as he quietly put on his pants and went to Nina's room. Juliette heard him singing "Geduld, Geduld" to Nina loud enough that she assumed Peter meant it for her. She got out of bed, slipped on her nightgown, and watched from the hallway as Peter twirled the giggling girl around the room. Nina held her hands over her head, tipped her head back to magnify the sensation, and spied her mother before Peter did.

Juliette said, "Now, aren't you two having a good time!" from the open doorway.

"Like mother, like daughter!" Peter laughed, swinging Nina over to her. Juliette took her daughter—Nina reached out for her father.

"Your train leaves in an hour, so get ready—your suitcase is packed—Marcel will be here in a few minutes."

Ten minutes later, the knocker banged. Peter kissed Juliette, pecked Nina on the cheek as she struggled to escape her mother's arms, and followed Marcel to the car. Juliette watched him go, and Nina screamed to the point of panic as the Rolls drove out of sight.

Nina cried inconsolably, and Juliette put her to bed with a deep sadness that she tried to shake by singing a Brahms lullaby to her daughter. She sang until Nina fell asleep, but the sadness remained.

The train journey to Amiens was uneventful; the day was warm, and Peter decided to walk to the hotel. The suitcase was light, and it was a pleasant kilometre in the spring sunshine to the Hotel de Berny. Peter registered at the lobby desk, and the hôtelier handed him a sealed envelope. He stuffed it in his pocket and carried his suitcase to the same room he had occupied on his trip a year ago.

Peter tore open the end of the envelope and pulled out a folded sheet of paper. As he expected, it was a coded message. The letter was from his girlfriend, asking him to meet her under a bridge over the Somme River. He decoded it, and the instructions directed him to pick up a package late on Thursday afternoon. The drop location was a planter on a corner a block from his hotel, but it warned if someone had crushed the pansies, he should leave. He burned the note and the envelope in an ashtray and flushed the ashes down the toilet.

The following morning's rehearsal went well, and Peter tried to leave the church immediately after, but Monsieur Renaud intercepted Peter before he got out of sight. He pulled him into a nave off the main gallery and whispered, "I tried singing while having sex, and it works! My voice improves every time I do it."

"Your wife no longer hates your singing?" Peter whispered.

"She does," Monsieur Renaud replied, "but my mistress doesn't!"

"I see." Peter smiled. He indicated he must go by pointing at the door and left Maestro Renaud trying to find words to a question.

He walked to the hotel, ate a late lunch, paid the restaurant bill, and left for the corner with the planter. The sun was warm; he wore a light jacket and whistled part of the "Geduld" aria from Bach's masterpiece.

When he reached the planter, the pansies were alive and well, but he decided to look around before he looked for the drop. He leaned against a light pole for a few minutes, whistling, watching people walk by in the spring sunshine. Nothing was out of place…he had followed all of Marcel's rules when he turned around and swept his hand over the loose dirt. The end of a brown envelope appeared just under the surface; he withdrew it, brushed it off and smoothed the earth. He slipped it into the inside pocket of his jacket and turned to leave.

Grey-uniformed Gestapo officers came at him from every escape route. Terror froze his brain as two officers grabbed his arms, and a third pulled the envelope from his jacket. The officer stepped back, opened it and took ten seconds to look through the contents. His accomplices searched Peter for weapons, pulled his identification papers and wallet out of his pockets, looked at them, and then handed everything to the officer with the envelope.

The Gestapo officer said, "You are under arrest for treason against the Third Reich!" He waved without waiting for a reply, a grey Gestapo car drove up to the curb, and the men holding Peter's arms pushed him into the rear seat.

Terror dominated Peter's mind, and panic reigned when the car drove through the Amiens Prison gates. Peter tried but couldn't control his fear as two Gestapo officers led him into the prison and down worn stone stairs. One of the officers stopped outside a door, and the other pushed Peter into a room where a man who looked like a senior Gestapo officer sat behind an oak desk strong enough to support a house. Light came from a dirty light fixture hung from the ceiling, a small window high on the wall behind the officer, and a dim reading lamp on the desk. The officer ordered Peter to hand him his papers, then talked as he examined them. "Wallonian. You have a German name, so can I assume you speak German as well as French?" He spoke in German.

"Yes, I do."

The officer looked into Peter's eyes. "Then listen to me very carefully. First, you must accept that your life is over—you will be dead before the day ends because you are a spy with no uniform. The penalty for treason is death, and I am authorized to carry it out immediately."

During the short pause meant to increase the tension, Peter resolved to tell this man nothing.

The officer began speaking again. "You have a choice of two ways to die—one is with a bullet in your brain, and I believe that to be painless, but of course, I cannot be sure. However, I know from experience your only other choice means a great deal of unbearable pain. Either way, the final outcome for you and me will be the same."

Peter was alert enough to know that this man had given this well-rehearsed speech many times, but knowing that didn't lessen the impact. Despite his determination to stand, Peter felt his knees buckle. The man behind him caught his arm.

The Gestapo officer behind the desk leaned back, and his young face became Peter's focal point. The officer deftly moved a pencil through his fingers, flipping it back and forth across his hand. "The easy death will result from you telling me precisely what I want to know." He leaned across the desk, his face in the shadows, his voice coming out of the gloom. "If you attempt to lie to me, the pain will be terrible!"

He put the pencil on the desk and picked up the letter Peter had taken from the planter. As he moved his head, the light played back and forth on his face—he seemed bored.

"I know the information in this envelope came from a Résistance cell because I caught the man who left it there. You will meet him when this interview is over."

He stood up and smiled; light from the overhead fixture bounced off his perfect white teeth.

"You will decode this letter, and you will give me the names and addresses of all the people who direct you. I want to know where you were going with these papers and who is waiting for them."

Peter was silent, hardly able to breathe. Somehow, he must bear the unbearable.

The officer looked at his watch, then at Peter.

"I will not wait more than a few more seconds." He said the words without emotion, clearly not expecting Peter to answer.

Peter waited in terrified silence, and a few seconds later, the Gestapo officer shouted, "Komm 'rein!"

Two men entered the room, stood beside Peter, and saluted the officer. One of them carried a short wooden club. The man that had brought him there stepped away.

"Show the young man what is ahead of him if he continues this foolishness."

The blow to Peter's wrist came so swiftly that he gasped and cried out, instinctively grasping his forearm. The second man pinned Peter's arms behind his back. The club struck his head, blinding his right eye, then expertly broke several ribs. Peter's legs buckled, but the man holding his arms didn't let him fall. The room swayed; the club struck Peter's right kneecap, breaking it.

Peter screamed, lost in a world of pain. He was vaguely aware that the club pulled back to hit the other knee, and that the officer behind the desk extended his arm, saying, "That's enough for now."

Peter fell to the floor, gasping, crying, praying for merciful death. He couldn't focus his eyes, and he couldn't move. And he couldn't stop his bladder and bowels from emptying themselves.

The officer leaned over the desk. "We are leaving temporarily to say hello to the old man who dropped the envelope. You should reconsider my offer before we return."

The men left the room, leaving Peter lying in his excrement. With every movement, pain shot through his body. He lay still and tried to breathe from his diaphragm, as Juliette had done when Nina was born, but it didn't help. His thoughts turned to Juliette and Nina, and he sobbed, cried aloud, and tried to remember a prayer from his childhood.

Fifteen minutes and an eternity of pain passed before the officer returned. He stepped over Peter and stood so that the light from the window silhouetted his upper body in a bright band of suspended dust. "Give me one name, and I promise the pain will stop!"

Peter continued to cry but resolved to say nothing. The officer called the men, and Peter screamed in anticipation of the blows, but none came. They each took one of his arms and dragged him out of the room and down the hall. His body revolted; he threw up his lunch, and every time his stomach heaved, a flash of blinding pain filled his brain. He screamed until his beautiful voice began to break.

The men dragged him into a room with a table and four wooden chairs. They used leather straps to tie Peter to one of the crude chairs, but he had no more strength to scream; he couldn't resist; he couldn't raise his head.

The officer grabbed his hair, pulled his head upright, and looked into Peter's eyes without a human expression on his face.

"Give me a name!" The demon said it without a twinge of mercy or empathy.

The officer stepped back and pointed. Peter followed his finger and recognized the old man with the hooknose, tied in a chair, blood covering his face. He had no shoes... and no toenails on his bloody feet. Hooknose looked dead until his head turned and looked at Peter through bloodshot eyes. Peter thought he saw a flicker of a smile.

"You will soon look like him if you don't give me a name!"

Peter began to sob but shook his head and said, "No."

The man who had used the club removed Peter's shoes and socks, and the other handed him a pair of needle-nosed pliers. Peter tried to move his feet away, but the leather straps held them tightly to the legs of the chair. The man squeezed Peter's foot in his strong fingers....

Obersturmbandführer Alex Küster tackled the endless paperwork piled up in his office. These were papers only he could see and touch, and there were more of them every day. Deeply engrossed in his work, he heard the first screams through the building's central heating system, which unfortunately carried the sounds from the torture room in the basement to his office on the second floor. Typically, he drowned them out by playing the radio at high volume, and he reached for the switch to turn it on, but before the tubes warmed, he heard the screams again and turned the switch off. He stood up, took the belt with his holstered pistol down from a wooden peg beside his jacket, and ran out the door, leaving his coat on its hanger, yanking the DWM Luger pistol from its holster before dropping the belt.

The torture rooms were directly below the prison commander's office, two floors down, and it took Küster scarcely thirty seconds to reach the room.

He sucked in his breath, said, "Mein Gott! Nein!" then shouted at the Gestapo officer, "Kriminalkommissar Gärtner, what the hell are you doing?"

Gärtner laughed, "What am I doing? You know perfectly well what I do!" He pointed at Peter and the old man. "These men are traitors and spies, and it is my duty to extract information from them!"

Küster grimaced, and the young officer's smile faded.

The Obersturmbandführer demanded, "And have you gotten your information?" through grinding teeth.

"Neither of them has said anything yet, but I assure you that eventually, they will tell me what I want to know!" He looked lasciviously at Peter, who used the last of his strength to laugh before shifting his gaze to Alex. His eyes focused on the gun in his friend's hand, then on his face. Alex looked down at the DWM Luger pistol, and Peter smiled.

Küster smoothly raised his Luger, flicking the safety off as he found his target, and the smiles on the three Gestapo men's faces faded. He waved the gun past their heads, stopped at Peter and fired. Peter's head jerked sideways, and before the sound of the gunshot died, another one blasted the men's eardrums, and the smile on the old man's face faded into peace. Küster turned to Gärtner and snarled, waving the gun in his young face, "I hate you and your kind! You will leave my prison within the next two minutes, or I swear to God, I will shoot you!"

Alex waited with Peter until the Gestapo men left his prison, put his hand on Peter's cheek, then returned to his office, slamming the door and screaming at the wall. When his assistant came running in, Küster had his pistol in one hand and his belt in the other. He shouted, "Get out! Go home! Get out of my sight!"

The man turned, ran, stumbled, and nearly fell as he left the outer office.

Alex Küster fired his gun into the stone wall until it was empty, showering granite fragments and pieces of lead across the room, then threw the pistol at the opposite wall. He collapsed into his chair and cried.

Finally, Küster slept. Waking an hour before dawn, he retrieved his pistol and drove to the railway station.

Chapter Thirty

Good Friday 1942

Die Wilden fressen einander, und die Zahmen betrügen einander.
(Wild animals eat one another; tame ones betray one another.)
Arthur Schopenhauer

AT TEN O'CLOCK ON GOOD FRIDAY MORNING, Jean Renaud called Jacques Durand. Veronique answered the phone just as they were going to mass and passed it to Jacques.

"Good morning, Monsieur Durand. I hope you are feeling well," Jean Renaud began, "I'm calling to ask whether you know where I can find Peter. He isn't in his hotel or the church, and the performance begins in three hours. He was supposed to run through a rehearsal with me an hour ago."

Jacques said nothing for a long time, prompting Monsieur Renaud to ask, "Monsieur Durand, are you there?"

"I'm still here. I'm trying to figure out where Peter might be, but unfortunately, I have no idea at all."

Renaud said, "Just a moment, someone is at my door." With a thud, he laid the phone on his desk, and Jacques heard him open the door. He heard loud voices, and then Jean Renaud shouting, "Peter Durand is not a spy; he is a musician!" Heavy boots approached the phone, and the line went dead.

"Who was that, dear?" Veronique asked as she came back into the room with her coat on. She said tentatively, "If we don't hurry, we'll be late for..." The expression on Jacques' face stopped her.

"That was the conductor of Peter's St. Matthew Passion. Peter has disappeared."

"Disappeared? Peter would never disappear!"

"No, he wouldn't..." Jacques hesitated before he went on. "While

I was on the phone, someone came to Monsieur Renaud's door, and I overheard Renaud say that Peter was not a spy. Someone, not Renaud, hung up the phone."

Veronique sat in a chair as her knees weakened. Jacques sat beside her.

"We must assume the worst—they would torture him—he would tell them what he knows about our organization."

"They may not have caught him," She said desperately, "They could have been looking for him, and he may be hiding somewhere."

Jacques shook his head, and Veronique broke into tears. "What have we done? We've killed our son!"

Jacques fought tears in his own eyes. "No! You must never say that. If our son is dead, Hitler killed him! We knew this might happen..." He wiped his eyes with his sleeve... "If he is dead, his will be the first life we've lost, and it is now our job to make it the last."

"He may not be dead—maybe you can still save him."

"We must hope he is dead," said Jacques miserably. "They would have tortured him until he broke, and now they will come for us. We must all go to Switzerland!"

Jacques shifted gears. "Marcel and Juliette haven't yet left for Antwerp. I will send him to get her and Nina. We must leave as soon as possible. Don't bother packing."

The telephone's clanging ring interrupted him—he picked it up and said, "Durand here!"

"Monsieur Durand, Alex Küster here. It is urgent that we meet."

"Where are you?"

" I am at the Brussels train station. There is a restaurant across the street, and I need you to meet me there before you do anything. Time is valuable, and you must not waste it."

Jacques hesitated, then said, "I will bring my driver, Marcel."

"Yes," said Alex, "but not in the restaurant. He must remain inconspicuous and see that we are not interrupted."

The line went dead.

Half an hour later, Jacques went into the almost empty restaurant. There were a few late risers eating crêpes and drinking coffee, but only one man was sitting alone, and he was wearing a grey SS uniform.

"Good morning, Obersturmbandführer Küster." Jacques offered him his hand, dreading the reason for the meeting.

Küster said, "Is there anything the waiter can get for you, Monsieur Durand? I've already eaten."

Jacques shook his head as he sat down. "I'm afraid I know why you are here. Monsieur Renaud called looking for Peter."

"I am the bearer of bad news," Küster said, "Please call me Alex, as Peter did." As Alex fiddled with a table knife, Jacques felt his heart break—Küster had used the past tense for Peter.

"I don't know how to start. I became close to your son-in-law."

The colour drained from Jacques' face. "He is dead, isn't he?"

Alex leaned across the table. "The Gestapo was waiting when Peter picked up a drop from the Résistance—you have a rat in your cellar. I usually hear about such things in time to do something, but this time, I was not informed, and that makes me nervous." He folded his hands, rubbing them together in what was a nervous habit. "They took him to Amiens Prison, where I am the director. The Gestapo uses the cellar below my office to...the polite word is interrogate... prisoners. The honest word would be torture."

Küster looked into Jacques' eyes with pity. "I recognized Peter's voice and ran to the interrogation room, but I was too late." He folded his hands so tight the knuckles whitened. "I had to shoot Peter and his friend." His voice cracked. "I hope you can forgive me—I will never forgive myself. I couldn't shoot his tormentors without compromising our greater cause, and there are too many of them for so few to make a difference."

Jacques said evenly, "I know you did what is best, and if I had your courage, I would have done the same. Thank you for that mercy."

Alex went on, still speaking very quietly. "Peter was a brave man." He paused, and his voice broke when he continued, "Neither Peter nor the old man said a word during the interrogation—I questioned the Gestapo officer, and I will guarantee that."

Jacques nodded slowly. "I wondered at Peter's admiration of you, and now I know why."

Alex stood, and Jacques stood with him. The SS officer said, "If we leave together, it may not look appropriate, but if I leave without you, will your man at the door do something rash?"

"He knows who you are. You will be safe." Jacques touched Küster's arm before he could turn. "Thank you, Alex, and may God help you."

Obersturmbandführer Küster slid the brim of his hat through his fingers and shook Jacques' hand. "I hope that the next time we meet, it will be under better circumstances."

Jacques waited five minutes after Alex exited the restaurant, and Marcel met him at the door. Jacques said, "We'll talk in the car."

As they drove home, when Jacques began to tell Marcel the story, Marcel pulled the car over. As Jacques spoke, Marcel sat with his shoulders rounded and his head down. When Jacques finished, Marcel asked him to drive, but Jacques said, "I think we'll stay here for a few minutes."

Marcel pulled the Rolls into the yard and parked in front of the main entrance. Veronique opened the door before they were out of the car.

"What did you find out?" Her tone was so desperately full of hope it was pitiful. She walked with them into the house. No one spoke until they were in the living room.

Jacques hesitated, then decided to tell the truth. Veronique's eyes filled with tears as he related as much detail as he could. Trembling, she asked, "Did they torture him?"

"No," he lied, "but Küster knew he couldn't save him from it and shot both Peter and another man they were torturing. They didn't suffer."

Veronique cried out, put both hands on her face and slumped back in her chair. Jacques said nothing as he waited for her cries to subside. Finally, she asked, "Do you trust this man? He could have shot Peter as a spy, and now…"

Jacques cut Veronique off, something he never did… "Küster is not who he appears to be, and I believe he would have saved Peter if it had been possible, even at the cost of his own life. He assured me that neither the other man nor Peter had said a word. The Gestapo told him they had learned nothing, which was part of why Küster met me. I believe he had no choice, and I trust him."

"Poor Juliette," Veronique wiped her face with her sleeve and controlled her sobbing. "We have to tell her as soon as possible."

Jacques opened his mouth to answer, but the clang of the telephone interrupted him. Marcel picked it up, waited while the person on the other end spoke and then said, "We're on our way." As he placed the receiver in its cradle, he said, "That was Juliette. Gestapo officers are in her house; they are arresting her."

Marcel stopped the Rolls Royce behind two Gestapo cars, and Jacques ran through the open front door. Juliette sat on the sofa in the living room; an officer watched her. Nina stood beside her mother's leg with her thumb in her mouth.

Jacques addressed the young man in a tone that left no doubt of his state of mind. "Who is in charge here?"

An officer appeared in the hall and said, "I am Kriminalsekretär Schwenke, and I presume you are Jacques Durand? I allowed your daughter to call you out of courtesy, and now that you are here... I have a few questions."

"Yes, I am Jacques Durand, and I want to know what's going on. My son-in-law is missing, and now you are here in his home. I want an explanation!"

"You are entitled to nothing, Monsieur Durand... and I will ask the questions. Your son-in-law is a traitor, and we will search this house until we find what we are looking for! And then we will take you and your daughter to Gestapo headquarters for questioning!"

"That is a lie!" Jacques shouted, pointing his finger at the officer. "Peter would never betray his country or his family, and you will not take my daughter anywhere!" He walked over to the telephone in the hall, picked up the receiver, and dialled.

The officer pushed the receiver button down. "Your lawyer cannot help you,"

Jacques spoke softly, "You know very well who I am, as I know who you are, and if you try to stop me, you will learn what I can do!"

The officer's face betrayed his hate, but he lifted his finger and stepped aside. Jacques dialled a series of numbers, explained the situation into the telephone and then gestured to Schwenke, holding the receiver in his outstretched hand.

"Kriminalinspektor Müller wants to speak with you."

The young officer hesitated, took the receiver, listened for a few seconds, said, "Jawohl, Herr Kriminalinspektor," and put the receiver back in its cradle. He called out to the men in the house and turned to Jacques. "I assure you I will be back."

Jacques looked deep into the Gestapo officer's eyes as he said, "I will inform Kriminalinspektor Müller of your threat when I have dinner with him this weekend." Jacques smiled. The Kriminalsekretär's face reddened, and he marched out of the house with his men. Marcel shut the door behind them.

Jacques turned to Juliette. "You and Nina are coming to our house for a while. I will cancel your performances, and you must pack for a long stay."

Juliette looked at her father and didn't question him. She was too terrified to speak.

Juliette screamed, her screams gradually turning to a mournful wail until she collapsed in a chair. Marcel had taken Nina out to play in the yard, but Jacques could hear his granddaughter crying to get into the house, shouting, "Mama! Mama!" at the top of her lungs. When a relenting Marcel brought Nina inside, she ran to her mother and climbed on her lap. Juliette put her arms around Nina and rocked her as they both cried. Nina's thumb found her mouth, and her mother left it there.

Chapter Thirty-One

Spring 1942

Wenn die Ratte sterben will, beißt sie die Katze in den Schwanz.
(If a rat wants to die, it bites the cat's tail.)

JULIETTE SPENT TWO DAYS ALTERNATELY CRYING AND SLEEPING, occasionally visited by Veronique and Nina. The day after Peter died, Juliette couldn't speak without crying, but on Easter Sunday, she ran out of tears and slept through the night and most of the next day. Late Easter Monday morning, Juliette soaked in a bath until the water cooled, then dressed. At eleven o'clock, she came down for breakfast with a rage in her soul that overwhelmed her broken heart. Jacques came out of his office and sat down opposite his daughter.

He watched her eat, and she frequently looked up at him but said nothing. Veronique left them alone at the table in front of the window, the sun streaming in through the white curtains. Finally, Juliette looked at him and said, "Daddy, I don't blame you." She wiped her mouth with a white linen napkin.

Jacques said, "I must take some of the blame—there is a rat in that cell, and I should have smelled it."

Juliette smiled, but there was no joy in it. "I will help you find the rat—and the only condition I have is that I want to watch him die!"

"Juliette, you must not let this make you bitter; it would do no good and would be a loss your mother and I could not bear."

She stopped eating, paused, squeezed her fork so hard her knuckles whitened, and said, "I am going to have my revenge with or without you! I will kill Nazis until there are no more to kill! I am going to join the real Résistance and make those bastards Pay. I want a gun, and I want Marcel to teach me how to use it!"

A look of panic crossed Jacques's face. "Juliette, think! The best way to get even is to sing—stay the course we have steered until now—you can hurt them much deeper than anyone, including Marcel. It accomplishes little to kill a few soldiers in an army of millions!"

Juliette crossed her arms and leaned back. She smiled but, as before, with no pleasure.

"I'm singing in Nürnberg early in May. Who am I bringing back?"

Jacques returned her smile, but his was warm and full of hope. He was obviously excited at Juliette's sudden reversal.

"You won't have heard of the Uranprojekt. I don't understand it myself, but it involves splitting uranium atoms to create power. Most scientists disagree, but I have heard that British and American physicists, and one or two German scientists, believe splitting a uranium atom could create a tremendous explosion… perhaps enough to level an entire city!"

"That doesn't sound possible, but does Hitler…" Juliette was suddenly interested.

"Yes, you are asking the right question… Does Hitler believe it? Is he building such a bomb?" Jacques watched the light return to Juliette's eyes and had to control the urge to laugh.

"The British are quite sure that Hitler is working toward this bomb, but there is no evidence. However, if he does build it… Juliette, imagine the power to incinerate an entire city in that man's hands!"

Juliette felt excitement growing in her gut, or was it something else? She said, "No one man should have that power, let alone a megalomaniac like Hitler! But how does that affect me? How can I help?"

"First—and there can be no compromise on this—your revenge for Peter must wait. Hitler's Jew hunt has gutted the Uranprojekt, but despite that, it continues, and you can help stop it."

Juliette felt her soul revive, resurrected by her excitement. Jacques saw it, didn't try to hide his gratification, and went on.

"When Hitler became chancellor, most of the leading Jewish physicists left Germany, and he conscripted many of those who stayed into the Wehrmacht. For that and other more complicated reasons connected with something called radiation, the program might die a natural death. But in any case, we need to know what they have accomplished and what their intentions are."

Juliette opened her mouth to speak, but Jacques held his hand in the universal stop sign.

"At the top level, there is a man in the project who is willing to go to America where his knowledge could be put to better use." He leaned ahead, "And you will bring him to us."

"Could the Americans build such a bomb?"

"No one knows for sure, but Albert Einstein, the man who discovered this awful power, left Germany for America when German President Paul Von Hindenburg appointed Hitler chancellor in January 1933. At the time, most of the top German physicists were Jews, and many followed him. No one has heard from them since." He smiled as though he knew something more.

"The United States wants our man as soon as we can get him there, even though he isn't a scientist—actually, he's an administrator. He is one-quarter Jewish, and his wife is one-eighth Jewish. The SS took her parents away, and she wants both of them to get out. You will take them to Switzerland with you."

"Is the plan similar to what we did with Peter's sister and her husband, with a twist, of course?"

"Of course!" Jacques chuckled.

Juliette folded her hands in front of her, trying to control her careening emotions. "Is Uncle Hébert coming to hear me sing again? I assume that's why I'm singing in Zürich a few days after my last performance in Nürnberg."

"Yes, but there is a risk, at least as high as the first time you crossed into Switzerland. You must not let your anger and ego overcome your sense of reason. You may not be ready to cross the border again yet."

Juliette lost the composure she was trying to control.

"I don't care what happens to me now—I want to hurt the Nazis—I want to destroy them! I might settle for dropping one of those Uran bombs on Berlin, but only if it killed every Nazi in that evil city!"

Jacques was quiet for a few seconds, and when he finally spoke, it was softly.

"That is precisely what I am afraid of—you will not listen to the voice of reason—you are a danger to yourself and others!"

Stunned, Juliette reran the words she had used and regretted every one of them. She suddenly realized she was becoming her enemy.

"I'm sorry, Papa. You are right, of course, and I will control myself."

"Control is not a substitute for a cure. You are sick with grief, mentally unwell, and many people's lives are at stake. Control is not enough—you must change your attitude before we can even think about this mission!"

Juliette worked with her accompanist on Gilda, her role in the opera Rigoletto, concentrating on her technique, hoping to restore the beauty her grief had taken. She simultaneously struggled to relieve the unbearable ache in her heart, but anger always smouldered in the depths, sometimes flaring to the surface of her soul.

When Marcel accompanied Juliette to Nürnberg early in May, they registered in the Pfälzerhof hotel. The following morning, a Monday, was the first rehearsal. It was a rare warm sunny day, and Juliette hummed to herself as she and Marcel walked to the opera house.

"I'm so glad to see you happy, Juliette. It's the first time I've heard you humming for the love of it in a very long time."

"You mean since Peter died." Juliette pulled on his arm. "You can say it, Marcel. I'm through grieving; now it's time to get even!" Marcel reached for her hand, but she pulled it away. "Give me a little more time, Marcel. There is nothing in my heart now but hate—I can't help hating everything German, including singing for the bastards in their damned theatres."

They took a shortcut through the side yard of the hotel. The Pfälzerhof was at the end of Am Gräslein, a dead-end street. The street annoyingly led away from the theatre and the downtown area, but a narrow path between buildings served as a shortcut, and Juliette walked single file behind Marcel to the intersecting street. Once on the brick sidewalk, she walked beside him, taking his hand as she habitually did but then pulling it away.

Marcel said quietly, "You do understand that the people who killed Peter don't represent the people here?"

Juliette replied, "Yes, I understand that intellectually, but emotionally, I can't differentiate."

"Do you remember why we sent Yvonne to England?"

Juliette nodded. "How could I forget?"

"Yvonne testifies this week, and we still have hope it will lead to something. The question isn't whether the German people would be outraged or that the army would revolt—both are givens; the question is whether the British politicians will believe Yvonne and support the German people."

"Okay, I understand." She looked at him and said, "I know you love me, Marcel." She blurted it out, then quickly turned her head away.

Marcel tripped over the edge of a sidewalk brick and caught himself before he fell. He tried to stop walking, but Juliette walked ahead, and he had to skip to draw even with her.

He caught her arm. "How long have you known?"

She stopped and faced him. "Since soon after I married Peter...." He let her arm go, and she looked deep into his eyes... "Maybe sooner. How long have you known?"

"I don't know..." He shook his head. "It seems as though I've always loved you."

Marcel tried to hold her hand again, but she pulled away and began walking.

Juliette talked as she walked. "Marcel, please don't give up on me. I loved Peter with all my heart, and there was no room for you. Now he's gone, but my heart isn't empty; it's full of sadness and hate. I know you will fill it when that is gone, but now there's only this burning hatred for my enemies and a broken heart. I need to grieve—but I also need to fight!" She finally stopped and turned. "Will you wait for me?"

"Until I kill every one of those bastards for you!"

They walked to the opera house in silence, entering by the familiar stage door. The rehearsal was at ten, giving Juliette a half-hour to warm up her voice. The General Music Director, Alphons Dressel, gave her the key to her private studio, and she warmed her voice using arpeggios and phrases from Rigoletto.

Marcel waited outside the door until she finished, and then they headed for the rehearsal room, down a long hall to a door marked 'Probebühne 2.' Everything was familiar; Marcel took his usual position in a corner where he had a view of the entire rehearsal room. Herr Dressel introduced Juliette to the tenor who would sing the Duke and the baritone who would sing Rigoletto. The tenor was as handsome and tall as Peter had been, and he whispered in her ear as they embraced, "Perhaps we could get together later?" Juliette restrained the urge to whack him and held the equally handsome baritone a tiny bit longer than she had the tenor. He kissed her cheeks and said, "toi, toi, toi," customary in every German theatre. When they parted, Herr Dressel introduced the other principals.

The niceties out of the way, Juliette sat with Marcel through the first act and watched the ensemble work. The tenor's rendition of Questa o quella brought memories of Peter flooding back. His voice was eerily similar to Peter's, and he moved very much like him. Marcel became increasingly nervous as the aria went on, and when the tenor hit the final ringing high note perfectly and in full voice despite it being a staging rehearsal, he squirmed and crossed his arms. Juliette caught herself reaching for Marcel's hand, and instead leaned her head on his shoulder.

Rigoletto's second scene takes place outside Rigoletto's home, where Gilda first sings a touching duet with her father, followed by a love scene with the philandering Duke. Halfway through the love scene, a wave of grief suddenly overwhelmed Juliette, her voice broke, and tears fell in torrents. She sobbed, "I can't do it!" and ran out of the rehearsal room. Marcel followed her, leaving the tenor standing with his mouth open.

Juliette stopped outside the door to her dressing room and leaned against the wall to wait for Marcel. She knew he would come, and as he approached, she slid down the wall and put her arms on her raised knees. Marcel slid down to crouch beside her.

"I can't do it…that tenor reminds me of Peter… When he sings, I hear Peter!"

Marcel said, "Peter was a brave man; you must understand that he suffered so we can carry on, not so you can satisfy a need for revenge. He could have told them what they wanted to know, and we would either be dead or safely in Switzerland." He turned to face Juliette. "Don't make his sacrifice worth less than it was. We have an important job to do, and you must sing with this tenor for us to do it. If you really want to get even, go in there and do your job!" He put his hand on her shoulder. "Let me get the justice you want—I know how, and I swear I will do it."

Juliette stood up without saying a word, and Marcel followed her.

She walked back into the rehearsal room and finished the duet, and when it was time for the one o'clock food break, Herr Dressel walked to the Menza with Juliette and Marcel.

Juliette said, "I will not give you any more trouble, Herr Dressel."

"It hadn't occurred to me that you would, and I have never heard a more sympathetic or beautiful Gilda; I feel privileged to work with you."

Herr Dressel didn't miss the look she gave Marcel nor the squeeze she gave his hand.

Juliette rehearsed every day during the week, but early Sunday morning, she and Marcel took the train to Heilbronn to visit Pastor Bergman and Maria. They arrived in time for the morning service at Pastor Bergamn's Renaissance church, and Erik and Marita Stephanie caught up to them as they climbed the stone steps.

They hugged, and Marita asked Juliette how Peter and Nina were doing; Juliette ruined her day by bluntly whispering, "The Gestapo killed Peter. Papa won't tell me, but I'm sure they tortured him."

Marita gasped and tried to speak but couldn't.

Erik started to speak, "My God, Juliette..." but Marcel poked him, and he stopped.

Juliette opened her mouth, but Marcel took her arm and guided her farther up the stone steps to where Pastor Bergman greeted his flock. Juliette resisted at first but then, realizing what she had done, hurried to meet the pastor. Matthias Bergman took Juliette's hand and said, "I'm so happy to see you, Juliette, and I'm looking forward to dinner together. Maria will be so happy to see you."

Juliette couldn't mask her surprise. She opened her mouth to ask the obvious question, but Marcel answered Pastor Bergman before she could. He touched Juliette's shoulder and said, over the top of her head, "Of course, we are also looking forward to it." Marcel took Juliette's arm and guided her up the last two steps and through the massive open doors. Erik and Marita hurried to catch up with them, and they walked into the church together.

Juliette avoided any reference to Peter in her Kaffeeklatsch conversation after the service. She chatted with Marita about Nina, and Marita updated her on Elke and Brigitte. Marcel and Erik stood to one side and talked about flying at night.

Once outside, Juliette and Marita walked ahead of Erik and Marcel. No one mentioned Peter, even when everyone was safely inside the Bergman home.

Marita helped Maria carry everything to the table, and then Matthias asked everyone to bow their heads while he said grace.

"Our Father in heaven, please help us in this, our hour of need. We have lost a beloved friend, Peter Schweitzer, and we need your help understanding why such things keep happening. Thousands die every day, and we need to know how to help end this." He paused, then added, "We are grateful for the wonderful food Maria has prepared, and we thank you both for it. Amen."

The 'amen' went around the table, and when Matthias lifted his head, everyone began eating, making small talk about children, food shortages, and the weather.

Juliette lost interest in her food and the chatter, put her fork down, looked around the table, and stopped the conversation when she said, "I would like to talk about Peter, but first, I want to clear something up." She paused, and the room was silent. "The Gestapo in Amiens killed him because he was working for the Résistance, and they caught Peter because a French traitor ratted on him. The Gestapo tortured him, and it must have been terrible because Daddy won't tell me anything." She looked around the table until her flashing eyes rested on Matthias.

"Right now, I don't see God anywhere, and it's for sure He won't listen to me. You still have faith, and I want you to talk to Him for me. Tell God to help me kill the people who tortured and killed Peter, preferably as painfully as those bastards killed the man who loved me!"

Tears ran down her cheeks, but her voice didn't falter. "Ask God to help me destroy the Nazi evil and the monster who leads it."

No one chewed or swallowed; there was no sound of breathing.

Marcel broke the silence when he stood and raised his glass. "A toast to Peter."

"And to the long and painful death of his murderers!" Juliette exclaimed.

"To the just and painful death of Peter's murderers!" Erik added, "And when Juliette finishes with them, may they burn in hell!"

Everyone but Matthias stood up and said, "May they burn in hell!"

Finally, Matthias said, "Normally, I don't condone violence, but in this violent world where there don't seem to be any rules, I can imagine a God who would delight in answering Juliette's prayer." He stood up and raised his glass. "May God appropriately punish the wicked and reward the virtuous." He drank, and everyone drank with him.

Erik said, "Matthias, sometimes you surprise me." and raised his glass to him.

Marcel looked at Erik curiously. "I can't figure you out, Erik. You just wished your comrades-in-arms in hell, although not before Juliette gets to torture them. How do you reconcile that with your job?"

Erik squared his shoulders and put both hands on the table. "My job is to stop as many bombers as I can from slaughtering innocent people with their bombs, and I will do it as long as they continue to fly over our cities." He pointed at the table with his index finger, using it for emphasis. "The Gestapo is equally my enemy—and I don't know one man in the Wehrmacht who wouldn't shoot them if he thought he could get away with it!"

Marcel asked, "What about the SS... Do you want to kill them too?"

Erik sat back in his chair, shook his head, and answered, "The Waffen SS is an elite band of soldiers—probably the best in the world. There certainly are criminals among them, but generally, they are professional soldiers fighting against other soldiers. However, parts of the Waffen SS, the SS, and the SD are as bad or perhaps worse than the Gestapo. I have no idea how anyone could figure out who's a bad guy and who's better or worse."

Marcel nodded. "I see; everyone in the Gestapo is evil and worthy of death, but only some in the SS, and we don't know which ones." He paused for a few seconds, then went on.

"Have you heard anything about the Nazis killing Jews in gas rooms at Auschwitz?"

The room was silent.

Matthias said, "I have heard rumours. Do you have evidence that this is happening?"

Juliette eagerly jumped in. "I brought an escaped Auschwitz prisoner across the border into Belgium. The Résistance smuggled her to England, and she is testifying there this week. She brought documents containing signatures and names of victims—and photographs of women stripped naked and forced into a room where Guards put gas in the vents. Witnesses wrote that hundreds of women screamed for over ten minutes before they died. Half the people gassed in the group that Yvonne was supposed to accompany were children and older women. From the photograph, we estimate that the room is capable of gassing five hundred to a thousand people at a time, and the documents show that they are filling the room three times a day!"

Erik asked quietly, "What do they do with the bodies?"

Marcel answered, "We have pictures of that, too. They dump the bodies into a trench. According to the documents, they soak the bodies in gasoline, burn them, and cover them with dirt. And we have evidence that they are building crematoriums to completely destroy the evidence that these people ever lived."

Maria sobbed. "How can they kill women and their children?"

Marita abruptly left the room. Erik stood to follow her but stopped when Matthias spoke.

"I can't understand how God could allow this. How can He let this happen if He is merciful and all-powerful?"

Marcel shrugged. "Perhaps this is our responsibility. He gave us the tools to stop it; it's up to us to use them."

"Marcel," Juliette rapped his arm with her clenched hand, "you are an atheist. You don't believe in God, and now, neither do I."

"No," said Marcel. "I have no belief one way or the other—I believe there may be a God, but perhaps there is not. I cannot reconcile what is happening with the existence of an omnipotent being who has the power to stop it."

Juliette said, "You are far too generous!"

Matthias said, "You might doubt the existence of God, but I know you both to be Godly. Every day, I must adjust my idea of who God is; this distressing news of Peter is forcing me to reassess my belief in who He is." He looked expectantly at Marcel. "But enough philosophy—we should talk about what you want us to do."

"Please excuse me," Erik stood up. "I must go find Marita, and it is best that I do not hear the discussion." He left, and Maria followed him.

Marcel watched them go before he turned to Matthias. "We have a man and his wife who must get to England. They will travel together, and we will use two cars to get them to Switzerland. If you can, you must hold them somewhere away from our hotel until it's time to go. It worked perfectly last time, so we decided that Juliette's uncle Hébert would come from Zürich to hear Juliette sing and take us back with him."

"May I ask what this man and his wife mean to the British?"

Marcel said, "He works on the Uranprojekt, a project to create a powerful electric generator called a reactor, which could also lead to the creation of a super-bomb—a single bomb that could destroy a large city. We believe they already have a working reactor, and the Allies need to know whether Hitler is working on a bomb. This man is some sort of manager with knowledge of their progress. He is one-quarter Jewish, his wife is one-eighth, and they are nervous."

Matthias nodded and said, "Yes, I can take care of that, but if you could limit the time here to a week or less, that would make it simpler and more comfortable, especially for the woman."

Marcel said, "Two or three days at most. They will take their holidays here on a wine-tasting trip along the Neckar River. That is all arranged, and I have their papers. It may even be possible to keep them in a hotel, but we must prepare for the worst."

Marita, Maria, and Erik returned, and although they had lost their appetite for dinner, no one refused Maria's offer of dessert. Juliette went to the kitchen with Maria and Marita, and they chattered as they prepared strawberries and whipped cream. They carried the treasures to the table, and everyone sweetened them by adding more calories, but Marcel made it an art.

Juliette watched Marcel clean the whipped cream off his strawberries, licking the last bit from his spoon. He carefully mixed honey, cream, and red berries in the exact proportion he wanted, then methodically cut the strawberries into small pieces. She laughed to herself and was about to speak when Marita abruptly asked Marcel, "Do you think Monica could be in Auschwitz?"

Marcel put his spoon down. "No. I don't know exactly where she is, but as far as we know, she is in a work camp near Berlin."

Marita hadn't touched her strawberries. "I think about her every day and pray for her every night after I tuck Elke and Brigitte in bed."

Juliette and Marcel walked back to the train station in silence. The intense late afternoon sun warmed them as they walked with their arms locked. Marcel shortened his pace to match Juliette's, and they walked in step, laughing when they lost the synchronization. Finally, Juliette gave up and slowed down.

"You had that all arranged, didn't you?" she asked Marcel with a hint of accusation.

"I'm afraid so. Everything but your cry for blood."

"I'm sorry about that. When I saw Erik's uniform, I saw a German officer who could have killed Peter. It won't happen again."

"You will have to control yourself, Juliette. Many lives depend on you."

Juliette searched for an answer while looking at her feet.

Marcel put his finger under her chin. "If you do something to get yourself killed, I won't be able to live without you. Do you understand me?"

Juliette stared into his eyes. "Yes, I understand. I love you too, but you must wait."

Marcel took her arm, smiled, started walking, and said, "Until hell freezes, Ma chéri, until hell freezes!"

Chapter Thirty-Two

June 1942

Eine Frau kann jederzeit hundert Männer täuschen, aber nicht einmal eine einzige Frau.
(A woman can fool a hundred men anytime, but not one woman one time)
Michèle Morgan

JACQUES FOLLOWED YVONNE'S PROGRESS, and the Résistance informed him the day she crossed the channel in a French fishing boat, transferring to a British fisherman somewhere in the middle. The British received documents and photographs a week before Yvonne's arrival and immediately set up a secret Commission to examine them and interview Yvonne.

And that was it; Jacques heard nothing of the outcome, and no stories of the atrocities committed in Auschwitz appeared in any of the world's newspapers. The war continued with ever-increasing intensity, and three weeks later, Yvonne landed at Pier 21 in Halifax, Canada. She stopped at the first post box and mailed the letter she had written while on the ship, addressed to Jacques Durand.

Jacques dialed a memorized nimber and a familiar voice said, "Hier ist Kriminaldirektor Richter," as he always did.

"Guten Abend, Kriminaldirektor Richter, Jacques Durand here."

Major Richter, head of the Gestapo in Heilbronn, answered eagerly, "Ah, Monsieur Durand, I have been anticipating your call."

"I am calling regarding the transport of the articles we discussed—I will have a perfect opportunity in about two weeks."

Richter's voice rose slightly. "Excellent! Excellent! May I ask what the opportunity involves?"

"My daughter is currently singing in Nürnberg, and her godfather is picking her up after the last performance. He will take her to Zürich, where she will sing again in a few weeks. Her entourage is extensive, and he will bring two cars to carry everything. There will be space for your items if you wish."

The ensuing silence was short but revealing. "I can arrange that, but there may be items we must leave behind. Some are much too large to fit into a car."

Jacques had expected that. "The rigid parts are a problem, but there is little value in them, and I have people who can build new ones later as needed. If you could remove the problem items and roll the articles in protective tubes no more than ten centimetres in diameter, we can take all of them. We have equipped the cars to carry such packages inconspicuously."

Richter became excited again. "If you are certain of that, this will be much simpler than I thought. Yes, we can have the articles ready for pickup in two weeks, and I will transfer the funds you require before they leave here."

It was Jacques' turn to be silent, but only for a few seconds. "You must understand that there can be no problems at the border. I will give you a list of the people travelling, and you must see that the crossing goes smoothly. Herr Kriminaldirektor, do I make myself clear?"

"Yes, I understand, and a mutual friend will take care of that—I have no authority at the border, and some of the articles belong to him."

Jacques slowed his speech. "My daughter will be in one of the cars, and if anything should go wrong, I will lose all interest in preserving the items already in my care. She is very dear to me, and the price for harming her is more than you can bear."

"I assure you, Monsieur Durand, that no harm will come to your daughter or anyone travelling with her. If they have the proper papers, no one will question them."

Jacques returned to his friendly tone. "I accept your guarantee, and you may rest assured that your items are safe with me. I stake my reputation on it."

"You are pledging much more than your reputation, Monsieur

Durand," Major Richter paused to let it sink in. "I bid you a pleasant evening and your daughter a pleasant journey to Zürich."

"Do you trust him?" Veronique asked. Nina sat on her grandmother's lap.

"I trust his greed. I have more than a million Swiss francs in paintings that belong to him already in our care, and he understands the consequences if anything should go wrong. We will take another million francs in paintings and jewels from Heilbronn to Switzerland, and his partner in all this is the head of the SS in Munich. If this goes wrong, they will lose more than two million francs, and, in that case, I believe our friend in Munich will find a way to kill him. The Nazi gangster's world is unforgiving."

Veronique tried rearranging Nina on her lap, but she wriggled out of her arms and slid to the floor. She leaned against her grandmother's legs and put her thumb in her mouth.

"And if the Germans win the war? When they discover the British government owns all those paintings, will they kill us?"

"The Allies will ultimately destroy Germany...Hitler sealed his and his country's fate when he attacked Russia and declared war on the Americans. By the time they figure out what we've done, it will hopefully be too late to get revenge or paintings."

Nina decided she wanted back on Veronique's lap. Her patient grandmother picked her up. "Where are the paintings now?"

"They're in a salt mine in Neckarsulm, on the eastern side of Heilbronn. Salt mines are usually very dry—I think it's because sodium chloride absorbs moisture. The Nazis built a vault in one of the abandoned tunnels, disguised the entrance, and filled it with loot plundered from the Jews. They catalogued the items, but a few SS and Gestapo officers have secured their future by keeping certain items out of the system. They're the ones who guard the loot, which is a bit like putting a wolf in charge of the sheep."

Nina whined when Veronique stood up. "I'm going to take this little bundle to bed. Would her grandfather like to give her a good-night kiss?"

Jacques stood, and Nina reached for him. He took her from Veronique, kissed her, squeezed her in a hug, then gave her back. He said, "Bonne nuit, ma chérie" and Nina said, "Bonne nuit, pépé."

The final performance of Rigoletto went better than Juliette dared hope. The tenor played the Duke as the ass he was supposed to be, and Juliette concentrated on Gilda's relationship with Rigoletto, her opera father. Discovering her father's plot to kill her lover, Gilda substitutes herself for the Duke, becoming the assassin's victim in his stead. Rigoletto realizes his mistake too late.

Juliette thought of her real-life father and shared Rigoletto's pain when he opened the sack that was supposed to contain the dead Duke. The final duet, sung with Gilda's dying breaths while lying in her father's arms, brought the house to tears, and following the final curtain, most of the audience openly wept. Juliette took her curtain call late, taking time to get control of her emotions. She succeeded until she left the stage after her last bow, when she threw herself in Marcel's arms, crying, "Oh, Marcel, when will it be over?"

On the street outside the stage entrance, a beautiful new Mercedes waited at the curb, and when they came out, Uncle Hébert opened the rear door, jumped out, hugged Juliette, and shook Marcel's hand.

He said, "Juliette, you made me cry for the first time in many years...I wish your father had heard that performance."

"Thank you, Uncle Hébert. I wish he could hear me sing too. Perhaps... when the war is over." She smiled and slid into the seat. As the chauffeur turned around, Juliette recognized him.

"Charles! Is that you, Charles?"

He smiled, his white teeth whiter against his black skin. "We will have time to catch up in Zürich." He quickly added, "Last week, I married a Swiss Mädel who says I'm her Swiss chocolate man!" He laughed and faced the front as he put the car in gear.

At the hotel, Uncle Hébert followed Juliette to her room. She sat on the bed, leaving the comfortable chair for her godfather, and when he was settled, she said, "Okay, Uncle, tell me what we do next."

"I can tell you some of it, but not all."

"Fun and games again? One of my best qualities is my ability to keep a secret."

"Yes, dear, I do know that. But, as your father has no doubt told you, what you don't know can't kill your accomplices. You must have faith in your father." He waited a couple of seconds, and when Juliette showed no inclination to interrupt him, he went on.

"You will ride in the first car with Charles and me. Your makeup lady, who should arrive at any moment, will ride with us. My chauffeur will drive the second car carrying Marcel and your coach."

"Who is the scientist—the chauffeur or the coach?" Juliette asked with a wink.

"My dear, I don't know what you're talking about."

Oskar and Karin Krüger arrived ten minutes after Juliette arrived in her room. Karin was a tall, powerfully built woman with a pleasant face. Oskar was half a head shorter than his wife, wore a soft grey hat to cover his balding head, and small round glasses that almost touched his eyeballs, magnifying them several times. His pointed nose, his complete lack of a chin on his triangular face, and the grey hat gave him a naturally comical appearance—he looked like a giant mouse.

It was almost too much for Juliette when Oskar spoke; she froze her smile and controlled the urge to laugh.

He squeaked, "I don't know how to thank you, young lady. It seems you are prepared to risk your life to rescue my wife and me."

Juliette could not suppress a chuckle, but she found words that suited. "Me? I'm not going to risk my life, and neither are you. I'm going to Zürich to sing." She continued to smile, knowing no one would guess that Oskar and Karin were husband and wife, and no one could appear less vital to anything than Oskar did.

Karin took over with a beautiful contralto speaking voice, "I don't think that is quite true. We must take the risk, but you have a choice. I admire your courage, and I thank you for it."

"Thank you, Karin, but I am not a movie heroine, and I'm certainly not courageous. I do this partly because my diva status comes with certain privileges, and because I have good reasons to hate the Nazis."

"Now, let's get to business." Marcel cut in before Juliette could go on, "I have written down all the details of your lives, and you have travel visas for Switzerland, but first, we will have to get you out of Germany. No one will be looking for you, but there will be questions at the border, so memorize who you are."

Karin asked Juliette, "What does your costume and makeup person do?"

"She cleans and irons my costumes, sews for me, helps me put on my makeup, and generally keeps track of everything. I am a diva, and you are my ersatz mother. You've been with me for a while, and you know me very well." Juliette made it up as she talked. This majestic woman would never be believable as a maid. "Yes—you must treat me as though you were the boss. My daddy has hired you to look after me, and that's what you do!"

"What about your vocal coach?" squeaked Oskar, "How does he fit in?"

Juliette laughed. "He teaches her to sing her roles..." She giggled, put her finger in the air and said, "Maybe we should think of something else."

"He could be your accountant." Marcel chuckled, "You're always in financial trouble with one government or another."

"Yes," he squeaked, "I'm an outstanding accountant. That is what I do in the Uranprojekt. I can fix whatever problems you have with any government, especially the Germans."

Juliette laughed. "In a few days, you will be in England, and my problem is with the Belgian government." She looked at him curiously. "But tell me, why would the British want an accountant?"

"I have the records with me. Every detail about every Reichsmark spent on the Uranprojekt is in these books. No one spent a Pfennig on that project without my permission!" He went to a bag he had been carrying and withdrew four thick ledgers.

Marcel said, "No one told me about this... Tell me about the ledgers!"

On anyone else, Oskar's smug look would have been offensive. "These ledgers detail everything purchased for the project since 1939. Each ledger is a full year except the last one, and it is complete up to the day I left, the twenty-ninth of May." When Marcel didn't ask the obvious question, Oskar said, "Don't worry, there are two sets of books… the originals are still in my office. No one knows I have them."

Marcel stretched out his hands. "Give me the ledgers—I'll return in about an hour."

Juliette, her accountant, and her lady-in-waiting spent the remainder of the evening going over who they were until they began speaking and acting their parts naturally. Marcel didn't return until long after they were asleep.

Without saying why, Jacques pushed the date to cross into Switzerland forward so they could spend a day travelling through the hills south of Nürnberg in the two Mercedes cars. They stopped at the Wartberg restaurant outside Heilbronn to enjoy the view of the city while they ate a light lunch.

The drive in the afternoon sunshine was pleasant, and they were in excellent spirits when they went for their evening meal in the Pfälzerhof dining room. Afterwards, Marcel asked for a conference in the privacy of his room.

He began, "The Gestapo or the SS were watching us today. They sat at a corner table in the Wartberg restaurant and, at varying times, followed our cars. That was not supposed to happen, but we suspected it might—that was the reason for the delay. We've changed our plans slightly, and we now know that we must be on our toes at the border. Expect the baggage and cars to be searched, and the guards will closely examine your papers."

Juliette spoke up, "Isn't that expected?"

"Yes, normally…" Something bothered Marcel… "There were agreements made—but somehow, a rat has gotten into the ship. We will give him some cheese, and then, while he's eating it, we will sneak past him."

Karin and Oskar didn't flinch at the news.

Juliette asked Karin, "You aren't afraid, are you? The border guards are trained to recognize fear."

Karin answered, "Oskar's brother and his parents are in Dachau; they killed my best friend during Kristallnacht, and we believe her husband is now in Treblinka—perhaps he is dead. What good comes from fear? At least we have a chance."

Marcel stopped the discussion. "Nothing will happen to anyone if we keep our heads."

Late the following morning, they left for Switzerland. The drive through the countryside went smoothly until the last few kilometres when they caught up to four German Lastwagen, black smoke pouring from their exhausts and moving at a snail's pace. The crooked road offered no place to pass, and the Mercedes' occupants were becoming ill from the exhaust smoke when they finally reached the border.

At the crossing, Hébert's cars had to wait while SS border guards searched the Lastwagen, lifting the floor mats in the cabs, probing under the seats, and banging steel bars on the load beds. Uncle Hébert instructed Charles to honk his horn, and the noise got an SS officer's attention. Hébert rolled down his window and, following a short conversation, put something in the officer's hand.

The young man put the article in his pocket, went to the guard and spoke to him. Seconds later, they waved the trucks ahead, and the Mercedes cars pulled up to the barrier.

Marcel's chauffeur handed the SS officer his papers, neatly packed in a leather pouch. As the officer went through them, Juliette overheard talk about the weather and the number of trucks making fortunes hauling contraband.

Oskar got out and stood beside Marcel while the officer checked his documents. The officer asked Oskar, "What is the purpose of your visit to Switzerland?"

"I am Mademoiselle Juliette Durand's personal assistant and book-keeper," he pointed toward Juliette. "I will be taking care of some banking business for her."

The young man's eyes lit up, and he lost all interest in Oskar. "Is she in the other car?" he asked eagerly.

"Why yes, she is. We're returning from Nürnberg, where she sang Gilda in the opera Rigoletto. Do you know it?"

The young man handed Oskar his papers. "No, I don't know any operas, but I do know Mademoiselle Durand!"

"Oh yes, you must be the young man she has spoken of so many times. Would you like me to formally introduce you to her?"

"I would be delighted." The young man became flustered. "I forgot to give her my name the last time I saw her—would you have a pencil and paper?"

Oskar fetched his leather case, took out a blank piece of paper and a sharp pencil. Juliette smiled as she watched the young man in a grey SS uniform lay his MP40 machine pistol on the rear fender while he spread the paper on the trunk cover to write his name. Oskar took it to Juliette, and she pretended to examine it.

Oskar grinned widely. "This young man says he knows you from the last time you crossed here. He wants me to introduce you to him."

Juliette squealed through the open window. Her door flew open, and she scrambled out of the car, running clumsily in her heels. She tripped at precisely the right time, throwing her arms around the young soldier to keep from falling. He stumbled, grabbed her around the waist and began stuttering. She kissed him full on the lips; he kissed her clumsily, groaned, and Juliette pushed him against the car to prevent him from collapsing. When she let him go, she said in terrible German laced with a thick French accent, "I knew you would be a fantastic kisser, Hans Feldman."

Hans's partner stepped between them, handed Hans his machine pistol, then turned to Juliette and said, "Papier bitte!"

He followed her to her car door. She leaned in, lifted her buttocks while she searched for her purse, finally found it, and began to open it.

Hans yelled, "No!" and grabbed the purse before Juliette undid the clasp. He examined the bag, turned it around, carefully opened it and passed it back to Juliette.

She smiled at Hans with a touch of disdain, handed his partner her comb, a bottle of perfume, a beautiful lace handkerchief... and finally when his hands were full, she found her passport and Swiss visa. She held them in front of him, smiling sweetly but with a bit of sarcasm around the edges. He carefully laid the toiletry articles on the car's roof while he examined her passport.

A senior SS officer approached with a group of four soldiers. "What is the problem here? Why aren't you searching these cars?" He stopped in front of Juliette and was about to speak again when she threw her arms around him. "Oh, Frederick, I am so glad to see you. Everything is all mixed up—please help me!"

He gently took her to one side and said quietly, "I know you are innocent my dear, but a reliable source has told us that these two cars are smuggling art treasures out of Germany. We will find them and punish the guilty parties, but you will be safe with me!" He waved to Hans and said, "You will take care of these ladies while we search the cars." Hans beamed.

The soldiers opened the engine compartments and the trunks of both cars. They pulled out the suitcases and searched through everything, leaving clothing scattered on the ground. When they found nothing, they removed the rear seats and the floor mats down to the bare metal. They pulled the panels from the doors but still found nothing. One of the officers went back to the building and returned with a mirror. He ordered Hans's partner to lie beside the cars and crawl along in the dirt, tilting the mirror while he shone a flashlight on it. It took him twenty minutes, and he found nothing.

Hébert Gronau was a man with a pleasant demeanour, but he lost every sign of it as the SS soldiers systematically tore his cars apart. He looked at Frederick and asked politely, "May I use your telephone, sir?"

Frederick deliberated, then shrugged, "Why not? The Bundeswehr pays for it."

Hébert walked over to the building with one of the SS soldiers, and, a few minutes later, the soldier returned without Herr Gronau.

"You are wanted on the telephone, sir."

When his boss didn't move, he said, "It's Hauptmajor Thurm calling from München, sir." Frederick hesitated. "He said you were to come sofort, sir."

Three minutes later, Frederick, red-faced and apoplectic, returned with Hébert.

"Put the cars back as they were!" He shouted at his men, straining to control his rage as he said, "And when you're done, let them go."

Juliette tried to keep from smiling, but Frederick caught her and scowled. She wiggled her fingers at him, but he ignored her. He marched back to the building, leaving six soldiers to reassemble the cars.

Hébert put Marcel in charge of the rebuilding and asked both chauffeurs to help. When the cars were reinstated to Marcel's satisfaction, he and the chauffeurs shook hands with the soldiers and thanked them for their cooperation. Hans waved at Juliette as she drove away, and when she blew him a kiss through the rear window, Hans's partner knocked his hat off.

The cars pulled into a parking lot at the foot of a steep hill on the outskirts of Zürich, and parked beside a familiar-looking truck with German plates.

Juliette watched Marcel leave the other Mercedes and shake hands with the driver. They chatted for a moment, and then the driver used a wrench to remove a heavy steel plate bolted on the rear of the truck bed. He reached into the void behind where the plate had been, pulled out a long metal tube and handed it to Marcel. He loaded it into the Mercedes' trunk and then returned to take a second tube from the driver. Altogether, eight tubes went into the two Mercedes.

The driver crawled under the truck, worked with the wrench for a few minutes, and slid a rectangular package into Marcel's waiting hands. Marcel passed it to Oskar in the rear seat of the Mercedes, followed by three canvas bags.

Juliette got out of the car and intercepted Marcel. "Paintings, jewellery, and four journals. Am I right?"

"Possibly," he said, "and I would like to compliment you on your performance at the border. Bravo, ma chérie!"

Juliette was on a roll. "The cars weren't supposed to be searched. Someone double-crossed us, didn't they?"

"I would rather say that they underestimated your father, and I would not want to be the man who did that. He wanted to blackmail Jacques by throwing you in jail, and my guess is that he would have traded you for something quite valuable."

Chapter Thirty-Three

May 1943

Freunde können und müssen Geheimnisse voreinander haben; sie sind einander doch kein Geheimnis.
(Friends can and must have shared secrets; between them, they are indeed not secrets.)
Goethe

Juliette reserved the summer of 1942 for family time with Nina and much-needed rest for herself. Jacques sold Juliette's house, and she moved back into her room at Avenue de Saturne 6. The summer passed, and autumn became a damp, bone-chilling winter. Juliette sang as often as she could, mainly in Germany, and her expeditions to snatch people from the clutches of the Nazis became almost routine. It was exceptional when she returned from Germany without a new coach, wardrobe expert, or a mistress who looked after her needs.

On the fifth of May 1943, on one of Juliette's few trips with no 'special' deliverables, Hébert Gronau picked up Juliette and Marcel at the train station in Zürich. Hébert's house was comfortable, most would say opulent, and he welcomed Juliette and Marcel warmly. The housemaid showed them to a room with a double bed, but Marcel corrected her. She left, chattering in bad French about her terrible mistake, and returned with a key to a separate room for Marcel.

Dinner with Hébert was a semiformal occasion—Marcel wore a vest and tie, and Juliette wore a pink dress with a white floral pattern. It almost covered her shoes, and the neckline buttoned to her chin.

The small talk was over before they finished the baked snail and cheese appetizers, and Hébert took advantage of the pause before the soup.

"I am sorry that I assumed you two were together. I apologize for any embarrassment it may have caused, but I excuse myself because it is obvious to everyone who knows you that you are in love."

Marcel's face turned crimson, but he said nothing. Juliette laughed softly. "Yes, I do love Marcel, and I'm sure he feels the same about me, but I still can't get past Peter's memory. I've known that Marcel cared for me since I married Peter, but my heart has no room for anything but hatred for the Nazis and revenge."

Hébert spread his hands. "I've lost two wives, one after only three years of marriage, and I know how devastating that is." He looked at Juliette and said desperately, "Juliette, you must forget about revenge! Life is too short to waste, and every day that passes, you and Marcel deny yourselves a day of joy you will never recover."

Juliette looked down at the table, and Marcel spoke up.

"I feel the same need for revenge. I intend to kill the men who tortured Peter, and if I have my way, their death will not be an easy one. We must have justice first and love later because if we choose love first, justice will never follow!"

"Love later? What nonsense! Do you think you can make up for lost time? Of course, you can't, and no one can count on tomorrow!"

Hébert turned his concentration to Juliette. "Here and now is all that any of us has. God will not help you get revenge; He will not give you back the time you've lost, and this vendetta will devour both of you. Stop now, live today. Sleep together tonight—enjoy the love you both feel!"

He waited as the maid served the soup, then went on. "The soup is here. I apologize for the interference, but I care for you both. I see you missing out on your wonderful youth, just as I squandered mine." He lifted his glass, full of red wine. "Damn the war!" He touched their glasses.

"Damn the war!"

Zerbinetta turned out to be every bit as fearsome as Juliette had anticipated it would be when she first saw the score of Ariadne auf Naxos. Juliette thought she had mastered Zerbinetta's aria scene standing at the piano, but when she began flitting around on the stage like a butterfly going from blossom to blossom, the aria became a beast. The German stage director had no sympathy and insisted on complete run-throughs from the first day. Juliette left out phrases and sang half-voice, commonly known as "marking," but to no avail—her voice revolted. She knew that if she continued punishing her vocal cords, they would give up, probably for months. Juliette told the director she couldn't continue working this way—she must learn his staging in sections.

The stage director ignored her pleas to break the aria into segments and assemble them when her voice had 'sung them in.' He reacted as most non-singing directors would—he maintained that her problem was psychological, suggesting positive thinking and confidence in her ability to do what he wanted as a cure. Finally, in a screaming match, Juliette broke off all civilized relations with the Regisseur and headed for the theatre manager's office.

She had made her feelings toward the director known to everyone within a thousand metres of the stage, and prepared herself to meet a forewarned manager. Juliette evaluated her position as she marched down the wide hallway but stopped at the certainty that she was the only soprano the manager could find who would even attempt to sing the role. All her weapons loaded for a fight, Juliette marched into the manager's office without knocking.

The theatre manager was a thin, medium-height man with a large French nose and sparkling eyes. Before Juliette could begin delivering her tirade, Jules Martin reached for her hand and said, "Ah! Mademoiselle Durand, may I offer you a cognac?" He bowed, brushing his lips across the back of her hand. He turned, lifted a decanter from the shelf, and pleasantly said, "I'm going to have one myself."

Juliette cancelled the tirade and nodded, and he poured two glasses. "I expect we will both need this. I heard that you banged heads with Herr Schmidt."

"He's been here?"

Doctor Jules Martin smiled with a generous dose of warmth. "Yes, he was here this morning before rehearsal, but I'm talking about the recent screaming. He believes you need psychiatric help—what do you think we should do?"

Juliette took a sip of her cognac to buy a little time to adjust... this silver-tongued man deserved the truth.

"Herr Schmidt is an arrogant bully, and I cannot sing with him directing me! I can sing the role and do the staging he wants, but I must come to it in steps without brutalizing my voice! He is asking me to do things that are impossible without a great deal of practice. When he introduces complicated and intense physical activity into extremely difficult passages, I must have the staging natural and automatic before working the coloratura phrases into my voice!"

The man smiled so warmly that Juliette had to return it. When he spoke, the combination made her skin pleasantly tingle.

"Yes, of course, I understand what you are saying, and I will make a change. Would you be happy if I changed the director, but just for your scenes? Your new director would work exclusively with you, using the staging outlined by Herr Schmidt."

Juliette felt the cognac's warmth working its way down to her toes. Her will to fight became the opposite.

"That depends... Who?" she asked cautiously.

"Malcolm Dégenis. He is a young Canadian, and I hired him as an assistant director when I had a similar problem. He works successfully with another director who is more difficult than Herr Schmidt; he is talented."

Juliette was aware she had crossed to the other side when she said, "Do you mean talented at working with difficult sopranos?" but didn't care.

Jules laughed. "Yes, he does have a wonderful personality that sopranos seem to like, perhaps because he loves women—you could even say he is blessed with a woman's artistic sensitivity." He put his glass down and leaned forward, stopping Juliette's sarcastic comment in her throat.

"He is very noticeably homosexual. Will that disturb you?"

Juliette answered quickly. "No, of course not! It might be nice to work with someone who likes me for something besides imagining me in their bed!"

Juliette finished the last drop, looked at her empty glass and said,

"You are very good at this, aren't you?"

"Mademoiselle?"

"Manipulating problem singers?..."

"Sometimes, but singers are the least of my problems—now I have to tell Herr Schmidt that he can't practise psychiatry on you." He chuckled a little too loud. "No German stage director wants to hear that!"

Juliette stood and immediately had to sit again to stop the room from spinning.

Jules laughed. "Perhaps we should have a cup of coffee before you go back to rehearsals?"

"Do you get all of your sopranos drunk?"

He blushed. "No, my wife would react badly to that. However, perhaps we should each have a cup of coffee and discuss another, more permanent contract."

Juliette nodded, and Jules filled a kettle and set it on a hotplate. She said, "You know I can't discuss money. My father does all that, but I can discuss what roles you want me to sing."

Jules and Juliette spent the entire hour left in the Mittagspause talking about potential roles, and when the Pause was over at three, she went directly to the stage, almost sober. When Juliette walked out of the wings, a young man crossed to meet her. He bypassed Juliette's hand and hugged her. Barely taller than she was and no wider, they flowed together like butter in a mould, and she liked him at once. He stepped back and wiped his pants with his hands as though he would prefer to brush a skirt.

"I'm so sorry I was forward with you, darling." He fiddled with his fingers on her wrist, avoiding eye contact. "I've heard you sing and watched you from afar, and I'm in love with your voice!"

Juliette laughed and wrapped her fingers around his hand so that he would stop tickling her. "I think we will become good friends, Malcolm." She put her finger on her lip and whispered, "When did the manager tell you we would be working together?"

"Oh, he told me this morning when I arrived." Malcolm said pleasantly, "Shall we begin?"

He crossed his arms over his chest and put a finger on his lip. "Just to review where we are: Ariadne is alone on the island of Naxos, jilted by Theseus after they slew the Minotaur monster together—a ghastly beast! She assumed they would become lovers since they had performed such magnanimous feats together, but Theseus had other monsters to kill and left her alone on Naxos. In true Wagnerian style, Ariadne is depressed. As a matter of fact, for the entire opera, she is either asleep, complaining, or threatening to kill herself!"

He laughed, clapped his hands to congratulate himself, then went on before Juliette could comment. "Zerbinetta, Harlekin, and their simple cohorts are trying to cheer poor Ariadne up, but their comedy bores her. Zerbinetta changes course—she breaks away, deciding to explain the rules of life to Ariadne, woman to woman, according to her flirtatious experience."

Malcolm looked around…they were alone except for the accompanist, who was filing her nails.

"You may sing the beginning vigorously, as Maestro Strauss has written it—Herr Schmidt has designed the appropriate vigorous activities." Malcolm danced gracefully in a circle around the imaginary rock on which Ariadne was sulking. He stopped in front of Juliette.

"But then, Herr Schmidt and I must diverge slightly. I would rather you flitted around with your voice and let the action dominate. There is no need to give much of your voice capital—we both know you will need it later. You must concentrate on the movement until it becomes yours. You must imagine it in your sleep!"

He looked mischievously at Juliette. "Can you flirt with your voice?"

Juliette immediately felt a sense of relief; she knew precisely what he meant.

The accompanist began at the beginning, and Malcolm gracefully danced the staging with Juliette. When she reached the spot Malcolm had indicated she should flirt, Juliette clipped the phrases seductively, changing her approach to the aria. At the end of the first third, with her voice still fresh, Malcolm stopped everything with a wave.

"Now, you are going to get serious with the middle section. Zerbinetta is a nymphomaniac who interprets fidelity as sleeping with the same man twice in a row! In truth, no man could satisfy her, and she flits here and there like a bee collecting nectar in a clover field. You must approach this as Zerbinetta, a bundle of nerves, always looking for the man who can keep up with her urges but never finding him. She is all the joy of sex personified and never serious." He smiled at Juliette. "Can you do that?"

"I'm afraid so…lately, I'm a natural at 'never serious.'"

Juliette enjoyed the two weeks of rehearsals and spent her free time with Malcolm and Marcel. When Malcolm was in the Menza with them, Juliette couldn't help but notice that the other cast and stage crew avoided sitting near them.

She decided to experiment and sat at one end of a table set for six. Two chorus members joined her but picked up their plates and changed tables when Malcolm arrived. When the dining room became packed, several men left without eating rather than sitting at one of the available places at Malcolm's table.

"They hate me," Malcolm stated flatly, watching a man standing with his plate in his hand, waiting for a place at another table.

"They don't hate you, Malcolm," Juliette put her hand on his, covering it, "You can't hate someone you don't know. They are embarrassed to the point where they can't face you. They don't know what to expect, so they deal with their fear and ignorance by avoiding you."

"How can I change that?"

"If you knew that, you could make the Nazis accept the Jews, and the English forgive the Germans—and the war would be over tomorrow. I know what a great person you are. You have helped me so much that I can never repay you."

Malcolm smiled, and Marcel added, "I hope this doesn't embarrass you, but Juliette told me she thinks of you as her very best friend."

Malcolm moved as though he would stand up but settled back into his chair. "That's exactly how I feel about her! I love her to death!"

Juliette's affectionate laugh drew the attention of everyone in the room.

Chapter Thirty-Four

22–29 May 1943

Was einem bösen Weib, 'nem Feind, man in den Rachen wirft, das nenn'
ich Kosten. Beim guten Gäste oder Freund dagegen nenn' ich Gewinn, was
man für ihn verbraucht.
(The revenge one takes against a bad wife or an enemy; I call that cost.
Whatever one gives to friends and guests, I call that profit.)
Titus Maccius Plautus

THE PREMIÈRE WAS A SENSATION, and before she went out for her third curtain call, Juliette ran backstage to find Malcolm. Over his protests, she took his hand and dragged him on the stage with her. He clumsily bent at the waist, and when he straightened, Juliette wrapped her arms around him and kissed him. She stood back and graciously swept her arm in his direction—the audience roared, and Juliette clapped with them.

Juliette and Marcel decided not to wait for the car. They would walk fifteen minutes to Hébert's home to change for the party—the May evening was warm, the walk would clear some cobwebs, and Juliette would have a private moment with Marcel. As they exited the stage door and turned down the narrow alley leading to the street, Juliette started to speak, but Marcel raised his hand for her to stop and listen.

A muffled plea for help came from behind the building, and Marcel ran toward the sound, his hand diving into his pocket. Juliette did her best to keep up, but she was several steps behind by the time Marcel rounded the corner of the opera house. When she passed the corner, she heard him say, "Oh my God," and saw that he had pulled the Beretta out of his pocket. He fired it twice in the air, then pointed the pistol at three men bent over a form lying on the ground.

The men, all brown-shirted German soldiers, slowly straightened, raising their hands. Juliette ran to the still body. She knelt and put her hand under his head. His face looked like tenderized meat, but he forced a painful smile and raised his hand.

"Juliette," he said, "I am so glad to see you!"

"Malcolm..." She hung her head, sobbing..., "What have they done to you?" She looked up in time to see the largest of the three SA soldiers unsnap his holster and move to pull out his Walther P38, then hesitate when he saw Marcel's smile.

Marcel motioned the Beretta's barrel to the pistol in the fat man's holster. "Do it, and pray for good luck... You will need a miracle!"

The fat man returned the smile, showing his crooked, nicotine-stained teeth. He changed his mind, carefully buttoned the holster, and slowly raised his hands.

The light from a streetlamp shone into the corner, full on his face, sending a shock through Juliette. She laid Malcolm's head on the ground, stood and walked purposefully over to the fat brown-shirted SA officer. Now certain who he was, she spit in his face and turned to Marcel.

She put out her hand, shouted, "Give me your gun!" and stepped toward him. Marcel stepped aside, taking her out of his line of fire and keeping the SA officers in front of him.

"That's the bastard who raped me on Kristallnacht..." Her voice became a scream... "Give...me...that...gun!" She pointed at the fat officer. "He must die, and I will kill him!"

Marcel put his hand out to stop her from getting between him and the SA soldiers, and she stood still. "Not this way, Juliette! He will get what's coming to him, but not now, not like this!" He waved his gun toward the street without looking away from the soldiers. "Get out of here, or I will give her the gun!" They fled, their running footfalls fading in the distance.

Juliette, furious, the rape refreshing itself in her mind, hissed, "We'll talk about this later," and returned to Malcolm.

Marcel carried Malcolm into the theatre—to the sofa in the lounge. Juliette went to the bathroom and brought back three damp towels. She gently cleaned the blood and dirt from Malcolm's face.

Marcel said, "I'm calling Hébert—we are getting you to a hospital!" He headed for the hallway—to a phone he had noted earlier, but Malcolm stopped him with a desperate plea.

"No, no hospital! There's nothing broken—I'll be alright."

Juliette stopped working on his face. "This isn't the first time someone has beaten you, is it?"

"No, I've lost count of them."

Juliette shouted at Marcel, "Why didn't you let me shoot them? If you didn't have the nerve, you should have given me the gun!"

"It is not a question of nerve. There is a time and a place," Marcel said firmly, "and that was neither. This country is not at war, and we would be in jail for the rest of our lives if either of us had shot those bastards." He raised his voice. "You must let me take care of these things! You know nothing of how this works, and you are getting in my way!" He walked out of the room, fists clenched.

Tears running down her cheeks, Juliette looked down at Malcolm, and he said, "He's never put you in your place before, has he?"

"No, he hasn't." She bowed her head.

"Has anyone?"

Juliette searched her memory, realized she knew the answer and shook her head.

Marcel returned ten minutes later with Hébert's chauffeur, and they carried Malcolm to the car. They laid him across the back seat with his head on Juliette's lap, and Marcel sat silently in the front seat.

Marcel suspected the SA officers had leave that would keep them in Zürich until the end of the week, and he started his hunt in the bars and brothels. He began his stalk near the opera house and patiently worked his way out. On Thursday night, an hour before midnight, Marcel found them sitting at a window in an upscale restaurant called the Rathauskeller.

He didn't have to wait long; five minutes later, three SA Brownshirts opened the heavy door and stepped onto the street. He followed, staying in the shadows. They stopped outside a bar...Marcel expected them to go in, but they set up a stand in an alley out of sight, smoking a steady string of cigarettes and laughing occasionally. Marcel set up his stand half a block away.

A half-hour later, two young men walked out of the bar. Clearly enjoying one another's company, they walked down the street hand in hand, and the SA trio followed them. The hunters paced themselves to catch the two men opposite a path that led downhill to a park along the lake. Surrounding them with their guns drawn, they laughed as they prodded their victims toward the water. Marcel cut across the park lawn, running to reach the bottom of the hill ahead of them, and set up his ambush in the dark shadows between two massive oak trees. When the soldiers arrived, pushing their victims ahead of them, they forced the two young men to the ground near the oaks. The big man straddled the smaller of the victims and pressed his gun against the side of his head.

"On your knees, you pervert!" He unbuttoned his fly; his partners giggled self-consciously and backed away, dragging the second victim toward the oaks.

Marcel stepped silently out of the shadows, drove his double-edged knife into the nearest man's neck, then whipped the handle sideways, cutting off his windpipe. He stepped over him, reached the second man just as he turned and, in a smooth motion, drew the knife across the stunned man's throat. Before the dying officer struck the ground, Marcel was on the back of the big man, his blade at the fat man's throat.

"You have three seconds to put the gun down—one, two..." The terrified man threw the gun; it landed near his intended victim's petrified partner, sitting on the ground a few feet away.

Marcel grabbed the SA officer by his hair and jerked his head back, exposing his throat to the knife—he used just enough pressure to cut through the skin on the fat man's neck and start a trickle of blood. The young victim rolled over, away from his tormentor, and Marcel said, "You can kill him with this knife or take the gun out of my right pocket and shoot him; the choice is yours!"

The young man stood up and moved close to his tormentor, who began to cry, pleading, "Please don't! We weren't going to hurt you—we were just going to have a little fun!"

The young man spat in the SA officer's face and searched for Marcel's gun.

His companion stood up. "Please don't kill him, James; he isn't worth it!"

"I beg to differ." Marcel turned to look at the young man who had found the Beretta and was trying to figure out how it worked. "I am going to kill him if you don't. However, your claim is more immediate, so I am giving you the first opportunity.

He glanced at the young man holding the Beretta. "If you don't want to do it, I don't mind—although I do have one request. Would you help me drag them to the water?"

The young man put the little pistol back in Marcel's pocket, shook his head and looked at the ground. Marcel drew the knife across the fat man's throat. He fell on his face, kicking, trying to stop the blood with his hands. Marcel rolled him over with his foot and snarled, "That's for Juliette!" The man's eyes slowly lost focus, and finally, his hands fell still.

Marcel and one of the young men dragged the heavy load ten metres down the hill to the water, leaving a trail of blood on the grass. The friends pulled the other men to the lake and rolled them into the water. A sprinkle of rain began to fall, then rapidly increased, washing the blood toward the lake.

"It's going to pour—we should go home," Marcel said quietly, "Thank you for your help, but perhaps you should buy one of these." He reached for his Beretta, and the man who had been the fat officer's intended victim inspected the tiny pistol before handing it back. He leaned over and picked up the heavy 9mm Walther the fat officer had thrown away.

Marcel smiled. "That will work."

Three days later, Juliette was browsing the local paper when she asked Marcel to stop reading his book and come over to her chair. The fat SA officer's gruesome picture was on the front page, along with his two comrades—there was no doubt about their identities. The headline shouted, "THREE GERMAN SA OFFICERS BRUTALLY MUR-DERED!"

"Do you know anything about this?"

Marcel leaned over to look at the newspaper. He took it from her, looked closely at the pictures, then handed it back. "Yes, that certainly does look brutal!

Malcolm took the paper from Juliette, stared at the picture, then looked at Marcel, who returned to his book.

CHAPTER THIRTY-FIVE

St Valentine's Day, February 1944

Die höchste Kunst des Betruges ist, scheinbar in die gestellte Falle zu gehen.
(The highest art of deception is to appear to step into the trap.)
François VI, Herzog de La Rochefoucauld

AUTUMN 1943 WAS A HAPPY TIME for Juliette and Nina, a time when they became close friends. Juliette taught her daughter new words every day, and, at two-and-a-half, she could recite the alphabet and speak like an adult. She hated baby talk and refused to respond to it, correcting those who tried to use it. On Christmas 1943, Nina asked how the baby Jesus was born.

Veronique laughed as she bragged about her granddaughter to Jacques. "That girl is not a child...she is a short adult! She asked me yesterday to explain who God was, and when I tried, she looked at me as though I were crazy and left in a huff. I expect you will have to try it soon, so good luck."

"Someone would have to explain it to me first." Sitting in her comfortable chair beside her father, Juliette spread her hands and said, "I haven't seen much evidence of God in the last few years. Now, the devil—he's out in the open; he's a vermin named Hitler."

Veronique touched her daughter's hand. "Juliette, please try to be happy—you're so bitter you frighten me. Perhaps if you returned to church..."

Juliette's voice rose. "No, I no longer believe in God and would feel like a hypocrite. If a God existed, Nina's father wouldn't be dead!"

"But perhaps if you pray, God will help you find peace, even if you think you don't believe in him. It doesn't hurt to pray, even if you have doubts."

Juliette wanted the discussion over. "The God you pray to has shown he isn't interested in me, and He won't help me because I want to see Peter's murderers dead! And I want to kill them with my own hands! When you pray, will you ask your God to help me with that?"

Veronique had been hooking a picture to hang in the foyer; it was a picture of a little girl singing as she skipped through a field of buttercups. Without looking up from her work, she asked Juliette, "What about Marcel—how long do you expect him to wait?"

"Mother, Peter has only been gone… It's too soon!"

Veronique put down her handiwork. "Juliette, I am going to give you a piece of advice. That man has loved you since before you went to Germany to sing. You broke his heart when you married Peter; Marcel tried hard but couldn't let go. He loved Peter because you loved him; no other man I know would have done that! He is waiting for you, and he is the best thing that has ever happened to this family. Stop chasing this terrible revenge… Marcel is where you will find peace and happiness."

Sadness softened Juliette's voice. "Mother, I love him too, but Peter filled my life so completely… You don't know what I lost because you didn't know him as I did. He carried insects out of the house, letting them go rather than killing them. He didn't swear, and he never drank too much. He made love to me as though I were the most precious thing in the world." She wiped her wet face with her hands. "Can anyone, even Marcel, follow that?"

Veronique put her finger under her daughter's chin, tilted her face upward, and said quietly, "You must let him go, darling—you must give Marcel a chance."

Juliette broke away and ran outside to where Marcel played with Nina. She looked at him, cried out, picked up Nina, and took her into the house. Juliette glanced at her mother as they met in the doorway, took Nina to her room, and lay down on the bed with her. Nina stroked Juliette's hair until her mother cried herself to sleep.

Juliette sang over thirty concerts each year in small and large churches and had sung almost half of the two hundred and nine published Bach cantatas when she was invited to sing the Fifty-First in the Amiens Cathedral. She had sung that particular cantata once before and loved it, primarily because only an exceptional soprano can do justice to the work. But the trumpet part steals the show; it is a beast and is considered the limiting factor for the tempo. If the soloists and the small ensemble are in tune with one another, the piece is magical. When Monique Desjardins told Juliette that Monsieur Renaud had lost his soprano to illness and wanted her to sing it in the Amiens cathedral on the thirteenth of February, she was so excited she screamed into the telephone.

Of course, her first concern was the trumpet soloist. She did not want to sing the trumpet/soprano duet slowly. But when Juliette called Maestro Renaud to sort out rehearsal times, he assured Juliette that the trumpet would be worthy of her capabilities. Hearing the understated excitement in Renaud's voice, she sensed that the trumpet would likely be better than average.

Juliette, afraid that she, not the trumpet, would be the tempo-limiting factor, decided to work the piece until it was a part of her at any tempo. Peter had set the family standard for Amiens, and she was determined not to let him down.

Two days before Juliette was to leave, her father asked her to come to his office. Marcel sat in a deep leather chair; Juliette sat beside him in the mate to it.

"As you undoubtedly expected," said Jacques, "I am responsible for the cantata you will sing on Sunday."

Juliette smiled sarcastically, and her father continued.

"I am getting close to finding the rat embedded in the Amiens cell. The woman who helped Peter set up the cell will meet you on Monday and give you information about the traitor's identity. She will only give it to you, and you must go alone. She is afraid to talk to anyone else—she trusts you because of your close connection to Peter." Jacques stopped and waited for Juliette's response. She forced her excitement into the background; she wanted to hear the whole story.

"Tell me everything, Daddy; I know you, and you have a plan!"

"I don't like this, but Peter trusted this woman, and she trusted him. She wants you to know something more than the obvious, and MI6 is interested in what she has to say. This might involve a whole network of cells!"

Marcel sat back, his brow wrinkled. He rubbed his chin and said, "I don't like it either. Why does this woman need to talk to Juliette? And why alone? I've tried to imagine a scenario where that would be necessary, and there is no good one! This information should go directly to MI6 and the Résistance. This woman is the head of one of their cells… why wouldn't they take care of this traitor internally, or at least use the radio to pass the information on to MI6?"

Juliette answered before her father could.

"Perhaps she wants to protect her identity, which is normal considering the business she is in. I must meet with her, and when I have the traitor's identity, Marcel can decide where we go from there."

Marcel shook his head. "This is a trap!" He leaned toward Jacques. "Jacques, they want Juliette so they can get to you!" He waved a hand in frustration. "Don't use Juliette to find this rat—I am working on it with the Résistance, and in the past few days, we've gotten much closer. Give me a little more time!"

Juliette stood up and almost stamped her foot but caught herself in time. "No, you will not stop me from doing this! I will find out who betrayed Peter, and then we will take care of him! I will meet with this woman!"

Jacques answered quickly. "I'm afraid I agree with Marcel, Juliette. We believe we are getting close, and this meeting is an unnecessary risk."

Juliette stared into her father's eyes, choosing her words carefully.

"Papa, I must meet this woman! I promise you and Marcel will be the first to know what she knows! Please, Papa, she is a woman like I am—if Marcel is near, what could happen?"

Jacques stared at his daughter for a long moment, then held up his hand to signal defeat. "All right, I knew what your answer would be, and that's why I arranged for you to sing in Amiens. Your mother and I discussed this, and we decided you must make the final decision. We suspect this informer has cost several lives, and there is no reason to believe it won't be more. We must catch him as soon as we can—every day he's free puts lives at risk, and it is for that reason I am allowing you to go. However, I want you and Marcel to assess the risk once you are in Amiens, and if Marcel still smells a rat, you must promise me that you will get out of there!"

Marcel sighed, "I will do my best to check everything out before the meeting, and I will be close when it takes place." He stood up. "Now, Nina is waiting for me to play with her." He turned to Juliette. "I didn't ask her, but I assume you are welcome to play with us if you like."

Marcel held the door open for Juliette, and she skipped through ahead of him.

Juliette and Marcel arrived at the Hotel de Berny at noon on Saturday, checked in, ate lunch, and then went to the cathedral.

Monsieur Renaud met Juliette at the door.

"Mademoiselle Durand, I am so happy to finally meet you!" He kissed her hand. "Peter told me so much about you." His face darkened, and his voice saddened, "I am so sorry for your loss. Both the voice and the man were too good for this world—selfish angels called him to sing with them."

Juliette graciously pulled her hand back. She fought her tears and silently cursed Renaud for causing them. "Monsieur Renaud, it is a loss I can never replace, and if I catch those angels, I will send them to hell!"

Marcel shifted his feet.

Renaud looked at Juliette with genuine pity, then pivoted the mood with a wide smile.

"Could I speak with you privately before the rehearsal?"

Juliette nodded, and he led the way to his office. Marcel remained outside, taking Renaud's hint when he closed the door in his face.

The maestro motioned Juliette to an uncomfortable Louis XVI chair and said, "Mademoiselle Durand, I have no doubt of your ability to sing this cantata, and I want to tell you that I will give you whatever you need. We will take the tempi you choose—my orchestra and I are as flexible as we need to be, as is the trumpet. We are here to make notations in my score."

Juliette rarely changed anything Bach wrote, and she liked the Peters edition they would use. She waved the suggestion off. "Peter said you were one of the best conductors he had ever worked with. He loved how you played Bach's St. John Passion, and I respect his judgment. There will be no changes from the Peters score unless you want to make them. I will take your tempi; you should play it according to your interpretation. If you are agreeable, I won't take liberties that you don't."

The maestro tucked his chin into his neck and laughed.

"You are a very rare soprano indeed. I have done this twice before with the soprano who fell ill and a different trumpet than we will have for the performance, and both times, it took an hour to write all the details that the soprano and trumpet wanted."

"I have also done it before," Juliette smiled evocatively, "and found that the limitation on the opening movement tempo and the final duet is with the trumpet; I bow to his preferences."

He thoughtfully rubbed his chin, prompting her to ask, "Will there be anything else, Monsieur Renaud?"

The maestro sat against the edge of his desk, both feet on the floor, his hands gripping the rim. "I would like to speak to you on a very delicate subject. Your husband helped me with my singing, ultimately improving my relationships with my wife and my mistress. Since I can no longer thank him in person, I will thank you. I understand you originated the solution common to both problems."

Juliette laughed, put her hands together on her lap and tried to think of what Peter had told him. Nothing came to mind, so she said, "Monsieur, I have no idea what you are talking about." She curiously tilted her head.

Monsieur Renaud rested his thumb along his pointed chin and rubbed his lower lip with his index finger, deep in thought.

"I should not have brought this up—I now regret it, but I have gone too far to stop. Please forgive me if you find what I am about to say offensive."

He stood away from the desk and began pacing. Juliette waited, her curiosity growing.

"Peter told me how you taught him to sing Bach." He turned to watch Juliette's reaction.

She laughed like a barmaid on Saturday night. "Oh yes, I remember that lesson fondly! I don't remember caring whether or not he learned to sing Bach, but it did turn out to have that benefit."

Monsieur Renaud laughed with Juliette. "My wife agrees with you.

She used to hate my singing, but now she's my biggest fan—if you understand my meaning?"

Juliette smiled and stood up. He took her hand and kissed it. "I am so glad Peter and I could help, Monsieur Renaud. Please give my regards to your wife and your mistress."

Renaud was about to speak when Juliette stood. He took the hint, closed his mouth and opened the door for her.

Marcel walked beside Juliette, following Maestro Renaud to the practice room.

Juliette smiled as they walked. Looking straight ahead, she asked, "Marcel, can you sing?"

"Not a bit... Why do you ask?"

"Just curious." She took his arm, and Monsieur Renaud chuckled.

"It is a pity, though. But I promise I will teach you someday."

The rehearsal began at precisely three in the afternoon. When Juliette arrived, two violins, a viola, and a bass continuo were waiting for her and the trumpet player. The soloists took their places, and Maestro Renaud entered. Juliette stood and opened her score, the trumpet player cleared his trumpet, and Monsieur Renaud began the piece. The tempo was faster than Juliette had ever heard it played, but she had practised it at even more extreme speeds to eliminate any tension in her voice. Consequently, she could easily sing it at the tempo Maestro Renaud set, and when the trumpet began, it became clear to Juliette that the conductor had not told her everything.

They blazed through the aria, every note clean, and when the movement finished, Juliette was sure she heard Maestro Renaud giggle. His face glowed with excitement as she began her difficult recitative. He played it so slowly that it tested Juliette's breathing, but they flowed effortlessly together, and Renaud's interpretation was nothing short of incredible.

At the rehearsal's conclusion, the instrumentalists stamped their feet and shouted their approval, and Juliette experienced something she hadn't felt since Peter died.

The performance on Sunday was equal to the rehearsal, and Juliette and Marcel went back to the hotel on a high note.

When Marcel picked up the key, the desk manager handed him an envelope that he put in his pocket without glancing at it.

When they entered Juliette's room, Marcel opened the letter as the door clicked into place. He read, "Lundi, 17:00, Le Porc Saint-Leu, Quai Bélu, Simone." It was written in plain language, setting off an alarm in his head.

He put the letter down and said, "She wants to meet you at a restaurant on the Quai Bélu, about a thirty-minute walk from here, at five tomorrow afternoon." He breathed deeply, "Don't do it, Juliette—let's catch the train tomorrow morning. You've done more than your share, and judging from what I just heard, you should sing, not fight." Marcel's eyes began to glisten. "Please, Juliette, I have a bad feeling—come home with me!"

Juliette took his hand and separated his fingers, locking his big hand in both of hers.

"I can't, Marcel... I must finish this. This woman is taking an enormous risk to meet me, and I can't let her down." She looked into his eyes, "Please forgive me, but I will make it up to you someday."

Marcel retrieved his hand and headed for the door without looking back. He paused with his hand on the lever. "We should be there a half-hour early so I can watch things for a while before the meeting. I will stay out of sight, but I will be there. I will do my best to protect you."

Juliette smiled. "I know you will—I know that you will always protect me."

He pushed the lever down and opened the door without looking at her.

The fourteenth day of February, a day set aside for lovers, was a dark, cold day with a damp feeling of snow in the air. Juliette and Marcel ate a late breakfast in the hotel dining room, forgetting, or not admitting, that it was St. Valentine's Day. They ate slowly and sat there for an hour, sipping weak coffee, talking about Nina, singing, and the war. Finally, they went to their rooms, and at four o'clock, they met in the lobby. She wore a long wool dress, long stockings, and a warm woollen coat. It had begun to snow, and the damp cold cut through to her bones.

Juliette had to walk fast to keep up with Marcel, warming her blood. They crossed the Somme bridge, and when they had almost reached the end of the Quai Bélu, Marcel stopped the frantic pace, took her hand, and they began to stroll like lovers. Juliette didn't try to pull her hand away.

At the end of the Quai, Marcel stopped and explained, "The restaurant is a hundred metres down the pier, and I'm going to let you walk the rest of the way alone. I will be watching, but you won't see me. When you get to the restaurant, look at the menu before entering. Take your time, hesitate, as though you can't make up your mind. Don't look around while you are outside; I will do that, and if I see a problem, I will come to you."

He appeared to be thinking of something, and Juliette waited. Finally, he shook it off and went on.

"There will be a menu on the maître d's desk, and while you are looking at it, I want you to search the room with your eyes, not your head. If you see any sign of SS, Gestapo, or German soldiers, turn and leave as though the prices are too high or you've lost interest in eating. I will follow you back to the bridge." Marcel looked at her with deep concern. "Should I repeat any of it?"

"No, I've got it. Where should I sit if everything is right?"

"Sit with your back to the wall, facing the door. If no free tables allow you to do that, don't sit down—leave at once!"

"How do I find Simone? I have no idea what she looks like."

"She will find you."

Juliette did precisely as Marcel instructed. When she reached the maître d', she checked the room for German soldiers or men who might be Gestapo. A mixture of men and women occupied four tables, and one table had two of each. Two other tables had only women, and an old man sat alone at another. Juliette listened to the muffled conversations—no one spoke German—there were no accents. She pointed the maître d' to the table she wanted and instructed him to send Simone when she arrived. She ordered a glass of white table wine.

Twenty minutes later, a woman five or six years older and slightly smaller than Juliette entered the restaurant and spoke to the maître d.' He picked up a menu and guided her to Juliette's table.

Juliette stood and offered her hand, and the woman took it self-consciously, half-bowing. "Please sit down, Simone. My husband has told me about you, and I feel as though I know you."

The woman, her back stiff, obviously nervous, slipped past Juliette to a chair on her right. After a moment's pause, and without looking into Juliette's eyes, she said, "I asked you here because I had no choice."

The woman's insecurity frightened Juliette. She put her hand on Simone's, and it was ice cold. When she looked into Simone's eyes, the woman shifted her gaze past Juliette into the room.

"Somehow, the Milice discovered that my husband and I were building a Résistance cell in Amiens." Simone looked down at the table. "They took us to a farmhouse south of here."

She looked into Juliette's eyes for the first time. "They told us what we must do, or they would take our children. René refused—he was very reckless—and a Gestapo officer shot our three-year-old daughter before our eyes."

Tears fell from Simone's eyes and rolled in rivers down her cheeks. "I died in that farmyard. When René tried to save our daughter, the Bosch shot him. I fell—I couldn't stand—they picked me up and took me to the house. The farmer and his wife are loyal to the Pétain Vichy—and the Vichy Milice are worse Hitler fanatics than the Gestapo."

She looked at Juliette through her tears. "They will kill my other children if I don't do what they ask!"

Juliette was terrified. She felt her heart skip beats and feared it would stop.

"I was the one who trapped your husband." She looked deep into Juliette's eyes. "But to save my children, I also had to sacrifice my father."

"Why are you telling me this?" Juliette asked, close to panic, terrified of the answer.

"Because those men and women are Vichy Milice, and the men will arrest you when I give them the signal."

"But I've done nothing!" Juliette picked up her purse and started to walk around the table. Simone grabbed her wrist, and three men stood up.

"I put papers in your coat pocket when I sat down—pictures and documents that will incriminate you."

The men approached Juliette; a couple from another table guarded the door with guns drawn.

"Mademoiselle Durand," said one of the men in native French, "you are under arrest for treason against the lawful government of France—you will come with me." He flashed a document, but Juliette couldn't focus on it. The men took her arms and pulled her out of the restaurant to cars waiting on the Quai. They pushed her into the backseat of a black Citroen; one arresting man sat on each side of her. She thought of Marcel, and had to force herself not to look for him. Fear froze her heart; she silently prayed for death.

Chapter Thirty-Six

14–15 February 1944

Seelenruhe bekommt man erst wenn man aufhört zu hoffen.
(Peace first comes to one's soul when all hope has gone.)

GRADUALLY, JULIETTE'S BREATHING and heart rate returned to normal. Her fear remained, but the panic evaporated, and, as the car drove through the gates at the Amiens Prison, her mind switched to survival. She noted everything around her with unusual clarity, details she would carry forever. She read and memorized the car's license number as one of the men beside her led her around the rear bumper and toward a heavy door. The other man opened it, and Juliette memorized both faces when he pushed her through it. She counted the stairs leading down to the cellar—18 stone steps. Two guards led her through another massive door, between rows of cells and through a third sliding cell door built into a ceiling-to-floor wall of bars. The men withdrew without a word, leaving a single light bulb burning in her cell.

Juliette looked around the cell at a small window and decided it was after six, quitting time for Germans. If they were going to torture her, they would wait until morning. She began to figure out how she would spend the night there. A narrow cot hung from two hinges, and two chains mortared into the wall a metre above them. Two neatly folded blankets lay at the foot of the thin mattress. A sink with a single tap was bolted in an outside corner, and a high, small, barred window in the centre of the outer wall gave the only natural light. A hole in the other outside corner served as a toilet.

She sat on the bed to organize her thoughts, and a voice asked, "Why are you here?" The voice spoke in a whisper.

She answered, "They think I'm Résistance."

"Are you?"

Juliette decided the voice belonged to a woman, but it was so rough and low she wasn't sure.

She said, without hesitation, "I am now! What's your name?"

"Simone... Yours?"

"Juliette." She had forgotten the first rule.

Simone reminded her, "If you want to be in the Résistance, you have to learn not to give your real name. But I suppose it doesn't matter now; we will both be dead soon."

"I doubt they will let me live past tomorrow...." Juliette's voice broke a little... "And they already know my name."

"It doesn't matter; they plan to execute all Résistance prisoners at the end of this week anyway. The scuttle is that the French Pétain government wants the Gestapo out of the building, so the bastards decided to kill all their prisoners."

"How many Gestapo prisoners are there?"

"I think a hundred, maybe more... I wish it could happen tonight. I have nothing more to live for."

Juliette's throat constricted. Her voice broke when she spoke. She suddenly thought of Marcel and Uncle Hébert's advice. "I have a wonderful little girl and a man who loves me."

The voice said nothing. Juliette listened but heard only a weak cough and raspy breathing.

"Are you alright?"

"Yes, I'm fine." Simone coughed, and Juliette waited.

"I had a husband and two children, but the Nazis shot them because the village had hidden Jews from the hunters. I was visiting friends on a farm near the village, and we escaped by fleeing into the forest. The Résistance found us, and I have worked for them since then, but although I am responsible for quite a few dead Germans, it is still not enough. My only regret is that I won't live to kill more of them!"

Juliette unfolded the blankets, spread one out on the mattress, and laid the other so she could pull it over her when she crawled into the bed.

"I want to kill Germans too..." She slid under the blanket... "They tortured and killed my husband, and they raped me. A friend got the man who raped me and two of his friends, but I want to kill the man who tortured my husband. I believe that man is in this building."

"It won't help, Juliette. I have killed many Germans, and it hasn't helped—the pain is still there."

Juliette began to cry softly. She was so close… and yet…

"Crying won't help either; I've cried until I don't have any more tears. Even when the pricks torture me, I can't cry, and my screams are gone too." There was a moment of quiet. "Sometimes, I welcome the pain."

Juliette pulled the blanket to her chin.

She spent the night listening to the sounds of the prison, wondering if she would die here. Someone wept; a man far away screamed until his voice failed. Simone was quiet.

Juliette tried to remember the pain of childbirth but couldn't. Before Nina was born, the midwife assured her the pain was not a problem, and she would forget it once she had her little bundle of joy. Following Nina's birth, the doctor assured her that no pain compares to the pain of childbirth and congratulated her with the caveat that he had never heard such screaming! Cheerfully, he assured her that birthing a baby is the most horrible pain a human can endure, and he would never lose his amazement that women continued to let men make them pregnant.

Curled in the fetal position, shivering, cold to the bone, Juliette decided that anyone inflicting pain on her would pay with their hearing.

The morning light filtering through the narrow window high in the wall triggered the sounds of prisoners waking. As the sounds resonated from the stone walls, Juliette began warming up her voice, starting with soft sounds in the middle range and increasing the volume and breadth until she was singing with her full voice. Not caring who was listening, she sang Violetta's aria of freedom from start to finish, nailing every high note.

A ripple of applause ran up and down the hallway, and when it stopped, Simone said, "Thank you, Juliette, I will now die happy—I have heard an angel sing."

Juliette looked out the window at snowflakes falling past, and something in her stirred as she said, "We will not die!" She thought of her father, "I still have an ace to play!"

Veronique picked up the telephone. "Durand."

Marcel sucked in his breath, "Veronique, I need to speak to Jacques."

That was enough for Veronique—she called Jacques to the phone without saying a word to Marcel. The assumption was always that the Nazis were listening.

"Yes, this is Jacques Durand."

Marcel said, "Your daughter has had some difficulty and needs immediate help. She has the problem we feared, and I don't have the tools to help her."

The line was silent, then, "Do you know where she is?"

"She ran off with two men in dark suits. It's a safe bet they're up to no good, probably in the same house Peter used to live in." Marcel paused. When Jacques said nothing, he continued, "If you want to avoid pain, you should contact the men's fathers and clarify the consequences of their son's actions."

"I will do that at once. Meanwhile, I want you to go to the address I gave you and call me from there." Jacques hung up the telephone.

Veronique punched Jacques on the arm and cried out, "They caught her, didn't they? Tell me the truth!"

Jacques took her hands in his, as much to protect himself as to comfort her. "Yes, the Gestapo has her, and she is in Amiens Prison. I doubt I will get her out today, but I will get her out! I will make calls, and I guarantee you on all the trinkets in the cathedral, she will not be tortured or killed!" He held her close and said, "I have the power to save her. Please believe me—I need you to be strong!"

Veronique hugged him hard, then released him. "Have you already planned for this?" She looked up into his eyes. He knew he couldn't hide anything from her.

"Yes, I knew this might happen—we have an enemy in the Brussels Gestapo, and we know who he is. I met him when Peter died, and he is determined to destroy me." Jacques put his hands on her shoulders;

he must have her trust. "The Maquis have plans for him, and he won't bother us much longer. But, for the moment, I must outmaneuver him." He let her go and began to pace.

"Marcel will join the Résistance and help them attack the prison during an airstrike the British have planned. During the attack, Marcel will find Juliette."

"An airstrike? British airplanes will bomb the prison when Juliette is in there?"

"It will be a precision strike aimed at the guards' barracks and dining hall. They'll blow holes in the outer walls so the Maquisard, the fighters in the Résistance, can attack the prison and free the Résistance prisoners.

The desperation in his wife's face compelled Jacques to quickly add, "Juliette will be in the section reserved for Gestapo Résistance prisoners. It's in the cellar, a safe distance from the bombers' targets." He watched the panic in Veronique's eyes gradually fade.

"Are they sending bombers just to rescue Juliette?" she asked, skeptical, "You said they planned the raid two weeks ago. How could they know that the Gestapo would capture her?"

"Juliette is a bonus, but an important one. The bombers are coming to save a hundred Résistance prisoners scheduled for execution on Saturday—among them several British agents."

"If the bombers fail, will the Gestapo kill Juliette?"

"Veronique, listen to me. It might be difficult to believe, but I can protect Juliette. If anyone hurts her, I will destroy a hundred million francs of loot that some important Nazis are counting on when the Germans lose the war. When Stalingrad fell over a year ago, and the German army began to retreat from Russia, my Nazi clients gave me addresses in South America and Asia where I am to send their assets. If anyone hurts Juliette, they know how I will react!"

Veronique kissed her husband. "Darling, if anything goes wrong, I won't hold it against you..."

Jacques knew that his wife had just lied to him.

Chapter Thirty-Seven

14–17 February 1944

Entschlossenheit im Unglück ist immer der halbe Weg zur Rettung.
(Decisiveness in a disaster is already halfway to salvation.)
Johann Heinrich Pestalozzi

Alex Küster's adjutant leaned against the door jamb and said breathlessly, "The Gestapo has captured Juliette Durand and is accusing her of crimes against the Third Reich! Gärtner set a trap yesterday, and now he's got her in the cellar. He's planning to interrogate her this morning."

Obersturmbandführer Alex Küster quickly stood, supporting his upper body on knuckles pressed against the hard wood of his desk.

"Take two guards with you—tell them to draw their weapons and bring that bastard here. If he resists, I order you to shoot him!"

The adjutant didn't have to ask who the 'bastard' was. "Jawohl, Herr Obersturmbandführer!" He saluted, turned on his heel, and Küster heard the staccato click of his black boots on the stone stair. Five minutes later, the adjutant tapped on the doorjamb to get his commander's attention.

"Gärtner is here, sir."

"Send him in and close the door."

The adjutant followed Gärtner through the door, smiling behind his back, and when his boss used his hand to shoo him out, he shut the door a little harder than necessary.

"What in hell are you up to, Gärtner?"

"It's Kriminalkommissar Gärtner, sir," he said, giving a smart "Heil Hitler" salute to drive his point home. He held it, trying to force Küster to return it.

Alex Küster, who outranked the Gestapo officer, made a half-hearted effort at a regulation Wehrmacht salute but remained in his chair, smiling coldly and staring at Gärtner until he lowered his stiff arm. Obersturmbandführer Küster replaced his icy smile with something more dangerous.

He rose from his chair and leaned across the desk, supporting his upper body with straight arms and hard knuckles on the edge of the desk. Speaking in a tone that left no doubt about the consequences of disobeying him, he said, "Mademoiselle Durand may stay in her cell for the time being, but you are not to touch her. If you or any other person harms her, I will teach you something about the art of inflicting pain before personally escorting you to the Russian front, where I will give you to the first Russian soldiers I see!"

Gärtner turned red. He screamed, spit flying from his mouth, "You have no authority to give me orders!"

Küster sat down, dialled nine numbers on his telephone, and said into the mouthpiece, "Ich habe den kleinen Scheisser vor mir... warte," and passed the telephone receiver to Gärtner, who tentatively took it from him.

He said, "Hier ist Kriminalkommissar Gärtner," trying too hard to sound confident.

The one-way conversation lasted twenty seconds, after which Gärtner said, "Jawohl, Herr Kriminaldirektor... ich verstehe, Herr Kriminaldirektor... zum Befehl, Herr Kriminaldirektor!"

Küster heard the line click dead before a now pale Gärtner took the receiver from his ear.

"Get out of here, Kriminalkommissar; you are stinking up my office!"

"You can't stop Saturday from coming. I have orders not to kill that whore, but we will see who wins on Saturday!" Gärtner didn't salute as he pushed the door-latch down and swung the door against the wall with a bang. He left it open and clicked his heels on every step until he was out of Alex's hearing. Küster dialled nine numbers again, and the line came alive after two rings. "Durand."

"Küster here." Alex knew no one was monitoring his phone—he was the one monitoring every phone in the building but his—but he knew that the Brussels Gestapo might be listening. He also knew they would not interfere. "I'm afraid your daughter is in my prison, but she is safe and well, and no one will harm her."

"Will Juliette be protected?"

"I will personally take care of her—as long as I'm alive, no harm will come to her."

"Thank you for that, Alex...I will do what I can on this end."

"I will see that your daughter gets to her friends, and I assume someone will be there to take her home."

Jacques was quiet before he spoke. "Yes, I will tell him to expect you—and that you will give Juliette to him." He paused, then said, "I will never be able to repay you, Alex. May God go with you." And then he added, speaking slowly, "You can tell your friends that their assets are safe as long as my daughter is unharmed."

Alex said, "That has been taken care of," and hung up the phone. He let his mind go to England, where the pilots would probably be in the briefing room. Through his window, he could see snowflakes drifting down from a low, lead-gray sky, and although he had never flown a plane, Alex couldn't imagine a low-level bombing attack in this weather.

08:00, 15 February 1944. Hunsdon, Hertfordshire, England

Group Captain Pickhard of 140 Wing stood before the men who would fly eighteen Mosquito aircraft he had chosen from four of his squadrons. They were the crème de la crème of RAF low level pilots.

"Gentlemen," he said, "we will not fly in this weather, but we will fly our next operation on or before Friday. This one is unique. I will review the details on the morning of the mission, but you must stay sober and keen until we fly, and I hereby cancel all leave until the operation is over."

Every man in the room—thirty-six of them—groaned. The group captain continued, "First, I caution you against any outside discussion of the mission. On our way in, we will be vulnerable for an extended period, and if the Germans get wind of what we are up to, we are all dead men—as are a hundred French Résistance fighters.

"This is going to be a test of us all, and even if we succeed, we will get no credit for it. Everything connected with it is top secret, and the War Department will bury this mission so deep Sherlock Holmes couldn't find it!"

He waited for the men to get their comments over with and began again.

"The Gestapo is holding a hundred Résistance fighters in the Amiens prison, and they will execute them at dawn on Saturday if we don't do something about it... and British agents are among them. The Résistance must liberate the prisoners before then, but they can't take the prison without help. And that's where we come in."

He pointed a tapered hardwood stick at an aerial photograph of a sprawling group of buildings surrounded by stone walls, tapping it at each point they would attack.

"We will blow holes in the walls, here, here, and here..." He touched the east wall and the north wall in two places. "We will kill as many guards as we can by bombing the dining hall and barracks, then knock down the end wall of the prison without killing the inmates." He rapped the pointer on the targets and then looked around the room at the young, confident faces, all of whom seemed to accept that they could actually accomplish that miraculous feat.

He turned to face the men and added a caveat: "If we are unsuccessful in doing that, we will have to destroy the prison!"

He waited for the men to digest the implications. The room was hushed, except for one airman in the back. Larry Inman said softly, "Hoolllyyyy shit!" and his navigator said, "Amen, brother!"

Larry's hand shot up.

"What is it, Larry?" The group captain hadn't asked for and didn't welcome questions.

"I'm from Canada, sir, from a small town. Although we are just colonial hicks, most of us use our heads to think, among other things. And my head says that killing people because we can't rescue them is as dumb as burning down a forest because it's a fire hazard! A guy I know did that, and the police put him in a building with bars on the windows!"

The men recited, "Yours is not to reason why..." and Group Captain Pickhard spread his arms in a bid for quiet.

"The reason, if indeed there is one we mortals can understand, is top secret and above my rank, but I will give you a possibility. There could be people in that prison who know something so important that if they aren't in the hands of our friends, as they will be if we do our job, they can do a lot of damage. Perhaps MI6 believes that burying whatever those people know is worth a few hundred lives. Those people could be the reason for the raid—and the hundred Résistance fighters we save could be nothing more than a bonus, a convenient excuse to cover the real reason for the raid."

Pickhard looked around the quiet room, waited, then closed with...

"Enough speculation—we will never know the truth, and the people who do know will take it to their grave. Do your job, keep your opinions to yourself, and we will all go home sooner!"

Larry opened his mouth; Pickhard looked straight at him, and he closed it.

"Dismissed!" Pickhard saluted; the men stood as one, returned the salute, and their commanding officer left the room.

In an emergency, Jacques' instructions to Marcel were to check out of the hotel, take the train to Saint Quentin, then to Amiens, and wear a tartan scarf at Amiens station. If the clocks at the ends of the station disagree by five minutes, he must get on a train to Brussels—If the clocks agree, someone will contact him—wait there until they do.

When he stepped onto the platform, Marcel checked the clocks; the time was identical. He was turning to locate the exits when a beautiful young woman threw her arms around him and kissed him hard on the mouth. She left him no choice; he wrapped his arms around her and kissed her passionately. She pulled back, grabbed his arms, and looked up into his face.

"I'm so glad you've come back!" she said, "I missed you so much!" She hugged him again, and he returned her affection. Clinging to his arm, she steered him toward the exit and a little Renault parked directly across the street.

"I'm sorry I attacked you." She shifted smoothly through the gears.

"I'm not," Marcel grinned.

"My name is—"

"Simone?"

"I was going to say Michelle Lapointe, but you can call me Simone if you like. I am a member of the Maquisard, the branch of the Résistance that does the dirty work. We are now an active army, using real names and armbands when we fight. Even the Germans expect an Allied landing within a few days or weeks, and we are prepared to fight in the open when that happens."

"Do you openly fight the Germans now?" he asked.

She smiled at him. "You will see me fight—I've been in the Résistance since the Germans invaded France, but the Maquisard is a relatively new bunch, concealed until now. But we are all well-armed and trained fighters, and we will be the Free French Army when the final battle for France begins!"

All that was missing was a waving flag and the Marseillaise. Marcel said nothing until they arrived at a small farmhouse on the side of a narrow road.

The windows were small; the interior of the house was dark. Michelle led him into the kitchen and motioned for him to sit down. Two men joined Marcel on the other side of the table, and Michelle introduced them as Guy and Richard. They had grown short black beards and were medium build and a few centimetres shorter than Marcel. She pointed out, "Guy is my husband."

Marcel smiled and said, "You had better watch that wife of yours— she runs around kissing strange men!"

Guy slapped her bottom, and she returned the affection by slapping his face hard enough to make her point.

Guy jerked his thumb toward her and rubbed his red face. "You see what I have to put up with?"

"I should be so lucky," said Marcel, and Michelle gave him a wink.

Guy stretched his arms across the table and intertwined his fingers. "I will explain the situation. First—we have been expecting you; we know who you are, and you should know that we are the Maquisard, the fighting arm of the Résistance. There are more than a hundred thousand of us at this moment, and we are organizing an army called the Forces Françaises de l'Intérieur. The Allies will land in France in the next few months, and then we will openly fight the Germans in an organized way. Neither you nor the woman you guard so well will be able to return to Brussels until the Germans leave; until then, you must fight with us."

Marcel smiled and sat back in his chair. "I know how to fight, but I've seen very little combat so far."

"That is not a problem... You will learn quickly." Guy slapped the table. "If you don't, we will give your parents one of our nice medals in your name."

Everyone laughed.

"We are going to attack the Amiens prison. Our objective is to find and rescue our people while you save your Juliette. I want you to fight with our unit."

"You are well informed," said Marcel.

"We are very good at what we do. Our intelligence is excellent, but, unfortunately, more than half of France supports the Germans. The Milice has infiltrated our organization, and several of them are in the Amiens Prison posing as Résistance while working for the Gestapo, and they are creating havoc! We have lost many men and women to those traitors. They are responsible for coercing the young lady who met with Juliette."

"You know about that?"

"We were at the Le Porc Saint Lieu—the old man in the corner was ours, but of course, he could do nothing to help."

Marcel remembered an old man with a cane struggling out the door and down the Quai.

"The Milice shot her husband and one of her three children, and the Gestapo tortured and killed her father. Her two remaining children are with the Milice traitors, and the Gestapo is using them to persuade her to cooperate—we will take care of that situation when the time is right."

"And the attack?" Marcel was openly skeptical. "You're going to need big guns to break those walls!"

Guy shook his head. "We will use British bombs! When the weather clears, the RAF will blow holes in the north and east perimeter walls and destroy the towers, gun positions, the dining hall and the barracks. As for the prisoners, the bombers will also blow out the north and eastern ends of the building, giving them an escape route and a way for us to get in and open the cells."

The excitement on Marcel's face disappeared. "But that will kill some of the prisoners!"

"Perhaps, but only a few. We presume those prisoners would rather die with a chance of escape than stay where they are."

"Do you know where Juliette is?"

Guy smiled confidently. "Yes, we do, and I will take you to her. Her father has seen that she is untouched. No one will molest her; the SS would kill the molester on the spot and receive the Iron Cross for it. We know the exact cell, and it is far enough away that a direct hit on the building would not injure her. However, there is something further that you should know."

Marcel waited for the bad news.

"If the airstrikes are unsuccessful, or if our following attack fails, the bombers will destroy the entire prison."

The blood drained from Marcel's face.

"There are people in that prison who we do not want to escape and others who must—and there are some we want dead. The Milice have infiltrated the Résistance prisoners, and we know who they are. They must die one way or another, preferably after interrogation. We will try to kill or capture them when we enter the prison, but the bombers will kill everyone if we can't reach them."

"My God, how can you kill everyone in the prison?"

"Your Juliette might survive if she is in her cell. It's a small room with very thick walls. We will look for her when the bombers leave, but we won't have much time. Our men will set up strategic ambushes to stop reinforcements from interrupting us, but it's only a matter of time before we must retreat."

Marcel didn't speak, so he went on.

"We have given the Milice a special code they believe is the escape word. If it is convenient, we will bring them with us for later interrogation... otherwise... " He indicated the slitting of a throat.

Marcel asked, "What is your rank in this new army, Guy?"

"I am a senior commander—I would be a captain or a major in a regular army." He waited, but Marcel was satisfied.

"I will have a hundred men hidden in barns close to the prison, and another fifty will ambush German reinforcements that come by road. We will blow up the railway tracks in several strategic places to stop those who would come by train."

Marcel sat back. "I have one more question. The British would need to know the building's construction—do they have that?"

Guy smiled. "Our friend inside the prison is Dominique Penchard, and he has a helpful ally in a high position. We have the building plans, exact dimensions of the outside walls, location and nature of the defence—down to the guards' duty roster. "

As the days counted down, everyone became nervous that the weather might not cooperate in time. The night of Thursday, the seventeenth, at the last possible moment and despite the continuing bad weather, fifty men of Guy's group assembled in a barn a hundred metres from the north wall of the prison, and another fifty waited in two barns farther east. Guy gave Marcel a Sten gun and four magazines to add to the Beretta in his pocket.

A white blanket of snow covered everything.

Chapter Thirty-Eight

18 February 1944

Weiberrache hat keine Grenzen.
(A woman's revenge has no limits.)

THREE DAYS CAME AND WENT; the sun didn't shine, and Juliette had nothing to do but watch snowflakes fall past the window. She tried counting them to relieve the boredom and fell asleep. The only break in the monotony came twice a day when a young French guard brought what passed for food and once a day when Juliette washed with cold water in front of the tiny sink. Twice, the guards took Simone away, and when she returned, she said they had raped her.

No one spoke to Juliette except Simone and the young man who brought her food she could barely eat. On the second day, Juliette complained, and the young man informed her that her treatment was more like a guest than a prisoner. He showed her what Simone and the other prisoners ate, and Juliette made him give Simone her ration while she gladly ate the thin potato soup—proof that her papa was watching over her.

Four days passed, and still no sun. The morning crept by; the dull light lingered, time slowed to a crawl. Every time Juliette looked through the tiny pane of glass, snowflakes fell between the bars, a steady parade of big, white snowflakes slipping and sliding down a gray wall. She was crossing the room on her way to the cot when the door opened, and a young uniformed Gestapo officer entered the cell. He motioned toward the door and said, "Follow me."

She followed the officer down a hallway toward the other end of the building and stopped at a heavy door. The officer knocked and, without waiting for a response, pushed Juliette through the door ahead of him. She took two steps and froze.

"Kriminalkommissar Kristof Gärtner!" She gasped, "You're the horny twit on the train!"

He stood, red-faced, strode across the room and struck Juliette full on the chin, twisting her mouth and cutting her tongue between her teeth. She fell sideways, and the young escort expertly caught her, righting her just in time to receive a blow on her left breast. She cried out, and again, the young man caught her before she fell. She spat blood on the floor but kept most of it in the side of her mouth.

Gärtner leaned over so that his face was inches from hers. "Your father can't save you now! You made a fool of me on the train, but you will beg me to kill you before this day is through!" He smiled, "My instructions are not to kill you—but there are things worse than death. You will beg for it like your Saujude husband did!"

Juliette screamed and spat as hard as she could. Blood and spit covered his face and rolled down his neck onto the collar of his clean uniform. He slapped her with his open hand, and she would have fallen had the young man holding her arms not held her upright.

Juliette's words slurred through her gritted teeth. "I swear on the Virgin Mary... I will kill you!"

Gärtner's scorn-filled laughter echoed from the stone walls of the cellar. "You will kill me?" His voice dropped to a vicious whisper. "No, my Jew-loving whore..." He squeezed Juliette's jaw between his powerful fingers and said into her eyes... "Fuck the orders. I will kill you as I killed your coward Saujude!" He released her jaw with a savage twist.

Kriminalkommissar Gärtner proved to be a slow learner; Juliette's tongue and the inside of her cheek were bleeding copiously, and again, she showered his face and the front of his uniform. He swung at her; she pulled her head back; the blow glanced off her forehead. He turned away, searching for something to wipe his face, screaming so violently Juliette was sure he had injured his vocal cords.

He said hoarsely, "Take her to the room and strip her. Do not touch her; she is mine!"

Alex Küster looked at his adjutant with an expression that said, "Don't ask…" as he said insistently, "I'm ordering you to go home for the rest of the day!"

"Yes, sir. Is there anything I can do for you before I go?"

"Jonathon, no, just go, and thank you for your help. I know this hasn't been easy for you, and there will be questions, but you must remain professional, as you have always been."

Jonathon put on his hat and coat, returned to stand in the door frame and saluted his boss smartly. Alex returned the military salute, then shook the young man's hand and said, "Thank you again, Jonathon."

Küster listened to his adjutant's boots on the stone step until he heard the heavy door at the bottom of the steps close behind him.

He rotated the dial on the telephone until the memorized numbers started the hummed dashes. The sound stopped, and he heard a voice say, "Oui…"

"Küster here…Les oiseaux vont-ils voler?"

"Peut-être," said the voice.

Küster replaced the receiver and stared at the wall. "Perhaps" wasn't good enough—if the birds didn't fly, over one hundred people would die the following day at dawn, and he had no doubt Juliette would be among them. If they did fly, he had work to do. He decided to wait a few minutes before going to Juliette's cell.

09:00, 18 February 1944. Hunsdon, Hertfordshire, England

The airmen gathered in the briefing room. None of them had left the base since the initial briefing, and security was the tightest the crews had ever seen. MPs were everywhere; nothing moved without written orders from God.

Group Captain Pickhard began the briefing.

"Gentlemen, we will go to Amiens this morning. The code name is Operation Jericho, and you are never to speak of this mission to anyone, no matter the outcome. There will be no medals, no commendations—only the satisfaction of a job well done."

A murmur ran through the room, and the airmen looked at one another, some shaking their heads, others looking at the floor. Many moved their lips as they recited a prayer. It was snowing, with a hundred feet of clear air under the solid overcast, not enough room to safely fly between the clouds and the ground, certainly not at two-hundred-and-fifty miles per hour.

"We have reliable information—there is no doubt the prisoners will be executed tomorrow at dawn. We must succeed today, and your best may not be good enough. But, if you accomplish your mission, a hundred of the bravest men and women in this war will not die!"

He searched each face to find hopelessness or fear but saw only resolve to get it done. He had picked his crews well. There were better pilots and navigators but no better men!

"I will fly lead this morning." The men shifted uneasily in their seats for the first time since the briefing started. Group Captain Pickhard had never flown a low-level mission with the squadron, and although he had been taking low-level training at Hatfield Base, none of the pilots in 487 Squadron had flown with him on an operation this close to the ground or this dangerous. His pilot skills were nothing short of phenomenal, and, as a leader, no man could fault him. But flying fifty feet above the ground at two hundred and fifty miles an hour, climbing to clear cows in a field, was a skill few men possessed—At those altitudes, trees and telephone poles are above the plane. This morning, they would skim the ground in a snowstorm with less than a quarter-mile of visibility—three seconds ahead of the airplane.

Pickhard continued, "I will lead a flight of three planes. I want Larry on my right wing and Webb on my left. We will fly an inverted V formation, with the centre aircraft trailing, and I will trust the two best low-level pilots in the squadron to keep me out of the trees."

The men laughed nervously. The Group Captain paused to look at the young faces, wondering which of them would die this afternoon, and who would drink in the pub tonight, raising glasses and singing songs for those who didn't make it.

"The flying orders are in your packets. 464 Squadron will lead the way with two groups of three aircraft that will remain in visual contact with one another. If anyone loses contact with their wingman for any reason, they must pull up into the soup and return to base. Do not hesitate; it is only a matter of seconds before you either hit one of your friends or something fastened to the ground. If you stick to the rules, some of us will make it to the target, and we will get the job done!"

Group Captain Pickhard introduced the navigation briefer and closed with the usual, "Good hunting, gentlemen!"

A Gestapo officer waiting outside Gärtner's door joined Juliette's procession. The trio walked down the hall and entered a large room with a table and four rough wooden chairs. One of the officers closed the door, and the other stepped behind Juliette, pinning her arms behind her. The man facing her put one hand on either side of the buttons holding the front of her dress together and pulled, popping buttons down to her navel. She screamed as loud as she could, focusing on the young man's right ear. The stone walls magnified the sound, and he stepped back, covering his ears.

"Scheisse!" Alex Küster looked at his watch, grabbed his coat and leather gun belt, pulled a desk drawer open, stuffed two extra magazines in his pocket and ran down the stairs. He slowed a little at the first landing and heard the sound of the door to the interrogation room opening.

The officer holding Juliette's arms relaxed slightly—she twisted free, ran to a corner and pulled a chair in front of her. She spat blood on the floor.

The men laughed at her as they approached from both sides. She picked the younger, smaller one and lunged at his neck. He set himself and caught her in midair, but before he had her intentions figured out, she had set her teeth in his neck. He cursed, wrenched himself away from her, and her perfect sharp teeth tore a piece out of his flesh. He let go of her and clutched at his throat; blood poured down his neck.

The second officer wrapped his arms around Juliette's waist, but she grabbed the table. He braced his feet to pull, and Juliette suddenly let go. The young man fell backward, knocking a chair over and breaking its rungs. He released Juliette's waist in time to break the fall with his hands—Juliette twisted around on top of him, sinking her teeth into the bulge of flesh above his elbow, torquing her head from side to side to tear a piece out of his tough muscle. He screamed, and Juliette spat flesh and blood onto the floor.

Strong hands picked her up, threw her against the edge of the table, and Juliette felt a rib crack. She gasped, and turned just in time to meet Gärtner's fist full on her nose. Blood splattered everywhere, dotting her attacker's uniform. Pain blurred Juliette's vision; she was falling, knowing this was the end. When her body hit the floor, the bloody officers pounced.

11:00, 18 February 1944. Hunsdon, Hertfordshire, England

The first trio of mosquitoes lifted off into an east wind, skimming the bottom of the clouds as they turned to a southeasterly heading. The cloud bottoms were up to five hundred feet, higher than Larry had expected. He throttled back to two hundred and fifty miles per hour indicated airspeed. Wing Commander Pickhard and Flight Lieutenant Webb flew in formation on his left, following his lead. Half a mile behind them, three more Mosquitos from their squadron followed in their wake. The eastern suburbs of London swept under them as they prepared for the turn at Littlehampton, south of Brighton.

A squadron of Typhoon fighters and a single pathfinder mosquito waited for their charges at ten thousand feet, well above the clouds. The second pathfinder, flying with the attack group, was equipped with GEE, a navigation system that used three fixed stations broadcasting radio signals to triangulate the aircraft's position. This new technology was the key to organizing the mission. The green tube display in the pathfinder's cockpit showed the distance from the mosquito to each of the three stations, and, using that information, the navigator calculated the plane's position with remarkable accuracy. The pathfinder mosquito's navigator couldn't see the ground but knew when his aircraft was precisely over the rendezvous point, and each mosquito in the group had the pathfinder on its radar.

"Passing point one... now," Danny spoke over the squadron frequency. He used the pathfinder blip to verify his position.

"Ailsome" was the code name Danny expected from the escorts, and "Ailsome overhead" came back immediately.

"We have our friends," said Danny over the frequency. A succession of clicks acknowledged receipt of the information. The exchange would be nonsense to the Germans listening to it, but their radar would tell them something was happening, and they would scramble a few fighters.

The clouds suddenly lifted to two thousand feet, but Larry stayed under five hundred, gradually dropping as he approached the French coast. He crossed the land at less than a hundred feet—under German radar—and immediately, the soup fell to just above his canopy.

The concussion of the gunshot stunned everyone in the room, and a circle of blood appeared on the front of the youngest Gestapo officer's tunic as he fell in a heap. Another shot—his partner followed his descent, blood and brain spraying from the exit wound in his head.

Leutnant Gärtner had dropped to the floor and now struggled to get his Walther P38 out of his holster and into his hand. As he desperately tried to raise it, a bullet crushed the bones in his right knee. He screamed, dropped the pistol, and a black boot kicked it away from him.

Juliette looked up from her hands and knees, gradually focusing her eyes. A man in an SS uniform quietly closed the door, and when he turned, she recognized him.

"Alex Küster," she said weakly, trying to pull herself up using the edge of the table. He helped her sit on an upright chair.

"It looks like I got here just in time," said Alex Küster, somewhat cheerfully. He examined her wounds while he talked. "Another minute, and you would have deprived me of the pleasure of killing those bastards!"

She fought to keep from laughing and to catch her breath. Her ribs hurt like hell when she tried to speak, and she gave up.

Alex spoke, still cheerful, "It's good to see you again, but the circumstances could have been more pleasant. Do you feel well enough to kill this piece of shit?" Pointing with the barrel of his Walther, Alex indicated Leutnant Gärtner, sitting in his pee on the floor, holding his mangled knee and crying in a feeble, childish voice.

"Of course, I will do it if you like, but you should know that he was the one who tortured Peter—and I'm sure you will appreciate the poetic justice—he did it in this room."

Blood covered Juliette's face; her little nose was swollen and crooked. She spat blood on the floor, held out her hand, and Obersturmbandführer Küster placed his gun in it.

"How does it work?"

"Just point it at where you want to hit him and pull the trigger. Be careful; the safety is off."

Juliette carefully aimed at her victim's head. She closed one eye, sighted along the top of the barrel, pulled the trigger, and shot the concrete floor. The bullet ricocheted around the room, narrowly missing Alex. Juliette lowered the gun, squeezed one eye shut and stuck her tongue out of the corner of her mouth as she slowly lifted the pistol.

Küster pushed down on the barrel. "Maybe you should aim at something bigger. You don't have to kill him with one shot; you've got eight more in the gun, and I have two spare magazines in my pocket."

Gärtner turned away; Juliette aimed at his back. He squeezed himself into the fetal position, crying, "Please don't kill me. Please don't kill me! Please!"

"May I make a recommendation, my dear?" Alex pleasantly smiled as Juliette stuck out her bloody tongue and closed one eye.

"What?" she asked without changing her position.

"Try holding the gun with both hands. Extend your arms and point the gun with both eyes open. Just look down the barrel at your target and slowly squeeze the trigger." Juliette looked sideways at him, and he demonstrated, then added, "Try to keep your eyes open when you fire. It's more fun when you see the bullets hit."

Juliette relaxed, lowered the gun, then raised it again, arms outstretched, using both hands.

"Perfect!"

Gärtner whined pitifully as he stretched his arm toward Juliette as though hoping to block the bullet. He turned his head away and closed his eyes.

She squeezed, the gun jumped, and she saw the cloud of smoke and flame that followed the shot out of the barrel. Milliseconds later, the bullet's impact broke Gärtner's spine. His legs straightened reflexively, and he rolled onto his back. His mouth moved, but no sound came out.

Juliette turned to Alex. "How was that? Frankly, I think I could get quite good at this!"

Gärtner gasped. She looked at him through a curtain of hate.

"You're going to have to shoot him again," said Alex, "Try his heart. If he has one, he'll die quickly."

"What if I don't want him to die quickly? ...I want to tell him about Peter!"

"In that case, shoot him in the stomach."

"How long will it take him to die?"

Alex rubbed the short stubble on his chin. "He's young, but his knee is bleeding quite badly, and he is probably bleeding internally from the back shot. I would say a half-hour, give or take a few minutes. But before you begin, I will explain our situation."

Alex took the gun, reloaded the magazine with a handful of loose bullets, took Leutnant Gärtner's pistol and put it in his belt. He looked through the young officer's pockets but found no spare magazines.

"The British are going to bomb the prison in..." He looked at his watch... "a little over half an hour. When the bombing is over, I will see that you get safely clear of the prison, and I would appreciate it if you could identify me to your friends as one of the good guys."

Juliette's eyes shone. "Is Marcel going to rescue me?"

"That is the plan, my dear." Alex took her hand and kissed it. "I will leave now and come back with clothes for you."

Juliette touched his arm. "There is a woman in the cell next to mine. Her name is Simone, and I promised I would save her. Is there any way...?"

"Of course. I'll be back in ten minutes." He pointed at the dying Gestapo officer. "Enjoy yourself." As an afterthought, "Remember, he won't feel anything below his waist."

11:35, 18 February 1944. A mosquito en route to Amiens Prison.

"Turn left to six two degrees... three–two–now." Larry turned smoothly, giving his wingmen time to see him. He could see Pickhard's

'F' clearly marked on the fuselage on his left but had no time to find Webb. He completed the gentle turn, and Danny pointed his gloved finger. "Follow that road until I tell you to turn. You will turn ninety degrees to the right in… twelve minutes… Mark!"

The ground flew past in a blur; visibility was under half a mile in the snow; trees and poles that lined the road flew past like closely spaced pickets on a fence. Larry concentrated on a point halfway to the limit of his vision, just under the clouds, keeping the obstacles as far below him as possible without flying into the soup. Pickhard's mosquito flew on the other side of the road and slightly behind—still no Webb in sight.

What seemed to Larry like seconds later, Danny said, "Turn right to one-four-five in… two minutes… Mark!"

A small town appeared dead ahead—a church steeple poked into the clouds.

"Turn right… three–two–now!" Danny left enough room for Webb and Pickhard's aircraft on the outside of the turn so they could stay in formation without hitting the steeple. With the shorter inside track, Larry cut the throttle slightly so that he didn't lose Pickhard and, turn completed, found himself on the right-hand side of another road.

"Follow that road for two minutes." Danny didn't turn his head to look at his pilot.

"Roger," said Larry to himself. Picking up the mike was out of the question. His eyes were dry from the strain, and he had to force himself to relax his hand on the stick. The road was relatively straight, but now, with under five hundred yards of visibility, he had no room for the tiniest error. He kept the aircraft steady at two-hundred-fifty mph and dared not look sideways to see if Pickhard and Webb had made it around the turn.

As if he had read his mind, Danny said, "Webb bought it on the turn…hit a pole and tore off a wing. Pickhard is still on station!"

Ten seconds later, Danny said, "That's Doullens. Last turn… Turn right one hundred five degrees to two-fifty… three–two–now!" Larry dropped the right wing to a thirty-degree bank, turned a little over ninety degrees, and straightened out to follow another straight road.

"Two minutes down that road to bingo," said Danny.

When Alex returned with Simone, Juliette sat on the table, swinging her legs back and forth over her bloody victim.

"He was hardly any fun at all... " She looked down at her husband's torturer... spat a gob of blood she had saved for him... "He only lasted a few minutes." Sick to her stomach, she forced a smile when she looked at Alex and Simone, then vomited a stream that hit the bottom of the wall two metres away.

As though God had been listening to Larry's prayers, the clouds moved up, the snow stopped, and he could see the target three miles ahead of his mosquito.

Pickhard's navigator came on the radio. "Leader one. The attack sequence begins in five–four–three–two–one–now!" Larry slowed during the countdown to pull in behind Captain Pickhard, flying straight at the eastern wall of the prison, aimed at a point just north of the centre.

Pickhard's bombs dropped short, with the closest to the wall still ten feet away. Danny opened the bomb bay and held his hand on the bomb release—Larry flew so low over the wall he had to pull up to avoid hitting the prison's roof. Danny flipped the bomb release a short second before the wall slid under the nose, and Larry needn't have worried about clearing the roof—the mosquito jumped fifty feet when four five-hundred-pound bombs dropped clear and slammed against the wall. The blow started their eleven-second fuse timers.

Alex pulled the women to the floor as the sound of two-thousand horsepower Rolls-Royce Merlin engines turning big propellers drifted inside the prison. Juliette and Simone crouched under the table, arms over their head as the bombers flew over.

The first explosion shook the prison... then two more... and then bomb blasts so close together it was impossible to count them. Juliette shouted, "What's happening?" and raised her head to locate Alex. He was sitting calmly in a chair.

"That, my dear, was the sound of very large bombs blowing walls down. Now, they will bomb the end wall of this building, and we had better hope they know what they're doing!"

The bomb blasts lasted six minutes, but it seemed much longer to everyone in the prison. The last bombs detonated very close to Juliette's, Simone's and Alex Küster's hiding place, followed by what could only be the sound of flying rubble as the building fell apart. Juliette could feel her heart pounding as the roar of engines and propellers receded. She looked at Alex; he nodded, and she and Simone crawled out from under the table and scampered through the door behind him.

Chunks of building filled the cellar stairway, and Alex motioned Simone and Juliette to stop and wait. He ran in the direction of the cells. Two shots rang out after he rounded the corner, followed a minute later by another. When he returned, Juliette asked, "What did you do?"

"The Résistance prisoners are free."

He led the way over the rubble to the light at the top of the stairs.

The entire end of the prison was gone; two floors and the roof hung in space, barely supported by a cantilever anchored to the structure behind them. Guards knelt on the open floors, firing at prisoners escaping across the yard. Alex carefully picked his targets and killed three before pulling Juliette and Simone behind him.

Alex said, "Run to the north wall," stopped, knelt, and fired as they passed him, then sprinted across the yard behind them. Halfway to a breach in the north wall, Juliette heard a grunt behind her. She looked back to see Alex lying face down, blood pouring from a hole in the middle of his back. She stopped, returned to kneel beside him, and rolled him over. He said, "It's better this way—keep going—find Marcel!"

Circling east of the prison, Larry saw dozens of prisoners sprinting across the yard and machine guns in the guard tower mowing them down. He pointed his mosquito straight at the guardhouse, four machine guns firing, scattering pieces of men and tower over the yard. With its wings vertical and turning as tightly as the mosquito could, the 'G' load blurring his vision, Larry made a second pass to target the guards firing from the prison windows. He levelled the wings, kicked the rudders back and forth and swept the window openings clean.

In the middle of the chaos, Pickhard's navigator called off the backup strike that would destroy the prison. Mission accomplished—

prisoners escaping—the rest is up to the Résistance.

Simone threw herself beside Juliette, shouting, "Get his gun and start shooting—they're coming after us!"

Juliette found Alex's gun and the spare magazines. She stretched her arms in front of her, holding the pistol with both hands as Alex had taught her. Simone caught a guard running behind a group of prisoners with a three-shot burst. Juliette found a grey guard uniform and fired low as Alex had instructed her, aiming at the junction of his legs.

The man dropped, screaming. She fired again, aiming a little higher.

Bullets bounced off the dirt around the women. A group of guards charged at them, and they were close when Juliette caught one in the stomach while Simone shot another. The last three fell together as machine guns chattered on both sides of Juliette.

She heard a familiar voice say, "I see you've learned to play a new instrument," and a shock of joy ran through her. She turned to find Marcel beside her, changing the magazine on his Sten gun. He shot another guard trying to cross the yard behind the escaping prisoners, and she went back to the business of killing, emptying her last magazine at two guards in a window. Simone had picked the same target, and the guards disappeared.

No more guns shot at the prisoners from the floors, but a few still fired from the windows, and a stream of bullets still rained down from one of the towers.

A Mosquito bomber skimmed the north wall, flame and smoke spitting from the centre of the fuselage under the cockpit. The tower exploded in a shower of splintered lumber and fire, and the beautiful aircraft gracefully skipped over it, stood on its left wing, and turned through a tight 270-degree turn, its machine guns sweeping the windows before it jumped over the prison, skimming the roof.

The cacophony of the past minutes receded to sporadic shots, and Marcel said, "Run to the barn behind the prison—there is transport there!"

Juliette leaned over Alex and felt his neck for a pulse, but there was none. She kissed him, closed his eyes, and habitually crossed herself. Simone took Juliette's hand, pulled her down to a crouch, then turned her to face the hole in the north wall. Simone refused to let her stand up until they were through it and halfway across the field to the barn. They raced the rest of the way, side by side, adrenaline dulling the pain in Juliette's ribs. Two women took them to a small waiting Camion; one of them told Juliette and Simone to lie down in the back, and the other spread a tarp over them.

Larry followed Pickhard's Mosquito as he turned for the homeward leg at five-hundred feet. Before they completed the turn, a German FW 190 broke out of the clouds to Pickhard's right, less than a thousand yards away, and fired every gun it had at the mosquito, sawing the tail off the plane—Pickhard's Mosquito dove straight into the ground in a shower of flame and debris.

The Focke Wulf pilot had no time to congratulate himself on his phenomenal luck; he hadn't seen Larry turn slightly to the right and fire his machine guns, leading a stream of tracers into the German aircraft. Its pilot dead, the plane glided to the ground, smoke trailing it until it struck beside the railway track, scattering debris a hundred metres ahead of the impact.

Larry circled Pickard's burning airplane. As he saluted, he said, "I hope those Résistance people are worth it."

He climbed into the soup and turned the mosquito to the course for home.

"Amen to that," said Danny.

Chapter Thirty-Nine

Spring 1944

Die unmögliche plus Bestimmung ist gleich Erfolg.
(The impossible plus determination equals success.)

They bounced along in the *petit camion* for four hours before it squealed to a halt. The driver pulled the tarpaulin off the box, and directed them toward a small farmhouse. A Renault car parked beside the little truck, and three men and a woman got out. Juliette's heart jumped when she recognized Marcel. The men began a tour of the property, and the women entered the house.

The house was apparently empty, but Simone searched to be sure. Juliette found a pot of stew prepared but cold and tried to make a fire in the stove. Simone cleaned the table and found bowls and cutlery, then watched Juliette, who was getting more frustrated by the minute.

Simone knelt beside Juliette and asked, "Do you want me to teach you how to make a fire?"

Juliette threw a piece of wood across the room. "We may not know one another that long." She straightened her back and drew her foot back as if to kick the iron stove but thought better of it. She turned to face Simone and snarled, "Alright, show me!"

Simone slid the iron stew pot to one side and removed the round iron sections that provided access to the top of the firebox. As she worked, she asked, "Who was that SS officer?" as she twisted a sheet of newspaper into a loose tube.

"He was Obersturmbandführer Alex Küster. He saved my husband Peter when he was in Dachau after Kristallnacht, and last year—no, it's been almost two years—he had to shoot Peter to stop the Gestapo from torturing him."

Simone arranged four pieces of split dry softwood on the paper.

"Küster shot your husband?" She lit the paper on both ends and opened the draft on the door at the front.

"There was no way he could save him, so he ended his suffering."

Simone covered the dancing flames with the iron access covers, slid two pieces of dry hardwood in the front of the firebox, and turned to Juliette. Simone pointed to a loaf of bread and a butter crock, then pointed at the table. Juliette picked them up, then stood and watched Simone slide the stew pot over the rapidly heating firebox.

Simone said, "I suppose I must believe that, considering he saved you." The stove huffed and puffed flame and smoke out of every crack around the door; Simone closed the draft until the fire became a quiet, steady roar. "Another benefit could have been that Peter couldn't talk if Küster shot him... Don't you think?"

Before Juliette could challenge her, Marcel stepped into the room, set his Sten gun on the windowsill and looked at Juliette. "Was Gärtner your handiwork?"

Juliette nodded, laid the bread and butter on the table, then suddenly realized she hadn't cleaned her face. Her broken nose throbbed, and she started to feel the ache in her ribs as the adrenaline wore off. She tongued the hole where she had lost a tooth and walked past Marcel to find a bathroom, but there was none. One of the other men pointed outside, and tears began welling up in her eyes, blurring her vision.

"It's around the corner. If you want water, work the handle on the pump in the yard."

Juliette, tears running down her cheeks, rounded the corner, and there was indeed a tiny building. She opened the door and recognized the typical hole in the floor with places for her feet and handholds on the wall.

She wiped her face with her sleeve, said, "Oh, what the hell!" and pulled down her men's pants. Still crying, she removed her panties and, when she finished, carried them to the pump. She wet and wrung them repeatedly, then washed her face with them. Blood and dirt covered the panties on the first pass, but after rinsing and washing twice more, they and her face were clean, and the tears had stopped. She touched her tender, swollen nose, shrugged, and went inside, panties in her hand.

"Is there a mirror around here?" Juliette asked a woman she didn't know.

"My dear, you have a crooked nose," Juliette remembered the woman who had driven the Renault—Simone said that she was born with a Sten gun in her hand. "And if I don't straighten it, your nose will stay that way unless someone breaks it again."

Juliette found a mirror and yelped when she saw her nose. It was very big, very crooked, and her face was black and blue all around it. She opened her mouth, and a missing tooth left a conspicuous gap.

"I can straighten it for you." The woman pointed, "Your nose—I am a nurse—or, I was one once."

"Won't it hurt like hell?"

"Oh, yes, for sure!" She looked at Juliette with a smile in the corners of her mouth. "But, how long has it been since you were fall-down drunk?"

"Never," said Juliette, "Have you got enough liquor?"

The woman laughed, "Oh, I think so." She touched Juliette's face, examined the possibilities, then led her to the kitchen. Juliette's stomach gurgled at the smell of stew.

"I'm Michelle and the tall man is my husband, Guy," she said as they walked into the kitchen. "The other man is Richard." She glanced over her shoulder as she reached the now scorching stove. "We're all Résistance—well, right now, we are Maquisard."

The stew was delicious, and Juliette wanted seconds, but Michelle and Simone wouldn't let her have it... something about making a mess during the 'operation.'

She had drunk two glasses of wine and was already giddy when Guy brought in a bottle of cognac and set it on the table. She asked, "Is that all for me?"

"Yes, it's all for you." Simone filled a water glass, grinning as she handed it to her.

A half-hour later, Juliette had drunk a third of the bottle and was singing naughty French songs. Everyone except Marcel laughed with or at her.

Michelle looked into Juliette's eyes and said, "She's close."

Marcel poured Juliette another glass, watching her intently. She cocked her head to one side, winked at him, then drank it straight down.

"Why don't we sleep together tonight? There are too many people and not enough beds, and I haven't had any love for almost two years. Peter was good, but not that good!" She slurred the sentence.

Marcel ignored Juliette. "I will sleep on the floor here in the kitchen. The women can have the beds."

Juliette laughed at him and slapped his arm. "Oh, come on, Marcel, I've gotten the revenge out of my system; I'm okay now!" She pushed on his arm. "Don't be a spoil-sport!"

"No..." Marcel shook his head... "You are not okay."

Juliette screwed up her face like a child and wailed.

"Oh God, I feel like an animal! I'm a bad person, worse than that Gestapo boy..." She stood up and fell sideways into Marcel's arms.

"Hold her head still." Michelle gripped Juliette's nose with her fingers, pulled out on it, twisted, and pushed sideways. She slowly released it, and it remained perfectly straight. Everyone checked it out and agreed that it was indeed straight.

Juliette's face healed over the following weeks, and the proper colour returned to her cheeks. The weather improved—a warm March melted what remained of the winter snow.

Michelle and Juliette stayed at the house when Simone and the men went on missions. Simone left for several days at a time, but the men usually returned by morning. Michelle operated the radio and taught Juliette the basics of coding and decoding messages.

March became April, the snow disappeared, and Juliette spent hours exploring the woods near the house. At first, Simone or Michelle walked with her, teaching her how to travel quietly over the forest floor, avoiding noisy leaves and dry twigs. She learned to follow the terrain, up and down the hills, staying off the trails. In time, she could tell where she was by the slope of the ground and the vegetation. The Ardennes Forest in spring is dense and beautiful, broken only by the occasional stream or small field, and Juliette fell in love with it.

When Juliette began to go out alone, Marcel decided she needed to carry a gun. He gave her his Beretta, found a leather purse somewhere and sewed an easily accessible and inconspicuous pocket for the gun inside the flap. Juliette learned to find and draw the pistol in a fast, fluid motion without looking down.

Juliette practiced shooting with Simone until she had a reasonable chance of hitting a close target. On one of their trips to an opening in the woods they used as a shooting range, Simone brought a Sten gun, a British point-and-shoot no-frills machine gun. The thirty-two-round magazine snapped in and out in a second, and the simple action could empty it in less than three seconds. The first time Juliette fired it, she expected the light gun to kick, but to her delight, it pulled away from her. She learned to hold the little gun without tightening her grip and to fire without blinking, with both eyes open, guiding the barrel to the target. She was a natural and became a better shot than Simone.

"Do you still want to kill Germans?" asked Simone on one of their shooting days.

"Yes, I certainly do!" said Juliette, "I want to kill them all!"

"Do you still hate them for what they did to Peter? Isn't your vendetta over? I saw what you did to that Gestapo officer!"

They lay on a small dry knoll covered with needles. The ground was soft; the day was warm; the sun shone through the trees.

Juliette rolled over on her back and put her hands behind her head. "I don't think I can ever go back to Germany to live, even when the war's over. I have dear friends there, but I don't think I can ever face them again."

Simone said nothing for a few minutes. "I would give everything to have what you have. I wouldn't be carrying a gun or a grudge if I had a man like Marcel and a little girl waiting for me."

"Don't you still hate the Germans?"

"No, I fight now to win, not for revenge. It's different, and I think I'm more effective." Simone rolled over and propped her head up with her elbow. "Are you planning to sleep with Marcel, or will you continue this bullshit feeling sorry for yourself?"

Juliette was quiet. She turned to face Simone, ready for a fight, but

Simone was too fast. She said, "Juliette, if you don't do something soon, I'm going after him. I know he likes me, and I like him very much. I'm going to ask him to marry me, and if he says yes, I will be the happiest woman in the world."

Juliette stood up and slung her Sten gun over her shoulder. "Did Marcel put you up to this?"

"No, you know I wouldn't do that, and neither would he. Marcel loves you, but you are acting like a spoiled brat! You need a good spanking to wake you up, and I will give it to you if you don't take that man to your bed!"

They walked almost two kilometres back to the house through an intricate system of paths weaving through the woods. Marcel and Guy had hammered the point ad nauseum: "Avoid routine! Avoid patterns of behaviour!" So, they varied the route.

When the women returned, they found the men splitting wood and piling it in a lean-to at the back of the house. Michelle was inside listening to British radio; Vera Lynn was singing "White Cliffs of Dover," again. Juliette felt like tearing the antenna out of the attic.

She watched Marcel's naked back ripple as he swung a double-bitted axe at a piece of green maple standing on end on a chopping block. The sharp blade travelled in a smooth arc that terminated precisely in the stick's centre. He flipped the handle just as it struck, driving the pieces neatly apart, one on each side of the block.

Juliette felt something she had not felt in many months and recognized it at once.

Chapter Forty

May 1944

Mein!
(She's mein!)
Franz Schubert, Die Schöne Müllerin

Juliette said, as she watched Marcel swing the axe again, "You told me that the war would be over this summer—why are you splitting wood if we aren't going to be here next winter?"

Guy turned to answer her question. "This farm belongs to a friend who is serving with the Free French Army. His wife and two children live with her parents in the Southern Alps, and they will return when the Allies free Belgium. I promised him we would look after the cows and leave her with dry wood for the winter."

"What cows?"

"The farm owns a field a kilometre down the road." He pointed south, "The cows are in a pasture there...I check on them every day."

"Could Marcel take me down there?"

Guy shrugged. "It would save me a trip,"

Marcel smiled, put on his shirt, and took Juliette's hand. They walked on the dirt road in the direction of the cows.

"How do we check on the cows?" Juliette noticed the rays of sunshine filtering through the leaves, casting dancing shadows on the dirt road, and couldn't remember when she had seen anything so beautiful.

Marcel let her hand go, bent over, and picked up a stone. He threw it at a tree and missed by a lot.

"We check the fences and count the cows—there are supposed to be twenty-one."

"So, you've done this before?"

She waited while he searched for another stone, picking it out as though he wanted certain qualities in his throwing rocks.

"Yes, we check on the cows whenever we return from a mission…I checked them two days ago with Simone."

He threw the stone at another tree with the same result. Simone's name got Juliette's undivided attention. Shocked, she set her resolve in stone, and an excitement she hadn't felt in years tingled in her body.

The forest stopped five hundred metres from the farmhouse, and a field opened up on the west side of the road. Juliette quickly counted the cows.

She asked, "What kind of cows are they?"

"I don't know much about cows, but they look like brown cows to me," said Marcel seriously.

"Yes, I think you're right." Juliette stepped up on the bottom rail and leaned on the top log of the split-rail fence. Marcel threw another stone.

She stepped down, smiling. "If you don't need to see anything more, let's walk back through the woods. Simone and I go there to shoot, and I want to show you what I can do."

Marcel shrugged. "You haven't got a gun, have you?"

"Marcel, I always have a gun." She patted her purse.

Juliette led the way, quickly finding a path through the woods to the little knoll where she and Simone had been shooting the sten gun earlier in the day.

"See those spots on that tree?" she said proudly, "I made those with Simone's Sten gun."

Marcel walked over to the tree Juliette had killed. He touched the holes. "You're kidding me! Even Simone can't shoot that well! In fact," he grinned, "I don't think I could do that with a Sten gun unless…" he put a finger in one of the holes… "I was standing right beside the tree." He grinned from ear to ear.

She pushed on his chest, and he staggered back.

"Are you calling me a liar?"

He backed up two steps, opened his mouth to speak, and she pushed him again.

"No, but you may have overestimated the distance." He continued backward, and Juliette continued to push him.

"I was standing right over there." She pointed to the top of the knoll, now less than twenty feet away. "I'll show you my boot prints." She pushed him again. He backed up half the distance, and she shoved him hard just as he lifted a foot and staggered. Off-balance and confused, he fell backward onto the soft ground. She threw herself on his chest and kissed him on the mouth, prying his lips open with her tongue.

"It's time, Marcel Guignard! I want you to make love to me!" She kissed him again, terrified he would push her away, but this time, Marcel's mouth opened without coaxing.

Juliette rolled off his chest and began taking off her dress. He pulled it over her head, and she turned so he could unfasten her bra. He removed his shirt, threw it down where he knew they would be lying, unbuckled his belt, dropped his pants, and turned back to her. She removed her panties and ran into his arms.

He asked in her ear, "Are you sure about this?" and she pulled his head down and kissed him.

He removed his underwear; she pushed him down and lay on top.

He was not at all like Peter. He had a big chest and a narrow waist. His arms were muscular, and his chest was hairy. She felt an excitement that she had forgotten or perhaps never experienced.

Marcel took her small buttocks in his strong hands and pressed her against him, stroking her body up and down. Juliette cried out softly each time he surged in her. He kept moving until she let out a long moan and collapsed, still pressing her hips down, moving slowly. Finally, she arched her back and pushed on his chest.

Her tears fell on his neck.

Marcel asked quietly, "Did I hurt you, Juliette?"

She shook her head. He stroked her with his hand, feeling for the small of her back with his fingers and gently kneading it.

Marcel ran his other hand through her hair. "I've loved you forever, Juliette, and I was beginning to...."

She snuggled her face against his neck and kissed him. "I know, darling; I almost lost you, and I've been a fool!"

The sun was low, and the air cooled quickly. Marcel was warm, but Juliette's back became cold. She stood up and put on her boots.

"Just boots?" Marcel asked, "You really should put on a few more clothes." He smiled up at her.

"We're not going back yet. Come over to the brook with me."

He shook his head.

"I'll wash you..."

Marcel stood up and followed her.

A small, clear brook ran through the forest twenty metres from where they lay. Juliette bent over and touched her fingers in the water.

"It's as cold as you think it is!" Juliette announced as she knelt to remove her boots. She stepped into the water; pain shot through her feet, and then they went numb. When she finished washing, she walked up the bank toward Marcel, and he looked at her with a crooked grin.

"You don't expect me to do that, do you?" He turned away, ready to bolt. She dove at him, and he ran into the water. He knelt and washed himself from the hips down, swearing and complaining, until Juliette came to help.

They dressed, and Juliette wrapped her arms around one of his, walking with her shadow completely covered by Marcel's.

"I am so happy. The war is almost over, and nothing will happen to us here." She looked up at him; he stopped and looked into her eyes.

"Juliette, the Germans are not done yet... in fact, they are more dangerous with their backs against the wall. They will cause a lot more misery before they're finished."

"But not to me!"

Marcel started walking again and was silent until they reached the house.

Chapter Forty-One

A few weeks later

Wenn die Buben Soldaten spielen, so gibt's Krieg.
(When boys play soldier, war follows)

Juliette had made up her mind. "I want to go on a mission. I can shoot as well as anyone here, and I want to fight."

Marcel put his fork down. "Juliette, the war will be over soon. The Allies will land in France any day now, and Belgium will be free before the end of the year. I can't allow you to take any risks." Marcel stood and filled his mug with water.

"I don't need your permission," Juliette said, her face red, "That's my decision, not yours!"

Guy corrected her, "No, it is my decision, and you are not going on any missions!"

She glared at the men, turned and charged out the door—slamming it so hard the wooden door frame rattled in the stone wall.

Juliette turned left on the road, uphill, away from the cows, walking fast at first but slowing as her temper cooled. When she reached the top of the long hill, she looked between the trees at the valley below, where the beginnings of the Meuse River flowed north, away from the forest, and her outburst lost its importance. The light was beginning to fade, and Juliette didn't want Marcel to leave before she saw him, so she turned to walk back down the hill.

The agony of the noisy, overworked twenty-seven horsepower air-cooled engine carried to Juliette well before the little Kubel-wagen came into view. It arrived sliding around the corner at the top of the hill, spraying dirt across the road as the driver drifted through the turn. The car had no roof, and Juliette heard the occupants' shrieks of youthful exuberance interspersed with laughter.

Juliette scrambled into the trees as the vehicle dragged its wheels as it tried to stop in a cloud of dust and gravel; the dirt road offered little braking traction, and it slid past her. The young man in the passenger seat jumped out of the sliding vehicle and fired a shot over Juliette's head.

"Halt, oder ich shiesse dich!"

Juliette froze, raised her hands, then turned to face the soldier. He was no more than sixteen and wore a satisfied smile as though he had just won the war all by himself.

The Kubelwagen's engine wheezed to a stop, and the boy's comrades hopped over the sides of the car to join him. The driver was a little older but still no more than eighteen.

The third boy, sitting in the rear seat, was a child—Juliette guessed he was not more than fourteen. His uniform was too big, and his rifle too heavy for his child's frame. Juliette doubted he even knew how to fire it. The way he held it, he obviously didn't plan to shoot anything in the near future.

The oldest member took charge.

"Let's have some fun!" He walked toward Juliette, nonchalantly carrying his old 'Karabiner 98,' a relic of the Great War, like a hero in a Western movie. He motioned with the rifle and said to Juliette, "Go up the hill into the trees."

Juliette looked at him, then at his rifle—she wasn't positive, but it appeared the safety was on. She turned and walked carefully between the trees, forcing the boys to follow in single file until the forest opened into a small clearing with a mossy floor. The lead boy called a halt, pointed his rifle at Juliette and ordered, "Kleider ab! Jetzt!"

Juliette stood still and waited. He repeated the command, and she said in French, "I don't understand."

He poked her with the rifle and repeated his demand, raising his voice, "Ausziehen! Jetzt!"

Juliette took her purse off her shoulder and held it against her stomach. The boy missed the sign when her eyes became large and bright, and her right hand slid under the flap.

In a final effort to defuse the situation, Juliette said in her best Prussian German, "That's enough, boys—the fun is over. Now, get back in your little car and drive away—everything will be fine." She wanted to say, "I won't tell your mothers," but decided against it.

The oldest boy turned to the other two standing behind him and laughed, but when the mixture of embarrassment and excitement on their faces became fear, he turned back to see Juliette holding a little gun in her hand. He had his rifle pointed at the ground with the safety on, and he was far too late lifting it. If the boy had just stood there like Juliette hoped he would, he might have lived to see another birthday. But when he moved to lift the gun like an American cowboy, Juliette pulled the trigger, and a neat hole appeared precisely where his heart would be, slightly to the left of the centre of his narrow chest. The second boy raised his rifle, and Juliette shouted, "Nein! Bitte…Tu's nicht!" However, the soldier, still a child, continued trying. She waited as long as she dared, but the young man was determined, and so Juliette fired her little gun again, and the child fell beside his dead comrade.

The third boy dropped his rifle on his feet, tears flowing down his face. "Bitte nicht shiessen!" he cried pitifully. He kicked his gun away as though it were a hateful thing, fell to his knees, and stretched his hands toward Juliette. "Bitte nicht shiessen!" He squeezed his eyes shut and collapsed on the ground, sobbing, beating on the moss with his hands. He repeated, "Ich will nicht sterben!" three times before Juliette reached him. He didn't want to die.

She put her pistol in its nest and lifted him by one arm. The boy's face screwed up in agony, and he sobbed as he begged her not to shoot him.

Juliette spoke quietly as she stood before him, removed his hat and stroked his head, "I want you to walk on the road with me. I promise that I'm not going to shoot you…I'm going to take you home and look after you."

The boy stopped crying, sucked in what he planned to be his final sob. She took his arm, turned him around, took a silk handkerchief out of her purse, wiped his face, and gave it to him.

"Wipe the dirt off your hands."

He did as she asked, still swallowing the occasional sob. He gave Juliette her handkerchief as he looked back toward his dead friends, and she gave him a brief minute before she took his hand and began walking down the hill.

It took ten minutes to reach the house, and the sun had gone when Juliette opened the door and followed the boy through it.

Marcel, Guy, and Richard sat at the table looking at a map, discussing the night's mission; Michelle was in the radio room. Simone sat at the table, darning a sock.

"Where did you get him?" Marcel asked as she urged the frightened boy into the room.

"He and his friends were going to have a little fun with me, but it didn't work out for them."

"Where are his friends?" asked Guy.

"I'm afraid they're dead... They're in the woods at the top of the hill, a hundred metres from the Kubelwagen they were driving."

Guy looked at Richard, and they both stood up. Guy said, "We will clean up the mess. Marcel, you do what you have to here."

Juliette ignored Guy's instruction to Marcel, pulled out a chair, told the boy to sit, and asked, "Are you hungry?" The boy nodded, and Juliette spooned stew into a bowl, cut a crooked piece of bread, buttered it and placed it on a small plate. She gave him a big spoon as she said, "It's going to be alright—eat your food."

Marcel said to Juliette in French, "What are you doing?"

She kept her eyes on the young German. He didn't react, so she assumed he hadn't understood Marcel's sarcasm. She turned to Marcel and said, as emphatically as she could, "I don't want to fight with you. He's scared to death, and you are frightening him."

"He doesn't understand French." The boy didn't lift his head.

"But your tone... If you want to talk about Daniel, we should go outside." Juliette's determination was etched on her face and in her heart.

"You've already named him! All right, we'll go outside. Watch that boy, Simone. He may be a child, but he is a German soldier!"

Simone nodded, looked at the boy shovelling stew into his mouth and smiled as she said, "Don't worry, I'll be careful."

Marcel held the door open for Juliette. "What were you thinking? Did you think you could bring him home like a stray puppy?

You hate Germans… Remember?" He followed her to the middle of the yard.

She said, a little too loud, "Neither you nor anyone else will touch that child!" When she paused, Marcel wisely waited until she went on, "He's mine, and I will take full responsibility for him!"

Marcel threw his hands in the air. "That 'child' is a German soldier—our enemy! Hell, Juliette, he's wearing a Wehrmacht uniform—think about what you are doing! Contrary to your expectations, this war is not over!"

She put her finger against his chest. "I will kill the person who touches that child! Do you understand?"

"Yes, I understand, but Guy will want to kill him if I don't do it before he returns." Marcel looked hard at her, and she waited, determined not to lose what she had found.

"There's been enough killing—I will leave and take him with me! The war is almost over, and this boy will not die!" Fighting back tears, Juliette turned to walk back into the house, but Marcel stopped her by gently touching her shoulder. She glared at him but felt a softness rising in her. His expression held no harshness, only his complete surrender to her, and like flipping a switch, the anger in her tears became love.

"I love you, Juliette." He held her arm gently. "We will find a way."

She spoke softly, wiping her face with her hand. "I love you too, but you can't kill Daniel in cold blood. If I must leave here and somehow find a way to live, I will, but I won't let anyone kill him. My heart can't take any more pain, especially from you!"

Marcel looked down, then raised his eyes to meet hers. "It's over five hundred kilometres to the Swiss border, but it may be possible for three of us to get there... but I need a day or two to work this out."

Juliette pulled Marcel's head down, kissed him, and said, "I love you, Marcel."

Guy and Richard stopped short when they returned to find the boy in his underwear, surrounded by Simone, Michelle, and Juliette. The women fussed around the boy; Juliette and Simone held up a pair of pants while Michelle marked them for alterations. Richard howled in protest, but Simone said, "You have more clothes than anyone here..." She pinned the cuffs on the pants... "and this boy has none—his uniform is in the stove. You can give up a shirt and a pair of pants."

Even less happy, Guy tried to get Marcel to step outside by motioning with his hand. He pointed to Juliette, then the door, but neither moved. He sat beside Marcel and whispered, "You and I both know the risk here..." Tension blurred his words; the boy noticed and looked at Marcel, then Juliette.

Marcel spoke softly, but loud enough that Juliette could hear. "There is no way I will fight Juliette on this. She cares for something in a way she hasn't since her husband died, and I won't take that away from her!"

Tears welled in Juliette's eyes.

Guy breathed slowly and looked away, calming himself. He took Marcel's tone of voice when he replied. "As your commander, I must give you two choices—either kill that soldier or leave and take him with you!" He let his gaze wander to Juliette. She was on her knees, helping Michelle, and she stood up to glare at him.

Marcel said, "I won't kill him, and neither will you. We might have to stay here for a week, but I will take responsibility for the boy until we leave. I want your word not to harm the boy."

Guy hesitated, looked at Juliette and said, "I agree; you will be responsible for the boy, and we will discuss this again in a few days." He paused with his eyes focused on Juliette's. "I will not guarantee anything, but he is safe for now." His voice softened. "I understand how you feel, and somehow, we must become human beings again, but it's too soon. He poses a danger if he decides to leave and go home or back to his unit. We can't guard him every minute, and he is still the enemy."

The boy sat on the floor as he waited for the women to finish sewing his clothes, seemingly unaware of the drama unfolding around him.

Everyone said a tearful goodbye when Simone left the group a few days after Daniel arrived, saying simply, "I've had enough...I must find peace."

Guy drove her to Florennes, and, over Marcel's objections, Michelle and Juliette decided to go for a walk with Daniel. Occasionally, German patrols drove on the road but never stopped when they saw the women.

Sometimes, they tooted their horn or shouted something, and the women always waved to boost the soldiers' egos.

It was May; the weather was glorious, and they had hardly put the house out of sight when a Kubelwagen loaded with four young soldiers stopped beside them. The soldier sitting in the front passenger seat beckoned them over. Juliette led the trio, and the soldier asked, "Do you speak German?"

Juliette added a heavy French accent and said, "Yes, I do a little."

He nodded. "Three days ago, a Kubelwagen like this with three soldiers in it drove down this road. Did you see it?"

Juliette turned to Michelle and Daniel and said in French, "He wants to know whether we've seen a German car like this one with three soldiers in it?" Michelle shook her head, and Daniel looked down at his boots and shyly stepped behind her.

Juliette glanced at Daniel, then looked at the soldier. "No, we didn't see it."

"Where do you live?" the young officer asked.

Juliette pointed in the direction of the farmhouse. "We live in the brick house down the road and look after the owner's cows. He is fighting for the Vichy French while his wife and children live with her parents."

The German officer seemed happy with that explanation. He tipped his hat and ordered the driver to go on. The little engine belched smoke and roared as the driver slipped the clutch.

When the Kubelwagen was out of sight, Juliette asked Daniel, "Why did you hide behind Michelle? You don't need to hide."

"Because my boots are Wehrmacht boots." Daniel looked down at them.

Michelle took Daniel's hand, and they continued their walk. "We'll have to do something about those boots."

Juliette smiled, squeezed Daniel's shoulder, and nodded.

Chapter Forty-Two

6 June 1944

Mit dem Kopf durch die Wand wird nicht gehen. Da siegt zum Schluss immer die Wand.
(Banging your head against a wall won't work; in the end, the wall always wins.)
Angela Merkel

THE MEN WENT ON ANOTHER ALL-NIGHT MISSION, and Richard wasn't with them when they arrived home. The women and Daniel were eating breakfast.

"What happened?" Michelle put her coffee down. "Where's Richard?"

Guy poured himself a cup of what passed for coffee and drank a sip before answering.

"We went to the river at Namur to destroy a barge loaded with ammunition. The guards spotted Richard just as he set the charges, and we had to detonate."

Juliette asked, incredulous, "You knew you would kill Richard when you blew up the barge?"

Guy shrugged. "It wasn't possible to save him—they were going to shoot him anyway." He looked at Marcel, who nodded and affirmed, "There was no choice… He would have done the same."

Juliette went to the stove, filled a pot half full of water and put it on the hot steel top over the firebox. She hid her face from Guy and Marcel as she put six eggs in the pot. A rooster and a dozen hens ran around the yard, and every morning, Juliette stole the hen's eggs.

Marcel joined her as she cut up a long loaf of bread, buttering the uneven slices and laying them in a heavy iron frying pan on the stove.

He said gently, "Richard died doing something he had to do—it's something we face every day."

"I know—it's not just Richard... I was thinking about Nina. What if I die? Even if I survive—will I ever see her again... Will you?"

"Yes, you will see her—that's why you must avoid the missions!" He added in a faraway tone, "Maybe it's time the war ended for you. Perhaps we should take Daniel to Switzerland to visit your Godfather."

"No, Guy said Daniel can stay. I won't go until we drive the Boche out of our country...I will not hide in Switzerland!"

May weather in Europe is usually the best of the year, and 1944 was no exception. The blossoming countryside ignored the war, and Juliette turned to nature while waiting for the German defeat. She told Marcel and Guy she didn't want to go on any missions.

When she wasn't walking in the forest, Juliette helped Michelle with coding—it took a lot of coordination to keep Guy's operations running smoothly—and taught Daniel to cook.

Juliette helped Michelle structure and code Guy's messages into one-minute segments sent hours or even days apart—the Germans had new equipment that could locate a transmitter within minutes. However, if they stuck to the protocol, they were relatively safe in the anonymity of the Ardennes Forest.

British Mosquitos flew high over the Résistance stations at night, transmitting coded voice messages on short-range VHF. A radio oper-ator, lying in the Mosquito's cramped bomb bay, collected and decoded messages broadcast from the ground, acting as a short-wave repeater to bases in England. The range of VHF frequencies was too short, and the mosquitoes moved too fast for the Germans to triangulate them or the ground stations effectively.

Early in May, Michelle received a message from one of the airborne repeater stations and reported to Guy, "The landing in France will happen very soon. We are 'code Vert,' designated to stop rail traffic when the landing begins. The preparation for the battle begins when Radio Londres broadcasts the first three lines of Paul Verlaine's poem Chanson d'Automne. Every day after that, we will receive five minutes of messages, and, eventually, one of them will be the next three lines of the poem, meaning the invasion is imminent, and we should begin our operation."

Marcel mused, "What does that mean? We've been attacking the rail lines for weeks now!"

Guy shrugged, "It means we must find a way to do more—we must try to cut every rail line between here, Brussels, and northern France. If we can stop the Germans from moving troops and equipment into France by rail, we will prevent them from reinforcing their defences at the beachhead."

Marcel shook his head. "We haven't got enough explosives to do that."

Guy said, "The Résistance has tried removing bolts and spikes from the outside rail on turns—and it worked…it derails the trains. If we do that, we can save our explosives for river barges and tunnels."

Marcel and Guy led their men on four raids in the next two weeks, attacking the main rail lines, delaying German troops for days using wrenches. They even blocked a tunnel by derailing a train in it.

When the Germans began inspecting the lines ahead of the trains, sympathetic machine shops devised a method to take the bolts out of rails and pull spikes without leaving any evidence. The shop cut the threads from bolts the Résistance used to replace the originals, and the centrifugal force of the locomotive pushing sideways slid the rails apart, separating the outside railand the train from the inside rail. They replaced spikes pulled from the ties with short-shanked false ones, and even a close inspection revealed nothing, but the track had little more than its weight on the slippery wooden railway tie to hold it in place.

On June 1, in their daily poetry readings, Radio Londres read the first three lines of Verlaine's poem, Chanson d'Automne, and on the fifth of June, read the following three lines announcing the imminent invasion. The French and Belgian Résistance increased their attacks in the days between the announcements, practicing for an all-or-nothing effort when the second announcement came.

Marcel and Guy's group destroyed a train, a bridge, or a barge almost every night, and when the second announcement came, they were as ready for the invasion as they could be.

The British, Canadians and Americans landed in Normandy on the morning following the second announcement, and clandestine radios over all of France and Belgium crackled with the news. Excited stations forwarded every detail of every skirmish from operator to operator. Guy forbade Michelle to use the radio except for emergencies, and she and Juliette listened as pointless chatter condemned cell after cell to death.

Despite the losses, it seemed everyone wanted to be in the Résistance now that winning was a certainty. Most Nazi collaborators stopped collaborating and began a restitution campaign, recognizing the danger they faced when the Germans retreated to their lairs. It was an excellent time to be a Résistance hero and the wrong time to talk to a German.

As July ended and August began, Guy commanded hundreds of Belgian and French Résistance soldiers. The first week of August was particularly active for the Résistance, and Guy's men attacked targets every night of the week.

Michelle often listened on the radio—a receiving radio sent no tattletale signal—sifting through increasingly heavy traffic as more and more amateurs obtained or built radios. Having little luck fighting the well-armed and elusive Résistance fighters, the SS took their rage out on the beginners—capturing, torturing, and killing hundreds of them.

Late in the night of August fifteenth, the crackle coming over Michelle's radio woke Juliette. The alarmed tone of the message indicated an emergency call, and knowing that Marcel and Guy were on a mission and could be in trouble, Juliette went into the radio room. She arrived just in time to hear Michelle send a short acknowledgment in open morse code, requesting the nature of the emergency. There followed a long explanation of something to do with German fuel-storage bunkers.

Michelle tried to calm the operator down, transmitting instructions and then repeating them to the confused operator on the other end. The amateur operator's keystroke was slow and filled with mistakes. The obviously confused person repeatedly asked Michelle to resend words and phrases. Juliette leaned against the doorjamb, Alarm bells sounding in her head, and she was on her way to stop Michelle from keying an answer to another question when Daniel, asleep on the floor under the table, screamed as the door shattered. Juliette turned and ran toward the door just as an SS soldier stepped over the threshold. Using the barrel of his MP40, he motioned her to stand beside Daniel, who crawled out from under the table. Two other soldiers, one an officer, joined the one holding the gun.

The officer asked, "Where are the men who live here with you?"

"There are no men; we are alone." She said it more loudly than intended and pulled Daniel close to her.

Juliette's voice was still ringing in the room when the officer nodded, and the butt of the nearest soldier's gun hit her on the side of the head. She staggered and fell, barely aware of Daniel charging at the man, shouting in Hamburg-accented Prussian German, "Leave her alone!" The soldier brought the butt of his gun down on Daniel's head, and he collapsed backward to lie beside Juliette.

Michelle gasped as she ran out of her room and saw Juliette on the floor. The soldier with the machine pistol aimed it at her.

The man in charge said, "Nicht schiessen," and stepped closer to Michelle. He asked, "Is there anyone else here?" And when no answer came, he drew his pistol and said, "Answer me, or I will shoot you!"

"No, we are alone." Michelle stared into the officer's eyes, loathing in her voice.

Despite her foggy brain, Juliette crawled to Daniel and rolled him over. He was unconscious but breathing, and she took him in her arms.

A fourth SS soldier entered the house carrying a machine pistol, and the officer with the Walther P38 in his hand holstered it and commanded the new soldier, "Shoot the boy and bring the women with you. The Junge is a Verweigerer and won't know anything." He said it as though this were just another day, and he wanted to get home to his wife, and then he left.

The soldier standing over the boy used his boot to force Juliette away from him, then fired a burst from his machine pistol into Daniel's chest. Juliette shouted, "No," struggled to her feet and tried to hit him. The soldier put the machine pistol in his left hand and hit her on the forehead with his right fist, knocking her backward toward the table—she grabbed a chair and stayed on her feet. Her purse hung from the back of the chair, and she moved her hand to it.

The other SS soldier took Michelle's arm and pushed her roughly toward the officer at the door. The officer instructed the soldier who had punched Juliette and was lifting his gun, "Fool…don't shoot her yet… she might know something!" The soldier moved toward Juliette, and she slung her purse over her shoulder as though she were going to church.

The SS soldiers pushed the women toward two gray cars parked on the road, and the group had almost reached them when Marcel and Guy appeared out of the gloom, standing fifty feet apart so the SS officers and their captives stood in their crossfire.

The Résistance had no way to look after prisoners. The solution to that problem was never to take any, and consequently, German soldiers knew what their fate would be if they surrendered to them. There were four well-trained SS soldiers, and they had women as shields, tipping the odds in their favour.

Two seconds passed, and all four officers made the same decision at the same time, but hadn't figured Juliette and her Beretta into the equation. She used their two seconds of indecision to remove her little gun from its pocket.

She shot the soldier beside her in the ear before he could lift his machine pistol, then fired at the man beside Michelle, hitting him in the chest as she dove sideways. Juliette fell to the ground as fast as gravity would take her, freeing Marcel and Guy to fire.

Everything was over in under three seconds; the last two SS officers lay on the ground in their death throes with bloody holes in their uniforms. As she got to her feet, the soldier Juliette had hit in the chest, the one who had shot Daniel, moved, and she shot him in the head, then spat on him.

Marcel ran to Juliette, but she turned before he got to her, and he followed her into the house. He stopped at the door; Juliette knelt beside Daniel, the boy's head cradled in her arms.

Marcel waited…she cried for five minutes, rocking back and forth, trying to sing a lullaby, but her voice failed her. She looked up at him, tears flowing in rivers down her cheeks.

"I can't do this anymore Marcel. Please, take me home!"

Chapter Forty-Three

September 1944

Der ewige Frieden findet man nur auf dem Friedhof.
(Eternal peace is only found in the cemetery.)

It proved surprisingly easy for Juliette and Marcel to cross the American lines. Since the Normandy landings, the Résistance had developed channels to freely move men and equipment through France and most of Belgium.

Trying to save themselves and their order of things, most Germans on and behind the front knew they were waging a losing battle. Although there were isolated atrocities, German officers began to understand the implications of defeat. When the inevitable played itself out, they did not want to face their victims' families and friends in court, especially with a gallows set up in the yard. The exceptions were the Gestapo and certain members of the SS who were the most entrenched fanatics and the slowest learners.

The Americans held Marcel and Juliette for a few days until they were satisfied they weren't a threat, then turned them over to British battle headquarters in Amiens. MI6 had an intense interest in Marcel and, with typical military efficiency, took only ten days to verify that he was indeed one of theirs. During that time, Marcel and Juliette stayed in a room above British intelligence offices in the Hotel de Berny.

On a beautiful sunny day, Juliette and Marcel sat on a bench beside a path in Amiens, watching the Somme River carry bits of flotsam past them. It was the third of September, and the British were at that moment driving their tanks down the streets of Brussels in front of cheering crowds. The only sounds of battle in Amiens were Allied planes flying overhead. Although only a few weeks had passed since Daniel's death, Juliette let the warm sunshine, a light breeze, and Marcel's presence beside her push her memories of war far away. She often tried to remember the details of Daniel's face, but her mind would only allow her a vague impression.

"It's terrible that we forget things like the loss and terror of war." Juliette kicked her foot at the ground, getting the toe of her shoe dirty. "It's as though Daniel, and Alex, and Peter…Juliette caught her breath at the start of a sob… It's as though they never existed. They're just vague pictures set in a piece of my life."

Marcel looked on the ground for something, found a small stone and threw it in the water.

"I don't think we could live with ourselves if we remembered every awful detail of the tragedies in our lives. There are some things I want to forget, but they won't go away."

Juliette watched the circle of ripples made by Marcel's stone expand in the water while moving slowly downstream.

"And now the members of the Résistance are taking their revenge."

Marcel found another stone. "What did you expect? You took your revenge against Gärtner, and I 'brutally' killed three SA soldiers for you. The Résistance must have their satisfaction, too. They call it, L'épuration Sauvage."

Juliette watched a piece of fabric floating down the lazy river that could be attached to a partially submerged body, but it was too far away to be sure. She pushed it to the back of her mind and said, "I can tell them that it doesn't work, no matter how many they kill. Revenge adds pain; it doesn't reduce it."

Marcel put his arm around Juliette's shoulder and pulled her close. He was silent, and she allowed him his reverie. Finally, he let her go and put his hands on the edge of the bench, leaning against them with stiff arms.

"The Résistance has been as brutal as the Milice—they are executing thousands without a trial, which has nothing to do with justice. Justice that is not revenge is hard because it is slow, but we must do it, or chaos will overwhelm us."

Juliette suddenly thought of the day she was captured and taken to

Amiens prison, and was surprised to feel something like sympathy for the woman who had trapped her.

She asked Marcel, "What about the woman who betrayed Peter and me... The one who lost her husband and a child?"

Marcel watched the river for a moment, then turned to her, "Guy told me the Maquis eventually exerted pressure on her. She stayed with the Milice but also reported to members of the Maquis, though not everyone trusted her, putting her in a terrible position."

"She's alive?" There was hope in her voice. "And her children?"

"To get her collaboration, the Maquis promised to rescue her kids when the Allies invaded, but as far as I know, they never did."

Marcel was silent, and Juliette knew he was holding something back. He looked at the water for a long time, and when she grew tired of waiting, she wrapped her hand around his arm and said, "I must know."

Marcel didn't look at Juliette. "The Maquis tried her for treason in their revenge court and found her guilty. They shot her."

Juliette leaned against Marcel and wept. She thought of the woman sitting across from her, remembering the lifeless agony in her eyes.

"She couldn't win, could she? They broke their word... the Maquis is replacing the Gestapo."

Juliette leaned against Marcel, crying for a reason she couldn't define. She watched a coloured leaf float past her, the first sign of autumn, and asked softly, "Do you know anything about Alex Küster? Why did he help Peter and me?"

Marcel leaned ahead, found a stone and pitched it underhand at the leaf, missing it. Juliette didn't know why, but she was glad; she wanted the leaf to survive.

"He was a member of the Schwartze Kapelle, a group dedicated to killing Hitler and deposing the Nazis."

"Yes, I know about them—Papa told me."

"Alex helped your father and me in our work and was instrumental in getting information the British needed to bomb the prison."

"Was it the Schwartze Kapelle that tried to kill Hitler in July? Was Alex part of the plot before he died?"

"Yes, and no. Alex wasn't involved directly in the twentieth of July attempt, the one you are referring to, but there were many others that he was probably involved in. Had Alex lived, he would have been arrested. On July twentieth and for weeks afterward, the Gestapo arrested the top people in the 'Kapelle,' including Admiral Canaris, the head of the Abwehr—the German intelligence department. Some believe he was the leader of the German resistance movement. They tortured him, got the names of others, murdered him in the worst way possible, then worked their way down. Thousands died, many, and perhaps most of them, innocent."

Marcel looked for another stone. "You will incriminate anyone when they are pulling out your toenails."

"Is that what Gärtner did to Peter?" Juliette asked the question so softly Marcel barely heard it.

"He was about to when Alex shot him."

"Why didn't he shoot that Gestapo animal instead?"

"Because Alex was the key to operations that would save hundreds of lives. If he had shot Gärtner, he couldn't have explained it, and the Gestapo would have arrested him before he and Peter had left the building. Alex knew too much; his arrest and torture would have been catastrophic for the movement and, incidentally, for your father and mother."

Juliette cried silently, her tears dropping on Marcel's legs. And then a horrible thought came out of nowhere. She said, "Perhaps the worst is yet to come; perhaps thousands more will die. Before he hangs, Hitler will execute the people in the work camps; then the Jews and Allies will blame all Germans and want revenge—and what will happen to Erik... Marita... their children...and Johann...?"

Marcel said quietly, "Where is my avenging angel? Germans raped you, murdered Peter... Why do you care what happens to them?"

"Having children mellows a woman."

"Children? My last count makes it one child—a wonderful little girl I can't wait to see."

She squeezed his arm. "I'm pregnant."

Marcel took Juliette's hand. "Are you sure?" His eyes became moist.

"Yes, I'm sure. I'm due in March or early April." Juliette lifted Marcel's hand and kissed it. "If it's a boy, we'll name him Peter. Will you make an honest woman of me?"

Marcel laughed, "I'll ask your father—what do you think he will say?"

"Whatever Mama says. But Papa and Mama love you almost as much as I do, so let's assume you're in."

"It's a deal then. Now, if we could stop this damned war! Brussels fell today, so we are making progress. I can take you home in a few days."

Juliette put her arms around Marcel's neck and squeezed so tight he cringed, but he kept the pain to himself. She spoke softly into his ear. "We've done our share—I need you to stay with me."

"Until hell freezes, ma Chérie… until hell freezes."

On the fifth of September, two days after the British army drove their tanks into Brussels, an MI6 car drove a joyful Marcel and Juliette to the front of Avenue Saturne 6. The weather was beautiful, precisely the setting Juliette had pictured for her homecoming.

She had telephoned her father and mother the day the British liberated the city, using a private line MI6 had made available to Marcel. Jacques and Veronique had been so excited they could barely control themselves, and Juliette had cried as she spoke to Nina.

Marcel walked ahead of Juliette, blocking her view of the door she knew her mother would open on her way to embrace her daughter. Jacques and Marcel would stand to one side...Jacques would embarrass Marcel with a hug and a kiss on each of his cheeks. Veronique and Juliette would cry.

Marcel didn't step aside. He stopped, turned, and grabbed Juliette's shoulders.

He was upset... this wasn't how it was supposed to go!

"Stay here! There's something wrong!" The tone of voice frightened Juliette, and she instinctively reached for the flap on her leather purse. Marcel waved frantically at the driver and withdrew his new Beretta from his jacket pocket. He put his hand in front of Juliette's face and pleaded, "Please, stay here, Juliette."

The driver joined him, his pistol drawn.

For the first time since she had known Marcel, Juliette followed his instructions. When Marcel and the driver approached, one on each side of the door, Juliette saw it was slightly open, splintered where force had broken the lock. She felt bile rising, burning her throat, and tears flowed in a sudden river. Her legs refused to move.

Marcel stood to one side as the driver kicked the door open, then disappeared inside with the driver on his heels. Juliette waited, arms at her side, the little pistol that lived in her purse hanging from her right hand. The longer she waited, the more she shook until, when Marcel finally appeared in the doorway, and she saw the shock and fury on his face, Juliette fell to her knees, sobbing. Sorrow overwhelmed her as the expression on his face destroyed what was left of her world!

Marcel slowly walked to her, tears running down his rough, bearded cheeks. He knelt beside her, wrapped his arms around her shoulders and sobbed.

"Mama? Nina?" Juliette whispered their names as she buried her face in his coat.

Marcel shook his head. His voice broke. "Everyone... They're all dead. The Gestapo killed them, and the bastards left a note."

"I want to see them." Juliette fought to get to her feet, but Marcel held her down.

"No, you can't—it's the work of a madman!"

Juliette thought about fighting him, but the expression on Marcel's face told her she would die if she went into the house. He scooped her into his arms and carried her, sobbing, to the waiting car. He put her in the back seat and said to the driver, who stood behind him with his gun still in his hand, "I will stay here; the trail is still fresh, and I want the man who is responsible. Take her to British Intelligence on Rue de la Roi. Accompany her inside and tell Captain Tomkin to send someone to gather evidence. I want the bastards who did this!"

As the car drove away, Juliette watched Marcel until she could no longer see him, and he didn't move. When she knew he couldn't hear her, she screamed, and the driver almost hit a tree growing on the edge of the street. He hunched his shoulders when she screamed a second time but kept the car on the road.

Captain Tomkin listened to the driver's story as he watched Juliette. Before the story was finished, the captain picked up the telephone, and almost immediately, a nurse and two men with a stretcher appeared, and the men helped her onto the stretcher. The nurse stabbed Juliette with a long needle, and before the syringe was empty, an overwhelming peace invaded her consciousness.

When Juliette woke, it was dark, and she was in a hospital bed. Marcel was asleep in a chair beside her, his hand covering hers.

She tried to sort out why she was in a bed, and then suddenly remembered. A close-up picture of Marcel's face rushed into her mind, anger and shock twisting it so she hardly recognized him. She tried to look past him but couldn't. She heard his words, "Everyone is dead!" and repeated them as she sobbed.

Marcel woke, stood, and grabbed her arms as she tried to get up. She knew she was screaming the words, but couldn't stop. He lay across her and cried like a broken-hearted child as he held her down, "I love you, Juliette. Please don't leave me! Don't give up!"

She wrapped her arms around him, and her screaming stopped. She said, "Stay here with me… They will kill you too! Please stay here!"

He said softly, "I must find them, Juliette. Go back to sleep…I swear I will find them."

The nurse pushed the door open, rolled Juliette on her side and stabbed her again. Marcel's face faded as she said, "No one can find them. They're gone! Everyone is dead!" She tried to say something else but lost the thought.

When Juliette woke, it was light, and Marcel stood beside her, holding a food tray. She looked at him and then at the nurse, who turned a noisy crank at the foot of the bed. The nurse was unarmed—a good omen

Marcel put the tray on her legs. She looked at him with a question ready to exit her lips but couldn't find any words.

Marcel said, "I love you. It's only been three days, but we can't wait… We need your help."

Juliette smiled and slurred, "Yes, it's time." She looked at the tray. A glass of apple juice, a glass of milk, a cup of coffee, and two croissants. MI6 had done their intelligence well.

She took a sip of milk, chased it with a slug of orange juice, and was suddenly ravenous.

Marcel said, "We have a lead on the bastards, but I can't do anything more without you. Do you think you can help me?"

Juliette swallowed, looked at Marcel and said, "Give me an hour to bathe and get dressed."

Marcel smiled. "Better yet, let's plan on starting tomorrow afternoon."

Chapter Forty-Four

September 1944

Revenge, when it's a gift, loses its sweetness.

THE FOLLOWING MORNING, Marcel led an unsteady Juliette to the light coming through the glass in the main doors that led outside British Intelligence Headquarters. Juliette stepped out of the MI6 building, stopped on the concrete landing and turned her face toward the sun's warmth. With her eyes closed, she said, "Marcel, Papa didn't tell me anything, and I don't know where anything is."

Marcel said, "I do," took her arm and guided her down the steps. "And yes, we have a lot of work to do."

At the walkway, Juliette stopped, turned to face Marcel and asked, "Why, Marcel? Why did they kill them?"

"Because they found out your father wasn't holding the treasure for them; he was holding it for British Intelligence. When the British Army came to town, Oberst Müller, your father's Gestapo ally, contacted Jacques to collect some of his loot and quickly figured out your father had tricked him—that Jacques worked for MI6. When Müller realized his pension and most of his fortune belonged to the British Government, he went crazy."

Juliette suddenly remembered her father's warning... that if the Nazis ever found out...

She said, "I hope it's a lot," and Marcel replied, "It is beyond your imagination."

Captain Tomkin reached across his small desk to shake Juliette's hand, and said in perfect French, "My condolences, Mademoiselle Durand; I am terribly sorry to intrude on your grief. I'm afraid your father has left us with a mountain of work, and we will need your help. Perhaps more importantly, we require your permission to sort it all out... Monsieur Durand's will is quite explicit..."

Juliette smiled as sweetly as she could manage. She saw a chance to make a deal and said, "First things first; I want certain heads delivered to me on British pikes. Specifically, I want everyone involved in my family's death delivered to me without conditions on what I can do to them."

Tomkin turned to Marcel. "That's his department," then turned back to Juliette. "I can't even talk about that, but I will say that you can trust us. We will see that you get the justice you want and deserve."

"Oh, I trust you, but I'm telling you that I won't be disappointed. The war isn't over for me until certain matters are resolved to my complete satisfaction."

Tomkin waved his hand to stop Juliette from saying anything more.

"I don't want to hear any details of what you two are up to. This is a branch of the British Government, and I'm not allowed to know anything about your shenanigans."

Tomkin changed gears. "So, what do you need at the moment? I have some papers for you to sign so we can get started on your father's affairs. Will you sign them before we deliver your heads?"

Juliette wanted to get out of there—bureaucracy wasn't something she did well, and financial matters were a complete mystery. She turned to Marcel.

"If I sign them and they take everything, what will I live on?"

Tomkin and Marcel exchanged looks. Marcel said, "My dear, aside from what the British are taking, you are rich beyond your imagination. You can choose to marry a prince if you like, but please remember the pauper who loves you and is living on meagre MI6 wages."

Juliette sat down and began signing a pile of papers without reading a single word written on them.

"You should read them, Mademoiselle," Tomkin slid another pair of sheets on the pile, separated by a piece of carbon paper.

"If you've cheated me, Marcel will cut your throat. I've seen his work... He's good at that."

Marcel gave his boss a Cheshire cat grin and said, "Don't test me on that." Tomkin smiled at Marcel, then turned to Juliette.

"Marcel and I have read every word. This bureaucracy will not cheat you, but certain Nazis will not take kindly to what we will do with their ill-gotten booty. Therefore, I have assigned a detail to protect you for the foreseeable future."

A week passed, and Juliette returned to what was now her house and home. She had a maid, cook and housekeeper who collectively spoke French, German, and English and didn't act at all like household help. The 'cook' could boil water and fry an egg but was still working on her toast. Juliette had no idea who they were or who paid them, but Marcel assured Juliette not to worry about that—they would be paid, and they had been vetted by Captain Tomkin's people. "But," he said, "only for allegiance to the crown… certainly not for their ability to do housework."

Marcel took over Juliette's father's office, and accountants and investigators became constant fixtures there and at a table set up in the drawing room that was constantly covered with papers. Six men, armed with machine guns and pistols, prowled the grounds day and night. No one got in or out without a thorough grilling.

Juliette slowly developed a routine. She slept wrapped around Marcel at night and in her father's big soft chair in front of a fire during the day, disturbed occasionally by Marcel when he needed her to sign a paper. When the sun shone, her preferred station was a rocking chair on the verandah wrapped in a cashmere shawl, and she was there when Marcel came through the open door to the terrace, dragging a wooden chair over to where she sat. He had no papers with him, and opened the conversation with, "Jean, head of the Résistance, is almost finished with the bastards who killed your family. It's time for you to meet them."

Juliette's heart jumped. "What does that mean?"

"It means that Jean and MI6 know whatever those animals know."

"And…" Juliette didn't feel the excitement she had expected.

"And as Tomkin promised, they are all yours if you want them. MI6 owes you and Jacques at least that much."

Juliette pulled her feet up onto the edge of the chair and wrapped her arms around her legs, resting her chin on a knee. "What do you think I should do?"

"The Maquis and the British Government will want them if you don't. There is a long line of people waiting for those animals—they've earned a lot of hate. I think you would be a better choice for them—if they had one."

"You didn't answer my question."

"I think you should meet them and make up your own mind. If you don't want to do what must be done, I would consider it an honour to do it for you."

Juliette put her feet on the floor and stood up. "Okay, I'll get my purse."

Marcel drove the Rolls Royce through the city streets, purposely detouring to the Rue de Louise, where he pointed out the Gestapo building, an innocuous eight-story structure. The main entrance was boarded shut with 'Stay Out—Danger of Mines' signs everywhere, written in three languages. All the bottom two floors' windows were boarded up, and graffiti unflattering to the 'Boche' decorated every square foot of the outside wall as far up as the good citizens of Brussels could reach. Marcel pulled to the curb opposite the building's main entrance.

"That's where Müller did his deeds. Fortunately, we had a spy in his office, and she minimized the damage." He nodded toward the building. "Unfortunately, she lost her husband, siblings and parents to the Nazis. They are now in a concentration camp or dead... No one knows for sure." He looked at Juliette. "She is a Jew, and to preserve her identity, she had to condemn some of her people to save others. She saved many more than she condemned!"

"She worked for MI6 and was in the same office as Oberst Müller?" Juliette suddenly felt ashamed; in the weeks since one of the two worst days of her life, she had thought she was the only person who had sacrificed so much. She asked, "What is she doing now?"

"She is still working for us. She smuggled a ledger out of Müller's office on the last day of German occupation—it has the names of every collaborator in the city. As Schwenke's, then Müller's assistant, she kept the books for a program that paid forty marks for every Jew a

Belgian citizen turned in, and consequently, we have a record of every mark paid and every person who got the money. She killed her boss, Kriminalsekretär Schwenke, the bastard who was in your house the morning we found out Peter died—and she killed him with a knife, a la 'yours truly.'"

"What will you do to the people who took the money for turning in Jews?"

"We gave the list to the Résistance and the Maquis, and they are working their way through it. When they're done, we'll take care of the survivors."

"What about the people we are going to visit?"

"A few of them are collaborators, but most are SS soldiers who worked for the Gestapo. Oberst Müller is among them, and it was he who murdered your family—he personally executed them. That's why I brought you to see this building. His office was on the eighth floor, and he tortured people in the cellar, like Gärtner."

Juliette felt her tears coming, along with a bitterness that threatened to extinguish her sense of reason.

"How many others did this man torture and kill?"

"Our agent, codename Olga, says thousands, and she would know. He tortured many of them personally... the man is full of hate for anyone who isn't an Aryan German like him. She said he even treated his own people like dirt under his feet, and no one will care what happens to him."

"Will she be there today? I want to meet her."

"No. Definitely not. When the soldiers found the hideout, she identified the people you have good reason to kill and those who did nothing wrong, and then she left. She doesn't want to be found, and you will never meet her."

"Tell me why Müller and his cohorts didn't escape to Germany?"

The car was so quiet Juliette could hear birds squawking as they fought with a squirrel over a piece of fruit.

"Müller is a true fanatic; he still believes the German army will defeat the Allies and return to rescue him. He and his men are in a cellar under one of the university buildings, and the institution is closed until this is over. They filled a room full of food close to toilets and water. They could have stayed there for at least a couple of months."

"What happened? How did you find them?"

"I didn't... the Résistance did. They used their special techniques on a few collaborators, and voila, they found someone who knew Müller's plan."

Marcel put the car in gear and smoothly accelerated.

"There were Blitzmädchen among the twenty-five people in the cellar, and Olga knew most of them. We're letting her question the women, but we know they took no part in the atrocities the Gestapo committed. Jean, head of the local Maquisard, wanted to keep everyone and try them for crimes against the Résistance, but British hospitality only goes so far! We took a few soldiers to our prison, but the ones still in the cellar were involved in your family's demise and await whatever fate you determine appropriate. You will decide whether you, the Maquis or British Justice get them. Jean has agreed to that."

"It's all so brutal. This war will never end if one side doesn't stop this tit-for-tat."

"We're almost there. Are you going soft on me?"

Juliette looked out the window. "No, I must avenge my family, or they will never rest."

Marcel stopped the car in front of the main campus building, behind a black Renault and two British army vehicles.

"That's Jean's car. He will want you to leave the bastards to him because he has special axes to grind...dozens of axes that include his wife and four children."

Juliette got out before Marcel rounded the long front of the car. She shut the door, he took her arm, and two men in plain clothes armed with sten guns attentively hovered around them as they walked to the main entrance. When Marcel was close enough for the guards at the door to recognize him, one of them grinned, touched his hat, and opened the door for Juliette.

Once inside, Juliette purposely walked two steps behind Marcel, who had magically produced a flashlight, as they negotiated a network of hallways, stopping at an unmarked door. Marcel opened it, and Juliette followed him down an endless stairway. They turned right at the bottom and passed through a room filled with pipes, valves, and what Juliette assumed was a furnace. It was cold, and the coal bins in the room were empty.

When Marcel opened the next door, the lights were on, and although the room was large, Juliette couldn't see any other way in or out. She counted eleven men chained to an iron heat pipe, their hands uncomfortably over their heads. They couldn't sit, and the steel bracelets cut into their wrists if they lowered their arms. Juliette felt a twinge of sympathy for the few who had ignored the pain and lowered their arms so their weight was on the pipes; their wrists looked like chopped meat. Others took the weight of their arms by holding onto the chain with their hands, but their sweaty faces and sunken eyes told Juliette they couldn't maintain that position much longer.

Only one man sat, and he was against the wall. His feet were bare, and he had bloody patches where his toenails should be. Half his fingers were crushed—likely victims of a hammer. Marcel pointed at him.

"That's what's left of Oberst Müller."

Juliette crossed the room and crouched in front of him. When he lifted his head, she saw that one of his eyes was swollen shut.

"You killed my parents and my daughter. Nina was only three years old."

He cocked his head to one side and looked at her. "Jacques Durand?"

She nodded.

"I lost my temper. I don't kill children except in special cases."

Juliette put her hand in her purse. Blind rage ruled for a short minute, and then Juliette took her hand back. She felt an urge to cry, thinking her tears might awaken enough empathy in this man that he would give her an explanation for why he had killed Nina that made human sense. But then, she thought, he isn't human; he's a predator without pity for his victims. He sincerely believes he has the right to torture and murder whomever he deems to deserve it. To break down in front of him would be the ultimate humiliation.

She asked him coldly, "Why did you do it? The war was, at that moment, over for you. What did you hope to gain by killing my family? Why didn't you surrender or, more logically, return to Germany with your staff?" Juliette's voice betrayed her anger but not the helplessness she felt. She knew Müller hoped she would shoot him… he was goading her to do it!

He looked at the wall at the other end of the room and recited his manifesto. "You will never defeat Hitler! He will return to rescue us, and together, we shall correct the mongrel mess that is Europe."

He turned his head to look into Juliette's eyes. "We trusted your father to guard the valuable assets we need to do our work, and he betrayed us! We trusted him with our priceless art and money. Jacques Durand pretended to be one of us; your father deceived us, and he deserved to die!"

Juliette sat on the dirty floor, crossed her legs, facing him with her purse between her thighs. She didn't care how dirty it was.

"Why did you kill my mother and daughter? Nina was only a baby!" She waited for him to say something, but he just hung his head. "Tell me, or I will shoot you!"

Juliette opened her purse, pulled out the pistol and pressed the barrel against his forehead.

Guns appeared in Marcel and Jean's hands, aimed at Müller.

Juliette raised her voice. "Aren't you afraid to die?"

"No, I hope you pull the trigger, but I doubt you will. I've seen enough death to know that it is nothing to fear… in most cases, death is a relief. If you don't kill me, someone else will, and that will end the pain. Even without the pain, dying would be better than rotting in jail, but I fear this will not soon be over." He raised his head. "Would it help you decide if I told you I killed your little girl first, in front of your father and mother? That your father was the last to die?"

Juliette locked her eyes on Müller's and held his gaze until he lowered his head.

"You know that Adolph Hitler won't rescue you, that he will die soon. The Russians are halfway through Poland and will be in Berlin in a few weeks or months. If the British and Americans don't get there first, the 'Bolsheviks' your hero calls Untermenschen will skin him alive, then drag his body through the streets. If the Americans get him first, they will parade him in front of their cameras and then hang him with the whole world watching!"

Spit ran out of the corner of Müller's mouth, his eyes bulged, and his face became as red as the blood seeping from a cut on his forehead. He shouted, "They will never catch Hitler! He has a plan, and he will rescue the cause. The Waffen SS will attack and drive the Allies back across the English Channel—those still alive! Hitler has a secret weapon, so fearful that he doesn't want to use it. But he will not allow you to invade Germany without unleashing its awful power! You are doomed to join your parents in hell!"

Juliette, shaking, stood up. "It's people like you and the monster you worship who caused this catastrophe, and you must pay so that others will hesitate. I hope with all my heart that there is a hell because there is not enough pain on earth to pay for what you've done!" He raised his head, and she looked into the eye that wasn't swollen shut. "You are an animal, and so are the men who follow you!" She pointed her little pistol at his genitals. "I have the right to inflict as much pain as I can..." She slowly squeezed the trigger, watching his eye, and smiled when she saw terror in it. She waited; he stared at her white finger. The hammer clicked on the empty chamber.

"...But that would make me a member of your club, wouldn't it?"

She relaxed and put the gun in her purse.

Juliette looked at Müller until he lowered his head, then turned to Marcel and said, "I don't want you to kill him."

She turned to Jean. "Jean, I am sorry..." She looked at him until he looked away, then said, "I understand how you feel—I have lost a child too. But we are not alone in that, and it would not be justice to kill him to satisfy only our vendetta. For all the crimes and for the victims and their families, he must face public justice, whatever that means."

She put her hand on Jean's chest. "We must go back to laws, discipline and sympathy, not revenge, chaos and hate. We must shout what he and others like him did from the rooftops, not bury it in cellars so their followers can deny the horrible facts. He shouldn't have the luxury of an easy death, and to me, hanging seems appropriate, but only after a fair trial that the society he has tried to destroy will see and record for history."

Jean smiled and took Juliette's hand. He kissed it and said, "Madame, I promise your wish shall be fulfilled."

Marcel led Juliette back through the string of rooms, up the long stairs and outside, into the sunlight. Juliette had her hand on the car's door handle when she changed her mind, turned and put her arms around Marcel's waist, looking up into his face. With tears in her eyes, she said to him, "I'm free now, and so are you...I don't need revenge...I need love." She touched his cheek. "I love you, and I won't survive if I lose you—let someone else finish this war." She took her little gun from her purse and put it in Marcel's big hand. "I don't need that anymore...I've got you."

Marcel put the pistol in his pocket, reached around Juliette to put his hand on the door handle and was opening it for her when she said, still with tears on her cheeks but with a wicked little smile, "I am going to teach you to sing Bach if it takes the rest of our lives!"

Marcel smiled a smile that told Juliette he knew. He said softly, "I'm sure it will take at least that long, but I'm not in a hurry."

Juliette slid into the seat and wiped her cheek with her sleeve. Her smile became a self-conscious laugh. "...You know about that, don't you?"

"Naturally...I'm a spy...I listen through keyholes!"

He checked that he wouldn't jamb anything in the door and gently closed it, then skipped as he rounded the rear of the car.

THE END

Message from the Author:

I hope you enjoyed the book, and I invite you to read the third one in the series, *Reap the Whirlwind*. But before you do, I have a favour to ask.

Most people pick books by looking at the cover, reading the blurb, and checking the reviews. I can control the first two, but the third is up to you, and your honest review will help others decide whether the book is for them. Most importantly, a good review, honestly written, is a justification for my writing. If you don't tell me whether you liked it or, shudders and shivers, not, I might assume you didn't, and that would be depressing.

If you are on Amazon, you can leave a review. Tell everyone what you liked or didn't like about the story or my writing.

Alternatively, if you aren't on Amazon or your review is rejected, use the links or the QR code to reach me and tell me whether you liked the book. Please give a rating, 1 to 5, and any comments you want to share, and I will submit an Editorial Review in your name.

thesongsofwar.com

Web site: *thesongsofwar.com.*
Facebook: *Robert Faulk, Author*
Email: *robertfaulk@thesongsofwar.com*

Join my newsletter on the website, by email, or on my Facebook page, and I promise to keep you updated on what I am doing. I will send you tidbits I cut from the books, historical context, and previews of new books I am writing.

Reap the Whirlwind

Book three in *The Songs of War* series is wrapped in British RAF General 'bomber' Harris's publicly stated objectives:

"The aim of the Combined Bomber Offensive...should be unambiguously stated [as] the destruction of German cities, the killing of German workers, and the disruption of civilized life throughout Germany...the destruction of houses, public utilities, transport and lives, the creation of a refugee problem on an unprecedented scale, and the breakdown of morale both at home and at the battle fronts by fear of extended and intensified bombing, are accepted and intended aims of our bombing policy. They are not by-products of attempts to hit factories." [Garret 1993, pp. 32–33].

Later in 1942: "We are going to scourge the Third Reich from end to end. We are bombing Germany city by city and ever more terribly in order to make it impossible for them to go on with the war. That is our object; we shall pursue it relentlessly." [Radio address, 28 July 1942].

From the Imperial War Museum: "The Nazis entered this war under the rather childish delusion that they were going to bomb everyone else, and nobody was going to bomb them. At Rotterdam, London, Warsaw and half a hundred other places, they put their rather naive theory into operation. They sowed the wind, and now they are going to *Reap the Whirlwind.*"

Despite horrifying losses, Allied bombers ravaged and burned Germany's cities, terrorizing the population, naively believing the people would turn against Hitler. Germany's helpless civilians had no route to a surrender—to whisper a word against Hitler was a death sentence—so they huddled in their shelters, cursing the *Englander* while the battle to kill them raged overhead.

Willy MacLaughlin, rear gunner on a Lancaster bomber, and Erik Stephanie, a Luftwaffe night fighter pilot, played a deadly 'cat and mouse' game in the dark skies over Europe while their women prayed that God would bring them safely home.

About the Author

Robert Faulk, a Canadian, born on a farm and educated in a small rural school, grew up in a world of hard workers—men and women who farmed the land and harvested the forests and the sea. He studied engineering in university and worked in construction before taking his wife and three children to Germany to pursue a career as an opera singer.

Over the next ten years in Europe, Robert met many Europeans willing to share still-fresh memories of the Second World War. Their stories, often traumatic and always deeply personal, expose the most devastating cost of any war—the human cost. Robert captures the spirit of these stories in a series of four books of historical fiction that he calls *The Songs of War.*